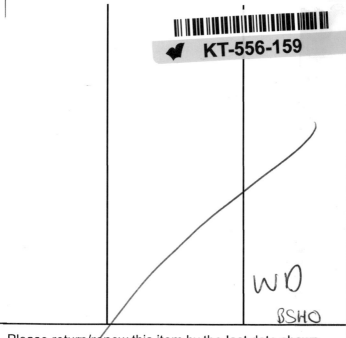

WO

BSHO

Please return/renew this item by the last date shown on this label, or on your self-service receipt.

To renew this item, visit **www.librarieswest.org.uk** or contact your library

Your borrower number and PIN are required.

Libraries**West**

THE ICELANDIC DOC'S BABY SURPRISE

LOUISA HEATON

CHRISTMAS WITH HER LOST-AND-FOUND LOVER

ANN McINTOSH

MILLS & BOON

First Published in Great Britain 2020
by Mills & Boon, an imprint of HarperCollins*Publishers*
1 London Bridge Street, London, SE1 9GF

The Icelandic Doc's Baby Surprise © 2020 by Louisa Heaton

Christmas with Her Lost-and-Found Lover © 2020 by Ann McIntosh

ISBN: 978-0-263-27984-9

MIX
Paper from
responsible sources
FSC™ C007454

This book is produced from independently certified FSC™ paper
to ensure responsible forest management.
For more information visit www.harpercollins.co.uk/green.

Printed and bound in Spain
by CPI, Barcelona

THE ICELANDIC DOC'S BABY SURPRISE

LOUISA HEATON

MILLS & BOON

For all of the strong women who inspire me to be my best.
xxx

CHAPTER ONE

DR MERRY BELL shook her head in dismay at the music coming from the taxi driver's radio. Cheesy Christmas music being played *here*? In Iceland?

She'd expected it in England. They'd been playing Christmas tunes on the radio since mid-November and she'd stopped listening to the radio in her car just because of that fact. Instead she'd loaded up a few podcasts and listened to those. Or audiobooks. Anything but the false jollity that the season brought with it.

It really was crazy the way people got so idiotic as December crept nearer. There was no appeal in it for her. Christmas only served to remind her of the worst mistake of her life.

Coming here to Iceland, somehow she'd expected something different. Traditional Icelandic music, maybe...

Merry stared resentfully out of the window of the taxi that was making slow progress up a snow-lined mountain pass. Tall banks of snow lay on either side and the white stuff was coming down heavily, in thick, large flakes, silently hitting the windshield before being pushed to one side by wipers that appeared to be struggling in the blizzard that had hit just after her plane had arrived in Reykjavik.

You didn't get to see snow like this in England.

Maybe I should try to appreciate it?

But she couldn't. Her mind was on other matters. Her destination, and the man at the centre of that destination—Dr Kristjan Gunnarsson. Now, there was a man who made her feel all hot and bothered. Made her blood pulse at an accelerated pace. A man who could melt all this snow just by sending one searing look its way.

Even now just the thought of seeing him again, of having to stand in front of him and tell him her news, made her thrum with a heat that was triple X-rated.

She thought of the last time they'd met. The last time she'd seen him he'd been naked in her bed, calling her back to him with a twinkle in those ice-blue eyes of his and a little curl of his beckoning finger.

Hawaii.

They'd both got carried away that last night. She'd thrown caution to the non-existent wind and decided to just let go and take a chance—after all, she'd never have to see the man ever again!

That had been the plan, anyway.

Before the medical conference had even started she'd gone for a walk on the beach and seen him emerging from the sea in a pair of trunks that had clung to his muscular thighs, water dripping down his broad, sculptured form.

She'd actually gasped to herself. James Bond and Mr Darcy emerging from the water had nothing on this guy! Watching Kristjan had been like watching the sea god Poseidon himself appearing from the waves. He'd run his hand over his hair, wiped the water from his face, and then he'd stood there, watching her, waiting for her to say something.

She'd wanted to say something cute, something amusing, but the only thing to come out of her mouth had been, 'The water looks good.'

And he'd replied, 'Just the water?' with a charming accent she hadn't quite been able to distinguish and a smirk that ought to have had a health warning attached to it.

Warning! May cause hot flushes and a racing heart.

That had been the start of it. The flirtation. She'd hoped that maybe he was just a tourist—but, no, he'd been part of the conference. He'd even been one of the speakers...talking about the social determinants of childhood health.

She'd sat in that room, watching him on the podium, his grey suit clinging in all the right places, his long blond hair restrained in a Viking plait down his back, and *tried* to concentrate on his words. But all she'd been able to think of was that first image she'd had of him...the shape of his well-hewn muscles, the droplets of water that had adhered to his pectorals, the way those trunks of his had clung to his body and what she would have given to run her fingers over his hot flesh...

Merry had never considered herself a lustful person, but looking at him, listening to him, had made her feel that way—naughty and excited, and her body had tingled in all the right places.

When his talk had been over her feet had propelled her towards him, to thank him for an inspiring talk, and he had turned to greet her, those sapphire eyes looking into her own molten brown ones, and she had felt like melting into a puddle under the intense heat of his gaze.

He'd bought her a drink. And then another. And she'd learned that they were both parentless. She'd been abandoned in a cardboard box outside the local vicar's house before some carol singers had arrived and found her there. That was how she'd got her name—Merry. And the paramedic who had been called out to her, who'd held her in the ambulance, his surname had been Bell. It had seemed apt, what with it being Christmas...

It hadn't been a great name for going through school, though. The jokes had never ended.

Kristjan's start in life had not been so terrible. He'd started out with a family but had lost his parents at an early age and ended up in the care system.

But sitting in that bar, sharing stories, had bonded them in a way she'd not expected. Before she'd known what she was doing she had told him her room number, and that had been the end—*the beginning?*—of that.

The hottest night of her life—and not just because they'd been in the tropics.

When she'd been married, sex had been quick and perfunctory and only for her husband's pleasure—and then he would fall asleep. With Kristjan it had been completely different, and he had made her body *sing*. Had shown her that her pleasure was just as important as his own.

Just thinking, even now, of how he had made her body feel, she experienced a feeling of heat and a blush stemming up from her very core. Thank goodness it was night-time, and the driver couldn't see the colour in her cheeks. Couldn't see as she shifted in her seat to try and pretend that she was just making herself more comfortable.

What would Kristjan say when he saw her? Would he be happy to see her? Or was she about to find out that the man she'd thought was impossibly single was actually married, with a wife he'd forgotten to tell her about? A *life* that she was about to turn upside down?

Because how could a man like that be single? It wasn't possible, was it? Unless he was one of those men who enjoyed his many conquests of women without any of the complications of a committed relationship?

Either way, he was about to get the news of a lifetime. Once she got to her B&B she'd change, shower, have something to eat and get an early night. Tomorrow she would see him. Tomorrow she would tell him and then be on her way.

She would have done the right thing. The moral thing. She neither wanted nor needed his interference in the matter, and if this was just about her she wouldn't be here at all.

Merry frowned, trying to see beyond the blizzard outside, trying to make some sense of the lights she saw in the distance. The taxi driver had collected her from the airport and told her that the trip to Snowy Peak was about two hours. All this time she'd seen nothing outside the window but a dark whiteness.

She only knew where he worked. He'd told her as they'd lain facing each other on soft white pillows, as his hand slid down her side into the dip of her stomach and then over the swell of her hip and thigh, before pulling her close, pressing her against him and beginning again.

She knew what she wanted to do. She wanted to keep it. But she didn't need *him*. She didn't need anyone and was more than happy to be everything this baby needed. Her child would not be left in a cardboard box, the way she had been. The only cardboard boxes her child would get close to would be the ones they used to play with. To make forts out of...or dens...or castles.

She suddenly became aware that the taxi had come to a stop. Merry frowned and leant forward. 'Something wrong?' Because it didn't look as if they'd arrived anywhere! The road ahead was hidden by the still falling snow and all around them it was dark.

'The road is too dangerous now. You must walk from here.'

She looked out at the snow, and then down at her trainers. All her luggage was in the boot of the car. It had been bad enough manhandling it through an airport, never mind up a mountain. Surely he wasn't serious?

'You are joking?'

The dark-haired driver turned around in his seat to face her. 'I do not joke. I am serious. I turn around here. Go back before road is impassable.'

'But…we're in the middle of nowhere!'

'Snowy Peak is top of this mountain. Ten minutes.'

'If it's just ten minutes then you can take me! I'm *paying* you to take me there.'

'Too steep like this. Snow too thick. Very dangerous. You must go on foot.'

Merry was exasperated. 'Seriously?'

'You want to crash? Fall down mountain? We do that if I drive you.'

She could see he was serious. She hadn't noticed the slow, steady climb of the car because she'd been so busy thinking about meeting up with Kristjan. But now she could see they were at an upward angle and that the road ahead, though thick with snow, looked sloped.

She could see a glow at the crest of the hill. Lights? From Snowy Peak? She knew the main hospital was there. Somewhere, anyway. And if it was only ten minutes…

She reluctantly thrust some money at the driver and he got out to help her get her bags from the boot.

The snow was coming down even more strongly, cold and wet, hitting her face. And, now she was out in it, it didn't seem as pretty as it had from inside the nice warm car. She was wearing the wrong shoes, the wrong clothes. And her suitcase wheels would be useless in the snow!

'Are you sure about this?' she yelled at the driver above the sound of the whistling wind.

'Yes. You go. Soon it will be too heavy.'

This wasn't too heavy already?

Merry slung one bag over her shoulder and tried to drag her suitcase behind her as she made her way up the road. The ice and snow beat against her face and hair and she could feel the cold soaking into her toes and clothes as she made slow headway through the storm. The thick tights she wore underneath her dress might as well have been the very lowest denier, because her legs felt bare in this intense cold.

Behind her, she saw the taillights of the taxi disappearing into the darkness of the night, and she swore before turning once again and plodding her way through the knee-high snow. She wanted to blame the driver, but even she could see how deep the snow was getting. Without a snowplough on the front of his vehicle, it was amazing that he'd been able to get this far as it was.

She was cold, and wet, and her legs were aching. But just when she thought she couldn't stand another moment in this weather she made the crest of the hill.

Spread out before her were the lights of Snowy Peak, warm yellow and white globes, and to one side a huge building that she saw was called the Snowy Peak Children's Hospital. She let out an exhausted breath on seeing it and trudged towards it, feeling relief that the taxi driver hadn't been kidding, even if he *had* just left her on the side of a snowy mountain at night.

With no idea of how to get to the B&B, she headed towards the hospital, a haven in the cold and the dark.

As she walked through the sliding doors, feeling a welcoming and pleasant gust of warm air from the heater above, she saw all eyes turn to her and realised just what she must look like…

Dr Kristjan Gunnarsson had been more than happy to push Aron's wheelchair towards the hospital shop. The little boy had waited days since his spinal surgery to get his first taste of a particular chocolate-covered fudge bar that had small bits of black liquorice suspended in its filling.

It wasn't something that they served on the hospital's healthy menu, and Kristjan had promised Aron a bar as soon as he was able to transfer himself to a wheelchair and stay in it for one hour without pain. That day had been today, and he'd never been prouder. In fact, Aron wanted to stay in the wheelchair until his mum arrived that night, so she could see him in it, too. He wanted it to be a surprise.

Now, with Aron chewing on his chocolatey snack, Kristjan was wheeling him back through the entrance foyer, towards the lifts that would take them back up to Aron's floor, when he became aware of the woman who had just trudged through the entrance doors, wheeling a snow-topped suitcase behind her. She'd stopped, propped the suitcase upright and was shaking the snow off her shoulders and her dark brown hair.

She looked miserably cold and wet and she was wearing totally the wrong things for winter in Iceland. Trainers, green tights, a yellow woollen dress and a short jacket. Only one woman he knew wore crazy clothes like that, but the last time he'd seen her she'd been in Hawaii, even though she lived in Brighton, England.

But now it would seem she was here.

Merry. *Dr* Merry Bell.

She hadn't spotted him yet, and he took a moment

to try and slow his breathing and appraise her. Her hair looked longer. He didn't remember it being that long the time they'd stood in the shower together, she with her hands up against the tiles and her back to him, when he'd lifted her hair away from her neck to kiss her hot skin...

Longing burned through him at the memory of that night and one morning they had spent together. She'd been unlike any woman he had ever met, and he'd left Hawaii—and her—with fond and extremely hot memories, knowing that it was probably for the best that she lived in another country.

She had been the first woman in his life who had made him yearn for more, but he didn't do full-on relationships—ever—and committing to more than one night with her would have broken all the rules he held himself accountable to. The rules that kept everyone at a distance—the way he liked them to be. Because then there would be no more pain. If he didn't get close and emotionally involved, he wouldn't have to face the losses that would come later.

But Hawaii had been—what? Roughly three months ago? What was she doing here? Was she here to work? There was a vacancy, but as far as he'd understood the hospital had chosen to wait until after Christmas to advertise.

He longed to go over to her and find out why she was here. As if his yearning had called out to her their eyes met and he felt the punch of it hit him in the gut.

And somewhere *lower.*

Her lips parted slightly, as if she was on the verge of saying something, but then she bit her lip and it was all he could do not to self-implode on the spot. He took a moment to gather himself, and used it to pretend he was just checking the brake on Aron's wheelchair.

Then he said, 'Excuse me, Aron, I won't be a moment.' And headed over to Merry.

As he got closer he could see the snow crystals still melting in her dark hair, and the way her make-up had smudged around her eyes, making them look smoky and sultry. He slowed as he got closer, taking his time to soak her up. She looked as if she needed a nice hot shower, and he could think of nothing better than taking her upstairs to the staff area, where there was a bathroom, and helping her off with her clothes. But he was on duty, and now was not the time for a seduction.

Was she aware that the outlines of her cold, peaked nipples were showing through her woollen dress?

He raised his eyes back up to her face. 'Hello, Merry.'

He could see she was just as disturbed by his presence as he was by hers, and it pleased him. He watched her cheeks flush with colour, and she pulled her jacket closed around her, as if it were a suit of armour.

'Hello, Kristjan.'

CHAPTER TWO

OKAY, SO SHE hadn't imagined it. Kristjan really was as stunning as she remembered. Tall and broad, muscular and strong. And looking just as luscious in clothes as he did out of them.

Don't think of him naked. That isn't helping!

She squeezed her eyes shut to try and dispel the image, but it was like trying to ignore an elephant in the room. You couldn't help but look at the huge grey creature. Only *her* elephant looked like a Viking out of time. He would look just as comfortable in a horned helmet, swinging a massive battle-axe, as he did in the bespoke suit, and that waistcoat he wore just emphasised his neat, flat stomach, under which she *knew* lay a set of perfectly moulded abs...

She forced herself to look elsewhere, and noticed that the hospital had a huge decorated Christmas tree in the centre of the entrance foyer and that 'White Christmas' was being piped out of hidden speakers.

Christmas. *Ugh.*

'To what do I owe the...pleasure?' asked Kristjan.

She could feel his eyes raking over her, and she wished again that she'd worn something a bit more suitable. She yanked once more at both sides of her jacket, to try and pull it closed. She hadn't expected to come straight from the airport and meet Kristjan. She'd expected the taxi to take her to the B&B she'd booked first, so she could settle in, get changed, and then meet Kristjan on *her* terms. She hadn't planned to be wearing her travelling clothes.

'The taxi driver made me walk up the last bit of the mountain. He was meant to be taking me to a B&B. I thought someone here might direct me to it...' She hoped she sounded as unbothered by him as she hoped.

Kristjan looked outside, assessing the weather. 'You came up the mountain in *this*?' he sounded angry.

'I didn't really have a choice in the matter. So...the Kerling B&B...?'

'This storm will go on for some time now, and I can't let you go outside in those cold, wet clothes—'

'You can't *let* me?' *Who did he think he was?*

'You can sleep here tonight.'

Sleep here? In the hospital? 'No. I can't.'

'There are plenty of beds in the on-call rooms.'

And she knew exactly what happened in on-call rooms.

She felt herself flush once again, knowing she did not want Kristjan to know where she was sleeping. He might expect something from her. A continuation of their bedtime adventures. And that wasn't what she was here for! In no way did she want or need any relationship with this man. Even if she *had* briefly entertained the idea of him hearing her news and sweeping her off her feet into the sunset, like men did in the movies.

No, he'd been fun for one night, when she'd thought she'd never see him again, and now it was more complicated than that she didn't need him making it worse, with his blue eyes and good intentions and beautifully honed muscles...

'I'd rather make my way to the B&B.'

'Why?' He looked amused and leaned in, whispering, 'You think I'm going to sneak into your on-call room in the middle of the night?'

She remembered how he'd whispered into her ear just what he was going to do to her that night in Hawaii, and she shivered at the memory.

'You're cold. Let's at least get you warm and dry and into a change of clothes.'

That *did* sound like a good idea, she had to admit. The clothes she had on were soaked, and she was freezing, and that couldn't be good for her condition. Not that he knew that. Not yet.

Reluctantly, she found herself agreeing. 'All right…'

He smiled and stepped forward to take her suitcase, then led her over to the lifts, where Aron waited. 'Aron, this is Dr Bell. Dr Bell—Aron Mikkelsson.'

The little boy in the wheelchair had chocolate at the sides of his mouth.

She smiled. 'Hello, Aron.'

'You are English?' Aron asked.

She was impressed that he knew some English and was willing to try it out on her. 'I am.'

'You know the Queen?' he asked, with excitement in his voice.

She laughed and shook her head. 'I'm afraid not, no.'

'Oh. Okay…'

She glanced at Kristjan as the doors to the lift opened and deliberately stood on the opposite side of Aron's wheelchair to create a distance between them once they were inside.

Kristjan pressed the button to take them up to the fourth floor of the hospital and they rode in silence.

She tried her hardest not to look at him. But her body was in perfect awareness of his proximity. Soon she couldn't stand it any more, and just had to have a quick glance.

Then she looked down at Aron and smiled. 'So, Aron, why are you here in the hospital?'

'He had an operation,' Kristjan answered.

'Oh?'

Aron just smiled, licking the chocolate from around his mouth.

'Removal of a malignant glial tumour,' Kristjan explained.

She nodded, then smiled again at Aron, because it was easier to look at the child than it was the man. The extremely virile man…

A quick glance at the left hand holding the handle of Aron's wheelchair showed no ring. Did that mean anything? He'd not been expecting her, so if he normally wore one he wouldn't have thought to hide it. This had to be normal, right? But not every married man wore a ring, and she had no idea if the traditions regarding marriage were different here in Iceland. Perhaps the men here didn't wear rings? Who knew?

The lift doors pinged open, revealing a corridor filled with tinsel and pictures on the wall of reindeer leaping through the snow and candy canes hanging from branches filled with fairy lights. The nurses' desk had a miniature Christmas tree, and more tinsel around the noticeboard, and in a corner by the linen cupboard was a stack of presents that almost reached the ceiling.

'Wait here. I'll just escort Aron back to his bed and get him comfortable.'

She nodded and watched Kristjan walk away, pushing the small boy's wheelchair. It felt odd to see him in this environment. She'd only ever seen him at the conference, presenting—or naked, of course. She'd almost forgotten he was a paediatric doctor, like her.

As they moved away she heard him say something to the boy. They both laughed and she smiled without realising it, watching them. He clearly got on well with the young lad, and she took a couple of steps forward so she could watch through the safety glass as he helped Aron out of his chair and safely back into bed. He passed Aron a book from his bedside, said something else, and then ruffled the boy's hair.

This was a different side to him, and it intrigued her greatly to see him with the boy. But that intrigue disturbed her. It shouldn't matter that he was great with kids. So she turned away and deliberately went over to the nurses' station, pretending to look through a bunch of leaflets that she thought were about vaccinations, so he wouldn't catch her watching him.

He had to be wondering why she was here. Was it too late to pretend that she was here for some other reason and then just go home again? He would never have to know! They'd never run into each other. He lived in Iceland. She in England—Brighton. The chances of them ever meeting again were slim...

But she knew she couldn't do that. Not to him and not to her baby. She had been abandoned and left without any parents. Growing up, she would have killed to know *something* about who her parents were! This baby in her belly had a father, and she knew *who* he was and *where* he was. Her child deserved to know its dad, too. Even if they hardly ever got to see one another.

That was how this was going to play out. That was her plan and she expected nothing else. She would tell him about the baby, and that she was going to keep it, and then she would go home. Start a life with her child back in Brighton. Her baby would know who it came from. Its mum and its dad. Her baby would have what she'd never had. And if her child ever wanted to go to Iceland... Well, they'd cross that bridge if they ever came to it.

She sensed his presence behind her before she turned to look at him.

'So...' he said.

'So...' She gave him a brief smile.

Now was not the time. Not like this. She was a mess, and shivering, and he was on duty. He deserved to hear this news when he had the time and the ability to sit and listen properly. Right now, she just wanted to get out of her wet clothes.

And into his arms? Imagine how good it would feel to press yourself against his hot, solid body...

'You mentioned somewhere I could get changed?' she said.

He gave a nod. 'Of course. Here—let me take that.' And he grabbed her wheeled suitcase and led the way.

She followed after him, admiring his restraint, not asking her questions. But, then again, he'd been good at holding off his own pleasure, making sure she was pleasured first... A shiver rippled down her spine and she rubbed at her arms to rid herself of the goosebumps that prickled over her skin.

He brought her to a door marked Aðeins Starfsfólk, pushing it open. Inside was what was obviously a staff-room, with lockers and a small kitchen area in one corner, and another door leading to a bathroom.

'Shower is through there. Want any help?'

She stared at him, her face flushing with heat, remembering that shower taken with him. 'No! Most definitely not!'

He laughed. 'I'm joking, Merry. I'm on duty. Relax.'

She let out a breath. Of course he was joking! She should have realised.

He grabbed a piece of paper off the small coffee table and scribbled a number on it. 'This is my mobile number. Get one of the nurses to contact me when you're done.'

She took the paper, but knew she wouldn't call him. Once she'd showered and changed she would be asking the nurses to direct her to her B&B. Then she would return tomorrow, to tell him about the baby.

'Thank you.'

'You're very welcome.'

He smiled at her for a moment and she allowed herself that moment to look into his eyes and wonder what it would be like to be more to him than a moment in time. To let herself be swept off her feet and into his bed again and who knew what afterwards?

But the moment passed as he pushed her case towards her hands.

'It's good to see you, Merry.'

She gave him a brief smile, then looked down and away. When she looked up again he'd gone, and the smack of disappointment that washed over her left her feeling confused and disturbed and lost all at once.

But Merry headed into the bathroom, closing and locking the door firmly behind her.

Rejuvenated, showered, warm and dry, she collected her things before heading out of the staff room, intent on asking a nurse for directions to her B&B.

But when she came hurrying out of the bathroom, ready to make her escape, she found Kristjan sitting on one of the couches, reading a newspaper that he put down at her appearance. He tilted his head to one side to look at her appraisingly and he smiled, standing, stretching to his full height.

She felt like a little elf before him. A naughty elf who had been caught trying to scurry out of the grotto without being seen by Santa Claus.

'You're here,' she said accusingly.

'I am.'

'But you're meant to be working.'

'And you're meant to be calling me. But I had a feeling you were going to leave without doing so—am I right?'

She coloured.

'What's going on, Merry? Why are you here?'

He genuinely seemed to want to know. Had he been worrying about it ever since he'd left her to take a shower? Could he not bear the thought of not knowing the answer?

She owed it to him. Why keep him waiting?

Because I didn't think it would happen like this.

She'd imagined sitting down with him in a coffee shop, or something—somewhere public, where neither of them could make a scene. Where she couldn't allow herself to fall into his arms. Because these last few weeks she'd been filled with a dizzying array of moods and emotions and she wasn't fully able to trust her body right now—*or* its responses.

One alarming change in particular had been to her sex drive. It hadn't taken her long to notice that it seemed to be on overdrive—she'd noticed every good-looking man at the airport and on the plane over here. And now she was with *him*. The man who had caused all this.

She was aware of everything about him. How he stood. His curious smile. The way his mouth was slightly curled. The way his hands sat on his hips as he stood there, looking at her with questioning eyes.

'I'm here to see you,' she said.

His eyes darkened. Was he pleased by her response? Or bothered by it?

'Why?' he asked. 'What we had in Hawaii was amazing, but it was finished when you walked out of your hotel room wearing that pretty blue dress.'

He remembered what she'd worn? That was nice...

'It's not finished.'

Kristjan smiled. 'Really? How so?' His voice was curious. 'I don't do long-term relationships, Merry. However, if you're interested in pursuing a purely sexual relationship, then I'm—'

'I'm pregnant, Kristjan. With your baby,' she added unnecessarily. Because what else would she be pregnant with?

She swallowed hard, awaiting his response, watching as myriad emotions played over his face. She saw shock. Surprise. Disbelief. He blinked, turned away, then instantly turned back again, as if he wanted to ask her a question, but nothing would come out of his mouth.

She'd never seen him unsure of anything. In all the time she had spent with him he had been surefooted, in control, had known exactly what he was doing at all times. This was a man who had stood at a podium in front of hundreds of other doctors and given his presentation assuredly, never faltering, never nervous—a man who'd had his audience in the palm of his hand. He had always seemed to know what was happening, and how, but now, in this very instant, he was floundering, and she could see how difficult he was finding that.

He was responding with the same emotions that she had felt when she'd watched that stick turn pink in her bathroom at home. Sheer disbelief...denial of the truth that had been right in front of her!

She was glad it wasn't easy for him, because it hadn't been easy for her.

And now he knew.

Her job was done.

I can go.

CHAPTER THREE

KRISTJAN COULD HEAR the cold wind whistling around the corner of the hospital, and through the window behind her he saw thick flakes of snow being blown this way, then that. She looked like an angel standing there, with that wintry backdrop and the tinsel around the window.

A very small angel.

Pregnant. With his baby.

His baby.

He felt a rush of emotions. Some that he could identify, others not so much. They rushed past so fast, just like the snow in the storm—there one minute, gone the next.

Never in his life had he expected a complication such as this. He loved kids—loved helping kids, making them better and sending them home—but he'd never thought to have one of his own.

Having a child meant having a relationship, making a commitment, and that was the sort of thing he had never aspired to—because wanting something like that opened you up to a whole new world of hurt, and the world was tough enough anyway. Being with someone else, in a relationship, meant knowing that you could lose them, and he'd already lost more than he cared to.

Only now—now that it had happened and Merry was standing before him, awaiting his reaction—he felt a stirring of something that he'd left well alone for a very long time. A feeling that he had kept locked away since he was very young, as soon as he had been capable of making such a decision.

His baby. *His.*

She had to be three months along. Heading into the second trimester. He looked down at her abdomen, but it was still flat. He watched her cover her abdomen with her hands, almost as if she could protect the baby from his stare.

'You want to keep it?'

He knew it was a horrible question to ask, but he figured she'd come all this way to tell him, so the likelihood that she did was strong. But he needed to know for sure. Needed her to say the words.

A look flashed in those chocolate eyes of hers. 'Yes. I do. I am. I need nothing from you, Kristjan. I just thought I'd do the right thing and let you know. And now that I have I can go home again.'

He frowned. Go home again? She had to be kidding? Down the mountain? In this? And they'd sorted nothing out. Nothing at all! What was going to happen in the future? With money. Visitation rights etc.

Why am I thinking about any of that? It's not like I'm going to be a full-time father. She lives in another country!

And that thought burrowed its way down into his soul like a root. It took hold of the desire he'd once hidden, then spread its tendrils throughout him and headed back up to the surface with tender green shoots, its leaves curling open in the light, revealing itself to him.

I can't let her go back. Not yet.

'Not in this weather, you can't. Have you looked outside? The mountain pass will be treacherous. People have died in less severe weather than this.'

She frowned, glancing out of the window. 'For how long? Till tomorrow?'

She really knew nothing about the weather patterns in his country. 'I'd say at least a few days.'

Her face registered her shock at his statement. 'A *few* days? But I'm booked on a flight home in two days!'

'You won't make it. We'll phone the airport and re-arrange your flight. Looks like you're going to be here over Christmas.'

'But...'

He could see the thoughts racing over her face as she looked from him to the window and back again. She really was beautiful. Even when she'd looked wet and be-draggled and freezing cold he'd wanted to take her in his arms and pull her towards him. To feel her soft body against his once more. All those feelings he'd stamped down since she left him in Hawaii had come rushing back.

And now that she was looking lost and hopeless... Well, that just made him want to look after her. Only he couldn't. Because she was pregnant with his child. Any move he made to restart what they'd finished in Hawaii would only make her think that they were in some sort of relationship—and they were not.

A baby, though...

That was huge. That was commitment on a grand scale. That was opening himself up to a world of pos-sible heartache and pain, and so far, for most of his life, he'd avoided that by staying single and only having to look after himself. It was a rule that he had kept to for all these years and it had served him well.

Now everything would change. If he got involved in this—*when* he got involved…

'I'll arrange lodgings for you,' he said.

'There won't be anything. It's December. All the rooms in the hotels have been taken by holidaymakers bringing their kids to Wonderland and I got the last room at the B&B, which was only available for two nights. I suppose I could ask them for space on the sofa or the floor after that… They're expecting me.'

Wonderland was the huge purpose-built village next to Snowy Peak that was a Christmas paradise for kids and their families. It brought in a lot of money and was good for the local economy, employing a lot of the locals who lived around the mountain.

He sighed, making a decision without thinking too hard about it. 'Then you'll stay with me.'

'What? I can't do that!'

'I won't have the mother of my child sleeping on a floor. Not when there's a perfectly good bed in my home.'

She looked at him uncertainly. She bit her bottom lip again in a way that was most disconcerting and did strange things to him below his belt.

'A spare bed?' she asked.

'You think I'm asking you to sleep with me?'

'Well…'

'Relax. I'm more than capable of resisting you. You'll be perfectly safe.'

He hoped he sounded believable, because he *knew* how she made him feel, and asking her to stay with him for the next few days was going to be…strange. Especially since he'd never let anyone into his own personal space before. Certainly not someone like her…

'I guess I should say thank you…'

'You're welcome.'

'Am I expected to sit around twiddling my thumbs with nothing to do, though?'

He thought for a moment. 'We can give you privileges at the hospital. You can work here. You're a paediatrician, and we need an extra person over the holidays anyway.'

She nodded. 'All right. I'll feel better if I'm earning my keep. That way I can pay you for board and lodging and food.'

'You don't need to do that.'

'Oh, but I do.'

He stared at her, mulling over the idea of going over to her, pulling her against his chest and kissing her until she stopped talking. He wasn't used to having people argue with him, and her determination to stand on her own two feet and pay him for staying at his place seemed to arouse his desire for her even more—which felt odd to him, because he never went back. He always moved forward.

But he held back. Considered her. The steady resolve in the eyes staring back at him was almost like a challenge. She was no walkover, was she?

'Then let's go see the Chief and get you set up. And then we'll need to get you out of those clothes.' He smiled, determined to put her on the back foot.

'I beg your pardon? These are perfectly acceptable—'

'And get you into some scrubs.' He grinned and held the door open for her. 'After you.'

He watched her as she walked past in her black polo neck and purple skirt, inhaling the scent of her shampoo. It was floral. He couldn't pick out which flower, but it was very nice…soft and gentle. The aroma warmed his senses, making him want to pick up a tress of her hair and inhale it some more.

Only he didn't do that.

He couldn't do that.

Instead, he kept control of his impulses and led her down to the Chief's office.

Merry picked up her first chart, gave it a brief scan, and then headed over to the bed. A really small little girl lay dwarfed in it, surrounded by teddy bears.

'Hello, there. My name is Dr Bell. Can you tell me your name, sweetheart?' She smiled at the little girl. It said on her chart that she was three years old, but she looked half that.

'Tinna.'

'Hello, Tinna!' She reached out to take hold of the little girl's fingers and shook her hand. 'Nice to meet you. Now…' she looked up at the child's parents, who had stood up on the other side of the bed on her arrival '…can you tell me what's brought you in here, today?'

The parents looked at each other and frowned. Clearly language was going to be a problem here. They obviously knew some basic English, but not much, and as she knew zero Icelandic they were in trouble.

She turned to look for help and saw Kristjan stroll over from another child's bedside.

'Need some assistance?'

Rankled, she pursed her lips. 'There seems to be a language barrier…'

'Ah. Okay. I'll translate for you.'

Which he did.

'She's had a seizure,' he said.

'Okay. When did that happen?'

'Just after dinner.'

'She wasn't choking on her food, or anything like that?'

The parents shook their heads.

'And has she had a seizure before?'

All of this information was in the notes, but she wanted to check and make sure. Sometimes parents remembered extra details on a subsequent retelling of events.

'No.'

'Okay… And how long did it last?'

'Not long. Maybe a half minute?'

'And she has Tay-Sachs?'

Tay-Sachs disease was an inherited condition that mainly affected babies and small children. It had no cure. It would stop the nerves from working, so that young sufferers would lose the ability to use their muscles, reach normal milestones. They would have swallowing difficulties, seizures, and the diseases would eventually be fatal. Not many Tay-Sachs sufferers made it past the age of five.

'Yes.'

'All right.' She put down the chart and sat on the edge of the bed. She smiled at Tinna. 'Okay, so we need to give you some medication to help stop what's happened to you today, so that hopefully it doesn't happen again. Is that all right, Tinna?'

'She wants to know if it will taste bad.'

She smiled. 'No, it won't. How do you feel right now?'

'Okay.'

She turned to the parents. 'Have you noticed any stiffness lately? Any speech problems? Swallowing difficulties?'

'A little.'

'Okay, so some physiotherapy might help her with that. Obviously we want Tinna to keep moving and be strong for as long as she can.'

'Is she going to be in hospital for a long time? They have family visiting, and it's Christmas soon, and they wonder if they'll be able to take her home?'

'I understand.' She turned to the parents once more, speaking low after Kristjan translated. 'I'd like to keep her in for at least twenty-four hours, just to be on the safe side. We'll get her on anti-seizure medication, and if she has no more seizures I don't see why you shouldn't be able to take her home.'

'Thank you, Doctor.'

'You're welcome.' She shook their hands, said goodbye to Tinna, and then went over with Kristjan to the doctors' station. He managed to dwarf everything, due to his size.

He smiled down at her. 'So, how did you feel your first consult went?'

'Fine. I feel really sorry for that little girl, though. And her poor parents. Tay-Sachs is awful… How do you cope as a parent, knowing your child won't live? It just doesn't seem right.'

She sat down and began inputting her notes, requesting medication for Tinna and asking for her family to be allowed to take her home afterwards. Today had been the child's first seizure, but it would be the start of many. Next time it might be breathing problems that brought Tinna in, and if she got pneumonia…

Merry tried to get rid of the sad thoughts in her head, but she couldn't, and she fought back the sudden sting of tears. A disease like Tay-Sachs was inherited. She had no idea of her own medical history! Her baby could get sick. Merry seemed healthy, and so did Kristjan—for now. But what about what the future held? Neither of them could know and that scared her.

'Are you all right?'

Kristjan's low voice sounded concerned. She forced a bright smile to her face and shrugged. 'I'm fine! What makes you think I'm not?'

'You suddenly stopped typing and you seemed to drift off for a moment.'

'I was thinking.'

'About...?'

What? Did he expect her to share every thought in her head? Who did he think he was? Just because she'd slept with him, and was now carrying his baby, did he think he suddenly had the right to know everything about her? Perhaps agreeing to stay with him was a bad idea. What did she know about him, really?

She couldn't tell him her doubts. How would that sound? *Oh, I don't want to come and stay at yours because you might be an axe murderer.*

'I'm just hungry. It's been a long day.'

He stared at her for a moment. 'Of course. I didn't think. Did you eat on the flight?'

'No, it was just a couple of hours.'

'Let me get you something now.'

'You don't have to do that!' she tried to protest.

But he was already up on his feet and looking taller than ever. He was like a wall—a mountain of a man, with a rugged exterior.

'Of course I do. You don't know where anything is yet. What do you want? Something savoury or something sweet?'

Well, she was so ravenous she would eat anything! 'Both!'

He smiled. 'A woman with a big appetite? I like that.'

Was he still talking about food? She couldn't tell. Not when he was looking at her like that. As if he could eat *her*!

She flushed, feeling the heat in her cheeks, and had to look away, resume her typing.

It was only as he was walking away that she stopped

to look at him. His bottom was neatly moulded by his trousers, atop his big, thick, muscular thighs. His plait of hair, tied neatly at the bottom with a twist of leather, reached almost halfway down his broad back.

She remembered what it had felt like to be pressed up against that hard body, and that stirred another type of hunger that she'd hoped she'd got a lid on.

She was going to be working and living with Dr Kristjan Gunnarsson for at least a few days. Maybe even a week! Over Christmas!

It wasn't that she had any family of her own to miss… And Merry figured he was almost her family now. No matter how the future played out, he would always be a part of her life because of their child.

How do I feel about that?

Kristjan was very pretty to look at and lust over, but what else was he? A good doctor, she supposed. He looked after sick kids, and you had to be pretty hard-core to do that. Being a paediatric doctor wasn't for wimps, so he had to be strong emotionally. And he was crazy good in bed…

She cursed and dismissed those intrusive, naughty, X-rated thoughts once again. She needed to be serious about this. Because she wasn't going to let him call the shots. This might be *their* baby, but it was *her* body, and *her* life, and no man—no matter how good-looking or how capable he was of giving her a screaming orgasm— was ever going to be in charge of how her life played out.

She'd given a man the ultimate control before.

No, I didn't give it to him. He took it.

So, there was no way she was going to let Kristjan Gunnarsson take anything away from her.

Ever.

CHAPTER FOUR

KRISTJAN HAD NEVER taken a woman to his home before. It was *his* space and his alone. The fact that he was now opening it up to Merry, the woman who was carrying his child, made him feel very strange indeed...

He watched her as she stepped inside, taking in the huge stone inglenook fireplace that dominated the room, the decorated Christmas tree that stood in the corner beside it. The floor-to-ceiling windows decorated with tiny white lights and the garlands of pine with frosted berries and silver ribbons.

What could he say? He loved Christmas. As his parents had, so many years ago. And he was determined each festive season to honour their memories by outdoing himself from the year before.

That was why he had so much Christmas decoration about the place. The true reason for going overboard at Christmas was that it allowed him to feel closer to them. To remember the way his mother had used to love decorating the tree with him. The way his father had pretended to be Santa.

And to pretend that he wasn't lonely he worked every Christmas in the hospital, with all those kids who didn't get the chance to go home. There was something special and heart-warming about being there at Christmas.

Merry stood by the mantelpiece, looking around her. 'You like Christmas?'

'You don't?'

'Not really.'

He thought everyone loved Christmas. 'Why not?'

She shrugged, but he figured she did know—she just didn't want to tell him. But then again, why would she? They barely knew one another. He'd invited a stranger to his home. To stay with him for a few days. And she was pregnant with his baby! How crazy was that?

'Let me give you the tour once I've lit the fire.'

He got the fire going, and once it was steadily roaring away he got up to show her around—the kitchen, the bathrooms, the spare bedroom. *His bedroom.*

She stood in the doorway of his bedroom and stared at the king-sized bed. He smiled at her discomfort. 'Don't worry. I don't have any plans to seduce you.'

Merry looked at him. 'Good, because I don't plan on being seduced.'

He walked right up to her, towering over her, and looked down at her beautiful face. 'Let's get you a drink.'

It felt good to be standing so close to her again and, despite his words, he couldn't help but think about what it would be like to kiss her again.

Perhaps she saw the thought in his eyes, because she turned away and headed down the stairs. At the bottom she stood there, fidgeting. 'You have a lovely home.'

He went down to stand beside her. 'Thank you.'

'Even if it *does* look like Santa threw up in here!'

Kristjan laughed. 'You'll get used to it. We Icelanders love Christmas.'

'I'm beginning to understand that.'

She straightened a little figurine he had displayed on

a windowsill. It was one of a herd of reindeer, pulling a sled holding a fat Santa and a ginormous sack of presents.

'By the time you leave here you will, too.'

'Oh, I don't think so.'

'No?'

She stared back. 'No.'

'My little ice queen... But we will melt your heart, don't worry.'

'It's fine the way it is. You mentioned a drink? Let me make it—what do you want?'

He raised an eyebrow. He wanted lots of things. Especially as he looked at her standing there, trying her hardest not to be charmed by his home. For instance, he wanted to undress her and make love to her in front of the fireplace. Or take her upstairs and reacquaint her with how good they were together in a shower. Or perhaps take her outside and introduce her to the wonders of a steamy hot tub...

But he also wanted to keep his head on his shoulders. 'Tea will be fine. Thank you.'

He followed her into the kitchen and watched her get acquainted with where he kept everything. She opened cupboards and drawers, and he found himself smiling at her obvious disgust that all his mugs looked like Christmas puddings because last week he'd swapped them with his normal ones for the festive season.

She looked at the box of teabags and scrunched up her face as she sniffed at it. 'What flavour is this tea?'

'Spiced apple and pear with ginger.'

'Seriously?'

'Wait till you try it. Don't add sugar—add a splash of this.' He passed her some maple syrup.

'You'll rot your teeth.'

'It's just for special occasions.'

'Such as?'

'*Christmas*, Merry. *Christmas*. Come on, tell me—why do you hate it so much? Because you were abandoned at Christmas? I seem to remember you telling me that.'

She passed him his tea and leant back against the kitchen counter. 'I used to love Christmas. The promise of it…what it meant.'

'So what happened?'

She shook her head, as if she couldn't quite believe she was going to tell him her story. 'A guy happened.'

He nodded in understanding. As he'd suspected. And that only gave strength as to his own reasons for staying single. *You let people in, you let yourself become vulnerable and people hurt you.* It always happened. Staying out of relationships was definitely the way to go.

But then he looked down at her belly. Thought about the baby growing there. He couldn't stay out of *that* relationship, could he? He might keep to himself, but he was a decent person and he would take care of his responsibilities.

'I apologise on behalf of all menfolk.' He smiled and raised his cup to her as if in a toast.

'And now another bloke has got me pregnant and I'm going to be a single mother.'

'It takes two, Merry. And we did use protection.'

'I know that!'

'You plan on staying in England?'

She laughed. 'You expect me to move to Iceland?'

'No.'

Yes.

The idea of knowing he would have a child in this world but not be able to see it was disturbing to him now that he thought about it. It had been a long time since he'd had a family, and now...

He smiled at himself—at the craziness of the situation. Just this morning it had been life as usual—no relationships, no commitments—and he had been happy. And tonight...? Tonight he was worrying about which country his child would live in, because he wanted to see it every day.

I do. I want to see it every day.

It would never have been his decision to be a father. He'd never wanted to get involved with anyone—that had always been his modus operandi. But now that it was a possibility—was *real*—he was surprised to discover he had opinions on the matter.

He was an all-in kind of a guy when he did something. He was fully committed to his work at the hospital. Being a paediatric doctor was his life! So the idea of only half-heartedly being a father was not one he could consolidate in his mind. That wasn't him. Sending money and birthday cards would not be enough. He wanted to be *involved*.

'Good. Because my life is in England,' Merry said.

'It could be here.'

'In the land of ice and snow? I don't think so!'

'You'll grow to love it. Trust me.'

'I'm not uprooting my entire life to move here because a *man* wants me to.'

'Then do it because the father of your child has asked you to.' He stared hard at her, wanting to show her he was serious.

She stared back at him and he could see that she was frightened. It was written all over her face. He didn't like seeing her scared. He didn't like seeing anyone feel that way. He fought the urge to cross over to her and pull her close, because he knew she didn't need that right now and would not appreciate it. She would view it as him trying to press his wishes on her.

A man had hurt her. Badly. He didn't know exactly how, but he did know that if he stood any chance of having his child in his life he needed to persuade this woman who stirred his blood that she could have a life *here*. He couldn't go to England. Iceland ran through his veins! He had history here. Roots. And…and it was a good place to raise a child.

I'm crazy to even consider this!

But he knew he had to.

Kristjan had lost the family he'd once had, and he had often yearned to have *someone*. When he had watched those other kids at the school gates running into their parents' loving arms. Watched them get scooped up and have kisses planted on their cheeks. He'd had that. Once.

His aunt and uncle had taken him in for a little while, but it had never been the same. They'd never wanted kids, and to suddenly find themselves parents had been a difficult transition for them.

They'd tried so *hard*. But he had known he was a burden to them. An extra struggle, both financial and emotional. He had felt like a spare part, and he'd been so desperate for love he had been left feeling angry. He'd rebelled as a teenager. That hadn't gone down well! Getting into trouble over silly things… he'd ended up in care. But that anger had fuelled him to stand alone and live his life *his* way.

He wanted more for his own child.

His child would have its father waiting for him or her at the school gates, and Kristjan knew he would be the type of father to scoop his child up into his arms and smother it with kisses!

'Let me prove it to you,' he said.

'Prove what?'

'That you and the baby could have a good life here in this country.'

She cradled her Christmas pudding mug in both hands and stared at him. Considered him. 'You *want* to be part of its life?'

'I do.'

Had she heard his voice waver? *He* had. But this *meant* something to him. Even with the short time he'd known about it, he knew he needed to be a part of this baby's life. 'Give me until the New Year. If you're not convinced, then go home to England and we'll sort something out.'

She stared at him for an age and he couldn't read her. Would she give him this chance? Would she stay?

He had no idea right now just how exactly he was going to prove to her that it would be worth her moving to another country on a permanent basis, but he knew he had to give it a try.

It was Christmas! The season of goodwill to all men and women—and babies. She *had* to give him a chance, right? She had to give him a chance to know his child. To *love* his child. Every day.

'All right.'

'All right?'

'I'll give you until the road clears, then I'm going. Understood?'

He nodded, knowing that the season and the weather were on his side. At this time of year most of the tourists has already arrived, well in advance of Christmas, and once the roads were impassable they would be like that for a long time. If he kept her busy with work, and showed her all the wonders of this place, then maybe she wouldn't have time to check weather reports and road conditions because she'd be falling in love.

He just had to show her the truth and the beauty of the place.

He would make her fall in love with being here.

A knock on the bedroom door had her slowly waking from a deep slumber. She'd never slept so well before. This bed was unbelievable! The mattress wasn't too hard, the blankets were thick and warm, and on top there was a pure white faux fur-lined topper.

After going into her room last night to settle down, she'd put on her pyjamas and then run her fingers through the topper as she passed by, unable to believe that this luxurious bedroom was to be hers! And the best part was it didn't look like a Christmas grotto in here. Kristjan's guest room had been minimally decorated—and that said a lot, considering how the rest of the house looked.

There were thick white candles on the windowsill, a garland of holly over the small fireplace that contained a log burner, and a set of snowmen like Russian dolls on her bedside table. That was it. She could cope with that amount of decoration. That was enough Christmas.

And so she'd gone to sleep and slept like the dead until now, when Kristjan had knocked at her door and woken her.

'Come in.'

He opened the door with a smile and brought in a breakfast tray, laid it on her lap. There were scrambled eggs and toast, hot chocolate in a mug shaped like a Christmas present, a bowl of muesli with a small jug of milk, and in a small bud vase a sprig of something that looked like mistletoe.

She picked it up and raised an eyebrow at him. 'What's this for?'

'For decoration. Don't eat that. It's poisonous.' He smiled.

She smiled back and propped herself up in bed properly, preparing to tuck herself in, then realised that he was just standing at the side of her bed staring at her, dressed in a very nice, *tight* pair of dark jeans and a checked shirt.

'Are you going to watch me eat?'

He sat on the edge of the bed and pinched a triangle of toast. 'No. I'm going to go and get my own breakfast in just a minute.'

'Right... Am I going to get breakfast in bed every morning?'

He smiled. 'Would that persuade you to stay?'

'I'm already staying.'

'I meant after.'

She took a sip of the hot chocolate. It was perfect. 'It will take more than a breakfast tray to get me to uproot everything.'

'Ah... Okay. And just what exactly *is* "everything"? Just so I know what I'm in competition with?'

She faltered before she responded. It wasn't as if she could say *family*. Her adoptive mother was dead. And her adoptive father... Well, he'd left years ago. When it had all got too much for him. He'd been a coward. He'd not been able to stay and watch the progression of the disease that had been slowly killing his wife and had instead left *her* to do so.

Life had been cruel to Merry. Her real mother had abandoned her and her adopted one had faded, day by day, until death had enveloped her with its icy grip and taken even that relationship away from her. It had made her think that maybe she was destined always to be alone?

That was why this was such a shock. The fact that Kristjan wanted to be involved with her baby. Was trying to keep her here. There wasn't much left for her at home any more, except bad memories. But...

'My friends. My *job*...'

He nodded and stood up again, swallowing the last of the toast he'd pinched, licking his fingertips to get at the melted butter, and she felt her loins curl with lust at the image. She knew what that tongue could do, applied to all the right places...

'All right. Enjoy your breakfast. We need to be at work in one hour.'

'Okay.'

He headed out of the bedroom.

'Kristjan?'

He turned. 'Yes?'

'Thank you. For breakfast in bed. It was very kind of you.'

He smiled at her and nodded. 'You're very welcome, Merry.' And then he was gone.

She heard his big form going down the stairs and she couldn't help but think, as she had last night, about what she'd agreed to. Staying here until after Christmas. Letting him try to show her that it might be worthwhile for her to stay here.

She didn't want to tell him that her home, back in Brighton, was a tiny flat with just a few pieces of furniture. A place she barely ever stayed at, because she worked so much. Or that her downstairs neighbour thought nothing of playing rock music into the early hours of the morning. Or that she'd lost most of her friends when she'd moved there to get away from her life with Mark.

Yes, she had her job—but she could do that anywhere.

Her colleagues were great, but she never socialised with them. Unless you counted the Christmas party, and she'd never really enjoyed that—watching people pair up with people they wouldn't normally look at, just because the Christmas spirit had got into them.

And now Kristjan wanted to try and give *her* some Christmas spirit. By showing her the joys of living in Snowy Peak.

He wanted to be part of this baby's life—which was something of a shock. A small part of her was pleased that he cared, but another part was terrified.

What if he was like her adoptive father? What if he left when the going got difficult? If it all got too hard?

Babies were hard work. It wasn't all cute pictures on social media showing sleeping babies inside giant flowers. It was explosive diarrhoea and spit-up, and crying into the long hours of the night.

Heck, what if *she* couldn't do it? Her own mother had failed and walked away. What was there to say that *she* would make a good mother? It was hardly in her genes, was it?

The fear of the future, of the unknown, cast a long, dark shadow…

CHAPTER FIVE

'ARE YOU READY? We need to get going.'

Merry was putting on her borrowed snow boots for the walk from Kristjan's house to the hospital. It had taken them a good twenty-minutes to get there last night in the thick snow, and she'd been amazed at the sight of the starry sky. It looked different here than it did in England—clearer…the stars brighter.

Walking behind the tall hulk that was Kristjan, she had struggled to keep up with him. He was used to this snow. She wasn't. A couple of times he'd had to stop to let her catch up, and at one point he'd had to take her hand and help her through a particularly deep patch of ice-white snow.

'Nearly ready. I just need my coat.'

'Wrap up warm—we're not going straight to the hospital.'

He pulled a thick knitted beanie hat onto his head and opened the door as she zipped up the coat he'd lent her.

'We're not?'

'No. We've been called out to an emergency.'

'Oh!'

She thought about that. An emergency? With the roads all blocked? How would they get there?

'What are you like with dogs?'

She raised her eyebrows. 'Dogs?'

He smiled enigmatically and went outside. Merry followed and a pack of nine dogs, all tethered to one another, came galloping around the end of the street, pulling a fur-lined sled behind it.

Merry stood watching in awe. The dogs were the kind of huskies that she'd seen on television once, in a mix of colours—grey, white, brown. The front dog, leading, was solid black and looked like a wolf.

'You've got to be kidding me?'

Kristjan grinned at her. 'I couldn't get any flying reindeer. Too short notice.'

She watched as Kristjan took control of the reins from the driver who had just stepped off.

'This is Henrik. He owns the pack.'

She looked at the dogs' owner, wondering what type of person had a pack of dogs at his beck and call?

'Are you coming?'

She could easily have just stood there, gawping at the dogs for ages, but she knew she had to get a grip. Somewhere there was a child, hurt or sick, and with every second she stood there, being amazed, that child suffered a little bit more.

She clambered onto the sled under the furs and found her feet touching boxes and packs. Lifting the furs, she saw that the sled was loaded with medical equipment.

'So, you always have this thing ready to go?'

Kristjan grinned and nodded. *'Yah!'* he yelled, and cracked the reins.

The dogs began to run and Merry gasped in delight as she was pulled down the centre of the street by the team of dogs. Powdery snow was spraying into her face, but it didn't matter. This was exhilarating!

They raced past shops and homes, all decorated for

Christmas. She saw fairy lights and Christmas trees everywhere. On one corner there was a giant snowman, and further down someone who clearly had a bit more skill in sculpting snow had made a snow castle worthy of a princess!

Soon the dogs had pulled them out of town and towards Wonderland, where all those tourists took their kids to meet Father Christmas and enjoy the Christmassy village. They passed through an arch made entirely out of reindeers' antlers and down what looked like it could have been a road before the snow hit.

Suddenly the dogs turned—guided by Kristjan, no doubt—and they went off-road, through a huge pile of snow that sprayed her face with more cold powder, and then moved onwards towards the dark pine trees and forest beyond.

Merry could barely breathe. This was unlike anything she had ever experienced! She'd thought it would be a bumpy ride, but it wasn't as bad as she'd expected, and she found she had to stifle the need to scream in delight and yell at Kristjan to go faster.

The bells on the dogs' reins jingled as they ran and now, up ahead, she could see a small campsite, where a fire was crackling away, sending a plume of smoke up and into the dark sky.

Of course, she thought. *They won't get daylight here until much later.*

Behind her, Kristjan must have pulled on the reins to make the dogs halt, as their run slowly became a trot, before they stilled, panting hot breaths into the icy air.

'You okay?' Kristjan stepped off the back of the sled and held out a gloved hand for her to get out.

'I'm good!'

She wanted to say more. To say that she'd found the experience on the sled exhilarating! But she knew they were here to work, and he would appreciate that even more.

'What are we here for?'

'Kid with a suspected broken leg.' He looked around him and saw a guy clambering out of one of the far tents and begin beckoning them. 'Grab the kit.'

Merry nodded and threw back the furs, grabbing the incident bag. She passed it to Kristjan, who slung it easily over his shoulder.

'Can you bring the Entonox?'

She picked up a smaller blue bag and tramped with him through the knee-high snow towards the man standing outside the tent.

'Egill?' asked Kristjan.

The man nodded. '*Já. Sonur minn er inni.*'

Egill held the tent flaps open for them both to enter, and Merry ducked her head and went in. The inside of the tent was warmer than she'd expected, and they both hurried over to the small boy who lay on the floor, on top of a couple of sleeping bags, with one leg raised on a pillow.

'Hey, there, little man. I'm Dr Gunnarsson, but you can call me Kristjan, and this here is Dr Merry Bell. She's English. You speak English?'

The boy nodded. 'A little.'

Merry knelt down beside the boy and smiled at him. 'What's your name?'

He looked shyly up at her. 'Arnar.'

'Can you tell us what happened, Arnar?' asked Kristjan, taking off his woollen gloves and putting on some medical ones.

'I try to climb tree.'

'And you fell?'

Arnar nodded his head and winced slightly.

Merry looked down at his legs, still clad in a thick snowsuit. 'How high were you in the tree?'

'The top.'

Merry turned to look at the boy's father. 'How high was that?'

'I guess about eight feet? I was in the tent making breakfast. I thought he was just playing. He'd been chasing rabbits.'

'Okay. Well, we're going to have to take a look at that leg, Arnar.'

The boy nodded.

'And we're going to have to cut open your suit, because we don't want to move your leg if we don't have to.'

Kristjan unzipped the medical bag and found the scissors and began gently cutting the suit from the ankle upwards. Whilst he did that, Merry continued with her questioning.

'Did you hit your head, Arnar?' She pointed at his skull.

'No.'

'You're sure? Can I take a look?'

She began to feel around the boy's skull, checking that there were no signs of fluid leaking from his ears or nose and constantly asking him questions as she worked, to check his level of consciousness and response. There were no visible wounds to his head or neck...nothing she could palpate amongst the bones. She gently checked his clavicles, and then both arms and his chest.

She turned to his father. 'Have you given him any painkillers?'

'We gave him some *ibúfen.*'

She frowned. 'Is that ibuprofen?'

Kristjan nodded. 'Look at this. Visible malformation of the lower leg towards the ankle. We need to splint him. Arnar? Merry is going to give you some medicine to breathe in. It's called Entonox and it's a painkiller, okay? It may make you feel a little woozy…*svimandi*…and it might give you a dry mouth, but that's okay. It will help, all right?'

'Okay.'

She unzipped the bag, attached a new mouthpiece to the tubing and passed it to Arnar. 'Okay, you breathe in and out with this…' Kristjan translated quietly as she spoke '…without removing your mouth from the mouthpiece. It's got a special two-way filter, so you just keep breathing…nice and steady. Can you hold this for me?'

She passed the child the Entonox, so he could hold it himself—that way she could help Kristjan with applying the splint and keep Arnar calm when his leg was moved.

'Now, we're going to move your leg to apply the splint and make sure you have good blood flow.' She smiled at the boy and then turned to look at Kristjan. 'Good dorsalis pulse?' she whispered.

He nodded, whispering back, 'Yes, but we still need to adjust the break by pulling on his foot.'

'Okay.' She turned back to Arnar. 'I'm going to hold your other hand, and I want you to try and relax, Arnar—okay? Keep breathing for me…that's it. Nice and deep. In and out.' She looked up at the boy's father. 'Egill, can you talk to him? About anything, really. Keep his mind off the adjustment.'

Egill nodded and knelt down by his son and began chatting in Icelandic.

Merry couldn't understand a word, but she helped Kristjan lay an inflatable splint under Arnar's leg and then watched as he took hold of the boy's foot and quickly, expertly, pulled it back into place.

Arnar groaned.

'Keep breathing in the gas!' she told him.

'You're doing great, Arnar!' said Kristjan. 'I'm just fastening the splint now, and then you're going to get a ride on a dog sled. Ever been on one of those?'

Arnar removed the mouthpiece and nodded. 'My dad has one.'

'They're great fun, aren't they? Merry took her first ride on one today, to get here and see you!'

The boy smiled at Merry, and then Kristjan scooped him up easily and carried him out to the sled.

The dogs lay in the snow, completely oblivious to the cold, their hot breath freezing in the air around them.

Merry helped wrap Arnar in furs and then fastened him to the sled with a couple of safety belts. She got in alongside him. 'Ready?'

He nodded, smiling, happy on the Entonox.

Kristjan clambered onto the back of the sled and called out to Egill. 'We'll be at the children's hospital in Snowy Peak. You know it?'

The father nodded. 'I'll follow. I have skis.'

'Okay.'

Kristjan cracked the reins and shouted to the dogs to get going and they all clambered to their feet and began to trot.

Kristjan guided the sled out of the trees towards Wonderland, in the direction of Snowy Peak. Merry found herself marvelling at the way people got around in Iceland without even thinking about it.

In England, snow had people hiding away indoors, moaning about the icy roads, being stranded on motorways, or complaining about the disgusting slush as everything melted away afterwards, saying that everything seemed to slow down or stop because of snow. But here they just adapted. The weather was expected to be like this, and they thought nothing of it. They had dogs, or sleds, or skis. Snow was a way of life here. Blocked roads? They didn't matter. They'd find another way. In Britain, if a road was blocked, someone would have to complain to the council before anything got done.

She took hold of Arnar's hand under the furs as they raced back to the hospital with their patient. She hoped he wouldn't need an operation. The bone hadn't broken the skin, but they had no real idea of how bad the break was or whether he'd need plates or pins.

He kept on taking the occasional suck of Entonox, especially if they bounced about as they went over some of the shallower bits of snow where there was less padding on the road.

They passed under the antler arch and she noticed a couple of people waving at them as they flew by. She and Arnar waved back, smiling, as they headed towards the busier roads of Snowy Peak. They passed a snow plough, with bells jingling on the front, and the driver waved at Arnar and tooted his horn in greeting.

Arnar looked up at her and smiled, and she couldn't help but smile back. The people here seemed so friendly! Maybe it was just the time of year, and people had a tendency to be nicer during the festive season, or perhaps that was just how they were. A small community who looked out for one another because they all knew how difficult life could be sometimes?

Kristjan wanted her to stay here. At least to consider it anyway. So he could see his child. So he could be a father.

She hadn't expected even to be thinking about this. Changing everything. Was it possible? Or was she just looking at everything with rose-tinted specs because she wanted to believe?

They slowed down as they got closer to the hospital

doors and Merry recognised Henrik, who had brought them the dog sled in the first place, coming out of the hospital, pushing an empty wheelchair with a leg rest. He was all wrapped up in a thick sheepskin coat.

He waved a greeting and the dogs barked at him in happy recognition.

'Here you go, Henrik! Back in one piece.'

'Thank you. How's the boy?'

'Suspected tib and fib fracture. We need to get him to X-Ray.'

'I've got the chair ready.'

'Good man. I never introduced you properly earlier... Henrik? This is Dr Merry Bell.'

She clambered down from the sled to shake his hand. 'Hello.'

He smiled. 'I'm the guy they come to when they want to attend a rapid response event. Mostly the dogs take tourists out, but in bad weather I keep them at my kennels for emergencies.'

Behind them Kristjan was lifting Arnar easily from the sled into the chair.

'Your dogs are wonderful. Very strong. Very quick.'

'The best hounds in Snowy Peak by far. The secret is to feed them reindeer.'

'*Reindeer?*' Merry felt her stomach churn at the thought.

'Because then they fly!' He boomed a laugh and clambered onto the sled, urging the dogs into a slow trot.

She turned to look at Kristjan and Arnar, who were both laughing at Henrik's joke. She pursed her lips, as if she was offended, but couldn't keep a straight face and laughed too.

'I guess I walked right into that one, huh?'

'You certainly did,' said Kristjan. 'Now, then, Arnar—

shall we get you registered and then take some pictures of your leg?'

Arnar pointed towards the doors. 'Let's go!'

Merry followed them inside.

'Look at that. He's fractured both the tibula and fibula shafts.' Kristjan pointed at the X-ray on the screen of the computer.

Merry sighed beside him. 'It's a comminuted fracture. He'll need surgery.'

A comminuted break meant that the bone had broken into more than two fragments.

'I'll get him referred to the surgeons. They'll need to come down and talk to Arnar's father.'

'Poor kid. He was just out there trying to have some fun.'

She was leaning over his shoulder to see the screen and he couldn't help but breathe in her scent. She smelt good enough to eat and it was highly distracting...

The time they'd spent together on that short trip to collect Arnar had been enlightening. He'd not been sure how she would react to the dog sled, but she'd seemed to enjoy every minute. At one point he'd looked down on her from his vantage point as he'd steered it and had seen a huge smile on her face, and he'd smiled himself at her pleasure.

It was important to him that she enjoyed her time here if he was to have any contact with his child, and he'd lain awake in bed last night, very much aware that she was in his guest bedroom, trying to figure out how he felt about having her there. Because if he had the baby in his life then she would be in his life too, and that would mean forming a commitment to someone else—something he had avoided at all costs.

Now it was unavoidable, and how did he feel about that? Everything had changed since yesterday. He'd expected a normal day at work and now this... A relationship was the last thing he wanted, and yet in the space of a few hours he'd gone from a confirmed bachelor to a prospective father, practically living with the mother of his child!

He certainly liked having Merry close. She stirred his blood like no other woman had ever done. He'd counted himself lucky that she lived in a whole other country, so he wouldn't be tempted to follow up how he'd felt about her in Hawaii, but... Even now he could easily turn her to face him and guide her lips to his—but they were at work, and there were boundaries, and...

Was it worth breaking all his rules for this woman? He had to remember what was important here. He was doing this for his *child*. Not for her. And, although she was staying in his home for now, she wouldn't always be. It was temporary. A means to an end, right now. He had to think of the bigger picture.

If only she wasn't so damned desirable!

With a growl, he pushed himself away from the screen, knowing he needed to get some space. Some perspective. She was getting under his skin and he didn't like it. He wasn't used to it.

'I'll go tell the father.'

'Okay.'

He stalked away, trying to work out why he felt so damned irritable all of a sudden. Was it because she had changed his entire future by turning up here? Because the news of her pregnancy had derailed everything he'd thought important? Perhaps he'd been a fool to think he could get through life without forming any meaningful attachments? But it had worked so far, and he'd thought he was doing fine—until she'd told him that she was expecting their baby, and then he'd jumped tracks. Just like that. The idea that she was carrying his daughter, or his son, had suddenly become the most important thing in his world, and he didn't want to let it go.

I want to be the best father there is. My child deserves it. I lost my parents. I can't let my son or daughter lose their father.

So he couldn't let her go, could he? And the inclement weather was doing him a huge favour! All he had to do now was work out how he was going to adapt to having Merry in his life. His body yearned for her in ways he couldn't imagine. His desire to touch her was incredibly strong…to absorb himself in her the way he had in Hawaii…

Perhaps if they slept together one more time he'd be able to get her out of his system?

Or was that the most ridiculous thought he'd ever had?

What if it worked the other way and it left him craving more? Because that was how he felt right now. Like an addict—wanting more. She was his drug. His oxygen…

After he'd spoken to Egill, Arnar's father, he left him in the capable hands of the paediatric surgeons and went to make himself a coffee. As he passed the ward he saw a male colleague talking to Merry, saw her laugh out loud at some sort of joke. He tried not to feel anything about that and headed up to the staffroom.

It was nothing. Just colleagues chatting. They were getting to know one another, that was all. She was fitting in at her temporary place of work. It was a normal thing to do. Making friends. But he hadn't known that Jóhann could even speak English!

As he sat with his cup of coffee he couldn't help but think about how *he* wanted to be the one to make her laugh, and that thought—that acknowledgement of his feelings—made him frown to himself and wonder just what the heck was going on in his head?

Because it wasn't normal.

Not for him.

He didn't care about that sort of thing.

He didn't care about having relationships.

Right?

'You cooked supper?'

Kristjan closed the front door behind him, stamping his feet on the mat to get rid of the excess snow, and then went over into the kitchen, where Merry stood, stirring a pot.

'Well, you made breakfast—it seemed only fair.'

'What is it?'

'Homemade minestrone soup and bread rolls that I made myself.'

She lifted a clean tea towel off the tray of rolls that were gently cooling on a rack, expecting to see him smile—only he didn't. Had she overstepped?

'I hope you don't mind. But you've been good enough to give me a place to stay—the least I can do is help out… especially since you won't let me pay you for board and lodging.'

He nodded, walking away from her, and pinched a satsuma from the fruit bowl and peeled it, popping chunks of it into his mouth. 'It's fine.'

'Really? You don't sound fine.'

'I am. It's just…an adjustment, that's all.'

She understood. 'Having someone live with you?' she asked.

He said nothing, just kept eating his satsuma.

'I get it. I do. If it's too much and you want me to go

to the B&B I can do that. I'll phone them later—after we've eaten.'

Considering she'd been shocked at his offer for her to stay with him, she now felt sad at the idea of moving out. Kristjan had such a lovely home—even if it did look like Santa's grotto. It was warm and comfortable and spacious. With huge comfy sofas, squishy pillows and blankets, roaring log fires. And it was the perfect situation for them to get to know each other a bit more.

She had no doubt that the B&B would struggle to be as comfortable as this place. But she would move if Kristjan was having second thoughts about inviting her into his home.

'No. Don't do that. Stay. Please.'

'Are you sure?'

He nodded. 'Yes.' He dropped the satsuma peel into the kitchen bin and then washed his hands, drying them on a towel patterned with snowmen.

She couldn't help but smile. Kristjan really loved Christmas, didn't he? He'd gone all out, putting to shame all those houses she'd seen at home, festooned in lights and outdoor decorations. They were nothing compared to Snowy Peak. They were nothing compared to Kristjan.

She tried her hardest not to stare at him, but it was difficult. She had been intimate with this man. He had seen her naked. Had stroked every inch of her skin. And she, in turn, knew every pore of his body. The feel of it. His solidity. His strength. How it felt to have him lie alongside her, to feel his arms wrapped around her body, to have his lips caressing her most intimate places...

Sometimes when she was with him it was all she could think of. And now she stood in the heart of his home, making dinner, filling the house with the aroma of delicious delights, and all she could think of was forgetting the soup, turning off the hob and stripping him naked right there and then.

But she knew she couldn't. It would be an impulsive mistake and she'd learned before that impulsiveness only got her into trouble.

'Why don't you take a seat and I'll serve this up?'

'Okay.'

She turned away from him as he sat down at the table, knowing she couldn't look at him a second more—because if she continued to look at him she wasn't sure she'd be able to control her impulses. Her desire for him went to her very core, and she knew she couldn't rely on desire, or lust, or anything like that. It was a fantasy. It wasn't real. Once the impulse went away you were left with nothing but a big mistake, and her child's future was not something she was willing to gamble with.

She'd already set the table—after rummaging through his cupboards to find crockery that didn't have a Christmas pattern on it. But it seemed Kristjan had swapped everything for the festive season, because all his plates and bowls and dishes were white with silver snowflakes painted on them, and she'd resigned herself to accepting the fact that if she was to stay here she'd have to get used to Christmas again. Because she sure as hell wasn't going to be able to avoid it!

Using a ladle, she scooped up the soup and filled two bowls to the top. She placed one in front of Kristjan and one in front of herself, then brought a small basket of her freshly made rolls over to the table.

'I hope you like soup?'

'I do. But I haven't had homemade soup for a long time.' He took a sip and gave a pleasantly surprised smile. 'This is delicious! How did you learn how to make it?'

'The internet!'

Kristjan had a healthy appetite. He polished off his first bowl and had a second. As well as two more bread rolls. She watched him eat it all with a warm, self-satisfied smile.

'I hope you've got room for dessert?'

He raised an eyebrow and looked at her.

She blushed and hurriedly got up from the table. 'Not that kind. The kind you eat.'

'That's what I was thinking of.'

She tried not to let him see how flustered she was and busied herself in the kitchen, putting their bowls into the dishwasher.

'It's not homemade. I bought it on the way home.'

'What is it?'

'Erm... I'm not sure how to pronounce it, but I saw it in a bakery. It's an oaty pastry with a fruity jam in latticework.' She pulled it from the fridge to show him.

'Ah. *Hjónabandssæla*.'

She frowned. 'What does that mean?'

'Wedded bliss.'

'You're kidding?'

'No.'

'Oh.'

She brought the pie to the table and sliced it, serving him a piece on a snowflake plate. Perhaps she should change the subject?

'Tell me why you love Christmas so much. It's a time for families and relationships, and you've told me you're not the relationship type.'

'You're right. I'm not.'

'So...why?'

'My parents loved it. They passed that love on to me, and after they died it just seemed the right thing to do. Go mad with the décor. It makes me feel close to them.

And it's a time for miracles, isn't it? People are happier at Christmas, and I like people to be happy.'

'I'm sorry about your parents.' She remembered what he'd told her that night in Hawaii. 'It was a car crash, wasn't it?'

'On the very mountain pass that you came up on, during a storm. You can see why I wasn't thrilled about you going out in it again.'

She nodded. No wonder he was tied to this place. Memories abounded for him. Whereas she'd always moved about. Her adoptive mother had gone from place to place, looking for the best medical help, although it had never been enough to stop what was happening to her.

'Tell me why *you* hate Christmas,' he said. 'Don't think I don't see you sneering at my decorations.' He smiled.

She gave a small laugh. 'I made the biggest mistake of my life one Christmas, and every year when it comes around it reminds me of that.'

'Will you tell me what happened, or do I have to guess?'

Merry sighed. 'I got married on Christmas Eve— really, really young, when I ought to have known better. I allowed myself to get swept up in the romance of an older man and the magic of the season and it all went wrong.'

'You're divorced?' He sounded surprised.

'I am.'

'Is this husband the man you mentioned earlier?'

She nodded. 'Yes. Mark. My biggest mistake. My biggest regret.'

'What happened?'

He seemed genuinely interested, and she figured there was no harm in telling him. Why not tell him?

He'd opened up his home to her—it was only fair she opened up in return. They were going to be in each other's lives for a long time.

'I met Mark at a club that I'd conned my way into, after saying I was much older than I was.'

'How old were you?'

'Eighteen. But you had to be twenty-one to get in. It was really claustrophobic in there. You couldn't move for people. It was dark, there were strobing lights, but I caught the eye of a bartender, who was doing all this amazing stuff with cocktails. Did you ever see that film where they throw everything about and mix drinks?'

Kristjan nodded.

'That was Mark. Only much cooler because I was seeing it in person. The second our eyes met I thought he seemed to be putting on a display just for me. He was slick and charming, wise and funny. We got talking. Then talking became flirting, and before I knew what was happening we were totally in lust and couldn't keep our hands off one another. He persuaded me to elope with him to Gretna Green and we got married on Christmas Eve.'

She remembered what that had felt like—the excitement, the thrill that she'd found someone who saw the real her and wanted to be with her. She'd been so used to being abandoned that finding someone who wanted to commit to her and love her had been intoxicating.

Kristjan sat listening, his face unreadable. 'And then what?'

She laughed cynically. 'We were filled with the joy of the festive season! Life was joyous! Good will to all men! We came back from an amazing honeymoon— a weekend in New York that we'd got at a bargain price through someone Mark knew—and then reality hit hard.

The bubble burst. He returned to work, I returned to medical school, and Mark became a different person.'

'How so?'

How much should she tell him? Did he need to know all her sordid secrets? Did he need to hear about how ashamed Mark had made her feel? How weak and pathetic? How he'd hated the time she'd spent away from him, surrounded by handsome younger guys?

'He became insanely jealous. Possessive. I couldn't go anywhere without him wanting to know where I was going, who I was going to speak to and whether the clothes I was wearing were appropriate. He tried to tell me what to wear, how to clean the flat, that my make-up wasn't necessary. He became this angry person I didn't recognise and I was afraid of him.'

She didn't mention the endless hours she'd spent stroking his ego to try and make him feel better. How she'd tell him over and over again how much she loved him to try and put the smile back on his face and get back the old Mark she'd first known. How puzzled she'd been, having not expected love to be this hard and this complicated.

'Was he violent?'

'Not to begin with. It started small. An accident at first, or so he claimed, and of course he was dreadfully sorry afterwards. I'd driven him so mad with jealousy, he couldn't help it, he said. If only I'd done this or done that... Basically, his anger was all my fault.'

That first time she'd been in so much shock she'd utterly convinced herself that his grovelling apology was real. That it truly had been a mistake and that maybe, just maybe, she *had* been the one at fault, driving him to this state.

Before knowing Mark she'd been absolutely certain of what she thought was acceptable in a relationship and what wasn't, and she'd felt sure that if a man ever hit her she would leave immediately. But when it had actually happened... It had been more complicated. And she'd thought she still loved him.

She'd been in turmoil, needing to speak to someone—anyone—and she'd finally confided in a friend. She had persuaded her it was dangerous to stay with Mark and, realising that her marriage, her dream, had failed, she'd felt devastated.

'Didn't you try to leave?'

'I *tried*. A fellow medical student offered me her floor to sleep on. But he tracked me down.'

She paused, thinking about that night when he'd found her. What he'd done to her. She'd been so scared, and when he'd threatened to kill himself if she didn't go back with him she'd been afraid of having his death on her conscience. So she'd gone back with him, thinking that this time it would be okay...they'd work on everything. He loved her!

But all he'd wanted was to get her on her own. To get his revenge for the humiliation she had laid upon him by leaving.

'He punished me for leaving, made me scared to make a second attempt. But the next day when he went to work I took my chance and went to the police. They got me a place at a women's refuge until I could get back on my feet again. So there you have it. I'm not a fan of Christmas and not a big fan of making rash decisions.'

'I'm sorry you got hurt.'

She shrugged. 'It wasn't your fault, was it?'

'Nor was it yours.'

Merry stared back at him, a little disconcerted. She'd always thought it *was* her fault. For Kristjan to say it wasn't, was... Well, she didn't know *what* to think.

He was surprising. This man she'd met in Hawaii, the man with whom she'd thought it would be fun to pass a hot night with, most definitely had more depth to him that she had first assumed. He wasn't just a plaything, a feast for her eyes and her senses. He was clever and kind and—dared she say it?—open-hearted.

Dr Kristjan Gunnarsson was most definitely turning out to be a surprise.

CHAPTER SIX

HE COULDN'T GET it out of his head. All that Merry had shared with him that night over dinner. Once again he lay in his bed, stewing over his emotions and feelings, trying to sort them and understand them.

That she had been treated so badly by a man… It was the kind of thing that made his blood boil and made him feel ashamed to be part of the same species.

He was glad she was out of it. He was glad that she had gone to the police. She must have felt so scared. So alone. He would never let anything like that happen to her again. Not if he was around—which he hoped to be. If she stayed…

But it was these protective feelings now being created in him that disturbed him. Those and the fact that she lay in bed in the room next to his with his baby in her belly.

He'd not expected to feel this way. Not expected to feel so strongly.

Unable to sleep, he threw off the thick blankets, pulled on a white tee shirt and went to get a drink of water from the kitchen. He didn't want to disturb her, so he tried his best to be quiet, but he knew he was wide awake and wouldn't sleep yet, so he started doing a bit of a work-out, hoping exercise and exhaustion would help him get a few hours' rest before tomorrow.

He worked his way through a few repetitions of sit-ups, plank side-dips and press-ups before starting a set of burpees. Then he got his weights out from behind the couch and began doing some arm curls.

It felt good to work off his frustration and his anger and finally, when he felt spent, he downed the rest of his water and turned to head back to his bedroom.

Merry stood watching him.

He hadn't heard her come out of her room.

'Sorry. Did I wake you?'

She shook her head. 'No, I was thirsty and I...er... didn't want to throw you off your rhythm.'

He shrugged. 'I couldn't sleep. What would you like? Water? Hot milk? I could do you some cocoa? Or a hot chocolate?'

'I don't feel thirsty any more.'

Really? Then why was she looking at him like that? With desire in her eyes and a gentle flush in her cheeks, her dark honeyed eyes all wide and alluring?

It was a temptation, her looking at him that way. He could feel the tension in the room. Was aware how few clothes either of them were wearing. They could be naked in seconds. He could show her all the delights he had dreamt of showing her since she'd started staying in his house.

He'd yearned for this woman after Hawaii, and been so thankful there was a huge body of water between them.

Now there wasn't.

But doing something about it would constitute—what?

They were already working together and almost living together. She was pregnant with his child. If he started to have sex with her too...

He didn't want her to misread the signals. Yes, he wanted her. He could feel his arousal now, just standing looking at her, and, boy, did he want to submit to his needs and desires. But it wouldn't just be sex, would it? Their relationship was complicated enough without them getting *involved*. He couldn't get into a physical relationship with this woman and then develop feelings for her, because then she would mean something special and what if he lost her?

Was he mistaking convenience for desire? And how could he forget what she'd told him? She'd admitted she'd fallen in lust with a man before and it had all gone wrong for her. And if this wasn't lust they were both feeling then he was the Pope.

He was trying to convince her to stay here permanently so he could see his child—so he could be a father every day and not just on holidays and birthdays. Did he really want to screw this up? Because if he got into a relationship with Merry and it failed then he would only have himself to blame when she went running back to England.

He walked over to her…hesitated, fighting his inner turmoil.

Don't kiss her. Don't kiss her. Don't kiss her.

'Goodnight, Merry. Sleep well.'

And with a great amount of determination and anguish he side-stepped her and went into his own bedroom, closing the door softly behind him.

Inside his room, he let out a huge breath of frustration and headed to his en-suite bathroom.

He most definitely needed a cold shower.

'Hello, I'm Dr Bell. Can you tell me what's brought you in today?'

Merry smiled at the family before her. A mum, a dad and a little girl. Kristjan had assigned a nurse to work with her and quietly translate as she talked with her patients.

'We saw our doctor this morning because Hekla had been suffering with bad tummy pains and occasional sickness.'

'Is that nausea or actual vomiting?'

'Being sick, yes. Not always. Sometimes. But it has been getting more frequent. He felt her tummy and said he could feel a lump, and then he referred us to come straight here.'

'Okay...'

Merry appraised Hekla. She was a very slim girl. Pale. Twelve years old. With lovely long, golden hair that she currently wore in plaits—one of which she was chewing the end of.

Her mother pulled it from her mouth.

'No other health worries that I should be aware of? No allergies?'

Mum shook her head. No.

'So, Hekla, can I take a look at you? Do you want to hop up onto this bed for me?'

Hekla used the footstool to get up onto the bed and sat on the edge.

'I'm going to listen to your chest first, okay?'

Merry used her stethoscope to listen to the girl's heart and lungs. They both sounded completely normal.

'And this little thing is a SATS monitor. It goes on your finger—see?' She slipped it on and pressed the button. 'This will tell me how much oxygen you're breathing in and your pulse rate, and on your other arm we'll do your blood pressure. The cuff will squeeze your arm tight, but it shouldn't hurt.'

She carried out her basic observations and happily they all came back normal.

Merry smiled at Hekla. She seemed quite anxious, but who wouldn't be if they felt ill and had been sent to hospital?

'Can you lie down for me? I'm going to feel your tummy—is that okay?' It was always important to her, when carrying out a physical examination on a child, that she told them what she was doing and they gave her permission.

'Yes.' Hekla lay down flat.

Merry began her assessment. First she visibly looked at the shape of the abdomen, to see whether there were any skin abnormalities or distention, but it looked fine. Then she began to palpate with her fingers, pressing and feeling the child's tummy, checking for masses or crepitus, and she instantly found what the doctor had. A mass about the size of a golf ball that shouldn't be there.

It was hard to feel, as it seemed to keep disappearing, and this made Merry suspect that it was probably in the digestive tract rather than attached to the abdominal wall. She unhooked her stethoscope from around her neck and listened to Hekla's bowel. It sounded normal, but something wasn't right.

'Okay, so I think we need to do a scan, Hekla. What we'll do is send you to another room where a big machine will take a picture of your tummy for us. Just to give us a clearer idea of what's going on. I think something might be blocking your tummy. You've not swallowed anything you shouldn't have?'

The young girl shook her head.

'Okay.' She pulled down Hekla's top and addressed the parents. 'We're going to send her to CT. You can both go with her. Once we get the result we might have a better idea of what's going on.'

'Thank you.'

'No problem.'

She left the family group in the cubicle and went to the doctors' station to call the scanning department and book Hekla in. Once that was done she called Olaf Ward, the children's ward, to make sure they had a bed, as she suspected Hekla would need surgery.

As she got off the phone Kristjan arrived at the desk, looking particularly delectable in a navy suit and waistcoat that emphasised the light blue of his eyes. Instantly her body went on high alert—the way it had last night, after she'd watched him exercise, when he'd walked right up to her and for a very brief moment she had thought—*hoped*—he would kiss her.

Her sex drive was high anyway, but pregnancy was making her feel as if it was firing on all cylinders—especially with him around, giving her her own private viewing of him working out. All those muscles working in perfect co-ordination… Flexing and tensing… Moving under his skin so smoothly that she had wanted to reach out and stroke him.

It had been difficult to get to sleep afterwards! Just the thought that he lay in the next room…

She'd heard him run the shower and had lain there fighting the urge to go join him, the way she had in Hawaii. But she'd had a stern talk with herself and told herself not to be so stupid! This lust she felt was a distraction and she was not here to act on it. She was here to decide if she was going to stay in Iceland or not. She was here to assess whether she could move her entire life over here. Not to dabble in sexual games with Kristjan. Even though that would be a welcome activity. After all, she knew what he was like in bed and she knew it would not be a disaster…

But sex complicated matters, didn't it? One-night

stands were fun, but they were fleeting, and there was nothing fleeting about their set-up right now. Getting into a relationship with Kristjan, even if it was just a sexual one, would just muddy the waters.

'Hey,' she said.

'Hey. How's it going? Your translator working out well for you?'

'Yes, Agnes is great. Just waiting for my patient to go to CT.'

'Ah. I've been up to check on Arnar and his leg. He's had his surgery and he's doing well. He's sitting up in bed playing computer games against one of the nurses.'

'Oh, that's good…'

Kristjan had big, wide hands. Strong. Capable. Nice clean nails. She couldn't stop looking at them. Remembering how they'd felt upon her body, how he'd cupped her breasts with them, how they'd slid so nicely down her back and over her bottom and held her against him. How was such a huge, strong man so gentle…?

'Merry? Are you okay?'

'Sorry—what?'

'I told you he should be going home today on crutches, but you seemed to be in another world.'

She smiled, feeling her cheeks flame red at her naughty thoughts. 'I am. I'm in Iceland.'

She got up and headed back to Hekla's cubicle, so she could escort her to the scanning department. It was easier to think without Kristjan around.

She left Hekla and her parents in the capable hands of the nurses on the CT unit and then went to sit in the doctor's booth to await the images on screen.

In front of her was a big window through which she could see the nurses getting Hekla into position and comfortable, with a pillow under her knees to support her.

Then they pressed a button or two and Hekla slid into the machine.

Merry looked at her computer screen, awaiting the images, and suddenly there they were, showing that Hekla had a six-centimetre mass in her duodenum, almost blocking the pyloric sphincter. No wonder the girl had pain and kept being sick.

But what was it? Was it malignant? No one would know until they opened her up. Hekla needed surgery.

Sighing, she got up to go talk to the parents.

'A what?'

The surgeon smiled. 'A trichobezoar.'

'A hairball?'

She remembered how Hekla had been chewing on the end of her plait. Was it really that she had consumed so much hair it had built up in her gut? Was it just a habit, or something more going on?

'Okay, thanks,' she said.

'I'll go and talk to the parents in case they have any questions about the surgery.'

'All right. I'll check on Hekla when she's brought back to the ward.'

She thanked him again and headed to the staffroom. It had been a long day and her feet felt tired and she was hungry. She thought of Hekla, chewing on her hair so much it had built up and blocked her insides. Poor thing!

But there was something else bothering her right now. She was having one or two cramping pains, and in the bathroom she noticed there was a spot of blood in her underwear.

Heart pounding, she stood there wondering what to do. Was she losing this baby…

No! This can't be happening! It can't!

This baby was her first opportunity to have an actual relation by blood! A child! Someone she could adore who would love her unconditionally in return. She might have been shocked to have discovered she was pregnant, but now that she'd lived with the idea for a while she couldn't bear the idea of losing it!

'Merry? You're white as snow. Are you all right?' Kristjan stood looking at her in the bathroom doorway.

'I'm spotting.'

He frowned. 'Any pain?'

'Some.' She could feel her fear rising. Her lower jaw beginning to tremble. She just wanted someone to hold her and tell her everything would be okay.

'We need to get you a scan.'

She nodded, feeling small and hopeless.

'Everything could still be fine.' He came towards her, took her hands in his, made her look into his eyes. 'You're going to be okay.'

'You can't know that.'

'I know. But you should try to remain positive.'

'I'm scared.'

He lowered her onto one of the couches. 'Sit here for a moment. I'll arrange everything.'

One of Kristjan's sonographer colleagues fitted them in immediately. And, after the longest twenty minutes of his life, worrying and waiting, he watched Merry finally lie herself down on the bed in an ultrasound room.

Kristjan switched off the lights. Should he hold her hand? He wasn't sure what the protocol was here. Where exactly he stood in his relationship with Merry. They were friends, he thought. They got on well and they had a searing attraction to one another that was often very distracting. They even lived together for now. But were they in a relationship?

That was something as yet undefined, and he didn't like it. For a man who always knew where he stood with everyone this was unfamiliar territory. Once upon a time it would have simply confirmed to him that his stance of not getting involved with people was the right thing, because it stopped all this worrying and wondering. But he wasn't that person any more. His child was in her belly and he was trying to persuade her to stay.

But most of all...he knew she must be scared. And probably believed herself to be alone here. With that thought, he took hold of her hand.

She turned in surprise to look at him.

'We're in this together, no matter what it shows,' he whispered.

Merry smiled, clearly grateful.

'How far along are you?' Magnús asked Merry.

'Um...coming up to fourteen weeks... I had a scan just before I came out here and the baby measured twelve weeks and six days.'

'Okay.'

Magnus was quiet for a moment as he squirted gel on her belly and moved the probe over her lower abdomen, frowning at the screen for a moment before turning it so they both could see.

'We have a heartbeat. Look.'

Kristjan stared in shock at the screen. That was his baby! Heart thundering away like a runaway train! It lay in Merry's womb like a curled bean and he could see it moving its arms and legs, as if it were trying to settle into a more comfortable position.

'Oh, my God! It's okay?'

'It's absolutely fine! Sometimes you can get a little

breakthrough bleeding. We don't always know why it happens, but it does.'

'So it's going to be all right?'

Merry squeezed his hand and he squeezed back.

'As long as you take things easy. Monitor the spotting. If it gets any worse you can come back. I'll just take some measurements to check baby's growth.' He smiled at Merry, then turned his smile on Kristjan. 'Who would have thought Mr Eternal Bachelor would father a child, hey?'

'Life happens, Magnús.'

'It certainly does.'

Merry gasped. 'It's moving! Jumping!'

Kristjan had no words. None he could say, anyway. At that moment of pure joy he was struck dumb, afraid to speak in case he wept, and he hadn't shed a tear since he was a small boy who had realised for the first time that he was all alone in the world.

He'd known that being a father mattered to him, but he hadn't realised just how much until he'd found Merry in the staffroom and she'd told him she was bleeding.

He'd seen many ultrasounds before, but nothing like this. Nothing that was *personal*. This was *his* baby. *His* child. *His* creation.

His family.

He squeezed her hand tightly and kissed the back of it.

'It's a good sign that the baby is healthy,' said Magnús. 'I'm just going to check the Nuchal Fold and then I'll take the measurements.'

Kristjan watched in fascination, unable to take his eyes off the screen, not wanting to miss a moment with his child. He could feel tears welling up and he surreptitiously wiped them away, hoping no one would say anything. It was too early to know whether he was having a boy or a girl, but this was still amazing.

Magnús focused on the baby's heart and played the heartbeat audibly, so they all could hear it as it roared away. A healthy heart. A perfect heart.

'This all looks good. Baby is measuring at just over thirteen weeks.'

'That seems about right,' answered Merry.

'Can we get a picture?' Kristjan asked.

'Sure.' Magnús printed a few off and then he was done, and giving Merry some blue paper towel to wipe up the gel from her abdomen. 'All looks good here. No problems that I can see.'

'Thank you, Magnús. It was very kind of you to fit us in.'

'No problem. I'll leave you two to get yourselves sorted out. See you later.' And he left the room.

Merry looked at him with a huge smile on her face. 'I think that was the most amazing thing I have ever seen!'

He smiled, overwhelmed. 'Me too.'

'Can we do this, Kristjan? Can we be the parents this baby needs?'

He didn't need to think about that. He knew he would sacrifice his life for his child if it needed it. 'Yes, we can. If we stay together.'

She nodded to show that she'd heard him. He wasn't sure she nodded to show she agreed with his statement. He still had no idea if she would remain in Iceland. He hoped so. He needed her to.

'Have you any plans for this evening, Merry?'

'Nothing except putting my feet up. Why?'

'There's something I want to show you.'

'Okay…'

'But let's go home and get changed first.'

* * *

'Wonderland? You're taking me to Wonderland?'

Wonderland was the big tourist attraction that sat alongside Snowy Peak. The place they'd raced through on the dog sled. And now they were approaching the big reindeer antler arch on a motorised snow sled.

Kristjan had arrived in front of his house with it and had asked her to hop on and put her arms around his waist if she needed to. She'd been wary of doing that, but the second they'd begun moving she'd clutched onto him, her arms wrapped around his waist, her face pressed into his back. For a few minutes she had allowed herself to close her eyes and just relax and enjoy the moment.

It was laughable, really. She was used to getting around places on foot or by car. Here, she'd been on a dog sled and now a snow sled! And they'd passed people wearing snowshoes and even a couple on skis!

Iceland in the winter was simply another world. Or at least it was up here in the mountains. She'd thought she'd hate not having many daylight hours, but she was getting used to the darkness and all the Christmas lights, and now Kristjan was about to throw her into a place that celebrated Christmas.

'This is a very special place to me,' he said.

He parked the snow sled to one side of the street and helped her off, and she took a moment to take in her surroundings.

Every building looked like a little gingerbread cabin. Only the snow on the roofs wasn't icing and the decorations weren't sweets. There were real lights and Christmas trees and candy canes. The streets were lit with electric candles and there was real holly and mistletoe. Everyone was dressed in winter gear—woolly hats and scarves and gloves—and from hidden speakers Christmas music played. Family groups walked from cabin to cabin, looking into shops full of wintry goodness, chocolates, gingerbread...

It was Christmas overload.

She was trying her best to hate it, and show her disapproval in her face, but it was hard to do because Kristjan was standing there looking at her with a smile as the snow gently fell in fat flakes and she couldn't help but laugh.

'What?' she said.

'You know you love it really.'

'Oh, *do* I?'

'You'll be singing Christmas carols before the night is out.'

'You want to put money on that?'

He grinned. 'Sure! I'll take that bet. How much?'

'If I sing a Christmas song before the night is over I'll work the entire day tomorrow dressed as an elf.'

'Done. Only not tomorrow. Tomorrow I want you to rest at home with your feet up.'

He held out his gloved hand for her to shake and she shook it, feeling confident about their wager. She'd never sung a Christmas song in her life! She knew the words to most of them, though. How could anyone not? They were shoved down your throat from early November.

'So...where exactly are we going?'

'The Elf Foundation.'

She raised an eyebrow. It sounded kitsch, whatever it was. 'Lead the way, my dear fellow.'

Kristjan performed a mock bow and began to walk across the street. She followed him, aware that some of the shop owners waved to Kristjan when they saw him pass.

'People know you? How often do you come here?'

'All will be revealed.'

'A man of mystery, eh?'

'Everyone has their secrets.' He smiled.

He led them past a shop that sold nothing but ornaments for Christmas trees, its window filled with miniature trains, nutcracker soldiers, reindeer and all manner of novelties. Another sold only Christmas jumpers, another only books, and at this window she stopped to look in.

Kristjan looked at her. 'Do you like books?'

'Are you kidding me? I *love* books! My favourite author is Nicola Drake. Look! They have her latest! I haven't read that yet.' Merry looked at the shop door and saw that it was closed already. 'Oh, damn! I might have to come back to get that.'

'Maybe Santa will bring it.'

'Maybe.' She turned away from the window and saw his face. 'Sorry. I'm putting a downer on the evening. You want to show me something that means a lot to you.'

She had no idea what the Elf Foundation could possibly mean to him. He was a doctor. A paediatrician. A grown man! What was he doing coming to this Christmas paradise where children outnumbered adults four to one? The Elf Foundation sounded like some silly factory shop where they got kids to help make toys, or something.

They rounded a corner and went down another street as the snow silently fell. Here she could see someone had tried to build a snowman, and it struck her that she had never done that as a kid. Mostly because there just hadn't been the kind of snow in England that had allowed her to do so. She could only remember it snowing heavily on a couple of occasions, and the snow had usually disappeared after a couple of hours.

As they passed she saw that one of the sticks that had

been used to make the snowman's arms had fallen off, so she stooped down to pick it up and reattach it.

'Getting into the Christmas spirit, Dr Bell?'

'No.' She smiled. 'I'm a doctor. I fix people. And this snowman needed my help.'

Kristjan laughed and steered her away from the snowman, grabbing her shoulders and positioning her in front of another cabin.

The Elf Foundation

She read the sign that was in English and Icelandic—Álfasjódurinn. There was some smaller text below it. As they got nearer it became clearer and she read it, in shock.

Founded by Dr Kristjan Gunnarsson

She turned to look at him, hoping he would give her some explanation, but he said nothing, simply smiled mysteriously and led her inside.

Warmth hit them both. Kristjan helped her off with her coat and hung it on a hook, and then she got the chance to take in just what she was seeing.

The place was mostly filled with kids, of all different ages, and just one or two adults—staff, they looked like—were helping to organise them on a stage. Some were dressed normally, others were in costume, and she guessed that they going to perform something along the lines of a nativity play.

But there was no Mary or Joseph or Wise Men here. One person looked like some kind of mountain troll, dressed in camouflage or hunting gear, and one was dressed in a furry black outfit with a hunchback.

She felt completely confused.

'Kristjan! You're here!' One of the staff came over, a big smile on her face, and greeted Kristjan, clapping him on the back.

'Of course, Gúdrun. I wouldn't miss it! Can I introduce you to Dr Merry Bell? She's an elf, too, but she only speaks English.'

Gúdrun raised her eyebrows and smiled a greeting at Merry. 'Nice to meet you. Are you here to watch the show?' she asked in English with a thick Icelandic accent.

'Er... I guess I am!'

'Okay! We have saved seats near the front, as always, Kristjan. Give us half an hour and we'll be ready!'

Gúdrun was distracted then, by one of the boys who was moving a piece of staging that looked like a mountain.

'No, no, Bjarki! Put that back!'

Merry gave a short laugh. 'What *is* going on? And why did you say I was an elf?'

Kristjan smiled. 'All will be revealed!'

'And will you also tell me why your name is on the sign outside?'

He nodded. 'Later. After you've seen the show. Now, let me get you a drink from the kitchen. Would you like something hot?'

'Chocolate, if they've got it.'

'They have. They also do a mean *kjötsúpa* here. It's lamb soup.'

She thought it was probably very nice, but she hadn't been that keen on the idea of meat in her pregnancy so far. 'Would you mind if I stuck to the hot chocolate?'

'Not at all. Wait here and I'll go get some.'

She tried to stay out of the way as the kids and the staff prepared the set pieces on the stage and arranged and rearranged the seats in front of it. She sat down on one, settling in the cushions.

Clearly this was their first night presenting this play— whatever it was about—and nerves and excitement were high.

She watched all the excited kids, wondering if their parents were coming to watch them in the play, and it brought back memories of being at school herself, knowing that whether she was a bit-part player or in the lead role, as she once had been in a school production of *Romeo and Juliet*, there would never be anyone in the audience cheering her on.

Her adoptive mother had never wanted to show up at school events, so self-conscious about the disease ravaging her body, and her adoptive father had run out on them years before, when the Motor Neurone Disease had been diagnosed. So Merry had learnt to be independent, and proud of herself, and when the audiences clapped at the end, no matter how small a part she'd played, she'd always believed they were clapping just for her.

She hoped these kids had people coming in to cheer them on. People to wait for them after the play and give them a big hug, telling them how proud they were and then saying, *Let's go home and sit by a Christmas tree and wonder about the presents underneath.*

The doors opened and adults began to file in, clearly filled with anticipation.

Kristjan found her and passed her a hot mug. 'Be careful.'

'What's under your arm?'

'This?' He placed his own drink on the floor. 'A footstool. So you can put your feet up. You're meant to be resting, remember?'

'I'm fine!'

'And we're keeping you that way. Allow me to spoil you, Merry. I don't do this for everyone.'

She smiled. 'Really? What about your patients?'

He thought for a moment. 'They're different. Now, come on. Feet up!'

She rested them on the footstool. 'You're very bossy. Is that because your name is on the door?'

'Perhaps.'

'And what play are we about to see?'

'It's the story of *Gryla, Leppaludi and the Yule Lads*.'

She frowned. 'I've never heard of that before. What's it about?'

'Wait and see.'

The lights went down and the audience became quiet as music began and the curtains were pulled open to reveal two giant puppets that looked like trolls—one female and hunchbacked and ugly, the other male, taller and equally repulsive.

The crowd *oohed* and *booed* and Merry decided these must be the bad guys.

'Leppaludi! I'm hungry! Bring me some children to eat!'

Leppaludi sat down on his haunches. 'I'm tired! Go fetch them yourself!'

Before she knew it Merry was absorbed in the play about two trolls who ate children, lived in a cave and had thirteen sons called the Yule Lads. Each of these sons was incredibly mischievous, and they stole things and harassed the local villagers close to their cave on the thirteen nights before Christmas. The parents in the village used fear of the Yule Lads to make their children behave. The first, Sheep-Cote Clod, would try to steal milk from the sheep. Stubby would steal food, another would slam doors, and another would spy through windows and steal the children's toys. Each of them was naughtier, uglier and smellier than the last.

The play was funny and scary and so much fun!

Merry was thoroughly enjoying herself, and when the play came to an end the audience got to their feet and gave all the child actors a huge round of applause. Merry didn't know any of them, but she was proud of them for putting on such a good show, and she was so engrossed in clapping them when they came on stage to take a bow that she was startled to realise that Kristjan was walking up the steps onto the stage, clearly about to make a speech.

She listened, enraptured.

'Good evening, ladies and gentlemen, and welcome to The Elf Foundation. I'm sure we can all agree that the children tonight put on a great play—let's show them our appreciation one more time.'

Everybody cheered and clapped.

'The Elf Foundation is a very special place to me. I wanted to create a place where any disadvantaged child, or child with a chronic or terminal illness could come to enjoy Wonderland and Christmas.'

Merry held her breath.

'I lost my parents at a very young age and I was very lonely. I didn't want other children to feel isolated the way I had felt. I wanted them to feel part of something. Part of a community. Part of something special. So I built The Elf Foundation. A place for children who felt isolated like I was. A place where they could come and learn through music and movement and then show others that they're just as important as those with families, or without health problems. Every child who appeared on stage tonight has a difficult story. Some have families but can't be with them. Some were completely abandoned. Some were chronically ill. But they all have come together to give joy to others at Christmas. Just like Santa's elves. And now I hope you will join with me in giving back to these children by singing a song to them and making a donation afterwards, if you can, so that we can continue to provide a place for these children here. Thank you very much—and if you look under your chairs you should find the lyrics to the song!'

Merry could feel her heart melting. That Kristjan should do something like this! Use his pain and his tragic past to create something so worthwhile! What a wonderfully kind and compassionate thing to do!

She reached under her seat and found the lyric sheet. In the corner, someone began playing a piano, and before she knew it, she was singing 'Winter Wonderland'.

It was only when they got to the chorus that Kristjan met her eye and winked at her, and she felt her heart pound, her feelings for him deepening as her understanding of him grew, and then realised with a start that he had won the bet. She was singing a Christmas song before the night was out. He'd done it. He'd managed to make her like Christmas.

Was it because this was so different from all the Christmases she had experienced as a child? Because here, despite the snow and the cold and the ice, there was real warmth and—dared she say it?—love and affection? Affection between children who didn't know each other. Who had come to put on this show for other people who *had* families and love, to make them smile? To make them *happy*?

It was such a selfless thing to do, and she knew she wanted to know more about Kristjan's Elf Foundation. She wanted to be involved—she wanted to be a part of this.

Could she do that if she lived in England?

Probably not.

When the song was over there were more loud cheers and clapping, and Kristjan stepped back so that the children could take their final bow. Then he was coming back down the stairs towards her, smiling as he stood in front of her.

'Well? What did you think?'

'It was amazing, Kristjan! I loved it. That you've done this…' She became lost for words, felt tears prick her eyes, and she hated it that she was probably going to cry in front of him again. She *never* cried. She'd always seen crying as a weakness. So she struggled to get control of herself. To take a deep breath. 'I'm very impressed.'

He nodded. 'Good. And you sang!'

'Yes. I did.'

'So you'll dress as an elf the next time you're at work?'

'I will.'

Kristjan grinned. 'I can't wait to see it.'

She laughed, all the tension leaving her body as she saw the delight and mischief in his eyes. 'No. Neither can I.'

There'd been no more bleeding and the cramping had stopped. Merry had spent her day searching for causes and had discovered there were many benign reasons— a cervical polyp, heavy lifting, excessive exercise. Perhaps the plane trip and dragging her suitcase up the mountain had contributed? Or the dogsled ride? It could have been anything. But she had been reassured by the scan that everything was all right and she felt ready to get back to work.

The elf costume hung on the back of the staffroom door. Kristjan had found it for her in a cupboard next to a Santa costume—'For Christmas Day. We hand out gifts to those kids still here.'

'Do you dress up as Santa?'

'I do so proudly.' Kristjan had passed her the costume. 'Off you go. I'll take a picture when you're done. We wouldn't want to forget this.'

'Hmm...'

She took the costume now and went into a changing room. There was a green hat with a white feather that looked more akin to something Robin Hood might have worn, a green velvet tunic with big red buttons, some weird, poufy green breeches, red-and-white-striped tights, like candy canes, and green bootees with bells on.

Merry looked at her reflection in the mirror and sighed—but she was also smiling. Was this the Christmas thaw? A few days ago she wouldn't have been caught dead wearing this stuff, but now... She was beginning to realise she didn't want to be the Grinch. She was beginning to see Christmas as something that could bring a smile to her face, and a part of her wanted that very much!

It had been exhausting to hate Christmas! And how much of that had been caused by Mark? Selfish, awful Mark.

But now she was here, in the land of Christmas, and she had Kristjan nearby, and a baby to grow, and everything seemed hopeful right now. It was a time of goodwill.

Yes, maybe some bad things had happened to her at Christmas, but that wasn't the season's fault. That didn't mean she couldn't turn it around and refuse to be a slave to her past. It was a time for new beginnings. To let go of the past and begin anew. If Kristjan could take *his* tragic past and make something positive out of it, like The Elf Foundation, then why couldn't she?

She stepped out of the changing room and saw Kristjan had a big grin on his face.

'Smile!' He lifted his mobile phone to take a picture.

Merry laughed. 'These shoes are very apt for a name like Dr Bell. The kids will think I'm making it up.' She pointed her foot to make the bells jingle.

'I think you look and sound delightful,' he replied.

'Thank you.' She walked with him to the lifts and travelled down to their ward, where Agnes, her nurse and translator, was waiting for her.

'You look…very nice.' Agnes smiled.

'I lost a bet. Now, who's first on the list today?'

She went to grab the patient file at the top of the intray, but Agnes got there first.

'Dr Gunnarsson said I'm not to let you work too hard today.'

Oh, did he, now? Merry turned to look at him and he shrugged.

'I'm taking care of both of you. Don't get angry.'

'I'm a grown woman. I'm quite capable of judging what I can and cannot do.'

'I know. But this isn't just about you any more, so I'd like to think I have a say.'

Irritatingly, he smiled at her before walking away.

Merry shook her head in exasperation, then smiled at Agnes, grabbed the top file from her and gazed at the details.

Ingestion of a foreign object

'Okay! Let's go!' She jingled her way to the waiting room and called out her patient's name. 'Darri Edvardsson?'

A mum, a dad and a little boy aged about five stood up.

She smiled at them. 'Hi, I'm Dr Bell. Let's see if we can sort out your problem.'

'Are you a real elf?' asked Darri.

'I am.' She smiled, thinking of the elves last night. She was one of them. One of the abandoned. And she was trying to make other people's lives better. Yes, she was an elf.

'Okay, then—it says here that you've swallowed something you shouldn't?' She was getting used to Agnes's low voice, quickly translating everything at her side, but she was beginning to wish she had the ability to speak the language herself. Maybe she should try to learn it if she stayed?

Darri's mother spoke up. 'He was playing with his toys, trying to build a crane out of those metal bits and pieces. He put a piece in his mouth as he tightened a bolt and somehow he swallowed it. I blame the cat for scaring him.'

'The cat?' Merry frowned.

'She jumped down from the window and startled him. Will he be okay? Will it pass normally?'

'Well, how big was this piece that you swallowed, Darri?'

'About this big.'

Darri showed her with his fingers, indicating a piece four, maybe five centimetres long.

'And did it have smooth edges? Was it rounded?'

'I don't know for sure,' he said.

'Well, I guess we'd better take an X-ray.'

'You don't think he'll need surgery, do you?' asked the mother.

'I'll need to see the films before I can answer that, but at the moment he seems fine. He's not vomiting...he's not in any pain. It all looks good, so far.'

'All right...'

'I'll just go and make that referral—I won't be long.'

She jingled her way back to the doctors' desk, rang through to the X-ray department and booked Darri in. There was a wait of about half an hour, but she wasn't unduly worried. The piece of metal would probably pass straight through.

She heard Kristjan laugh from another cubicle and it made her smile. Who'd have thought that a man like him would have so much depth to his character? When she'd first met him she'd pegged him as the kind of guy you just had a quick fling with. He was fun, and sexy as hell, and she'd thought she'd never run into him again—which had been good because he hadn't seemed like the type of guy who did commitment.

And yet here he was. Opening up his home to her. Accepting her pregnancy and getting teary-eyed at the sight of their baby on the ultrasound screen. He'd opened up a place for orphaned children to go at Christmas. He cared for sick children and made them better. He was funny, kind, charismatic—and he *cared*.

I like him. I like him very much.

Which was disturbing in all manner of ways.

It wasn't meant to be happening. Her plan for a quick visit, announcing the news and then returning to England was now all skewed. And she was beginning to like certain things.

They were friends—and that was good, because they'd need to be if the future became more uncertain. She still wasn't sure what she was going to do. Stay? Or go back home?

She was going to be a mother, and her baby would have a chance to know both its parents if she stayed. Shouldn't she do what was right for her child? Shouldn't that be her top priority as a parent? You made sacrifices for your children, didn't you?

As her mother had done for her, by giving her up in the hope that she would have a better life than the one she could give her. That was what she had to believe had been the motive for her mother leaving her on a vicar's doorstep.

And her adoptive mother had done all she could to raise her before she'd got sick, and she had been devastated when Merry had become her carer at such a young age. That was why Merry had chosen to go into medicine. She'd hated feeling she couldn't do more. Couldn't understand what was truly going on.

Merry wanted to give her child what she had never had—a proper family. And by staying here in Iceland she could do that.

But...

But she'd never considered giving up her old life. There wasn't much at home, but it *was* home. *Home.*

Everything was familiar there—her job was there. They'd been good when she'd rung to say she was stuck in Iceland for a few days, and she'd felt terribly guilty about letting them down.

But which was more important? Her job? Or her child's future?

It was a no-brainer when she put it in such stark terms as that, even if in reality it would be hard.

Although she *was* beginning to love it here. The place and the people were beginning to make her consider the move as a real possibility.

And Kristjan...?

He was at the heart of the matter. He had feelings she had to take into consideration, too. He wanted to be a dad. She could see that, and that was fantastic. She'd not known what to expect from his reaction when she'd first come here.

Could she imagine walking away?

Right there and then, she wasn't sure that she could.

Her feelings for him were growing. Multiplying. And as they did so her fears grew with them.

What if this turned out to be a big mistake?

CHAPTER SEVEN

'I THOUGHT YOU might like to go out for a meal tonight.' Kristjan leaned on the doctors' desk where Merry was typing some patient notes into the computer system.

She looked up and laughed when she saw he was wearing the Santa costume—from the red hat and white beard down to the big black boots.

He had to give it to her—she had kept her word about wearing an elf costume, despite her feelings about Christmas, and she seemed to be taking it in her stride. He also had to admit that he *liked* seeing her dressed up as an elf! She looked more whimsical and beautiful than ever, and it made him smile to hear her feet making jingling noises as she walked about the department.

The patients loved it, too—especially some of the younger ones—and one or two had even asked where Santa was. Hence the costume. He had decided to join in, and he loved how her smile now made him feel all warm on the inside.

'Dinner?'

She seemed to think about it.

'Do we get to wear our own clothes or do we have to stay in costume?'

He grinned. 'Costume would be fun, but I'll let you decide. I'm up for either.'

'Well, much as I've enjoyed being Merry the Elf today, I'm kind of looking forward to putting on something that doesn't itch so much.'

'Okay. I've got us reservations at eight o'clock at Ingrid's. It's a restaurant in town.'

'Sounds great. Thanks.'

'I thought it might give us a chance to talk about how things are going.'

Her smile faltered. 'Is there anything in particular that you want to talk about?'

'No. I just thought that usually when we get home from work we eat and then go to sleep. It might be nice to go out…have someone else cook and clean up whilst you're meant to be resting.' He smiled. 'And, you know… I think going out for dinner is what normal people do, but I'm not sure.'

She nodded, smiling. 'I've heard of the practice.'

'We might like it.'

'We might.'

He was still smiling at her, and she was smiling back, and he realised that they were so absorbed in one another that other members of staff were glancing at them with amused looks on their faces. It certainly hadn't taken long for the hospital grapevine to do its thing.

Kristjan stood up straight, adjusted his scratchy white beard and his big fake belly, and headed off to treat another patient. He felt good because she'd agreed to eat out with him. They needed to get to know one another better and time was running out. He had no idea if she was going to leave or not, and he figured if he knew more about her he might find the thing that would make her want to stay.

Who'd have thought it? The eternal bachelor was trying to make a relationship work.

The only question was…what type of relationship would it be?

What to wear?

Kristjan had said they were going out for dinner, and Merry wanted to dress up nicely for the occasion, but she didn't want him to think that she was dressing up for *him*. This wasn't a romantic date or anything. They weren't trying to *court* one another. It was like Kristjan had said. They were just going to get to know one another better.

So, what sort of dress should she wear to dinner with a friend? There wasn't much in her luggage, and she'd hardly had time to go shopping for clothes, but there was a simple black dress that she'd put in her suitcase just in case she had to meet Kristjan at a place such as a restaurant.

It will have to do.

Merry slipped into it and stared at her reflection in the bedroom mirror. It still fitted all right—her pregnancy wasn't showing too much yet, though she thought she could feel an extra rounding to her lower abdomen. Not much. But enough to notice a small change.

And my hair… I need to do something with my hair.

She pulled it back, then scrunched it up high, trying it one way, then another. In the end she just swept it up into a clip, added some small diamond stud earrings and put on some lipstick and eyeliner.

There. That's not too much. I don't look like I'm trying too hard.

She slipped into a pair of heels, sprayed her wrists with perfume without thinking about it, and stepped out into the living area to wait for Kristjan.

He was already there, dressed smartly in dark trousers and jacket and an ice-blue shirt that matched his eyes.

He took her breath away, standing there like that, looking so smart and formal, and when he smiled it went straight to her heart and it began to pound faster.

'You look beautiful, Merry.'

'This old thing? Oh, I've had it for years,' she replied, suddenly nervous.

It's not a date. It's not a date. It's not a date...

She distracted herself from his appreciative gaze by picking up her bag and coat.

'Here. I got you something.' He passed her a small parcel wrapped up in a gold paper and bow.

'For Christmas?'

'No. For now. For agreeing to stay. At least until the roads are clear.' He smiled.

'Oh... I feel bad that I haven't got you anything.'

'Just open it.'

With nervous fingers she undid the bow and carefully opened the paper to find the Nicola Drake book that she'd wanted.

'Kristjan! You shouldn't have!'

'I saw that you wanted it.'

How sweet was that? But, knowing she was in danger of being swept off her feet by this charming, sexy man, she refused to take her eyes off the book and look into Kristjan's face.

Because if she did she'd want to give him a kiss as a thank-you. And if she did that... Well, then they'd be close, pressed against each other, and she'd be inhaling his scent, feeling the solidity of his body, and her need for him might overcome all sensibility and they'd miss their dinner reservation!

'This is so kind of you. Thank you. Let me put it in my room, so I don't lose it, and then we can go.'

In her bedroom, she took a moment to rest against her bedroom wall and take a few deep breaths. What was he *doing* to her? Giving her thoughtful gifts... Dressing as Santa so she didn't feel silly being the only one in costume, even though she was the one that had lost the bet... Opening a foundation for orphaned kids...

What else would she learn about this man? There had to be a dark side. There always was. She had to remember that. She'd made rash decisions before about a man and look how *that* had turned out?

After giving herself a stern talking-to in the mirror, she pasted on a smile and headed out to join him. 'Are we ready?'

He gave a nod. 'We are. Ingrid's isn't far. But you won't be able to walk in those heels. Not in this snow.'

'I can put on the snow boots.'

He smiled. 'Those heels are nicer. We'll take the snow sled.'

She bit her lip as he helped her on with her coat, like a perfect gentleman. She was perfectly aware of him standing so close to her. She could even feel his warm breath on her bare shoulders, and it sent shivers to all those perfect places...

'Thank you.'

'Wait here. Let me bring it round from the shed.'

She waited, with butterflies in her stomach, as she heard the engine start up and the sound of the purring machine as it stopped outside the front door.

When he came in and offered her his arm he quickly grabbed a blanket from the back of the couch. 'So your legs don't get cold.'

He told her to sit side-saddle, draping the blanket over

her legs, and leaned in close to tuck the blanket around her thighs. Feeling his hands on her again almost doubled her heartbeat, and she badly hoped he wouldn't notice her reaction to him. Thankfully he got onto the sled himself, wrapped her arms around his waist and held her with one hand—surely only for extra security?—as they quickly motored to the restaurant.

Ingrid's really wasn't far. It was small. Cosy. Intimate. Full of dark corners and perfect for private conversations. But it was also very aware that it was Christmas, and there were huge garlands draping from the thick wooden beams, with frosted slivers of orange and cinnamon sticks and poinsettia-red ribbons. Candlesticks gleamed. Sconces glowed. And a cascade of silver and white baubles hung from the ceiling like drops of snow.

A waiter received them and seated them in a corner booth, and Merry smiled at the table decoration. Three white tealights floating in a bowl that looked as if it had been carved from a silver birch tree.

'This is nice. Have you been here before?'

'Once or twice. We had the staff Christmas party here last year.'

'Where are you having it this year?'

'Wonderland.'

'Oh.'

'You're very welcome to come. In fact, you should make sure you do. It'll be fun.'

'Well, we'll see…'

She pretended to straighten the cutlery, though it didn't need it. The table was perfect. As was this evening. As was *he*. Which was why she was trying to find fault with it. And she felt awful for doing so.

'What would you like to drink?'

'Oh, just a fruit juice or something will be fine.'

'I'll join you.'

'You don't have to.'

'I know, but I will. I *am* driving, after all.' He signalled to the waiter. 'Could we have two apple juices, please?'

'We have apple, pear and ginger? Will that be all right?' the waiter asked.

Kristjan looked at her for confirmation and she gave a brief nod.

When the waiter had left to get their drinks, Kristjan seemed keen to get the conversation going.

'I was very impressed that you stayed dressed as an elf all day.'

'Well, I'm a woman of my word.'

'I can see that—though I'm not sure anyone else would be able to wear it as well as you did.'

She smiled. 'And *you* made a good Santa.'

'Thank you.'

'Do you think you'll make a good father?'

The question was out before she could think about what she was asking, and her cheeks flamed red with heat.

But then she thought to herself, *Well, we wanted to get to know one another a bit more. We might as well discuss what's going to be important...*

'I hope so... Yes, I think I will be a great father. Given the opportunity.'

'You want to be involved?'

'How could I not? As soon as you told me about the baby I... And then when we saw the baby on the scan it was just...' He shook his head, clearly lost for words. 'I've never felt like that before.'

'It *was* amazing...'

She felt her heart soften at the thought of the ultrasound. To see her baby moving the way it had! Jumping, slipping, sliding, waving its arms and legs! Its little heart pounding away! A real person already! It was incredible, and it was all going on inside her body. She was creating—no, *growing* the future.

'How does it feel to know you'll soon have your very first blood relation?' he asked.

'I don't know. I veer from being amazed to incredulous to disbelieving from one moment to the next. I don't think I'll quite believe it's really there until I hold him or her in my arms.'

He nodded. 'I'll be honest with you… I never thought I wanted this until it happened, and now I just know that I want it more than anything.'

'I know what you mean. I'd resigned myself to being single for the rest of my life, maybe getting a cat or two, but…'

'You can still have a cat or two. We do have pets here in Iceland.'

'I'd much rather have my baby.'

She looked into his ice-blue eyes and saw exactly the same feeling mirrored back. He wanted this child as much as she did. It was a new opportunity for them both. But they needed to know how they would manage it. How it would work and who would have custody.

'Do you think it's a girl or a boy?' he asked.

'I don't know.' She'd had dreams of both. 'Do you want to find out before the birth?'

'Do *you* want to?' he replied.

'I think I'd like to know. So I can plan. Decorate a nursery. Do all that kind of thing.'

'Agree on names?'

The waiter arrived then, with their drinks on a tray, which he served up along with their menus, before disappearing again.

Merry liked it that he didn't get in the way, like in some places where the waiters were constantly in your face, asking questions. Did they want the wine list? Could they get them anything else? Did they like the food? She hated that.

To be fair, she didn't know if he would interrupt their meal or not, but from what she'd seen so far the staff here liked to disappear into the background and let the atmosphere and the restaurant speak for itself. Taking a sip of her drink, she nodded at how wonderful it was—sweet, with a kick of ginger that warmed the palette. 'You're thinking of traditional Icelandic names?' she asked.

'I like Icelandic names, but I'd rather pick one that we both agree on, whether it comes from my country or not.'

Damn. He was still being chivalrous. What was there not to like? Or to pick fault with? Perhaps he was too giving? Perhaps she had stumbled from one man who took and took to one who gave and gave? Was that why she was intrigued by him? Attracted to him? Because he was the polar opposite of Mark?

She would have to be careful. Very, very careful.

'I guess names can wait until we know what it is.'

'Agreed.'

They picked up their menus and she pretended to be studying the selection, but in reality she was stealing glances at him. Watching his eyes as he read the offerings, trying to see if she could detect any hint of nastiness in his features that might speak of someone with a hidden dark side. But she could see nothing but his eyes, which spoke of kindness and generosity and sex appeal. Come-to-bed eyes. Let-me-undress-you eyes. Let-me-make-you-feel-good eyes.

She'd looked so intensely into those eyes once. In Hawaii. Amazed by the man she'd been with. Kristjan. A tall Viking. With long blond hair that he wore in a plait down his back, a beard, *huge* muscles…

If it wasn't for the fact that he wore a suit and carried a cell phone she would have imagined he'd either stepped off a film set or off a longboat and mislaid his horned helmet and axe.

Perhaps it was the raw maleness of him. His outward appearance of someone who could take care of whoever he was with. Could offer protection.

Merry had never felt protected in her entire life. She'd been taken care of by her adoptive mother, but their roles had been so quickly reversed. She had never felt the way she did when she was with Kristjan.

'See anything you fancy?' he asked.

'I'm sorry—what?'

He looked at her with amusement. 'On the menu?'

'Oh, right. Sure. Erm…what do you recommend?'

'How are you with fish?'

'Good.'

'Okay. The scallops with a parsnip purée and pickled figs sound good.'

'Great.'

'Cod fillet for main? With garlic mash and champagne sauce?'

She nodded, and watched as he got the waiter's attention and gave their order. It was feeling as if they were on a date. Even though they'd both said it wasn't. But there was no way she was going to get into a relationship with this man. With *any* man, thank you very much. She couldn't afford the risk to her heart.

Did Kristjan constitute a risk? Was it wrong of her to judge him on another man's standards?

They were going to co-parent, so they were going to be involved with each other to some degree, but just how much would that be? Because if he was going to continue being chivalrous and lovely and kind and amazing, she didn't know how her poor little heart was going to end up!

Kristjan was intoxicating her.

She had butterflies in her stomach, performing a full aerobatic show.

She sipped at her juice. 'This place is nice.'

'It is. The chef is a very good friend.'

'Do you know *everybody* around here?'

'Well, when you don't have any family you make time for lots of other people.'

'And this is quite a small community?'

'Yes.'

'Do you ever find that restrictive? Knowing that everyone knows your business?'

'No. It's nice, in a way. People look out for one another here on the mountain. I know I could count on anyone to come to my rescue if I needed it.'

'You're lucky, then. I've always felt alone.'

'Is that why you got married so young, do you think? So you would have someone? To make a family?'

'Maybe... I was a bit of a daydreamer. And Mark seemed so much wiser. So distinguished. Perhaps I was looking for a father figure? I was a big romantic. I'm not now.'

'You don't make any time for romance?'

'No point. It never seems to end well. Every person I know who's in a relationship has problems and difficulties.'

'But isn't that part of human nature, though? We have problems and difficulties with our friends, too. In any type of relationship.'

'So why haven't *you* ever got involved with someone, then? What's stopped you?'

Kristjan shook his head. 'I loved my parents. When I lost them on the mountain pass it broke my heart and I swore I would never care for anyone like that ever again. Plus, I experienced a little of what you just talked about. I saw all these other people having problems, giving themselves and losing pieces of who they were just to fit into a relationship and make it work, and as I got older I decided I was *never* going to compromise who I was. I was never going to lose any pieces of myself. I was just going to be me.'

'So you've always been single? You've never been in a committed relationship?'

'No, and I never intended to be.'

'Until me.'

He smiled. 'Until you.'

The waiter arrived then, with their starters. 'Enjoy your meal,' he said.

Looking at her beautifully arranged plate of food, Merry could understand why some people took pictures of their meals. 'This looks lovely.'

But her appetite was wavering. He'd as good as told her that she was different. That she mattered. Although *was* it her? Or was it just the baby that changed everything? She hoped not. A small part of her—maybe even a large part—wanted to feel that *she* was the one making him change his beliefs. That they had something special.

The scallops were exquisite. Rich in flavour and perfect with the smooth and slightly sweet parsnip purée. And the pickled figs added the perfect sharpness to her palate.

'You don't feel like you've missed out?' she asked.

'What have I missed?'

'Camaraderie? Closeness? Intimacy?'

'I've experienced all of those.'

'Just not with the same person?'

'No.'

She sighed, not sure why this bothered her. Was it because he had no track record by which she could judge his ability to sustain a relationship? If he'd never had a committed relationship before, how could she tell how he would be? Would he get bored by the commitment after a few months, once the excitement of a new baby had worn off and the sleepless nights and the stinky nappies and the crying took its toll?

Maybe *this* was his big fault?

This was what was wrong with him?

She'd found it. His Achilles' heel.

'So you don't do commitment at all? You can see how this might bother me...what with you wanting to be an involved father and everything.'

'I've never been in a committed *romantic* relationship. But I was committed to my education and my training to be a doctor. I'm committed to my place of work. I'm committed to The Elf Foundation and have been for years. I'm committed to my friends. I can *do* commitment, Merry.' He dabbed at his mouth with his napkin. 'Can you?'

'Me?' Surely he didn't have a problem with *her* evidence of commitment? 'I got *married*!'

'Which, for very obvious reasons, didn't last. That wasn't your fault, but have you committed to anything since then? You're considering leaving your job, leaving your country...'

'That's what *you* want me to do!'

'I'm just saying...' He smiled, as if he had proved his point.

Kristjan really was the most infuriating man she had ever met. 'You've asked me to consider doing those things and I'm being open and considerate because of our situation.'

'Because at the moment you don't have a choice. The roads are impassable.'

'For *cars*. I'm sure I could use your snow sled to get down the mountain.'

His eyes darkened. 'It's too dangerous. Tell me you would never do that.'

She stared at him, then relented. 'Fine. I'd never do that.'

'Thank you. Look, I'm sorry I implied you weren't committed, but you did the same thing to me. I think we're both very tense because of what's happening. We both want to get this right and we're both committed in our own ways. Can we agree on that?'

She shrugged. 'We can't get this wrong, Kristjan. This is too important just to feel our way through and hope for the best. We have to be sure we know what we're doing.'

'I'm not sure parenting is like that. Have you ever met any parent who's *totally* in control of the situation?'

No, she hadn't. The parents she met in hospital, when their child was sick or injured, were most often out of their heads with worrying and fear. And her own adoptive mother had felt totally powerless as her disease had taken more and more away from her.

'We just have to do our best and work together—not against each other,' he said.

'And your first request is that I consider staying in Iceland permanently?'

'I would like you to consider it, yes. Can you see yourself giving up your job and your home in England?'

'I *have* thought about it.'

'And?'

'And I don't know. I really don't. I would so much love

the fairy tale! The happy family. Mum and dad in one house…a happy child. The white picket fence. Maybe a dog or something. But is that realistic?'

'There's nothing wrong with wanting the fairy tale.'

'But I can't have it. Because I don't want to get involved romantically ever again and you said you don't either. Do you think we could share a house but live independent lives?' She smiled sadly. 'Do you think I'd want our child to see you bringing home random women?'

'That wouldn't happen.'

'No? Have you *seen* you? Women notice you, Kristjan. You're pretty hard to miss.'

'My focus would be on my son or daughter.'

The words he was saying were great—but they weren't realistic, were they? He was a big, virile man and he would have needs. Did he think they could live together and every so often he would go out and meet someone, hook up with them at their place before coming home to her and the baby? That would make her feel…

What? Jealous? Because that was how the idea made her feel right now. Jealous and angry and upset and…

Disturbed by the emotion, she put her knife and fork together on her plate, indicating that she was finished with her first course.

She was feeling a bit sick. 'Excuse me. I just need to use the bathroom…'

He watched her go, frustrated with the turn of their conversation. He'd hoped to clear the air of a few things, but instead they'd just muddied the waters somehow. The conversation should have remained light and breezy, but it had got serious quite quickly.

They both had desires here—and he wasn't talking sexually, though that did complicate matters too. Because no matter how much he tried to ignore the feelings he had for Merry, they kept creeping back to the surface, and the fact that she was carrying his baby was making him feel all caveman-like and protective of her, too.

He'd never felt this way about a woman before. Perhaps that was why he'd been a little prickly this evening? Biting back when she'd accused him of never being committed to anything…

Because he *was* committed! To their baby. He was committed to providing that baby with the best life, and with two parents who would love it very much!

I'll apologise when she comes back.

They could start the conversation over. Start afresh. They were friends—that would be easy enough. He didn't like how it had made him feel to upset her. It was wrong. She was the mother of his child, and if they couldn't agree right now, how would it be when the baby was here and they had to make other decisions?

When she came back to the table he stood up and watched her settle into her chair, before sitting down once more across from her. She looked a little flushed in the candlelight.

'Are you all right?'

He needed to know that she was. They'd both had a difficult time lately, what with the scare and the whole change in circumstances for both of them. It was a lot to absorb.

She nodded, smiling.

'I'm sorry, Merry. I didn't mean to respond the way I did. I guess I'm just nervous.'

'Of the situation?'

'And of you.'

'*Me?*'

'I've never had someone important in my life since my

parents, and yet here you are, carrying the most precious cargo. My child. And I know that you could leave at any minute. Get on a plane and disappear from my life.' He reached out and took her hand across the table. Squeezed it. 'You've become special and I never expected that.'

'Because of the baby?'

'Yes.'

She nodded, squeezed his hand back, then reclaimed it to pick up her glass and sip at her drink. She looked a little annoyed, not meeting his eye, and he wasn't sure why. Hadn't he just told her what she wanted to hear? He was being honest with her. As far as he could be, anyway.

The waiter came and took their plates and disappeared once again.

He looked at Merry. She was so beautiful tonight. In that little black dress that showed the smooth curve of her shoulders and bare neck. The twinkle of her earrings drawing the eye to her soft skin. Of course she always looked beautiful. Every man in this place probably thought the same thing.

He was stepping out into new and unfamiliar territory here—caring for a woman in the way he knew he was starting to care for Merry. He'd told her it was simply because of the baby, but he'd been holding something back. He didn't want her to be confused about how he felt, but how could he tell her when he couldn't admit it out loud?

I guess I'm just going to have to try to be genuine and take it day by day.

'I want you to stay, but I know that you have a home and a life elsewhere. So I'll take the reindeer by the horns and trust you completely. If you say you're considering staying here, then that's good enough for now. We'll take each day as it comes.'

She nodded. 'We will.'

* * *

The main course was fabulous, but even better was the succulent dessert of *kleinur*—a pastry similar to a doughnut, filled with rhubarb curd and dusted in icing sugar.

After the slightly sticky start to their conversation, they'd veered onto safer topics, and now it was late and time for them to go home.

Merry yawned, beginning to feel the effects of the long day on a body that was already working overtime growing another person.

'Tired?' asked Kristjan.

'Ready for bed.'

She didn't see the way his pupils dilated briefly as she was putting on her coat, but she heard him thank the maître d' and then they stepped outside into the cold, dark night.

A frost was settling, making the snow crunchy underfoot. He escorted her safely across the ice and took her hand to help her onto the sled once more for the short trip back. He went to grab the blanket and put it over her lap again, but she remembered how it had felt to have him do that before, and she was still smarting from the fact that he'd told her this was all because of the baby and not her at all.

Kristjan studied her. 'Are you okay?' he asked, concern filling his face.

Her heart was pounding, her legs like jelly. 'Yes, I'm just tired. It's been a long day.'

'Let's get you home.'

She held on to him tightly as they drove back, laying her head gently against his back as he drove at a slow speed through the snow. Merry tried to absorb what it felt like to lay herself against him, how fabulous it was, how wonderfully solid and safe he made her feel, but all it did was bring tears to her eyes that she had to wipe away surreptitiously.

At the house, he escorted her in. She peeled off her heels, wincing, and settled onto the couch.

'Remind me never to wear heels again. My ankles are the size of beachballs.'

She propped herself up and tried to focus on rotating her sore ankles, rather than on the rest of her, but all the tingling and anticipation she'd felt as she'd lain against him, and the sense that she might lose him after all, and all the wanting, was hard to ignore.

'Okay, let's have a proper look at these, shall we?' he said, and he gently lifted her feet onto his lap.

She had such dainty feet. Pixie feet. Her toenails were painted a soft rose colour. He began to massage her skin, gently manipulating her ankles with smooth, steady strokes in the hope that it would feel good. The friction caused by his hands upon her warmed his touch, and soon his massaging strokes were not just encompassing her ankles, but her feet too, and her lower legs.

It was as if he felt hypnotised, drawn to touching her. To being in contact with her. As if he couldn't let go.

He wondered what would happen if his hands moved up her leg… Past her knee… Beyond the hemline of that little black dress that so beautifully showed off her shoulders and slim arms. There was a zip down the side… it would come off in one easy movement…

He brought his thoughts back to her feet, taming them, trying to throw cold water on them, but it was impossible! Touching her, holding her, was too much for his senses to handle. His blood was racing round his body and he needed to cool down before he made a terrible mistake.

With a growl, he got up, moving her feet to the couch, and stalked away from her.

'What's wrong?' she asked.

'Nothing.'

'There's something. Talk to me.'

He turned to look at her, and all he wanted to do was take her in his arms and take her to his bed. 'The truth?'

She nodded. 'The truth.'

'If I'd kept my hands upon you I wouldn't have wanted to stop.'

Her eyes widened at his statement and her lips parted. 'Oh.'

'And I don't think that would be wise for either of us right now, would it?' he said, annoyed with his reaction to her.

'I guess not…no.'

'So, if you don't mind, I think I'll go to bed. Alone.'

'All right.'

'Do you need anything?'

'Um… I don't think so. I'd like a glass of water, though, if that's not too much trouble?'

Water. He could do that. It was practical and it was safe and it had nothing to do with caressing her body and making her his. Unless he poured that glass of ice-cold water over her naked body… Would it make her nipples peak? Strain outward, ready for his warm mouth to envelop them? Would he be able to follow the rivulets of water with his tongue? He could take a cube of ice and run it down her…

Stop it!

He gritted his teeth as he got a glass of water and took it to her room, placing it down upon her table. He tried not to imagine her in the bed. Tried not to wonder if she slept naked or not. Tried not to inhale the scent of her perfume that lingered in the room.

He headed back out and walked around the edge of the living room without looking at her, not sure if his resolve would hold if he did. 'Goodnight, Merry.'

'Goodnight, Kristjan.'

He closed the door to his bedroom and leaned back on it, wishing it had a lock, before pulling his shirt free from his trousers and slowly getting undressed.

If he had any more cold showers he'd be totally made of ice.

Kristjan woke in the early hours and, being totally unable to get back to sleep, decided to go for a swim in Snowy Peak's geothermal outdoor community pool. What he needed was to work off some of the pent-up energy that had been simmering in him since last night. It was the kind of energy that he usually worked off in a much more satisfying way, but swimming, powering through a few lengths, would have to do.

When he arrived the surface of the water was as still as a millpond, and once he was stripped to his shorts he dived in and felt the heat of the thermal waters embrace him. At that early hour there was no one else there and he had the pool to himself. As he swam, his thoughts continued to rampage in his head.

Merry. The baby. How all this was going to work it-self out.

If she stayed, would she buy her own place? Would it be here, in Snowy Peak? Or would she prefer to be in Reykjavik, where there were more people? What if they had a huge falling out? Would she leave? Would she hold the threat of leaving over him for ever? And if she did leave would he follow? This community, these people, meant so much to him. His parents were buried here. He had history here. Roots.

But…

He couldn't imagine not being in his child's life.

The powerlessness, the uncertainty of it all, was immensely frustrating to him—a man who was used to being in control of everything. Perhaps that was why he'd wanted Merry last night—because he'd felt that if he could at least possess her, then she would be his? At least for a short time?

He didn't want a full-time relationship with her, did he?

Did he?

He took a deep breath and swam underwater for as long as he could, before finally breaking the surface and gasping for air, swimming in a front crawl towards the edge in powerful strokes, turning at the poolside and swimming out again, determined to exhaust himself before he returned home.

Because he liked the way she looked in the morning. The ruffled bed hair, the way she yawned, how gorgeous she was when she was all sleepy and tired… And then the transformation of this sleepy woman, who disappeared into her bedroom wearing pyjamas and emerged half an hour later perfectly groomed and smelling amazing!

He enjoyed the chats they would have as they walked to work…the way she'd wrap her hands around a take-out coffee cup…the way her lips would purse as she blew on her drink to cool it…

So many things were getting into his system, making him want to enjoy them more, and—dammit—he didn't know how he wanted to feel about that. This was just meant to be about the baby, but his thoughts were becoming about *her*, too.

He'd never been in a romantic relationship. Not one that had lasted for more than one night, anyway. He knew about attraction. He was a master of desire. But was he any good at doing more than that?

Spent, he pulled himself from the water, the heat rising in steam from his body, and grabbed a towel and headed inside to the changing rooms. His arms and legs hurt in a pleasant way. He'd got his blood moving. He'd had the workout he needed.

Well, the one he would *allow* himself to have.

Time to go back and face temptation all over again.

'You're up?'

Kristjan had come through the front door just as she was getting on her coat, ready for work.

'Yes. Where did you go? I was worried when you weren't here.'

'I left you a note.'

'You did? Where?'

'On the fridge.'

'I didn't see it.'

She went into the kitchen and saw that on the floor, almost out of view, was a green sticky note that must have fallen off the fridge earlier.

'Found it!'

He'd followed her into the kitchen, opened the fridge and was taking a huge glug of orange juice. 'How are the ankles today?'

'Oh, much better after resting, thank you.'

'You're feeling okay?'

'Absolutely.'

She watched him. He'd come in carrying a bag, and now he picked it up and headed into his own room. He certainly was a mystery man.

'Where did you go?' she called.

'For a swim.'

'In this weather?' she asked in surprise.

He emerged from his room. 'Geothermal pool. Keeps you nice and warm.'

'Oh. I didn't know you swam.'

'I do on occasion.' He smiled and grabbed his jacket. 'Ready?'

'Yes.'

It was a little weird this morning. She could feel the tension between them after last night. It had been hard to lie in her room, staring at the bedroom ceiling, knowing that just a few metres away Kristjan lay in his own bed, wishing he was in hers!

She'd wanted him there too, if she were brutally honest, but her logical mind had kept telling her that it was a good thing that he wasn't. That he had done the honourable thing. Because this situation wasn't about them satisfying their lustful urges for each other—this was about the baby and nothing more. If there'd been no pregnancy she wouldn't even *be* here. She never would have seen him again! He wouldn't have given her a second thought!

No, it was *good* that he was being sensible—because they both needed to be. Right?

Even if, looking at him right now, she could easily imagine what it might be like to throw caution to the wind and satisfy those urges that she was feeling towards him. She could rip off his jacket and push him up against the wall, begin pulling his shirt out from the waistband of his trousers and feel those rock-hard abs once again, and the heat of him in her hands, and...

'Let's go to work.'

She nodded, hoping her hot flush wasn't visible. Work was a good idea. They couldn't do anything at work.

At least that was what she kept repeating to herself as they tramped through the snow towards the hospital.

The department was busy, which was good, because it kept her occupied and kept her thoughts away from Kristjan. She'd sutured the arm of a twelve-year-old, diagnosed a four-year-old with asthma and another with chicken pox, and now she was seeing to a seven-year-old girl who'd been brought in by her mother because she'd been up all night with tummy pains and being sick.

It could simply be a bug, but children were very good at compensating when there was something else going on in their bodies, and it paid to be thorough. Merry had quickly come to realise that a mother's instinct was usually not wrong.

Would she have that herself? Was it something you learned or was it truly instinctual? She'd followed a hunch before, believed that Mark was her soulmate, that he would treat her as the love of his life until they were old and grey, and she'd got *that* wrong.

'I'm just going to have a feel of your tummy, Ingmar—is that okay?'

Ingmar nodded, looking pale and teary-eyed.

Merry observed the abdomen and then began to palpate. It quickly became apparent that Ingmar had pain over McBurney's Point, indicating that something was going on with her appendix.

'I think you have appendicitis—which means, Ingmar, that we're going to have to take the appendix out.'

Ingmar looked at her mother, terrified.

'Surgery?' the woman asked.

She nodded at the mum. 'I'm afraid so. It's the safest option. If the appendix ruptures it can cause considerable pain and further difficulties. We need to act sooner, rather than later. When did she last eat?'

'About six o'clock last night,' Agnes translated.

Over twelve hours—that was good. It would lessen any risk with the anaesthetic.

'Good. Okay, so nothing more to eat now, but she can have sips of water if she wants. I'll get a nurse to come and insert a cannula, and get some extra painkillers on board, and then I'll get the surgeons to come down and have a chat with you both.'

'Okay...'

'And I'll come and check on you in the ward afterwards, when it's all done. You'll be absolutely fine, Ingmar. You're in good hands.'

She laid her hand on the little girl's and gave it a quick squeeze, knowing exactly how Ingmar felt. She'd felt terrified herself when she'd had to have her own appendix out, aged twelve. Back then she'd already been looking after her mum, who had been in a wheelchair, and though Merry had been frightened about the pains she'd been having, she'd thought they were period pains, and had simply stayed quiet until she'd collapsed at the bottom of the stairs.

It had been a terrifying time, but she had lain in the hospital ward worrying more about her mum than herself.

Would Kristjan be at her bedside when she gave birth? Would he hold her hand and help her through her contractions? Would he care and fret and worry over her the way her mother had?

Or would he only be there because of the baby? Because that was what he had said when they were at Ingrid's restaurant last night. That was the true connection between them. The lust and desire they felt was just an urge they both wanted to scratch. Once the itch was gone, what would be left over?

He was on the phone at the doctors' desk, asking for a porter to be bleeped, and she waited for him to get off the phone before asking him her question.

'Do you want to be at the birth?'

He blinked. 'Of course I do!'

'Right. Okay.'

'Do you *want* me at the birth?'

She tried to picture it. Being in pain, struggling through contractions for hours and hours, puffing on gas and air. Doing it alone, with no one at her side, would be...*horrible*. She could hire a doula, but it wouldn't be the same as someone who cared. And she thought that he did—even if it was just for the baby.

'I do,' she said.

He smiled. 'Good.'

She looked down at her booted feet. *It was okay.*

'Have you ever had your appendix out?' she asked.

'No.'

'Ever been in hospital and had to have surgery?'

'No.'

So he *didn't* know what it was like, then.

'But I've sat by lots of bedsides until my patients have woken up and I can know that they're okay.'

Yes. She could imagine him doing that. He was attentive. She would give him that.

'You'll be a good birth partner, then?'

'I'd like to think so. Does that mean you've decided to stay?'

She took a moment to think about it. *Had* she made a decision? It would be hard to say yes, but a part of her really wanted to. Because then the responsibility for this new life would be shared, and she would have someone in her corner again. She'd forgotten what that was like...

I want to be loved.

'I don't know,' she said.

There were carollers in the hospital, in the main foyer, standing beneath the Christmas tree. They wore dark coats, red scarves, and each of them had on a Santa hat with a fluffy white bobble. Their beautiful voices were soaring to the heavens like angels.

Merry stood listening to them, imagining the carollers who had found her outside a vicar's house and what they must have thought...thinking of how carollers had always held a special place in her heart. They went from home to home to try and bring a little pleasure to people by singing their favourite Christmas tunes. It was probably why she'd so easily joined in with the singing at The Elf Foundation.

Right now they were singing an Icelandic version of 'Silent Night', and she wasn't sure whether it was the music, or whether it was the lead female singer, whose voice was absolutely amazing, soaring above the rest, but she felt tears prick the backs of her eyes.

It was such beautiful, heartfelt music.

She felt hands upon her shoulders and turned to see Kristjan there, just standing, listening to the singing, too.

'Isn't it wonderful?' she asked wistfully.

'It is. I thought you didn't like Christmas?'

She smiled and sniffed, wiping away her tears. 'I'm warming to it. And carollers have always been special to me.'

'Because they found you?'

'If they hadn't done what they chose to do I could have died out there in the cold.'

He didn't say anything. He didn't have to. She could feel his thumbs caressing her back.

They didn't need to speak. They just stood there, watching and listening, as the carollers went from 'Silent Night' to 'O Holy Night' and then 'Have Yourself A Merry Little Christmas'.

Merry let out a heavy sigh and turned to face him. 'I need to go and check on my patient. She should be out of surgery now and on the ward.'

'The appendectomy?'

She nodded.

'I'll come with you.'

They rode up in the lift together silently, with Merry very much aware she was in a contained space with Kristjan. He tended to fill small spaces—or at least, to her, he seemed to. It was hard not to be aware of him when he was around. But after the other night, and the way he had held her as they listened to the carol singing just now, it was as if she could still feel his hands upon her body. She craved more of that, and the fact that she knew he was having a hard time keeping his hands off her... Well, that just added to the tension.

It was a nice tension. Electric. Sexual. Her body tingled nicely in anticipation and there was something about knowing she was carrying his child that made her want him even more. She felt that maybe her feelings were moving beyond the sexual too. She liked him. *Really* liked him. She liked being around him. Her heart skipped a beat when she saw him. His smile warmed her...she found herself craving more.

But it was madness to think that they could create a decent relationship between them. Because he didn't do romance, or girlfriends, and she refused ever to get involved romantically with a man again. A relationship based on sexual attraction would never last, because *lust* never lasted, and if they screwed up the nice little friendship they'd got going on right now they'd never forgive themselves. Not when both of them wanted this baby to be brought up by two parents.

The lift doors pinged open and they headed to the recovery ward. Ingmar was in the first bed, with a nurse beside her taking her observations.

'How is she doing?' asked Merry.

'Very well. Temperature and blood pressure are normal. She's just starting to come round.'

'How long before she makes it onto Olaf Ward?'

'A couple of hours.'

'Has the surgeon spoken to the parents?'

'I believe so.'

Merry watched as Ingmar's eyelids flickered slightly before she went back to sleep again. It would take her a few moments to come around properly but children tended to sleep well after anaesthetic. The most important thing was that all had gone well.

She had no other patients in the recovery ward to check on, so she thanked the nurse and headed back to the lifts.

'I had my appendix out when I was twelve,' she said.

Kristjan raised an eyebrow. 'Really?'

'Yes. I remember being really worried about my mum, because she was going through a bad patch with her health.'

'A bad patch?'

'She had Motor Neurone Disease. She was diagnosed in her early forties with amyotrophic lateral sclerosis.'

'I'm sorry. Was it difficult?'

'Incredibly. I didn't know what to do, you know…? I was meant to be looking after her. Yet there I was in a hospital bed and she was having to cope at home all by herself.'

'A child shouldn't have to have such responsibilities.'

'I know—but I did. And it ended up giving me my purpose.'

'Medicine?'

She nodded. 'My mother tried her very best, even when she was at her absolute worst. I hope that I'm able to be the best mother I can be at all times.'

'As long as everyone does their best…that's all we can ask for.'

'Do you think my birth parents did their best? When they abandoned me?'

He thought for a moment. 'I have to hope so. Hope that their own situation wasn't optimal for raising a child and they gave you up so you'd have something better.'

'But why abandon me in the cold? Doesn't that strike you as uncaring? They could have left me at a hospital, or a fire station, or at a doctor's surgery.'

'Try to look on it with positivity. You may never know the real truth, so you have to choose to believe you were left where they knew you would be found quickly.'

'You're more forgiving than I.'

'It's something I learned to do long ago. Forgive the world.'

He was very sage, but since getting pregnant she'd begun to wonder about her real family. What might she be passing on to her baby genetically? She had no idea.

'I wonder how my child will remember me?'

'I'm sure they will love you very much.'

She smiled, grateful that he was trying to keep her cheered.

'You're worried about the baby, aren't you?' he asked.

She nodded. 'I think I'm more worried about doing it right. Being a mother.'

'We're doing everything we can to make sure he or she is given the best start in life. To make sure that our child is loved and cared for.'

'Are we?'

She wasn't sure if they were. She was still dithering, after all, about staying in Iceland. If she truly wanted to give their baby the best start and both parents wouldn't she have decided to stay by now? Would it be enough for her just to be a co-parent with Kristjan? Or would she spend a lifetime yearning for more, because her fear of loving him was too great?

He reached up to tuck a stray strand of hair behind her ear. He smiled gently at her. 'We are, Merry.'

She still wasn't sure. Something felt very wrong and she couldn't identify it yet. Kristjan's certainty was niggling her and she felt a wave of irritation sweep over her.

Just what the hell was she doing? She'd come all this way to Iceland to tell a man he was going to be a father and then go home. She hadn't intended to do any more than that. Didn't need a man to tell her what to do, and yet she had allowed Kristjan to persuade her to stay until the snow cleared. Then he had asked her to stay on after that and give up her life in the UK, and she was actually *considering* it! After vowing never to let a man call the shots in her life again! Here she was, pandering to what *Kristjan* wanted! She was making the same mistake again. Allowing her attraction to a man to muddy her thinking.

She took a step back. 'This is wrong.'

'What is?'

'This. The whole... *This!* I need some space. I need

some perspective. I need...' She saw the surprised look on his face. 'I need to get a clear head. Kristjan. I need to go home.'

'What? I thought you were going to—?'

'Stay? Yes, you thought that because I agreed to it and because I thought I had no choice. But staying here with you isn't allowing me to think straight!'

'Merry...'

'No! This is too much! Working with you, living with you, and now I'm going to raise a baby with you? It's too much, too fast!'

He let out a breath. 'You're panicking.'

'You bet your life I am!'

'What can I do to make this better?'

'Nothing! It's not up to you to make this better! It's not up to you to fix. I need to sort this out on my own!'

Kristjan stared straight at her. 'Why?'

She stared back, suddenly deflated. Confused. 'What do you mean, *why?*'

'Why do you have to sort it on your own? Could it be because that's what you've always done? And because this...this sharing responsibility with someone else... feels odd? *Terrifying?*'

How did he *know*? How did he know that she was scared?

Tears began to fall. From somewhere he produced a handkerchief and then he was guiding her over to a set of chairs.

'I'm scared, too. You think I know what I'm doing? I don't. But neither does any new parent. There's no manual here. There's no set of rules. Everybody makes it up as they go along, from minute to minute.'

Merry felt as if she was about to start hyperventilating, her breathing was coming so fast.

'That's the whole point! I can't get this wrong. I *can't*...'

She could no longer speak. Her breathing was too rapid and she was beginning to feel faint. Her hands were tingling with pins and needles and her chest hurt. It was as if there wasn't enough air.

'Merry?'

She flapped her hands in front of her face, to get more oxygen, but nothing seemed to be working and she couldn't speak to tell him.

But somehow he knew, and he scooped her up in his arms once again and backed through the doors to the recovery ward, laid her on a bed and got an oxygen mask over her mouth.

'Breathe for me, Merry. Breathe... You're having a panic attack.'

She clutched that mask as if it was her only lifeline in the world, sucking in huge lungsful of air as if it was her last ever chance.

'Steady breaths, now. In for five seconds...out for five. Come on, look at me. Look into my eyes and breathe with me. One...two...three...'

She latched on to his steely blue eyes. Once upon a time she would have thought that staring into his eyes was the wrong thing to do, but it was totally *right* now, as she tried to follow his instructions, and slowly, after a few minutes, her breathing became easier.

Her body began to tremble with all the adrenaline that had surged into it. She felt relieved, and also a little embarrassed that she had freaked out so suddenly, but being with him was raking up all these feelings, and she still had no clear answers. She felt as if someone was going to come along at any moment and say, *A baby? You can't have a baby! You have no idea of what you're doing!*

What if she couldn't do it?

She and Kristjan were going through all this and yet when it came along the baby might be too much for her. She might be like her birth mother and...

'Look at me, Merry. Breathe...'

She removed the oxygen mask. 'I'm sorry. I didn't mean to freak out.'

'It's okay.'

'You must think I'm being silly.'

'I don't.'

'What if I can't do this? Be a mum?' she whispered.

Kristjan smiled at her, nothing but kindness and empathy in his eyes.

He sat on the bed, stroked the side of her face and whispered back, 'Oh, Merry! But what if you *can*?'

CHAPTER EIGHT

'I WANT TO show you something. Are you up to going out?'

'Sure. Where are we going?'

Kristjan smiled at Merry, wanting it to be a surprise. 'Somewhere special.'

He helped her on with her coat, wrapped her scarf around her neck and pulled her woolly hat down over her head.

She smiled at him the entire time and he was glad that she was okay now, after her panic attack that afternoon.

He understood her freaking out. Sometimes he wished he could do the same thing, but she needed someone strong beside her whilst she worked through this. They both did. Luckily, they had each other. Although he didn't think Merry understood just how much he needed *her*, too. It was a realisation that totally freaked *him* out.

But he was managing. Minute by minute. Hour by hour.

After today he'd figured she needed to see something amazing. And tonight was meant to be a good night, by all accounts.

'Can you trust me?' he asked.

'It depends.'

'I want you to wear this blindfold.' He held up another scarf.

She laughed. 'This isn't *Fifty Shades*, Kristjan.'

He smiled. 'I know. This is nothing like that, but I want where we're going to be a surprise. I promise you'll be safe and if at any time you feel you need to take it off, then I won't stop you.'

She considered it for a moment. 'All right.'

So he tied the scarf around her eyes and guided her out of the house and onto the snow sled. 'Hold on tight—we're off for a short ride to the other side of Wonderland.'

'What's there?'

'Everything.' He knew she'd like it once she saw it. He knew she needed to see it, too.

Starting the engine, he drove them to the special place just beyond Wonderland. Here was the real countryside of Iceland, and there was one spot that lots of people went to, to see something really special as there was no other light pollution to get in the way.

Parked, he slowly helped her off the snow sled and gently guided her to where she needed to stand. He looked up at the sky above them, knowing that this would be perfect, and then he slowly removed the scarf from her eyes, watching her face attentively as he did so. He wanted to see her reaction. Wanted her to see the beauty. Wanted her to see what *he* saw.

'The Aurora Borealis!' she gasped.

Above them, green and blue waves arced across the sky as if blown by a solar wind, slowly dancing to an unknown tune, glimmering and flickering from dark green to light, as if mixed by invisible fingers. There was a hint of yellow at the outermost edges, swirling like mist.

'It's like magic!'

He watched her face, her smile, her awe. The gleam in her eyes at seeing such a natural wonder.

'Beautiful, indeed.'

He looked up, watching the lights as they rolled and flowed above them. They were caused by disturbances in the magnetosphere—charged particles emitting light and ionisation. He knew the science, he knew the facts, but it was still a wondrous display...almost mystical.

'This is amazing, Kristjan! Thank you!'

'You needed to see it. To see the wonder of the world. How beautiful it is. In our job we get to see a lot of pain. A lot of upset. It can be scary, and I don't want you to be scared ever again.'

She turned to him. Looked up into his eyes. He could see the lights reflected in her pupils. She looked as if she had magic swirling inside her, and in a way she did. She was growing their baby.

He couldn't help himself. He took a step towards her, cupped her face in his hands and brought her lips to his. They were soft. Warm. And she sank into him, against him, her tongue entwining with his as he deepened the kiss.

He didn't need the light show above. There were fire-works going off inside him. He'd dreamt of this. Wanted this ever since she'd walked through the doors of the hospital, freezing cold and dripping wet, dragging that suitcase. It had been a sweet torture to see her each day. An ache in his soul, an agony that he had to keep his distance—and, boy, had he tried! He had tried so hard. And now, in the night-time air, with wind so cold and biting it felt as if it was slicing at his skin, he was blissfully ignorant as his body temperature soared at her touch.

He hadn't kissed her like this since Hawaii. From that tropical beach to this heart of winter she made the rest of the world fall away, and all he could think of—all he knew as his lips joined with hers—was ecstasy.

'Merry...'

He traced his lips along the length of her jaw, down her neck, but that damned scarf was in the way! He wanted to rip it off her, just as much as he wanted to rip away all their clothes, but they were out in the freezing cold and that wouldn't do. He knew he needed to have her—he couldn't wait any longer.

Her pupils had grown large and dark, her lips were swollen from his kisses, and she looked at him in a daze.

'Take my hand.'

He guided her back to the snow sled, waited for her to get on it and wrap her arms around his waist, and then they were off—heading for home…where there was warmth and beds and a hot shower.

He reminded himself to be careful. Not to rush. He carried precious cargo with him and, although he was adept with a motorised sled, he'd seen plenty of ferocious injuries to kids who had come off them, or overturned them, or simply gone too fast and not read the lie of the land beneath the snow. There was a certain skill to it. A sixth sense, almost. You had to work *with* the snow, not against it.

The lights of the Borealis were left behind them as the lights and noise of Wonderland grew ever closer. He saw the happy families, heard the music. Normally he would have enjoyed it—slowed down and taken in the sight—but not tonight.

He felt her arms tighten around him and he pressed one gloved hand against hers, clutching it to his chest. He drove like that for quite a way, until he had to let go to steer them home. As they got closer and closer it was as if he could hear his heart thundering in his head. He felt hot. Ready to strip himself of his clothes and bury himself in her. To devour her. To be consumed by her.

He parked, helped her off and, still holding her hand,

led her inside. Once the door was closed he helped unwind her scarf and unzip her coat. Then he pulled off her woolly hat and he gazed at her with a smile. 'Are you sure?'

She nodded.

It was all the permission he needed.

She hadn't known what to expect when he'd blindfolded her. It had been a difficult day, what with her panic attack, but when he'd removed the scarf and she'd seen the Northern Lights... It had been as if a miracle had occurred in the sky. As if she was watching real magic. And, even though logically she knew there was a scientific reason for what had been happening, and that it could easily be explained, she'd preferred just to stand there and soak it in, wondering at the wonderful display it was, believing it would be the pinnacle of her evening.

She had been wrong.

Kristjan had kissed her. And it had been as if he had switched on fairy lights in her body. Because now she was burning hot and bright all over and she wanted him more than ever. The short ride back to the house had been wonderful—leaning into him, her arms wrapped around him—and he had taken her hand, and she had thought she could feel the thudding of his heart inside his chest.

And now they were inside, and he was kissing her again, and—*oh, my God*—it was everything. She felt dizzy and senseless and all of a quiver, with a sharp need that she knew could only be sated by him.

She needed his mouth upon her body. She needed him to touch her as she had never been touched before. And she reached down to lift up her jumper and toss it to one side.

Why am I wearing so many layers?

After the jumper there was a shirt, and beneath that a thermal top. There were jeans and her thick socks, and then there were all *his* clothes. They tried to shed them as fast as they could, but jeans got caught on ankles and needed a tug, which made them both laugh, and then he couldn't get his shirt off without undoing the cuffs. And although Merry had never imagined herself as a woman who might actually want to physically *rip* the clothes off another person, she found herself wanting to do that so badly!

And then finally—*finally!*—they were down to their underwear, and suddenly everything slowed right down... which was perfect.

He traced the strap of her bra from her shoulder down to her breast, his thumb brushing over her peaked nipple through the lace before he stooped to kiss and suck it through the thin material.

Oh, my God!

She arched back, thrusting her breasts further towards him, the agony and the ecstasy of it all making her act on animal instinct. She felt his thumbs hook into the sides of her knickers and he slowly slid them down her legs, his lips tracing a trail of soft, featherlight kisses over her belly and her abdomen and her sex, where his tongue lingered, licking and teasing as she quivered above him.

Why had she denied herself this? Why had she fought this for so long?

It had been impossible to forget how good it had been between them in Hawaii, and it had given her some delicious dreams in the weeks afterwards. Before she knew about the baby she had often thought about how it might be if they were ever to run into each other again.

Yet they had *both* tried to not do this. Tried not to sleep with one another again. Because they hadn't wanted to complicate matters. But here they were. He was lowering her down onto the rug in front of the fire that had been slowly kindling whilst they were out and she could feel its gentle warmth down one side of her body as Kristjan created a trail of pleasuring kisses.

His muscles gleamed and rippled in the firelight, his arms flexing with power as he held himself easily above her. The whiskers from his beard tickled her inner thighs and she felt him caress her lower abdomen, stroking tenderly with his fingertips where the baby was before he came up to kiss her again.

She could taste herself in his kiss and she responded fully, wanting more of him, wrapping her legs around his back and pulling him closer. 'I need you, Kristjan. Now.'

He gazed into her eyes for a moment. 'I don't have any protection on me.'

She smiled. 'You can't get me pregnant. I already am.'

'But what about—?'

'I'm clean. I haven't slept with anyone but you.'

She could see that he was deciding what to tell her. Whether to admit to the truth, or not. The truth won out. 'Nor me—not since Hawaii.'

She smiled. 'Really? There's been no one since me?'

He smiled back. 'No. But it would be irresponsible to assume...'

'Please, Kristjan... I need you *now*.'

When he entered her she felt the full length of him filling her up and she groaned, arching upwards, clutching him to her, pulling his lips down onto her own, needing to consume him as he consumed her.

His movements were slow and languid at first, so that she felt pleasure in every single millisecond, every delicious inch, before his movements got quicker and quicker and he clutched at her bottom, pulling her against him as he powered into her again and again.

Merry allowed herself to sink into it, her arms outstretched above her head, breathing hard and heavy with every thrust.

This was what sex was meant to be like.

Feeling the way she did right now, she knew that what she'd had before had been nothing. Mark had been a bad amateur, not really knowing how to pleasure a woman and only considerate of how *he* felt.

Kristjan took her to the brink, and each time she thought she might come he slowed it down and withdrew, kissing her, nibbling, licking, leaving her gasping with delight and desire, before plunging in again so that when she finally came, in a explosion of ecstasy, he came himself.

They lay spent together afterwards, wrapped in each other's arms on the rug in front of the gently crackling fire. Merry put her head on the rise and fall of his chest, her fingers tickling the chest hair there.

Everything ached in such a wonderful way. Her every nerve-ending was alive and shining bright like stars in a night sky. She fitted against him as if she had been made specifically just for him. She felt so happy. So content.

There was no need for talk. Their bodies had said everything they needed to say. And they fell asleep in front of the fire, wrapped together, legs entwined.

When she woke in the early hours of the morning, she found that Kristjan had got up already, but he had laid a lovely blanket of red and white over her and gently stoked the fire, laying it with fresh logs to keep her warm.

There was a note beside her.

Gone for a swim. Back soon. K

She smiled, pulling herself up into a seated position, clutching the blanket to her naked chest. She was hungry, and thirsty, and as if he had known what she would need there was a tray laid on the small coffee table. A pot of coffee. A pot of hot chocolate. Some pastries and a bowl of fresh fruit.

Thought you might need this. K

The note was stuck to one of the Christmas pudding mugs that she was now so familiar with seeing about the place.

She would eat and then grab a shower, she thought. Looking at the clock, she saw they had three hours before they both needed to be at work.

They had taken a huge step forward last night, and Kristjan had shown her that he wanted to be with her. That was massive. For both of them. It must have been so obvious that there was something simmering away between them. It had been palpable—even the people at work had noticed, she felt sure.

It was the beginning of something. A way forward. One step taken. All the pair of them could do was take it one day at a time.

Kristjan powered through the water in a front crawl, barely stopping, his arms slicing through the heated water of the geothermal pool as if they were blades. His chest was protesting and he was gasping for air, but it was as if he was punishing himself, seeing how far he could go, and for how long, without taking a breath, knowing he wouldn't stop until his body forced him to.

He had slept with Merry. And when he'd woken this morning he hadn't known how he felt about that.

The sex had been great. It had been before and he had no doubt that it always would be. But...

Relationships were never just about sex.

Relationships were...*expectations*.

When you were with someone, when you were committed, that other person expected certain things. By sleeping with Merry had he given her the impression that they were something bigger? Because last night, for him, it had been all about sating the lust that he'd felt since he'd laid eyes on her again and had started getting to know her a bit more. Since he'd had her in *his* house, in *his* guest bedroom, under *his* roof, knowing that she was carrying *his* baby...

His lungs burned and he stopped, gasping for air, steam rising from the warmth of his skin in the cold morning air. All around him snow lay on the surface at the poolside, on the benches where people could sit, on the rails where they draped their towels. It was freezing, and yet he felt none of it. His thoughts were enmeshed with what had happened and what it might mean.

Merry wouldn't expect anything of him, would she? She'd told him before that she would never make the same mistake again and get into a relationship simply because of lust—and wasn't *lust* the emotion that had driven them both last night?

He was in the clear, right? They'd both simply scratched an insatiable itch and now everything would be fine. They'd be clear-headed. Able to think straight.

But all his mind could focus on was a replay of last night. The way her skin had looked in the firelight. The smooth curves of her flesh. The softness. The roundness of her lower abdomen where their baby grew. The taste of her...

He felt his body stir in response and, feeling aggravated that it was doing that, he pulled himself from the water and lay down on the poolside, rolling himself in the snow. He'd hoped the shock of the cold would sort him out and cleave those thoughts from his brain as his body went into survival mode. Only it never happened.

He simply remembered her gasps. Her breathing. How she'd arched against him and how it had felt to hear her scream his name... Even now, his body reacted! He'd hoped that by being with her at last he would finally get some control back over his feelings, but it was as if she had fed them and they had grown and they wanted to be fed again.

Would it ever stop?

If she left—if she went back to the UK—would he finally feel his body chill out and stop reacting to the thought of her?

But I don't want her to go back to the UK.

Perhaps they both needed some space? She was living in his house. She was at his place of work. What if he found her another place to stay? He had lots of friends who might have a spare room or a couch...

But did he really want the mother of his baby sleeping on someone's couch? The answer was a resounding no. She deserved the comfort of her own bed.

Maybe I should be the one to move out?

He thought of perhaps spending a few nights in the on-call rooms. He'd done it before. And the hospital always got busier around the Christmas period—especially as the big day got closer. It would be a good reason to stay there without her thinking that he was avoiding her. And when he *had* to spend time with her he could take her to places that didn't involve being near a bedroom. Show her the local schools and nurseries. Give her an idea of what it would be like for their baby to live in Snowy Peak as it grew up. Prove to her that there was a *future* here.

It seemed reasonable to him. It certainly seemed like a plan. And he felt badly in need of one of those.

Kristjan draped his towel around his shoulders and brushed off some of the snow. Three days till Christmas. Their first Christmas together, the two of them alone. After this there would be a baby to consider.

He hoped that they would at least spend it sitting around the same table. The thought that they might not be able to…pained him. But he had to be realistic. He was getting too close to her. Letting his feelings for her overwhelm him. If he lost her and the baby now, how would that feel?

He stared at the snow-covered mountain.

No. It was already too much loss to contemplate. He couldn't lose them. No matter how damn scary it was to keep her close.

'He's had a fever for a couple of days, with a cold, but today his temperature has been sky-high, and he's all sleepy, so…'

'You did the right thing, bringing him in.' Kristjan re-assured the mother as he grabbed hold of an electronic thermometer to check the baby boy's temperature for himself.

He put on a single use cover and placed the probe in the boy's ear. It beeped and he checked the temperature. Thirty-nine point six.

'Hmm…that's very high. Just over a hundred and three. Has he had any rashes that you've noticed?'

'Not really. One or two spots, but…'

'Where?'

'On his belly.'

The baby was ten months old and currently wearing only a sleeveless vest over his nappy. Kristjan lifted the clothing and noticed a bit of a mottled discolouration on the baby's skin that didn't look good.

'Has he been having plenty of wet nappies?'

'Not as many as he usually does—but then he hasn't been drinking as much. What do you think it is? A virus?'

He hoped that was all it was, but right now Kristjan was worried about sepsis—a life-threatening reaction to an infection...the immune system overreacting. The baby was breathing quite rapidly. But he didn't want to alarm the mother unless he was sure.

'Was he born at term? After a healthy pregnancy?'

'He was born a month early.'

'Right. And he's up to date with his vaccinations?'

'Yes.'

'Okay. I'm worried that his body is overreacting to an infection, so what I'm going to do is admit him and give him strong antibiotics and some fluids.'

'You think it's serious?'

'It could be. It might be sepsis. And if it is then I want us to be fighting it as soon as we can, okay?'

'Okay.'

The mum looked worried, but she was remaining calm, which was great.

'I'm admitting him right now. A nurse will come in to start the antibiotics and she'll monitor him until we can get him up to a ward.'

'Thank you, Doctor.'

'No problem. You did a good thing bringing him in.'

He headed from the cubicle to chart the case immediately, to prescribe the antibiotics and to call up to not only the children's ward but also the intensive care unit, to make sure they had space if necessary—which they did. Then he asked a nurse to take a blood sample, so they could send it off for some rapid testing.

'I want observations every fifteen minutes.'

The nurse nodded.

'Good morning!' The voice came from behind him.

He looked up. *Merry.* 'Good morning.'

'You were gone when I woke up.'

She leaned in over the counter and he breathed in her perfume. It did some heady things to his senses, and it was all he could do not to reach over the counter and pull her closer.

'I went for a swim and then I came in early.'

'Thanks for leaving me some breakfast.'

Oh. He'd forgotten about that.

'No problem.'

He wished he'd been there to feed it to her. Mouthful by mouthful, teasing those lips of hers with strawberries and other delightful things.

He watched her look around them before leaning in closer and whispering, 'I had a good time last night.'

So did I. 'Me too.'

'And we're okay?'

He smiled. 'Of course. Why wouldn't we be?'

'Good. I thought I might cook you dinner tonight? And for dessert we could…'

Her voice trailed off and he knew what she was implying.

She meant sex. More sex. And normally he wasn't the type of guy who would turn down sex with a woman he really wanted.

'Sounds good. I'd love to stop and think about that a bit more thoroughly, but I've got a query sepsis case I need to process.'

She nodded, understanding instantly. 'Don't let me stop you.'

He grabbed the notes and headed off in the direction of the young baby's cubicle, to update the mother and get the antibiotics on board. He didn't need to do it himself—the nurse was more than capable—but he needed to get away. To keep his head clear and in the zone for treating patients.

He couldn't afford to be distracted.

In her lunch hour, Merry decided to go Christmas shopping. Christmas was only a couple of days away, and she felt she needed to get Kristjan a present or two. He'd done so much for her—giving her a place to stay, a job to go to—and he was still doing his best to get her to stay in Iceland.

He deserved a gift. Something thoughtful. Something that would make him smile. And perhaps after dinner tonight she would give him the best present of all...

It didn't take her long to find a shop that sold fancy underwear. Silk. Lace. She tried on one or two pieces before making her selection, and then headed off to get him something that he wouldn't be allowed to see until the twenty-fifth of December.

It was difficult. She wasn't sure what to get him. He had bookshelves, but they were mainly filled with medical books, and he played his music through a speaker, so there wasn't any music collection she could plough through. She knew he dressed well, and enjoyed swimming, his job...

Maybe something for The Elf Foundation?

A thought struck her, but she knew it wasn't something she could get sorted in a lunch hour. She needed to head back to the hospital, but when she got back she'd search the internet for someone to help her with her idea and make a few calls, put it into motion...

She felt very happy with her decision, and couldn't wait to see Kristjan's face when he found out. Now all she had to do was get through the afternoon, cook dinner, and then let him unwrap her like a very special present!

But first she had a list of patients. She picked up the chart at the top of the pile, checked that Agnes was free to accompany her, and then headed through to a cubicle, to see a woman sitting on the examination bed next to a little boy who was reading a book.

'Hello. I'm Dr Bell. What's brought you in here today?'

'I couldn't get in to see my local doctor, so I've brought my son here. He's got all these bruises. Look at them! On his arms...his legs. You should see the ones he has on his back! He wasn't like that when I dropped him off at his father's house a couple of days ago.'

Merry understood the subtext. This mother was suggesting that her ex-partner was either neglectful, or that he was abusing the boy. Well...it could be either of those—or neither. It could be something medical, she knew, but clearly the boy's mother hadn't considered that.

'I want you to take photographs. I've got some on my phone, but I want this reported!'

'Okay...well, let's take a look first, shall we?'

The boy's name was Tómas and he was six years of age. Old enough to co-operate, if he wasn't too scared.

'Hey, Tómas. Can I have a look at you?' she asked.

The boy nodded and put down his book.

'What are you reading?'

'It's about pirates. And a dragon.'

'Wow! Sounds amazing! You like to read?'

'Yes.'

'Me, too! But I can't remember the last book I read

that had a dragon in it. Or a pirate, for that matter. Is he a good pirate?'

'He's okay.'

The boy really did have some bruises on him, but they didn't look like hand marks, or the kind of bruises he'd get if someone had held him tightly. They were mostly small. The kind of bruises she'd expect a rough and tumble young boy to have. But he did have a lot, and the one on his side, near his back, was quite big.

'Did you fall over at your dad's?'

'No.'

'Did you play any sports?'

'We went ice-skating.'

'Sounds fun. And you didn't fall over there?'

'I nearly fell over. I hit the side of the rink when someone crashed into me.'

'Uh-huh…'

It could just be a collision injury, but Merry's sixth sense was tingling, telling her something wasn't right here. The boy looked quite pale, and he was a little underweight. If this was abuse, she'd be surprised.

'How have you been feeling lately, Tómas? Your usual self?'

'He's been tired,' the mother answered. 'Like he's got no energy. He wasn't very keen on going to his dad's… he wanted to stay home.'

More subtext. The mum was willing her to understand her suspicions.

'Is that right? You've been feeling tired? Sleepy?' asked Merry.

'Stuff hurts.'

'What stuff?'

Tómas shrugged. 'Everything.'

Merry looked at his mum. 'Do you brush his teeth for him?'

'No, he does it himself. He's always been very good at that.'

'When you brush your teeth, Tómas, do you notice any bleeding?'

'Only if he does it too hard,' the mum interrupted.

Merry felt around the boy's neck, checking for swollen lymph nodes, and found a couple in the boy's neck. This was definitely something.

'And he's normally fit and well?'

'Absolutely.'

'Okay. The nurse is going to perform a blood test. It's just a small needle—what we call a butterfly needle—and it won't hurt at all.'

'What are you checking for?' asked the mother.

'I want to check his red and white blood cells, and then I think we may need to get a haematologist to check the results, just to be on the safe side.'

'And then you'll report it?'

'Not yet. Let's see the results of the blood test first, okay?'

The boy's mum nodded reluctantly and Merry watched as Agnes took a sample of blood.

Tómas was very good. He was fascinated by the cold spray the nurse applied to the crook of his elbow and he even watched the needle go in.

'Is that my blood?' he askd.

'It is.'

'Wow!'

She labelled the bottles, marked the request form to check for a range of conditions, and then placed a plaster on his arm, once the bleeding had stopped. It took a little longer than normal, but she tried not to let it show

how that worried her. If she was right—and she sincerely hoped that she wasn't—then this wonderful little boy had a type of leukaemia.

'Okay, you can stay here. I'll just get these sent off to the path lab. Tómas? When I come back, I want you to tell me what's happened in your story.'

He smiled at her rather wanly. 'I will.'

Merry closed the curtain, her heart filling with dread as she popped the blood into the shuttle that would send the sample directly to the lab within seconds. When it had whooshed away in the tube, she sat down at the doctors' desk to write up her notes.

'How's it going?' Kristjan appeared from around the corner.

'Not great. How was your case? Was it sepsis?'

'No. I think it's just a nasty virus, but we're keeping the baby in to monitor him. What are you dealing with?'

She sighed and sagged in her chair. 'I'm hoping it's not a case of acute leukaemia.'

Kristjan frowned. 'I'm sorry… Need any help with it?'

'No. I've got the bloods sent off. But… You know when you have that feeling in your gut?'

'I do.'

'Well, I'm hoping mine is wrong.'

'Did you mark the tests as urgent?'

'Yeah.'

'Need a hug?'

She looked up at him and smiled. 'Yeah.'

Kristjan came from around to her side of the desk and wrapped her in a huge bear hug, pressing her gently against his chest so that she felt warm and protected and soothed by his presence. It was nice. It was *very* nice. And she really didn't want him to let go. How quickly she had begun to love being in his arms.

'Do we all get one of those?' asked Agnes, with a smile.

'If you need one,' answered Kristjan.

Merry inhaled his scent one last time, then pushed herself reluctantly away. 'Thanks.'

'No problem.'

'I guess all I can do is wait, huh?'

'And keep your fingers crossed.'

She nodded as he walked away to carry on with his own work, and for a brief moment she crossed her fingers and looked up at the big fat Santa ornament on the doctors' desk.

'If you've got anything to do with this whatsoever,' she whispered urgently, 'then please, *please*, I beg of you, give that family a happy Christmas.'

She wouldn't know if her plea was answered. At least not for a little while.

And when the haematologist himself came down with the results, a grim look on his face, Merry knew that not all prayers were answered.

'You need to do a bone marrow biopsy,' she said.

She just knew.

He nodded, face still grim.

'Okay. Let's go and tell them the news.'

CHAPTER NINE

TÓMAS'S CASE AFFECTED her all afternoon. It was horrible to hear such a life-changing diagnosis at any time of life, but that young... And so close to Christmas...

Merry wondered what kind of a time the family would have, knowing what their youngest child would face after the festive season.

Remission induction to start with, to kill the harmful cells in Tómas's bone marrow, restore the balance and hopefully relieve some of the symptoms. This would be done through blood transfusions, mostly, but it would leave the boy with no immune system.

Then there would be something they called 'consolidation,' to kill any remaining leukaemia cells, and finally maintenance, when he would receive regular chemotherapy treatments to stop the leukaemia from coming back.

His little body would come under attack from all the medication they'd have to give him, as well as steroids for a couple of years, but hopefully the treatment would work, and he wouldn't suffer any complications.

He and his family had a long road ahead of them, and as she'd worked Merry wondered how she would feel if *her* child ever got terribly sick like that? How would she cope? Would she feel powerless? At the mercy of other doctors and their opinions?

It was something she always tried to keep at the forefront of her mind when she dealt with patients and their families—how would *she* feel to be receiving this news and how would *she* want the doctors to speak to *her*? And now she was thinking would it be better to hear that news alone, or with Kristjan?

He would be strong, no doubt. He would support her, do everything that was needed. And, if either she or their child needed it, he'd be there to give one of those special hugs.

She could see so many benefits to being with him, but it didn't boil down just to pros and cons at the end of the day, did it? It came down to feelings, and hers were all over the place—betraying her, making her want him, making her desire more than they currently had. It was confusing. Dizzying.

She was dreaming of having the fairy tale. Of walking into the sunset with him. Getting her happy-ever-after. Didn't she deserve one after all this time?

So she was hopeful about the situation between herself and Kristjan. They'd turned a corner, hadn't they? Grown closer. Taken a big step in their relationship. And she knew that if she was going to enjoy this evening—which she very much hoped she would—she would have to shake off her feelings about Tómas. He had been sent home now, but would be back the next day for his bone marrow biopsy. All she could do was hope they'd caught it early and that treatment would be effective.

She got home ahead of Kristjan and began preparing their evening meal. She'd decided to try and make something traditional to Iceland. Something heart-warming that would show him that she cared and had made an effort.

Whilst it cooked she took the time to have a quick shower and shave her legs and paint her nails. She was just blowing air over her fingertips when she heard the front door open.

'I'm back!'

'I'll be out in just a minute!'

Excitement and anticipation filled her at the thought of the two of them alone once again. He'd left so early that morning—cheating her out of waking up in his arms—and then they'd spent the day at work, with stressful cases for both of them. Illness and disease didn't care what time of year it was. It happened no matter what. But she could make time and plan for enjoying herself, and she knew she wanted to take time to enjoy Kristjan.

Her nails now dry, she slipped a dress over the fancy underwear she'd bought earlier and padded out barefoot to greet him.

He was standing in the living area, on the rug they'd made love on the night before, loosening his tie. Smiling, she went over to him and went up on tiptoe to give him a welcoming kiss. His beard whiskers tickled for a moment, and then she helped him undo the tie, tossing it over the back of a chair.

'Welcome home.'

'Something smells good.'

'It's a fish stew. *Ploppfishur?*'

He laughed. 'Close enough. Do I have time to take a shower?'

She thought about it. She could turn the heat down a little on the stew. 'I could join you…'

He smiled. 'Really?'

'Mmm… Really.' She stepped closer and began undoing his shirt buttons. 'Let me help you with this shirt.'

Her fingers made quick work of the buttons, and she looked up at him and smiled as her hands dipped lower and lower with each button. Then she pulled his shirt from the waistband of his trousers.

'And with this belt…'

The belt undid easily, and she pulled it from the loops like a whip. Kristjan stared down at her, his breath quickening, as she peeled the shirt from his broad shoulders.

She took in the round curve of his deltoid muscles and leaned in to inhale his delicious scent and lay her lips upon the hot flesh of his chest. She pulled the shirt down his arms and let it drop to the floor, and then she hooked a finger into the top of his trousers and smiled at him.

'Come with me.'

Feeling her body tingling in anticipation, she led him towards his en-suite bathroom and reached in to turn on the shower. Then, with the hiss of the water behind them, she began to undo her dress, pulling loose the tie belt at the waist so that it fell open to reveal the black silk underwear she'd bought earlier.

'You like?'

'Very much so.' His voice husky.

'How about you take a closer look?'

She took his hands, lifted them to her breasts and let go, closing her eyes in delicious agony as she felt his thumbs sweep over her nipples before rising to pull the bra straps from her shoulders. He stepped closer, reaching round her to undo the hook at the back and then slip the bra off.

She smiled at him, hooked her thumbs in the waistband of her knickers and pulled them down, stepping neatly out of them and watching in delight as his gaze hungrily roamed her body.

When he made eye contact once again she stepped forward and undid the button and the zip of his trousers. She reached in beneath his underwear, to take him in her grasp.

He sucked in a breath and she stood there stroking him, feeling him swell in her firm grip, and she smiled like a devil, pleased with her own power.

This was like being back in Hawaii—that very first night when they had first met. They had been equals. Each taking their pleasure. Exploring one another for the first time. Learning what they liked.

Well, Merry knew what *he* liked. 'Do you want more?'

'I do.' His voice was rough, throaty.

She pulled her hand free and began to slide his trousers down, her mouth dropping kisses all the way down his chest, over his abdomen, whispering in featherlight touches over his obliques knowing he was ticklish there as she pulled down his underwear and took him in her mouth.

She had never felt more powerful than she did in that moment. Knowing he was at her mercy and he was all hers. She'd never had this before.

With her husband Mark she had been a passive participant. He'd never needed anything from her except her ability to lie there until he was done. He hadn't wanted her to touch him, to actively give him pleasure, and the first time she had tried he had scowled and told her that he didn't like it. That her being 'sexually aggressive' as he'd called it, turned him off. To him, the male was the leader during sex and she should know her place.

It had been a very unsatisfying sex life, and she had been glad when she'd been able to flee his grasp.

Meeting Kristjan in Hawaii had been a revelation for her. She had explored her own power and what she was capable of doing and it had been refreshing to discover that during intimacy she could ask for things. She could do things she had never tried before. And with every gasp of breath Kristjan had simply signalled to her that she was more powerful than she had ever believed.

Being intimate with Kristjan had given her power. She'd thrived on it. And in turn she'd been vulnerable and had opened up to Kristjan, who was so experienced in pleasuring a woman, and known that she could give up control and it would be okay. He'd made her feel safe. He'd made her feel adventurous. He'd made her feel *equal*.

Now she led Kristjan under the spray of water and their lips met. There was something delicious about the heat of the water on their alert, anticipatory bodies. Every nerve-ending was awaiting his touch as she felt the force and heat of the water pound down upon them, and she was barely aware of the coldness of the black marble tiles as Kristjan pressed her against them, her hands above her head as his lips traced the curve of her neck and shoulder. Her breasts were straining outward, desperate for the caress of his hands and mouth.

'Kristjan...' she breathed.

He lifted her up, pulled her legs around his waist as he thrust into her, grinding into her over and over.

Merry allowed herself to submit to all the delicious feelings in her body. Her tingling nerve-endings. The feel of his mouth upon hers. His large strong hands cupping her buttocks. The water raining down and the feel of him filling her, sliding in and out.

She could feel her orgasm coming, could feel her excitement building, and she clutched him ever tighter, urging him on. Suddenly her world exploded in a firework display of ecstasy and excitement, with Kristjan coming only seconds afterwards.

The water continued to pound down as he slowly lowered her feet to the floor of the shower and kissed her gently—her neck, her breasts, her mouth. And then he was holding her face, cupping it in his hands as he kissed her reverently.

'I've never had dessert before my main course before.'

Merry chuckled. 'And what did you think of it?'

He smiled, smoothing back her hair from her face. 'I could definitely make it a habit.'

They had both eaten ravenously afterwards, having second and even third helpings of Merry's fish stew. She was a good cook, and Kristjan liked it that she was trying new things.

Life was going well for them, he thought. They got on at home and at work. The sex was great! And he enjoyed her company even when they *weren't* lying in each other's arms.

But for now they were. Kristjan was spooning Merry's naked body once again, and the heat of their bodies was making them feel like one.

He could get used to this. Who knew there were delights to be had when you slept with a woman more than once? He'd always thought of sex as something that was a one-off experience. You had your fun and then you forgot about that woman because there was no point in carrying on. In fact, he'd told himself it was *dangerous* to do so.

He'd *never* done this! And he was surprised at how comfortable it made him feel, knowing he could take the time to explore Merry's body. To enjoy it. Even without sex there was something wonderful about just lying here in her arms. It made him feel...*valued*. It wasn't just a desirous wanting, or a need that he felt—though he did feel that too—it was as if she had *chosen* him. Out of all the men on the planet, she had chosen and found worth in *him*. Not just once. Not just in a fleeting sexual encounter never to be experienced again. But multiple times. She was staying. She wanted him.

At least for now, anyway.

'It's Christmas Eve tomorrow,' he said.

'I know. The year has gone so fast.'

'On Christmas Eve here, families usually give each other the gift of a book and sit and read in the evening.'

'They do? What kind of books do you like?'

'I don't know. I've only ever given books to patients before, and I only read for knowledge. It's been a long time since I had a family.'

She turned to look at him, stroked his face. 'You think of us as a family?'

'Aren't we? In some strange way?'

Merry smiled. 'I guess... I'll get you a book. Tell me what you like.'

'I don't know... Crime? Thriller?'

'I'll get you *something*.'

He kissed the tip of her nose. He was grateful to have her here, knowing it could still be fleeting. He thought about the news he'd heard just before he'd left work today. He had to tell her. It was the right thing to do.

'They think they'll be able to clear the mountain pass soon,' he told her.

She'd promised to stay until the roads cleared, but that had been before they'd got closer. Had she changed her mind? Did it even matter to her about the roads? She hadn't said anything.

Did he feel her stiffen slightly? Tense?

He sank his nose into her hair, breathed in her scent. Honey blossom. Meadows. She smelt of freedom and the warmth of summer.

'When?' she asked.

His heart sank. Did she still plan on leaving? Even though she lay here in his arms? He didn't want to lose her, but she was a free woman and he wouldn't tie her down. Mark had restricted her movements; he wouldn't do the same. He had to trust that she would make the right decision.

'I don't know. A nurse mentioned it. She's been hoping to get down to visit her family in Reykjavik.'

'Oh...'

She pulled his arm tighter around her waist and he took that moment to inhale her scent once again, telling himself that if he trapped the memory in his head he would always be able to feel her near. Always remember this moment in which he had held her in his arms. He hoped this wasn't the last time. But he wanted to be honest with her. He didn't want her to hear that he'd known about the roads and chosen not to tell her.

Kristjan closed his eyes, hoping for the peaceful oblivion of sleep, where none of this mattered. Where he didn't live in a world where she might leave him behind. Where he didn't feel the tight fear of her possible desertion in the pit of his gut. Didn't have that sick feeling that he had had recently, the more he had allowed himself to have feelings. The more he lost control.

But sleep wouldn't come.

And he lay there for hours, hoping that Merry wasn't already planning in her head for the time when they would separate. Hoping that telling her the news about the mountain pass wasn't the worst thing he'd ever done in his entire life.

CHAPTER TEN

CHRISTMAS EVE MORNING, and Merry didn't have work until the afternoon—which was good, as there were a few things she needed to sort out in order to give Kristjan the present she was organising. But as she bustled about from place to place in Snowy Peak she couldn't help but ruminate on the fact that he'd told her last night that the mountain pass might soon give safe passage through the mountain range and back to Reykjavik.

Where the airport was.

She could go home.

If I want to.

When she'd first got here it had been all she could think about, but now...? Now everything was muddled. Confused. She didn't know *what* she felt. Her feelings for Kristjan were complicated now, and their situation... She had no idea what to do for the best.

If she stayed, what would it mean for them? She *loved* it here in Snowy Peak. She could easily admit that she had fallen in love with the place—the area, the people, the hospital...

Kristjan?

She loved being with him. Loved being in his arms. Loved working with him.

But was it any more than that? Was she *in love* with him?

Merry didn't want to be. All these years of telling herself never to get involved with a man again and here she was—in deep with the father of her baby!

As she sat with a latte in one of the coffee shops, she watched the families passing by outside, doing last-minute shopping for friends and family. She watched mothers holding the hands of excited children. She watched fathers as they gave their children shoulder rides to keep them out of the snow. Watched how they would gather snowballs and throw them at each other.

Would this be her future, her baby's future, if she stayed here?

If she did stay, just what would she be committing to?

She and Kristjan hadn't made any rules, hadn't told each other what they were to one another. Was she reading too much into what was happening? Kristjan wasn't a man of commitment. He'd not told her they were exclusive or anything…

And if they cleared the mountain pass…if the first of the winter storms had really gone…what would she do? For her baby's sake?

Was having two parents the best thing? There were plenty of single parents out there doing a fabulous job of raising happy, well-adjusted children. There were children who split their time between parents and they were doing well too. It was what she had originally planned. But everything was different now. Kristjan was invested in their child and she wasn't sure her conscience would be clear if she denied him access to their baby.

But was she too focused on the idea that because she had no parents at all, two were better than one?

Right now, it was all fun and great sex—but what about when that wore off? She was wary of making the same mistake again, but she kept second-guessing herself. What if this *wasn't* a mistake? What if staying in Snowy Peak with Kristjan *could* be the best thing she ever did?

I still have time to think about it.

She headed to the shops, picked up the meat she would need: smoked lamb, ptarmigan—which was apparently the in thing here in Iceland—and ham. Then she picked up veggies from the market, some *laufabrauð*—leaf bread—from the bakery, and collected the ingredients for a traditional Icelandic rice pudding called *möndlu grautur.* She'd found the recipe after watching a television show, and had thought that a rice pudding made with whipped cream and almonds sounded amazing.

As she shopped, she developed the cosy warm feeling that she was just like everybody else. Domesticated and part of a family, so that she could create an amazing Icelandic Christmas for Kristjan. She wanted to do it. He'd put himself out by inviting her to stay—the least she could do was cook. And it felt good!

Back in the UK she'd often spent Christmas alone, cooking for one, or had made sure she took the day shift at work and had Christmas lunch there when she could grab it. Sometimes it had been nice. Other times Christmas had just proved to her what she *didn't* have.

Even the one Christmas she'd shared with Mark had been so...restrictive. They'd been on honeymoon, for goodness' sake, and yet Mark had wanted a Christmas like the ones he was used to having at home with his family. Because she had no family traditions of her own she had gone along with it, not aware of the reprisals until much later...

This Christmas she wanted to do something nice. Maybe start her own traditions. Because next Christmas she'd have a son or a daughter, and they might only be a few months old, but it would be their most special Christmas ever!

What did she want Christmas to mean to her child?

A special time, just for family, when they would wear matching cosy pyjamas and sip hot chocolate, maybe open just one gift from their Christmas stockings on Christmas Eve! Perhaps they would go to church and light candles and sing carols? Perhaps she would make a Christmas pudding and put a coin in it for one of them to find? Perhaps after Christmas dinner they would go out for a long walk, wrapped up tight in scarves and woolly hats, and perhaps they would have a pet dog to throw sticks for? And she would video the faces of her family as they unwrapped presents and spent the morning playing games and cooking Christmas dinner...and she'd wear a special Christmas apron and...

Listen to me! Perhaps I do love Christmas after all! Perhaps I do love Kristjan?

She checked her watch. Nearly time to head for home.

Home.

It could be. But even if she decided to stay in Snowy Peak, wasn't it presumptuous to assume that she and Kristjan would continue to live together? Wasn't it time she looked for her own place?

There was a local paper in the café that had properties listed in the back. It didn't mean anything...she was just checking out all her options.

She looked them over, circled a couple that could be promising, and then she headed back.

When she got to work, the majority of the staff were dressed in costumes.

Kristjan had on red Santa trousers held up by brown leather braces over a checked shirt, sleeves rolled up at the cuffs, looking like a Santa who'd just spent a couple of good hours in his workshop. The nurses were dressed as elves and angels and shepherds. She felt totally out of place in her normal everyday clothes, so she went and borrowed the elf outfit she'd worn before, when she'd lost that bet with Kristjan.

Christmas music played low in the background of the unit, and it was still—unsurprisingly—as busy as ever. Lots of kids were coming in with viruses, chest infections, and there was one case of chicken pox. She diagnosed a broken arm, a broken wrist, and referred one little boy for an endoscopy because he'd swallowed a coin that was now stuck in his oesophagus. She saw a bad case of nappy rash, consulted with an ophthalmologist because someone had scratched an eyeball on a thorny bush, and admitted one of her young patients she suspected had pneumonia.

She didn't like having to admit children at Christmas, but sometimes it was impossible not to, and she knew the hospital would do its very best to make the kids who were there enjoy the special day.

She was halfway through her shift when she received a call to her mobile phone, and she answered it after scurrying away to a private corner.

'Hello?'

'Dr Bell? It's Kari, from Viktorssons?'

Suddenly it came to her. 'The solicitors? Right!'

'I just wanted to let you know that we have the initial paperwork for you, as you requested, if you'd like to collect it?'

'Really? Oh, that's fabulous! Thank you. Unfortunately, I'm at work now, till late.'

'At the hospital?'

'Yes.'

'I can drop it in for you at Reception on my way home—it wouldn't be any trouble.'

'Kari, you've been an absolute lifesaver! Thank you for doing this. I know it was late notice, but I appreciate it.'

'No problem! Happy Christmas, Dr Bell.'

'You too, Kari.'

She ended the call and bit her lip with excitement, hoping that Kristjan would love what she had done. It had felt right. And, even if things didn't work out between them, it was still a good thing to do.

'Who are you talking to?'

She turned at the sound of Kristjan's voice. He was right behind her.

'No one.'

'All right…'

She could see he didn't believe her. Had he heard who she'd been speaking to?

'I'm finishing now. Heading home. Do you need me to pick anything up?' he asked.

'No, I think I got everything this morning. You could check on the lamb for me. It's in the slow cooker.'

'Will do. What time do you finish?'

'Six.'

'I'll have everything ready for then.'

She smiled. 'I'm meant to be getting it ready for *you*.'

'That's okay. Are we going to the big carol concert at Wonderland later? It starts at nine. The Elf Foundation are singing a couple of songs… I said we'd try to show support if we were free.'

'I'd love to.'

And she meant it. Even though she would have hated the idea of it when she'd first arrived here.

'Great. See you later.' And he leaned forward to kiss her.

One of the male nurses wolf-whistled the pair of them and Merry blushed red. Most of the staff here knew the situation between her and Kristjan and she'd made some very good friends here.

It would be a good place to settle down.

When he got home, Kristjan felt his stomach rumble in anticipation at the aroma when he walked through the front door. Everything was going perfectly. He and Merry were getting on great, and when he'd told her about the mountain pass, she hadn't said a single thing about leaving. That had to be good news, right?

In the kitchen, he got out the steamer and put on some of the vegetables, then made himself a coffee and went into the living room to have a five-minute sit-down.

He saw the local paper on the table and began to browse through it, reading about a court case that was ongoing in Reykjavik and a local dog-sledding endurance race that someone was undertaking to raise money for a brain cancer charity. He went from one story to the next, ignoring the television pages and the financial pages, and was about to close the paper again when he noticed that a couple of properties—local apartments for sale—had been circled.

He sat forward, reading intently.

Apartment for sale, leasehold
Two bedrooms, unfurnished
Parking space and small cellar.

Merry was looking for property? That was great news, wasn't it?

It meant she was planning on staying. It meant that

she saw a future for them as a family. That must have been why he'd heard her on the phone with a solicitor!

And it was then that he was suddenly hit with an overwhelming sense of responsibility to get this right that he almost couldn't catch his breath.

How much would it take for him to show that he was able to do this, to be the man they both needed? To be this honoured, to be trusted by her like this, was...unbelievable. All this time she had been alone in the world and now...

Could he do it? Was he capable of opening up his heart and letting them both in so much he wouldn't know where *he* ended and *they* began? If he was going to care for them the way they needed he would have to take action and show them just how committed he was. Prove it to them.

Kristjan got up and went into his bedroom to change.

If Merry could do this and be brave after all she'd been through, then so could he.

Kristjan had lit the candles on the table she'd prepared earlier in the day before going to work. Nat King Cole was playing from the speakers and she emerged to find him pouring some non-alcoholic wine into two glasses.

'To us!' he toasted.

She smiled. 'To us.' And she took a sip, wincing at the tang of the drink. 'Is this battery acid?'

'I hope not. I'd hate to need surgery to repair my stomach lining the day before Christmas.'

'I'll stick to fruit juice, I think.'

She went to the kitchen to pour herself an orange juice and dish up the food into serving bowls for the table. She was looking forward to it. She'd never had ptarmigan before, but assumed it would taste like any game bird. She hoped she could stomach at least a bite of it, not being very keen on meat at the moment.

'I picked you up some noodle soup and a chickpea and vegetable pot pie if you can't stomach the meat,' he said.

'Oh, that's very thoughtful of you. Thanks.'

'No problem. Shall we get started?'

She nodded and smiled as he pulled out her chair for her, and when she was seated comfortably he draped a red cloth napkin over her lap before kissing her on the lips.

'Happy Christmas, Merry.'

'Happy Christmas.'

They clinked glasses once again and, not knowing what to do, she was relieved when Kristjan took the lids off the bowls.

'Shall I serve?' he asked.

'Please.'

He served her a selection of everything and she was determined to try it all. She wasn't keen on the lamb or the ham and though she tried the ptarmigan it wasn't for her—not in her current condition, anyway—so she was relieved to have the alternatives he had so kindly provided.

They took their time over the meal, chatting about the medical cases they'd had in the past, and then Kristjan changed the topic of conversation.

'Tell me about your *best* Christmas.'

'My best one? I think it might be this one,' she said, feeling shy about admitting it.

'Really?' He seemed pleased. 'Didn't you get married at Christmas?'

'A few years ago today. Yes.'

'And that wasn't a good Christmas? Before it all went wrong?'

She shook her head. 'No. But I don't want to think about that time in my life. I've moved on. Everything's changed.'

'For the better?'

'I hope so.'

'So do I. In fact…' He got up from his seat at the table and came over to her, kneeling at her side as he took her hand in his.

What was he doing?

He looked as if he was going down on one knee, and men only tended to do that if they were tying their laces or proposing! And Kristjan's shoes did not have laces…

'Kristjan…'

He put his finger to her lips. 'Please. Let me speak. I've been thinking a lot just lately, and I've come to the conclusion that you and I have something amazing here. We understand each other, we share painful pasts, but more than that we're united in what we want for the future—for our child! Knowing that you're moving here permanently, giving up your old life for us, is—'

What the hell was he going on about?

She hadn't made a decision yet and he was thinking she would just do everything that he wanted? Had he never heard of compromise? Had he never heard of talking things through?

Her chair scraped back noisily as she got to her feet.

'*Stop! Stop it now!*'

A wave of anger washed over her at his presumption. How dared he?

'I never said I was moving here permanently, and you have no right to assume that's what I'm going to do! *I'm* the one in charge of my life! Not you! Do you think you can just get down on one knee and propose to me and assume everything has gone your way? You don't marry someone just because they're having your baby! You marry someone because you *love* them! Have you never listened to a word I've said?'

She threw down her napkin and stormed from the

room into the guest bedroom, slamming the door behind her, feeling fury and rage overwhelming her with their strength, along with a feeling of disbelief and injustice!

She'd told him about what had happened with Mark. How they'd got married in a rush, on a whim, with neither of them taking the time to think it through properly and how that had ended for her! Bruised and battered in a women's shelter, swearing off men *for life.*

And he thought proposing marriage to her was a *good* thing to do? On the anniversary of making the worst mistake of her life, he wanted her to make another one? He had *no idea* what he was doing! He was a relationship virgin.

You didn't propose marriage because there was a baby. You married because of love. You married because you couldn't live without the other person! You married because you wanted to be with that person for the rest of your life! To wake up with them and go to sleep with them every single day. To care for them when they were sick. To hold their hand when they were going through something hard. To give them your heart in the palm of your hand, knowing that they would keep it safe for as long as they lived.

He was proposing for all the wrong reasons. For convenience. Because she already lived in his house. Because she already shared his bed. Because she was already pregnant. Because of the baby. He wasn't proposing because he loved her!

And who says I'm staying?

This wasn't real yet. But he was trying to make it so. Trying to fix the holes in their relationship with a giant sticking plaster.

Well, plasters didn't heal anything. They just hid the

badness. And if this behaviour, this assumption, wasn't controlling, then she didn't know what was!

Tears trickled down her cheeks as she grabbed her clothes from the wardrobe and threw them on the bed, looking for the wheeled suitcase she'd put away only a few short weeks ago.

Did he not see how she felt? How she would be repeating the past if she jumped straight into a relationship with him? What they had together was fun and, yes, she enjoyed being with him—but was she ready to live a *life* with him?

She stopped to sniff. Wipe her nose.

He'd ruined *everything*!

There was a knock at her bedroom door and then he opened it. 'Merry...'

She saw him see the suitcase, the clothes, the fact that she was packing.

'You're not leaving?'

'Of course, I am! You don't get to have a say in what I do!'

'But, Merry, I—'

She held up her hands. 'I don't want to hear it, Kristjan! Why couldn't you have just...?' She ran out of words, frustrated at his clumsy attempt to advance their relationship into something it wasn't.

'It's Christmas Eve! Please...where will you go?'

'I'll find somewhere,' she said.

'But—'

'The mountain pass may be open. I'll ask around. But what I do and where I go is nothing to do with you.'

'You're carrying my child.'

'Oh, I know! I've almost uprooted everything because

of it. You persuaded me to stay because of it. You *assumed* because of it. Well, no more.'

'I can't let you wander the streets on Christmas Eve, Merry. And you can't go down that mountain pass if it isn't safe!'

She fastened the suitcase and shrugged on her coat. 'Just try to stop me!' she said, and she barged past, her heart breaking in her fury, storming to the front door and opening it.

Outside, snowflakes gently fell, slow and silent.

She turned. 'I thought you just might be different. But you men… You're all the same.'

And as she closed the door behind her the last thing she saw was the shocked and hurt look on Kristjan's face.

Nat King Cole crooned quietly from the speakers whilst Kristjan sat in his now very empty home, wondering just what the hell had happened.

She'd been planning to move to Iceland. She'd circled some properties in Snowy Peak. Had been speaking to a solicitor. He'd heard her on the phone. You didn't do that unless you were thinking of viewing those properties, and you only viewed properties if you were interested in moving. And the solicitor…? Well, that could have been for anything!

Had he read her wrong? They'd been getting along so well together. He'd thought…

What? What did I think—really?

Okay, perhaps a proposal had been jumping the gun somewhat, but he was new to this relationship malarkey and he hadn't really known what he was doing. But it hadn't really been about the proposal, or love, it had been about showing her that he was committed to her!

But what if she'd never wanted that?

He sat there for a moment, trying to see things from her point of view. She had discovered she was pregnant after a hot one-night stand in Hawaii and had come all this way to another country to tell the father—only to get stranded because of the snow. The father had invited her to stay and to work at his hospital, because he'd known she was a good doctor. But they hadn't been able to keep their hands off one another, and then the father had told her he would convince her to stay.

He had told her, he would convince her…

Was that it? Was that the crux of this matter? Had she felt as if a noose was tightening?

Merry had told him about Mark, about what had happened in her marriage. How her husband had been a controlling man, making all the decisions, telling her what to do.

She'd hated Christmas because she'd made a bad decision at Christmas, to marry a man on impulse. And he, Kristjan, had proposed on Christmas Eve—on impulse!

Oh, boy, am I an idiot!

And now she was out there, traipsing around in the snow, pregnant and with nowhere to go. On Christmas Eve!

In a daze, he walked into the guest room and looked around. The wardrobe doors still hung open, and a couple of coat hangers were lopsided. The chest of drawers wasn't closed properly, and she'd left the book she was reading on her nightstand.

He picked it up and looked at it. Books were special on Christmas Eve in Iceland. Families gave each other books to read the night before Christmas. He'd bought her this book, knowing she wanted it. He'd hoped she was reading it. There was a bookmark. No. It was an envelope.

He opened the book for a closer look and saw that the envelope had his name on it.

Merry Christmas, Kristjan!

He sat down on the edge of the bed and opened the envelope to find an official solicitor's letter confirming the fact that Dr Merry Bell was going to be financing, every year in perpetuity, a week at The Elf Foundation for one child who had no family of their own. It was to be called The Bell Prize.

Oh. That was why!

His heart swelled with gratitude that she would do this! That she would join him and provide a special time away for a child at the foundation that he had set up.

She cared. Just as much as he did.

And she was scared. Just as much as he was.

He could see that now.

And he'd gone storming in with his big boots. Thinking that commitment was what she needed to see. But what if he'd been wrong all this time? What if she'd needed to hear something more? Be shown something more?

I should have told her that I love her.

He couldn't lose her. She didn't deserve this and neither did he. He couldn't let things end this way. He had to tell her how he truly felt!

Kristjan didn't even have time to grab his jacket. He simply got up and left, slamming the door behind him, sending a shower of settled snow from his porch down onto his shoulders.

He ignored it.

The cold didn't matter.

What mattered more than anything was Merry.

* * *

She'd never imagined that she would be trudging through the snow again, cold and wet, dragging that damned wheeled suitcase behind her the way she had when she'd first arrived, but here she was.

Her first thought when she'd left Kristjan's house had been to tramp right up to the mountain pass and see if she could get down it. But she'd quickly got rid of that idea.

Yes, she would finally be out of Snowy Peak, but it had been a two-hour taxi ride from Reykjavik to get there, and she didn't fancy trudging for hours, seeing if she could hitch a ride from someone in a country she didn't know. And, though she was fairly certain she'd made a huge mistake in leaving Kristjan's house, where it was warm and dry, she didn't want to make another mistake. She knew the pass could be treacherous. It had taken the lives of both of his parents—she would never risk her child's life like that.

I need to find somewhere, but where?

She thought of looking for the B&B, or a pub, but she wasn't sure she wanted to be around people full of Christmas cheer right now—not when she was feeling so miserable and heartbroken. So she decided to head for the hospital. It would be the most sensible thing. Dry and warm and with plenty of beds. She could coop herself up in one of the on-call rooms and eat Christmas dinner in the café, or something.

But she didn't want anyone to know that she was there. She didn't want anyone telling Kristjan that that was where she was. So now she was going the back way to the hospital, slipping in through one of the back doors, using her key pass to get in and a utilities lift to get her up to the staff floor, where she took one of the on-call rooms, locking the door behind her and standing there in the dark.

The room was plain and simple. A bed and a bedside table. A lamp. A phone. In the window was a tinsel star— the only hint that elsewhere people were celebrating.

She didn't put the light on.

She didn't care.

All that mattered was that she was warm and dry. She would stay here until the mountain pass cleared and then she would go. She would not stay with another man who thought he was calling all the shots in her life. Who thought he could impose his will upon her life.

God only knew how he would be once their child came along. And to think she'd thought they could do this without love. Because now she knew you couldn't.

Kristjan! Why did you ruin everything?

Merry lay back on the bed, one hand over her eyes, trying not to cry. She'd thought they had a chance. She really had. They were perfectly matched as friends, as sexual partners, as work colleagues. And she *loved* him! He'd made her fall in love with him!

The connection they shared was like nothing she had ever felt before. She'd kept looking for his faults and had found none—but perhaps his fault was that he couldn't truly see what she wanted? What she needed to hear from him? Perhaps she was the one who had made a mistake? Willing, hoping for him to be different, perhaps she had seen things that weren't there?

All along it had been about the baby. That was what he had said. '*United in what we want for our child.*'

He'd not been proposing because he *loved* her. He'd not been proposing because he couldn't live without *her*!

All along it had been about the baby.

Perhaps he had slept with her because he'd thought that

by continuing that pleasure she would be swayed towards staying? Was that it? Had she been used so terribly? Was he like Mark? Acting a certain way to ensnare her and keep her here so he could have what *he* wanted? Had she made the same terrible mistake as before?

The thought sickened her.

She hoped not.

Because if she had then she really didn't think she'd want to see him ever again.

No matter how much it broke her heart.

'*Merry? Merry!*'

Kristjan trudged through the snow, calling her name, wondering where the hell she'd gone in such a short amount of time. In this cold. In this snow.

He'd wondered for just a brief moment, terrifyingly, if she'd tried to get down the mountain pass—but he'd dismissed that as being ridiculous. She wouldn't do that! It was dangerous and she wouldn't endanger their baby. But in his panic he'd had to check, and so he'd got out the snow sled and raced as fast as he dared to the mountain pass.

There had been no sign of her. No sign of anyone having trudged through the snow there recently.

No. So she had to be somewhere else. *Somewhere.*

He'd driven back to Snowy Peak, calling in at a couple of B&Bs to see if she'd shown up. He went to the hotels and asked, but no one had seen her, and that had been when he thought of The Elf Foundation. She must have gone there! It was the only place she knew, apart from the hospital.

So he'd motored through the snow, ignoring the cold and the strange looks he'd got from people for wearing only a long-sleeved shirt with no coat, and burst through the doors of the foundation.

The kids had been having their read-along. All sitting in a circle, reading their books, surrounded by chocolate and cake and buttery icing-sugar-covered delights.

They'd all looked up at him and what a sight he must have made! In trousers and a thin shirt with no coat, snow on his shoulders and in his hair and his beard.

'Has Dr Bell showed up here tonight?' he'd asked.

'Dr Bell?'

'The woman I came with the other day.'

'Sorry, no. We haven't seen her.'

'Oh.' The disappointment had been overwhelming. 'I'm sorry. I… I can't stay. Merry Christmas.'

'Merry Christmas, Dr Gunnarsson!'

So where was she? The hospital?

Again, he'd leapt onto the snow sled, knowing he had to put this right. Knowing he had to let her know how he truly felt.

The sled had carried him through fine snow and now he was trudging through the thick banks of it that lay up against the shops and doorways. His trousers were soaked, but he didn't care about any of that. It simply didn't matter.

When he got to the hospital, he ran up to a porter who stood by the reception desk chewing on a flapjack.

'Have you seen Dr Bell?'

'No, sorry.'

He ran over to the lifts, to see if he could find her up in the staffroom. The lift seemed to take an age to get there, and when it finally arrived he stood there as it rose upwards, tapping his feet, the breath huffing from his body impatiently, until finally the doors pinged open and he raced down the corridor, passing Agnes, who called out, 'Don't run!'

He slowed to a walking pace and threw open the door to the staffroom, expecting to see Merry, huddled up on the couch, red-eyed, maybe sipping a hot chocolate or something. But she wasn't there either.

He let out a huge breath.

Where *was* she?

He checked the on-call rooms, rattling at the door handles, but most were empty, or locked, indicating that someone was asleep in there. None had their lights on. And no one had seen her arrive.

She couldn't still be out there, could she? All alone? In the freezing cold?

He'd never forgive himself if something happened to either of them!

I'd never forgive myself... I love her. I can't lose her...

He suddenly realised he might have totally screwed up the one relationship in his life that he *did* want!

Had he, in his fumbling way, ruined what might have been his one true love? Ruined his future with the mother of his baby? He didn't want one without the other, and if he found her and she told him that she was moving back to the UK then he would follow her around the world, if it meant being in their lives. He'd let her call all the shots.

He couldn't do this without her. He couldn't live without her in his life.

I have to find her. I have to tell her everything.

CHAPTER ELEVEN

'MERRY?' THE DOORKNOB rattled slightly, then she heard a curse, and her name repeated at the door of another on-call room farther down the corridor.

Merry huddled underneath the covers, fighting her urge to go to him, praying for sleep to come and steal her away from the turmoil raging in her mind.

She couldn't quite believe that she was in another country, homeless and with no place to go, on Christmas Day. No one to celebrate with. Alone once again.

It shouldn't hurt this much. She'd had many Christmases alone—why should this one be any different?

Because I dared to dream, that's why.

Even though she'd told herself she wouldn't get involved, she had done it anyway. She'd told herself every day not to get too involved with Kristjan, that he wasn't the type of man who settled down, and that even though he might be a good doctor and a good father, it did not mean he would make a good partner for life. He'd not had any practice, had he?

And yet he had somehow got into her heart. Maybe it was the pregnancy hormones—maybe it wasn't. But he'd sneakily got under her defences and she had allowed him in, telling herself it was just sex, that it was sensible—

logical, even—to create a positive relationship with her child's father.

Perhaps it was a male thing to think you could call all the shots? Take control? Tell other people what to do? Perhaps because Kristjan hadn't had parents for a long time he was so used to calling the shots in his own life that he thought he could call them in hers?

She thought about that for a moment. It even caused her to sit up in bed.

He's so used to calling the shots in his own life...

Was that it? Was that the key to all this? What had he really done but ask her to consider staying here? For the baby. For him. For *them*.

He wouldn't have asked her to marry him on a whim—he would have considered it. Kristjan wasn't a man who casually got into relationships.

Have I misjudged him?

But he'd seemed pretty certain she was staying. As if the decision was a done deal. Where would he have got that idea when she hadn't actually confirmed or denied that...? And then she remembered the newspaper she'd brought home from the café. The properties she'd circled so idly, asking herself that if she was going to stay where would she choose? It had been a game, that was all!

But I left the paper on the table. I didn't clear it away. What if he saw it and thought...? Oh, no!

He'd thought she was staying because she'd left evidence to *make* him think that! He wasn't assuming anything about her at all!

And she'd not given him any time to explain. She'd panicked and run, feeling claustrophobic, feeling the ghosts of Christmases past coming to haunt her, telling her she was about to make the same mistake as she had with Mark.

Merry threw off the blankets and grabbed at her shoes. She had to catch up with him!

The suitcase could stay here. It would be safe. All she needed was her coat.

She shrugged into it and unlocked the on-call room door, dashed out into the corridor. It was empty, save for the fairy lights twinkling along the windowsills and a bare trolley bed that was out of use due to a broken bed-rail. She ran down the corridor and hit the lift button. It glowed brightly and on the display above the doors she saw that the lift was on the ground floor, but on its way up.

'Come on! Come on!'

When it finally arrived, she dashed inside and pressed the button for the ground floor, twisting her hands over and over as the numbers slowly went from four down to three, to two, to one and then to Ground Floor.

The doors slid open and the music of Christmas assailed her as she ran through the entrance foyer, past the carollers, and as she got to the front door she thought she saw him.

'*Kristjan!*'

He turned, saw her, and she watched him let out a breath. He looked positively freezing. And soaking wet.

He came running towards her and met her by the huge Christmas tree. He stopped about a metre away.

'I've been looking everywhere for you.'

'I was here.'

'I looked for you in the staffroom—'

'I was in an on-call room.'

'They were all empty or locked.'

'I was there all the time.'

He stared back at her. 'I never meant to assume that you were staying. I never meant to tell you what to do.'

'I know. I know you didn't. I got frightened—by everything. Frightened of making the same mistake. Of rushing into a relationship. Worried that we were together for the wrong reasons.'

'I want you here so that I can be a father, Merry.'

She nodded, knowing she had no right to expect him to love her.

Then he stepped closer, taking both her hands in his.

'But I also want you here because I'm in love with you and I don't want to be without you. If you need me to move to England with you then I will, because my home will be wherever you and our baby are. We can have an engagement that lasts years if you need to—if you're worried about marriage—or we can carry on as we are! When I tried to tell you before I got it wrong. I'm not used to this. I'm not used to wanting someone. So when you came into my life and threw all my rules and beliefs to one side I wasn't sure what to do.'

She smiled, her heart exploding with happiness. 'You *were* going to propose!'

He nodded. 'Yes. And I know you've done this before, but there's no rush for us to get married. We don't have to elope...we can wait as long as you want if you don't want to marry just yet. I just need you to know that that offer is on the table—always. For when you're ready. For when *you* decide.'

She hiccupped a laugh. He'd just told her everything she ever needed to hear.

'I've already decided, so ask me again.'

He brought her hands to his lips. Kissed them, then got down on one knee.

All around them people had stopped to watch, their faces full of smiles.

'Merry Bell. I love you so much and I want to continue

to love you for the rest of my life. Would you do me the honour of becoming my wife?'

Happy tears trickled down her cheeks. 'I will.'

She cupped his face with her hands and brought his lips up to hers, kissing him with great intent. She hoped he could feel just how much she loved him, too! He was her everything!

'We should wait until after the baby,' she said. 'I want to plan a proper wedding this time.'

'We'll do anything you want.'

She kissed him again. So happy! So pleased that she had found him here! So pleased that he had come looking for her! So pleased that she'd been wrong!

Around them, the onlookers clapped and cheered.

'I don't have a ring for you.' He looked uncertain. 'Does that bother you?'

She shook her head. 'Of course not!'

Suddenly he seemed to have a thought, and he swung his plait round to undo the leather tie at the bottom of it before taking her hand in his and tying the leather around her finger.

'There. That will have to do until I can find you the perfect ring.'

She beamed at her leather ring. 'I don't need the perfect ring. I have the perfect man and that's what matters.'

EPILOGUE

One year later

THEIR SON'S HAPPY burbling noises came over the baby monitor.

Merry turned to Kristjan and smiled. 'He's awake!'

She was so excited. Their first Christmas as a family! Einar was six months old and she'd been looking forward to this day ever since he was born.

They got up, putting on their matching Christmas pyjamas and robes, and headed to their son's room.

'Einar! Hello, lovely boy! Merry Christmas! It's Christmas Day!'

Merry scooped her son up into her arms and kissed him on the cheek. He was a big boy, just like his father, and there was nothing she loved more than going to fetch him from his crib each morning.

Einar grinned at her. Some dribble went down his chin before he nuzzled into her neck for a cuddle and she inhaled the delicious baby scent.

'Let's go and see what Santa has brought.'

She had to admit that they might have gone a tad overboard on presents for Einar, and that he was probably going to be more interested in ripping at the wrapping paper rather than in the actual toys, but she didn't care. She was determined to soak up every happy moment with her family.

Kristjan changed his son's nappy whilst she got Einar a Christmas onesie that made him look like a gingerbread man, and then they headed into the living room where the tree awaited, with presents underneath.

It looked like something on a Christmas card. Homely, traditional, festive… There were red and gold twinkling fairy lights, and by the fireplace was a large reindeer made out of sticks and wood, his belly filled with baubles, tinsel hanging from his antlers like icicles.

They all sat down by the fire.

'Look, Einar! Look at all your presents!'

He was sitting up all by himself. He'd started doing it earlier that week. Because he still had the occasional wobble, they surrounded him with pillows—just in case. He gurgled and chuckled, reaching for a low-hanging bauble.

'Try this, Einar. Your first Christmas present ever.'

She passed him a small, loosely wrapped present and he held it to him and laughed, his one solitary tooth just beginning to show.

Merry tried to show him how to open it, but of course she had to unwrap the whole thing. She revealed a big, squidgy penguin and Einar hugged it tight, dribbling over its head.

'Safe to say I think he likes it,' said Kristjan.

'Yep. Do you think we should do some more, or just let him get used to one at a time?'

'He seems happy with the penguin for now.'

She smiled, looking with adoration at her beautiful blue-eyed son. So like his father.

'I've got a gift for you,' she said to Kristjan, reaching for the gift she'd specially hidden under the tree yesterday.

Kristjan smiled and leaned forward to kiss her. 'Thank you. What is it?'

She laughed. 'Open it!'

He slid his finger under the tape and pulled it free to find an envelope inside. He opened that and pulled out a cream card, embossed with silver snowflakes. It was a save the date card. The date was in the middle of June.

He opened the card.

> *Save the Date!*
> *June 14th*
> *The wedding of*
> *Dr Merry Bell*
> *and Dr Kristjan Gunnarsson!*

He looked up at her, surprised. 'Really?'

'Yes. Let's do it, Kristjan! Let's get married!'

He pulled her towards him, locked his lips with hers and kissed her under the mistletoe that hung from the ceiling.

Merry felt so happy! This past year had been a whirl-wind, what with the pregnancy and getting used to being a mother. But she'd quickly come to realise that she thrived on being part of something—*a family*.

Kristjan made her happier than she had ever thought possible, and he had patiently waited for her to say when she was ready.

Well, now she was. She was more than ready and she wanted the whole world to know it.

'So is that a yes?' she asked, eyes sparkling.

He nodded. 'It's always been yes. I love you, Merry Bell.'

She beamed with happiness and kissed him once again.

* * * * *

CHRISTMAS
WITH HER
LOST-AND-FOUND
LOVER

ANN McINTOSH

MILLS & BOON

CHAPTER ONE

Dr. Elise van Hagan got the callout at seven thirty in the morning, just after coming back in from shoveling the side garden so Baxter, her golden retriever, could do his business. And then, with characteristic efficiency, she got ready and was out the door in just under ten minutes.

This despite the fact it had been ages since she'd last put on her rescue gear, her stomach was in knots, and her hands were shaking.

Tom Harding, head of the Banff volunteer search and rescue team, had been the one to call.

"There's been a barn collapse at Trail's End, and unfortunately Ben Sullivan was inside when it happened. Can you get up there and assess the situation for us? It'll take at least thirty minutes to get the team mobilized, and the helicopter pilot has final say on whether he'll even fly in this weather or not."

A small part of her was shouting she was the last person who should go. After all, she hadn't been on a rescue for almost a year. What possible help could she render, when she was out of practice and frankly terrified?

But she'd agreed, as Tom must've known she would. She was a doctor and a highly trained search and rescue team member, albeit now retired, so there was never any real debate about whether she would or not. Those, along with the thought of what Janice Sullivan, Ben's mother, must be going through, were all factors that galvanized her to push past her fears.

She didn't know how she'd react if something similar happened to her own son, Jeevan. Knowing the mental and emotional toll his eight-month research trip to Indonesia and Borneo had taken on her, she could only imagine the hell the other woman was going through.

For Elise, memories of past Christmas tragedies already marred the season. She could only hope this incident would have a happy ending.

The only questions regarding her capabilities were within her own mind, and she forced herself not to think about them but concentrate on getting to the site as quickly as possible. Letting her attention wander while she was riding her snowmobile through the gray predawn light and towing Baxter, safely secured in his enclosed sled, could lead to disaster. Especially on a gloomy morning, with sunrise still an hour or so away.

Of course, normally the fire rescue squad would have been called out under the circumstances, but there had been a blizzard in the Banff area the night before. Being on a rural roadway, neither Elise's house nor Trail's End—a husky rescue and dogsledding training camp—had been ploughed out yet. Therefore, Tom had been called on to see if the search and rescue squad could assist, but there were issues there, too.

The team on duty usually assembled at eight in the morning during the ski season, to be on call, so they would have to come in to base before being dispatched.

And if the pilot refused to fly until after the icy mist hanging low over the mountains burned off, there would be an additional delay.

Even coming as close as possible and then riding in on snowmobiles would take a long time to coordinate.

So Elise was it, until additional hands could be found and brought on board.

She just hoped there was something she could do—preferably that didn't involve actually going under any snow.

Instantly the memory came back, causing her to ease back on the throttle and slow the snowmobile until she got her anxiety under control. She still dreamed about it some nights: the roar of the avalanche, the sensation of losing her footing, falling and sliding. Being tumbled over and consumed by the snow. Encased, as though it planned on keeping her entombed forever.

Resolutely she pushed it all back, taking deep breaths, mentally distancing herself from the images. There was no trail to follow, and she had to have her head on straight so as not to crash. A blustery, post-blizzard wind was blowing, too, causing skirls of snow that further obscured her vision and stung her cheeks.

Trail's End property abutted her own but was over a ridge, and Elise had to avoid the trees and deeper drifts as she made her way up the side of the hill behind her property. Getting to the top, she paused, scanning the valley below.

It was still too dark to see much, but almost directly below her was the lodge Janice Sullivan lived in, which also housed the sled dog teams that came to train there. That was already lit up—down to the Christmas tree in the front window—and clearly visible, as were the two blocks of kennels, separated from the house by a field. The veterinary building, which Elise knew was behind the kennels, was a gray shadow in the snow, but just beyond, she could see lights bobbing around and hear voices.

That must be the damaged barn.

Aware of time ticking away, she plotted a path down the hill and set off as quickly as she dared.

As she neared the collapsed building, Janice ran to meet her, and Elise's heart ached in sympathy at the sight of the other woman's tear-ravaged face. Turning off the engine, Elise swung her leg over the seat and found herself engulfed in Janice's shaking arms.

"Oh, Elise. Thank God you're here. Please help him."

"I'll do my best, Jan." After giving the other woman a tight squeeze, Elise gently extricated herself, so as to take off her goggles and then release Baxter from the sled. "Did you see what happened?"

"No, I was in the kennels when I heard the crash and ran out. He...he's buried in there, and he isn't answering when we shout. He had a couple of dogs with him, and we've heard one barking, so we know at least one is still in there."

Finally getting the golden retriever free from the harness keeping him secured to the sled, Elise detached her rescue kit and medical bag. Baxter shook himself, then cast an alert glance at Elise, waiting for instructions.

"The back of the barn looks to be still standing. Is there a door or any windows in that wall?" she asked as she got the disaster response litter off the side of the sled. Putting the bags on it, she grabbed the attached strap.

"No," Janice replied, and they both started trotting toward the building, Baxter at Elise's side. "Only at the front, where the roof came down. It really was just a storage shed, with some old equipment and overflow supplies."

Three men were near the barn, all holding shovels. Two were looking toward the approaching women, while the third was stooping down, as though trying to see through the debris and snow into the damaged building. Something about the third man's posture, the shape of him—even through his snow gear—caused a shiver of recognition, but Elise ignored it, fully in rescue mode now.

"Tom told us not to do anything until you got here," Janice continued as they neared the men. "We were going to try to dig him out ourselves."

"I'm glad you listened. Digging willy-nilly could make the situation worse."

It was clear the front, left section of the barn's roof had collapsed inward, probably from the weight of the snow dumped by the blizzard. As the layers of snow were deposited, one on top of the other, they'd compressed, forming a solid mass. What had slid off and remained in front of the damaged barn wasn't a drift, but more like a jumbled heap of snow blocks.

Anyone under it at the time of the collapse would probably be seriously injured, if not dead. Time definitely was of the essence.

"I think I can see a gap, just there." The man who was bending down pointed. "That may be the way in, if we can widen it."

Elise froze, not from the words but from the voice, at once both familiar and strange. Deep and rhythmic, with the flavor of Trinidad in the way some words dipped and swung, it was one she'd never thought she would hear again and couldn't believe she was actually hearing.

It must be a mistake, a cosmic trick.

Then the man looked up and her heart stopped, while cold flashed sickeningly through her entire body. That icy stream had nothing to do with the weather, and everything to do with the dark eyes peering at her so intently.

It was him: Rohan.

And yet it wasn't.

Not the way she remembered him anyway. Older, which would make sense. But the features she could see—those between his cap and the scarf pulled up around his lower face—were ever so slightly askew, out of alignment. Yet it was so close a resemblance that, for an instant, she was thrown back in time to the first moment she'd seen him, in a club in Cambridge, Ontario.

He'd been so beautiful, his dark eyes flashing with amusement, his smile lighting his entire face. The first time their gazes met, the sexual attraction had been instantaneous and undeniable.

Just thinking about it now turned the ice in her veins to a wave of heat and caused a shiver of awareness to skitter along her spine.

Then she pulled herself together.

It couldn't be Rohan. He'd been dead for over twenty-seven years.

Also, there was not even a hint of recognition in his solemn, slightly questioning eyes.

Even in the predawn gloom, the similarities were so striking that the chance of the two men not being related were astronomical. Now wasn't the time to ask, but she might, later, after having a chance to think it through. Rohan's family had made it plain they wanted nothing to do with her, or with Jeevan.

Some things were better left in the past, where they couldn't foul the present.

Whoever this man was had no bearing on her mission to get to Ben as fast as she could, so she put all the questions and speculation aside, although her pulse still pounded from the unexpected encounter.

Grabbing her flashlight, she stooped beside him so as to see what he was pointing out.

"It looks like a clear space going into the structure," he said, taking her hand to guide the high-powered beam slightly to the right, to a jagged break in the mounds of snow. The unexpected touch of his fingers, even through their gloves, almost made her drop the flashlight. "That's the side that doesn't seem to have fallen all the way in."

"If the left wall gave way, rather than the roof itself, the trusses could have formed a pocket," she replied. "We need to get a path or tunnel cut to that section of wall, but we have to be careful."

"How do you want to proceed?"

"Let's just get going, Dr. van Hagan." One of the other men came forward, shovel in hand, scowling. "All this shilly-shallying is wasting time."

Both Elise and the man she'd been speaking to rose and moved to intercept the oncoming figure, but it was Elise who stepped into his path first.

Meeting his gaze, she said in a level, calm tone, "I'm trained in search and rescue, and I'm in charge here until my commander arrives. If you have a problem following my orders, I suggest you leave the vicinity."

"Don't be an ass, Trevor," Jan said. "Elise knows what she's doing, and if you muck this up and Ben gets hurt, I'll have your hide."

Trevor seemed set to argue, then just huffed and stepped back.

Elise turned slightly so she was addressing everyone. "I need to take a better look at the building. Baxter, search."

The golden immediately started up the snow pile, working back and forth, and Elise stepped back and to the side, until she could shine her light at what remained of the roof. Besides the conversation among the people outside and the croak of a raven in the distant trees, it had been silent. But just then, she heard a dog begin to howl from inside the building, the eerie sound raising gooseflesh along her arms and making the hair at her nape prickle.

The sooner she could get in there, the better.

Rohan Khan watched Elise step back from the building to get a better vantage point. Simultaneously he listened to the urgent, whispered conversation going on behind him.

"Are you sure she knows what to do? She's doing a lot of nothing right now."

"What do you want her to do, Trevor? Just barge through and risk bringing the rest of the barn down on Ben?" The anger in Jan's voice was clear. "Give her a chance to figure out the best way to get in there. We're lucky to have her here, both as a rescuer and an emergency doctor. If anyone can help Ben, it's her."

Rohan tuned them out, looking instead at the golden retriever up on the mound of snow. It was working along the side of the barn now, picking its way through the hard clumps of icy snow, nose down, tail up, the picture of total concentration.

The crunch of footsteps behind him alerted him to her approach, but she went swiftly by him to where the dog now sat, looking expectantly down at his mistress. When she immediately began to climb up the snowbank, Rohan instinctively moved to stand behind her, although he didn't know whether it was to help or to catch her if she fell.

She went up the slippery mass as sure-footed as a mountain goat, and Rohan heaved a silent sigh of relief when she got to the top.

Something about this woman had caught and held his attention from the first moment he'd looked up and found her staring back. He'd frozen, captured by the expression of shock on her face. Her pale eyes gleamed as they tracked over his face, and for the first time in years Rohan was aware of his scars and had to stop himself from covering the left side of his face. He'd been unable to make out the exact color of her eyes. Perhaps an icy blue, which would fit with the way she'd then shaken her head and turned away, as though dismissing his presence.

It had left him wondering what it was about him that had so surprised her. Was it his accent, or the darkness of his skin? While Calgary was a more multicultural city, maybe Banff residents weren't used to seeing someone like him among them. Or perhaps it was something as simple as her being aware that he was a stranger.

Whatever it was, that look she'd given him had garnered his full attention, and now he stared up at her as she surveyed the building from the high ground.

When she turned and started back down, calling the dog to follow, he automatically held up his hand, offering assistance.

It was ignored; she slid and slipped down the slope of snow, then jumped to the ground.

"There are no breaks in the roof here." She tried to sound matter-of-fact, but Rohan thought there was a slight tremor in her voice. "I'll have to get in through that gap you noticed. Luckily, it looks like there's the least amount of snow there, but we'll have to be extremely careful. This side of the roof is leaning on the snowpack at the front."

He nodded but found he was doing so to her back, as she'd already walked away. By the time he rejoined the others, she was saying, "Jan, call Tom and tell him I'm going in, and ask about an ETA for the team. You, and you—" she pointed to Rohan and Nathan "—come and help me dig."

"Hey, what about me?" Trevor growled but got a bland glance in return.

"You need to stand back and watch what's left of the roofline. If you see it start to shift or any snow sliding off, even a little, you shout so we can stop. This pile of snow is holding up the rest of the roof."

Under her direction, they widened the crack a little at a time, inch by inch, creating a tunnel.

"Don't go any wider," Elise directed, when Nathan started digging around the edges, probably to make it easier to go deeper. "I can get the litter through at that width, but we have to maintain the integrity of the pack."

Rohan lay on his belly and worked his way forward. The sun was coming up, and he thought the snow at the end of the crack looked lighter, almost ethereal, and realized he was right when a chunk fell off ahead of him, and he could see straight into what was left of the barn.

"I'm through," he called.

"Then back out," came the reply. "Quickly."

He did as she demanded and wasn't even on his feet when she was on her stomach and going forward. She'd tied a rope to her waist, and at the end was the litter holding her bags, but she waited until she was through the tunnel to pull it in behind her.

Rohan knelt to help feed it through, and before it began to move, he could hear her breath sawing in and out of her throat, as though she'd run a mile, rather than crawled three meters.

"Tom says they can't get here for at least another twenty minutes," Jan called so Elise could hear. "The copter is grounded until the fog lifts."

There was no answer except for a skitter of sound, and he couldn't stop himself from bending low to try to see what was happening.

He caught a flash of light as she picked her way through the rubble, then it disappeared.

Rohan's heart was pounding, and it seemed he wasn't the only one concerned, as her dog came and sat beside him, bending to look into the tunnel, too. Baxter whined so softly the sound hardly reached Rohan's ears. Reaching out, he ruffled the hair on the dog's chest.

"It'll be okay, boy," he said, hoping he was telling the truth.

CHAPTER TWO

THE INSIDE OF the barn was a jumble of broken boards and heaps of snow festooning an old tractor and sundry boxes and bags. Shining her light around, Elise picked her way over and around the wreckage, looking for Ben. She'd left the litter behind and was just carrying her medical kit. If she needed the litter, she'd have to find a way to maneuver it through the rubble, and it wouldn't be an easy task.

Getting Ben back to the tunnel in the snow on it would be even harder.

Through the gloom she heard a low growl and followed the sound. Ducking under a partially fallen roof truss, she found them on the other side, the dog standing beside Ben as though on guard. Even from a distance, Elise could see a small pool of blood beneath the young man's head, and there was a beam across his lower abdomen.

She pulled off her thermal gloves and stuffed them into one pocket, then reached into the other to get the package of surgical gloves she'd put in there for convenience. The need to get to Ben to properly determine his injuries was even more urgent, but when she stepped closer, the dog growled again.

"It's okay," Elise said soothingly. "I'm here to help."

"Do you see anything?" Janice's frantic shout made

the dog's head turn slightly, but it didn't budge from its position.

"I found Ben, but one of the dogs is guarding him and won't let me near," she called, as loud as she could without shouting. She neither wanted to scare the dog nor cause any vibrations. "Jan, call and tell them we need a medical evacuation by air, right away."

Just the fact Ben had been unconscious for as long as he had was a worry, and the longer it took to get him the medical attention he needed, the worse his prognosis would be. Gathering her courage, she took another small step forward, but the dog growled again. Louder this time.

Elise did the only thing she could think of, and called, "Bax, come."

She heard the scrabble of claws on ice immediately, as the golden made his way through the tunnel. It was as though he'd just been waiting for the command. If anything could calm the frightened husky, it would be Baxter. After they'd retired from the SAR team, she'd trained him to be an emotional support animal, and he was as excellent at it as he'd been in his previous position.

He was trained to work with humans, but with any luck, he'd allay the husky's fears and allow her to see to Ben.

It sounded as though Baxter was having a hard time navigating the rubble to approach her, if the sounds behind her were any indication. When he appeared by her side and the sounds continued, she risked taking her gaze off the husky for a quick glance behind her.

"What are you doing in here?" she demanded, as the man—whose name she didn't know and had refused, for some reason, to ask for—ducked under the truss and came toward her.

"It sounded like you needed help with the dog. She's

one of a group I brought up from Calgary and they're all just shy of feral, since they were rescued from a hoarding situation. She knows me. Don't you, sweetheart?"

He walked by, his shoulder brushing hers, and Elise shivered, both from the contact and the low crooning tone of his voice he used to speak to the dog.

"It's not safe for you to be in here," she said, struggling to keep her voice low, but sounding furious anyway.

He didn't even spare her a glance.

"Oh, it's not safe for any of us, is it?" he said, stooping down near the dog and seemingly addressing the words to it. "Which is why it's important we get Ben stabilized and out of here as quickly as possible."

She wanted to rail at him and tell him to leave, but she bit back the words on seeing the husky slowly start to relax, ears coming up, hackles subsiding. Bax moved in closer to the other dog, and between the man and the retriever, they managed to form a barrier shielding the husky from Ben.

"I think you can go to him," the man said softly as the husky sniffed at his outstretched hand. "She was scared, but she's doing a bit better now."

Elise held herself back from rushing, moving slowly so as not to upset the husky again. Kneeling beside Ben, she put the flashlight upright on the ground for illumination, then tore open the packet of gloves and quickly pulled them on.

Visual examination showed he wasn't dressed properly for the weather, with his coat unzipped and just a T-shirt beneath it. His skin was unnaturally pale, almost gray, and when she put her fingers to his neck, she found his skin was chilled.

But she could also see the slight rise and fall of his chest, with each slow breath.

Pulse weak and thready.

Pupils—thankfully—responsive, although the left was sluggish.

Taking the C-collar from her kit, she quickly fitted it around Ben's neck. It needed to be stabilized before she checked his head wound.

"How is he doing?"

The low words had her glancing up, and she shook her head. "Not too well."

Reaching under his head, she found the laceration, felt the give of the skull beneath.

"Depressed head fracture and hypothermia, at the very least," she said, running her hands over his chest, then his arms.

She thought his shirt would be caught under the beam lying over his abdomen, but when she tugged at it, it came loose easily. Lifting it, she examined his chest for bruises, gave a silent sigh of relief when there were none visible.

Bending lower, she looked along his body and realized the beam wasn't pinning him down but had caught on the old tractor tire alongside where he was lying.

"Thank goodness, I don't think he's trapped under here. Once I get the backboard on, I should be able to pull him free. I'll have to take a chance on exacerbating any injuries he may have to his legs, but we need to get him out of here ASAP."

"I'll get the litter," came the calm reply.

"Be careful," she instructed. "Try not to bump anything."

By the time he returned, she'd fitted the backboard and pulled Ben free of the beam. There was a definite compound fracture to his left femur, which made it even more imperative that they move as quickly as possible.

The man cleared a path below the truss and slid the litter through.

"I'll help you get him on," he said, ducking under the wood.

"I'm putting a pressure cuff on his leg, and then he'll be ready for transport."

"Okay," he said, stepping past where Elise was working, going deeper into the barn.

"What are you doing?" she asked, her voice sharp.

He didn't pause. "There's another dog in here, probably traumatized, if not injured, and I need to find it."

There was no give in his tone, which told her trying to make him stop would be futile, and she felt a spurt of anger.

"Be quick about it," she snapped. "And try not to bring the entire building down on us."

You insufferable man...

As if he were inclined to linger in a place that creaked and groaned and seemed set to come down around his ears!

But although her tone had him clenching his teeth, he couldn't blame her for being so testy. The situation was anything but cozy, and should he put a foot wrong or move something he shouldn't, he could cost them all their lives.

There was a slight noise behind him, and he turned to see Baxter and the female husky sniffing around. They were both going toward the undamaged part of the barn, picking their way through the snow and debris in their way. On a hunch, he followed.

Unerringly direct, they led Rohan past an old car at the back of the barn, to the second husky.

"I found him," he called, on seeing the trembling animal hiding beneath a low shelf. After a closer look, he added, "He's injured. There's blood on his side, although I can't see where it's coming from."

"Can you carry him out?"

"I'll need to muzzle him," he replied as the dog bared his teeth and gave a throaty warning. "Do you have a roll of gauze?"

"In my medical kit. But hurry. It sounds like the wind is picking up, and hopefully the helicopter will be here soon."

He knew what she meant. Although definitely not gale force, the wind was increasing the rattling of loose shutters and boards, the squeal of wood under unusual stresses. Picking his way back to her seemed to take forever, although it was less than a minute.

After he took off his thick gloves, it didn't take him long to grab the gauze and cut a length. Once back, he carefully approached the injured animal. The other dogs had stayed with the husky, and Rohan hoped the female wouldn't get upset if the male started struggling.

Thank goodness they were in the back of the building, away from the danger of hitting the wrong thing and shaking something loose.

Like the rest of the roof.

He put the flashlight down, where it would give him the most illumination. Making a loop with an overhand knot in the gauze, Rohan got close to the snarling animal and, with a flick of his wrist, slipped the loop over the animal's muzzle, then pulled it tight.

The husky tried to pull away and then, realizing that wouldn't work, brought both front paws up to its face, trying to scrape the gauze off. The motion seemed to cause it pain; it yelped and dropped its paws again.

"No, you don't," Rohan said, leaning in to tie the gauze in a knot behind the struggling dog's ears, holding the makeshift muzzle in place. "You're okay. I'm not going to hurt you, and you know that."

The dog gave him a wide-eyed glare, the whites showing all around his irises, as a few rage-filled bubbles frothed from its mouth.

As Rohan gave the dog a quick examination, there was a clatter from where Elise was.

"Are you okay?"

"Yes," she said, a little breathless. "Just getting Ben onto the litter. Are you ready to get out of here?"

"Yes," he replied. There was a laceration on the dog's side, and perhaps a broken rib, although it was hard to tell in the cramped quarters, and with no real time to spend. When it had railed back from the muzzle it also held its back leg up, so there could be some damage there, too.

"Sorry, fellow," he said to the dog, knowing he was going to cause him pain.

Rohan put back on his gloves before lifting the injured dog, careful to support him with an arm under his chest and the other just behind the hind legs. But it took some doing to pick up his flashlight from where he'd put it on the ground, and he had to carefully navigate back to Elise, since the light waved crazily about.

Elise had the litter facing out when he got back to their original position, Ben covered with an emergency blanket and strapped down, but neither she nor her light was there. The sun was up, and the room was a bit lighter, but not by much. The only light coming in was through the damaged roof, and with the sun low on the horizon at this time of year, the first rays didn't penetrate far.

Rohan felt a spurt of annoyance, caused by rising trepidation. She'd been hurrying him along, and now she had disappeared.

When he saw her light coming back, and she ducked under the truss, his relief was instantaneous and intense.

"I've cleared a path as best as I could back to the tunnel, but there are a couple of spots we'll have to carry him over," she said, putting the narrow piece of plywood she was carrying on the ground.

When she pulled another blanket from her kit and spread it on the wood, he was puzzled.

"What's that for?"

"For the dog," she said. "There's no way to carry him out, so we'll have to slide him."

Why hadn't he thought of that?

"You're right, of course. But take the wood to the tunnel. I'll carry him that far, then come back to help you with the litter."

Rohan followed her light along the path she'd cleared, and they deposited the dog in a small space next to their exit point.

As they headed back, a particularly strong gust of breeze had them both looking up at the roof leaning above them and made them move even faster.

Getting the litter across the floor was a chore, and Rohan knew he couldn't relax even when they finally made it back to the gap in the snow.

"You push the litter through," he suggested, wanting her out first. "And I'll bring up the rear with the dog."

"No," she argued. "You go first with the litter, and I'll manage the dog. It'll be quicker, and frankly, you shouldn't have been in here to begin with, so I want you out ASAP."

He hesitated, but then came the unmistakable sound of approaching rotors, and he reluctantly nodded.

Getting Ben Sullivan onto the helicopter had to be their first priority.

Yet the thought of leaving her behind left a sour taste in the back of his throat.

She'd bent to pull something from her bag at the foot of the litter, and when she straightened, their gazes collided.

Gray. Her eyes were gray, not blue as he'd thought before. And something in their serious, gleaming depths made his heart clench and then start to race.

Then she frowned and waved a hand at him, impatience written all over her expression.

"Get a move on. The copter's coming in for a landing."

They maneuvered the litter into the gap, carefully pushing it together, until Rohan had to lie on his belly to keep it moving forward, digging the toes of his boots into the slippery ground to get traction.

"I see it," yelled one of the men on the other side. "Just a little more, and I can get a hand to it."

"Go easy," Elise called back. "If it gets hung up on the sides, it could collapse the tunnel."

It slid through fairly smoothly, and Rohan levered to his feet once he was back on the other side of the snow-pack, as Janice and Nathan took charge of the litter. They took Elise's bags off, just as Baxter and the female husky came trotting out of the tunnel, linked by a makeshift leash of gauze tied to the husky's collar. Baxter had the other end in his mouth and led the compliant female out behind him.

Rohan knelt down and heard the board scraping across the ground. Elise had the piece of plywood with the dog lying on it, and she was pushing it along through the tunnel. Thank goodness the male husky wasn't struggling; he was most likely in pain and too afraid to move. Rohan watched it shuffle forward, time seeming to slow, so it moved only inches at a time.

The helicopter circled above, and the wind gusts increased, upping his stress levels, as the barn groaned like a dying beast.

Suddenly the wood's forward momentum in the tunnel ceased.

"Elise, are you okay?"

"It's stuck." Her words were calm, but Rohan thought there was a slight tremor in her voice. "I can't get it to move."

Without hesitation, he plunged back into the tunnel, crawling forward until he felt the edge of the board.

"It's stuck on some ice," he said, panting, scrabbling to get fingers under the board to lift it. Unlike the litter, which had runners on the bottom, the board wasn't faring so well on the rough terrain. "I've got the front lifted. Push."

The wood slid forward, just as someone outside the tunnel shone a flashlight in, giving Rohan some light to work with. He moved back and lifted again.

"Push."

Just as he said it, the sound of the rotors got louder, and there was a long, low creak, followed by a loud crash from within the barn. Instinctively Rohan ducked his head, thinking the tunnel was about to come down on them.

Thankfully it didn't.

"Everyone okay in there?"

Rohan lifted up onto his elbows to see over the dog, and met a wide, terrified stare. Elise's face was pallid, her lips pulled back in a grimace of fear and perhaps pain.

"Are you hurt?" She didn't reply. Didn't even blink. "Elise, are you hurt?"

As though being released from a trance, she shook her head, but the terror in her eyes didn't subside. It made him want to hold her, reassure her everything would be fine, but there was no way and no time for that. Getting out was imperative.

Rohan got his fingers back under the board and growled, "Then push, dammit."

She did.

It felt like an eternity before they were all safely on the other side of the tunnel. By then, the medical personnel were running toward them from the helicopter. Rohan held out a hand and helped the still-pale Elise to her feet. He couldn't help noticing the tremors running through her fingers, but her voice was calm and sure as she relayed to the EMTs her findings regarding the injured man.

Nathan and Trevor picked up the board with the husky and, on Rohan's request, headed off to the veterinarian center with it, while Jan made her way beside the litter to the helicopter.

At that point it was just the two of them left at the site of destruction, watching as Ben was loaded into the helicopter, Janice jumping in after him. The aircraft took off, and they watched it turn, heading for Banff.

Elise sighed. "That's that."

Rohan looked at her profile, able to truly study it for the first time.

Hers was a strong face—square of jaw, with high cheekbones and a prominent nose and chin—but it was also intriguingly feminine. As he watched, she reached up and pulled off her toque, revealing straight, light brown hair, up in a ponytail on the top of her head.

A few wisps had escaped the hair tie and fell along her cheek. Rohan had the ridiculous urge to tuck them back behind her ear. She did it herself, with an impatient brush of her fingers, and a warm shock of desire startled him so much he had to look away.

The sound of the rotors faded, and nearby, a raven croaked.

He cleared his throat before looking back at her, saying, "I should go to the vet center to see what I can do for that dog, but before I go, I realize we haven't been introduced properly. I'm Rohan. Rohan—"

"Khan," she finished for him, before slapping him, seemingly with all the force she could muster, across the face.

CHAPTER THREE

SHE'D HIT HIM as hard as she could, but nowhere as hard as she would have liked. Besides the thermal gloves she was wearing, Elise was shaking from a combination of adrenaline and rage.

Even so, seeing his head snap to the side was highly satisfying.

The shock on his face was even more so.

"What…?" Rohan's voice faded as he raised a hand to his face, his dark eyes wide and gleaming with a mixture of surprise and anger. "Why did you hit me?"

Elise drew herself up to her full height and tilted her head back so she could look down her nose at him. "That was for the twenty-seven years I thought you were dead, you worm."

Then, before he could respond, she grabbed her bags and marched off toward her snowmobile, surprised that the icy drifts she went through didn't melt with the heat of her rage.

"Wait," he called. She heard the crunch of his boots behind her and sped up. "Wait!"

That was what he'd said, just before he'd left her to go to Trinidad all those years ago:

"Wait for me, please? I'll only be gone for a couple of weeks, and then I'll be back, before Christmas."

Yet, even as she agreed she'd be there for him when he got back, a part of her was already braced for heartache.

She'd had no faith in his protestations of love, or the likelihood he'd return.

Life had already taught her how quickly and easily others could disappear, especially, it seemed, around the Christmas season.

And Rohan hadn't come back. Instead, she was told he'd died in a car crash, just days after getting to Trinidad.

And she'd believed it to be true all these years.

"What an idiot I was," she muttered to herself, just as he caught up to her near the snowmobile.

"What are you talking about?" It was clear he was trying to stay calm, but the words were little better than a growl, and when she spun around to face him, she could see the anger simmering in his eyes. "Do you know me?"

"Once upon a time, long ago, I thought I did. But that was before you and your family lied to me. My sister tried to warn me, before I took off with you that summer, but I wouldn't listen."

"But—"

In no mood to hear any more lies, Elise cut him off. "And now, *now*, you have the nerve to pretend you don't even know who I am? Or worse, actually *don't* remember me? You're a stinking *rat*."

"Just hold on a minute." His voice rose and Elise stiffened, giving him a narrow-eyed glare. "Will you stop haranguing me and give me a chance to speak?"

"Why, so you can spin some new lies?"

"No! So I can explain, or at least try to."

"What possible explanation could you give me that will make any damn sense?" The effects of temper and rapidly diminishing adrenaline were getting to her, and

Elise's anger peaked as she realized the backs of her eyes were stinging with tears. "You and your family lied, and for twenty-seven years I've thought you were dead. End of story. Full stop. There's no way to spin that to make yourself look anything but a liar and a rat."

Rohan held up his hand, and it gave her a brief moment of pleasure when she realized it was shaking. "Listen to me. In December, twenty-seven years ago, I was in a car crash and I suffered a traumatic brain injury and subsequent retrograde amnesia. When I woke up, I couldn't remember anything after the Victoria Day celebrations in May. I was shocked when they told me it was the end of the year, not the middle."

She didn't believe him—didn't want to believe him—until he put his hand to his face to briefly finger the scars there.

Then she realized why it had been so simple to dismiss the thought that it might actually be Rohan. What she'd thought of as differences were actually the end result of the accident—the changes brought on by scar tissue and reconstructive surgery.

As the anger waned and the adrenaline dump took hold, Elise swallowed against a rush of nausea and lowered herself to rest against the snowmobile seat, her legs suddenly turning to jelly.

"Are you okay?" he asked, reaching to steady her as her foot slipped and she grabbed the handlebar for balance.

The sensation of his fingers, so strong on her arm, made her shiver despite her inner turmoil. She pulled away.

"Those months, between June and December, were when we were together. We met two weeks before Canada Day."

They stared at each other, a strange current running between them. Elise's mind conjured memories, many of which she'd tried to forget but still crept their way into her head at the strangest times. Or sometimes invaded her dreams.

She'd held back from him then, even though they'd had a whirlwind summer romance that stretched into autumn and, he'd said, would last forever. He'd made it plain he was in love with her—said he loved her—and wanted to be with her, no matter the cost.

But Elise hadn't believed in everlasting love back then, and wouldn't commit to more than waiting to see what would come of it when he got back to Canada.

Rohan's face was pale. He once more touched his cheek, rubbing at it this time, as though talking about the past had awakened sensations in his flesh that had to be erased.

He swallowed, then asked, "What were we doing during that time? I tried to find out, but my roommate was working as an assistant at the Ridgetown vet school campus, and other friends said they hardly saw me, so they couldn't give me any information."

Heat warmed her cheeks as she recalled the hours spent making love with him, the sense of abandon she'd never experienced before then, and hadn't since. But that wasn't something she was willing to share, so she fell back on the mundane.

"We traveled mostly—to the Maritime provinces in summer, and up into Algonquin Park in fall. We'd decided to take some time off before you job-hunted and I started my residency. We went to places we'd always wanted to see and hadn't got to yet."

He nodded slowly, and she wondered what he was thinking. The Rohan of old had been very much an open book, willing to express every emotion as it surfaced.

This was a different person. One who was more contained and closed off than she remembered.

"Who told you I had died?"

From his tone you'd think they were discussing the weather, or he was asking for the time. It was so at odds with the vibrant, sometimes fiery young man she'd once known that the entire conversation felt surreal. She was talking to someone who spoke and looked like the Rohan she'd once cared for, but was, to all intents and purposes, a stranger.

"Your father. And your cousin Chandi confirmed it."

That got a reaction. A flash of anger tautened his face, and his fingers clenched and flexed.

"I'm sorry," he said, clearly back under control. His voice was bland, but she heard the sincerity in his words. "They had no right to deceive you that way."

Then he looked away, his lips tight, a frown wrinkling his brow. She thought perhaps he was going to elaborate, and they could talk through what had happened, but when he next spoke, it was to say, "I... I have to go and check on the husky that was injured. I'm really sorry."

And before she could answer, he turned and strode away.

For a moment all she could do was watch him go, stunned at his abrupt departure.

She still felt weak and confused, and in no condition to run after him. Nor did she want to. What she really wanted was a little time by herself to figure out what to do. Because if Rohan Khan thought their conversation was over, he was in for a huge surprise.

It really had only begun.

Rohan tried to maintain his composure, but inside he seethed, embarrassed and unsettled by the conversation he'd just had.

His cheek still stung slightly from the slap Elise had given him, but he didn't blame her for it. Not at all. She'd been deceived horribly, and had acted out of anger and shock.

Here was another instance of his father interfering in ways that hurt others, and doing so without a care for the consequences.

He'd always been like that—a controlling bully who did whatever he could to get his way. All his life Rohan had fought for his own autonomy, refusing to cede to his father's expectations, or give in when told he would never be good enough. Had the old man lied to Elise out of sheer malice, or as a way to get his son under his control?

There was no way to know, since his father now suffered from advanced dementia, and could provide no answer or explanations.

But Chandi probably could.

He had the urge to call her right away but knew he needed to cool down before he did. Chandi wasn't the kind to give up any information if she felt she was under attack, and once her back was up, she'd clam up out of spite.

Besides, he had the husky to see to, and he was glad of that.

Work, and interacting with the animals, always lowered Rohan's stress levels.

His affinity with animals was another thing his father never understood and had tried to interfere with.

"Study medicine," Dada had said incessantly.

"I plan to," was Rohan's standard reply as a teenager, knowing exactly what his father meant. "Animal medicine."

There had been threats to cut his oldest son off, refuse to pay for school or anything else. Rohan had almost given in, worn down by his father's bullying, but his grandfather, Baba, had stepped in, saying he would fund Rohan's education. Since the old man was the only person Rohan's father deferred to, it had thankfully worked out.

Rohan liked to think he would have taken his chances on his own if Baba hadn't paid for vet school, since caring for animals gave him a sense of purpose and satisfaction unlike anything else. Nothing in his life had ever given him the pleasure working with the animals did.

At least that he remembered.

The hole in his memory banks, which he thought he'd grown accustomed to and didn't matter anymore, suddenly gaped wide again. A blank space he knew had changed the trajectory of his life in ways he had never really understood, even as it had caused untold pain to himself and others.

Like Elise van Hagan.

He opened the door to the small clinic on the property, used by the vets that often traveled with the dogsled teams. Taking a deep breath of the antiseptic smell lowered his heart rate. Nathan and Trevor looked up and nodded a greeting. They already had the husky on an examination table, both standing alongside it, making sure the animal stayed put and kept calm.

Rohan nodded in return, turning his back to take off his jacket, trying to maintain an air of calm even as his stomach pitched and rolled like a dinghy at sea.

If he could just force himself to concentrate on the dog, on repairing whatever damage it had sustained, his insides would settle.

Yet the image of furious gray eyes, set in that startlingly lovely face, haunted him.

Should he try to contact her again, or leave well enough alone? As he hung up his coat, he pushed the question away, unwilling to dwell on it just then.

As Rohan began a more comprehensive examination of the husky, Trevor said, "Neither of us are vet techs, but we can help, if you need it."

"I think I'll be okay," Rohan replied, just as the door to the clinic opened and Elise walked in with her bags, followed by Baxter, again leading the second husky by its makeshift leash.

"I wasn't sure what to do with this girl," she said, her tone brisk. "Could one of you take charge of her for me, please?"

The dog on the table yelped as Rohan examined the hind leg, and Nathan and Trevor exchanged glances, as though asking each other who should let go of the animal to do as Elise asked.

To Rohan's surprise, Elise continued, "I also thought you might need a hand if you have to operate, Dr. Khan, since Janice is the only certified vet tech here. What have you found?"

She took off her gloves as she spoke, then shucked her hat, coat and scarf, moving with the fluid efficiency he was beginning to think was habitual.

Taken aback, as he thought she would have been on her way after their conversation, Rohan replied, "A couple of lacerations and a suspected broken rib. Plus, it feels like his cranial cruciate ligament is torn."

"So X-rays first, then," she said, walking over to the sink. "And then you'll know for sure."

"Yes," he replied, still shocked by her calm demeanor and willingness to help.

Perhaps it was his imagination, but the atmosphere in the room seemed to heat and thicken. He wasn't surprised at the alacrity with which Nathan and Trevor moved, and once Elise had commanded Bax to drop the gauze tethering the two dogs together, they took off with the husky in tow.

Leaving him alone with the woman Rohan was beginning to think was set on turning his calm, orderly life upside down.

CHAPTER FOUR

ELISE FINISHED SCRUBBING her hands, and after drying them, reached for a pair of gloves. The silence in the room was broken only by the click of Baxter's nails as he sniffed around, and the huffing breaths of the dog on the table.

She'd gotten a little shock of surprise when she saw Rohan, now without his thick coat. She didn't remember him being in such good shape when he was younger. But now, in jeans that hugged long, muscular legs, and a Henley shirt that displayed his wide chest to its best advantage, there was no denying he was downright toothsome.

But she refused to let the thought linger in her head.

She couldn't afford to be sidetracked by something as mundane as how well he'd aged.

"Will you sedate him before you x-ray?" she asked, avoiding looking at him. It had taken all her courage just to come after him, and using the dogs as an excuse seemed silly and transparent now.

Surely he must realize there was something else she had in mind?

But his voice was almost annoyingly calm when he replied, "Yes. It'll stop him from struggling and potentially hurting himself even more. Dealing with half-wild dogs like this is very different from the average family pet, although those can get testy, too."

"Okay. Just tell me what you need, and let's get to it."

When she turned, she found herself under the kind of intense scrutiny that made the hair on the back of her neck stir, and reminded her why she'd fallen for him all those years before.

He had the type of gaze that seemed able to see into and through you, sussing out all your deepest secrets. That hadn't changed in the slightest, although now it was solemn, serious, where before there had always been a little spark of laughter in his eyes. As though, no matter what he saw, he'd always be nonjudgmental and forgiving.

Loving.

That was definitely missing. But even without it, something stirred in her chest, and she tore her gaze away, examining the supplies, familiarizing herself with the clinic's layout, so as to not have to look at him anymore.

After commanding Bax to lie down, she easily found the sedative Rohan requested, and wheeled out the portable X-ray machine while he administered it. There was scant conversation between them, but after the first few fraught moments, they fell into an easy working rhythm.

She had some serious matters to discuss with him, but while he was setting up to operate, or was repairing the torn CCL the X-ray revealed, wasn't the time.

"Luckily there are no broken ribs," Rohan said as he looked at the chest X-ray. "He's obviously in some pain, but the bruising should heal without intervention."

Once they had the husky prepped, Rohan made the incision, and the surgery was underway. When she heard her phone ringing in her bag, she ignored it. If it was important, the person would leave a message.

They worked in relative silence until, as he was removing the torn ligament, Rohan said, "Thanks for offering to help with this. I could have managed on my own, but it's definitely easier with two sets of hands."

"Any medical procedure is, isn't it?" she replied, keeping her voice level, although being in such close proximity to him was difficult. While she could have left, giving herself time to process what had happened, she knew delaying the inevitable wouldn't help.

Besides, she wanted to get a handle on who this new Rohan was, since it was clear he was much different from the sunny young man she'd once known. Getting to know him a bit would, hopefully, give her an idea of how to move forward.

"You said you brought these dogs up from Calgary?" she asked, looking for an opening to ask him more personal questions.

He glanced up at her over his mask and nodded. Being on the other side of the table, with the bright light overhead, allowed her to see the lighter shading in his irises, which at a distance looked uniformly dark brown.

"We rescued them from a hoarding situation. Almost fifty dogs kept in a barn in horrible conditions. Ten of them were huskies, so we contacted Janice to see if she would take them. They need people who understand the breed to work with them so, hopefully, they can find new homes."

"Or maybe get taken on by one of the dogsled teams?"

The corners of his eyes crinkled as he said, "That would be even better, since they're not really used to being house pets, but most of them don't even know how to be dogs yet, much less working animals. The two that were with Ben this morning are, so far, the ones who've adapted best. Some of the others don't even want to go outdoors."

"That's so sad. Do you work with the rescue as their vet?"

"No, I'm a partner in a clinic in Calgary, and we sometimes do pro bono work for the rescue. They operate strictly on donations, so they're usually strapped for cash."

"That's nice of you."

He shrugged, checking the dog's meniscus for damage. "I like to give back to the community."

That sounded like the old Rohan, who'd been vocal about social activism. It was kind of nice to know that hadn't changed.

"What about you?" he asked, gaze still lowered to the surgical site in front of him. "I know you do search and rescue, and gathered you're an emergency room physician?"

The question surprised her. While she was focused on finding out about him, she hadn't considered he might be curious about her, too.

"Yes, I work in the emergency room, but I'm actually retired from search and rescue now."

Once more she was subjected to a moment of intense scrutiny. "Why did you give it up? From what I saw today, you're very good at it."

"It was time," she said, succinctly. "Also, Baxter had been injured, and they warned me that continuing a full schedule might eventually make him lame, so we retired together."

No way would she talk about the avalanche that had caused Bax's injury, and the nightmares that continued to haunt her. It was the first time in her life she'd given up anything out of fear, and she couldn't help the shame that swamped her every time she thought about it.

The meniscus was sound, so Rohan prepared to drill the holes necessary to anchor the sutures that would keep the bones aligned and stabilize the stifle.

"What happened to you after the accident? Did you come back to Canada after you recovered?"

Rohan's hands stilled for an instant, then started moving again.

"I had to have a number of operations, and some reconstructive surgery. It took me more than a year to get back to normal." He paused, as though considering what he'd just said. "Well, back to a new normal, anyway. Then I got a job as a government vet, figuring I'd stay in Trinidad rather than come back here."

There was a finality to his words. When he reached for the drill and asked Elise to hold the dog's leg so it didn't shift, she got the impression he didn't want to elaborate further. That he'd closed himself off in a way she knew he never would have years before.

As she watched Rohan's nimble fingers attach the sutures to the bone, she wondered where that man had gone, and if any of his old personality remained.

She hoped so, for all their sakes.

Rohan couldn't stop wondering why Elise van Hagan had come to offer her help, but as he answered her almost too casual questions, his curiosity was further piqued.

Was she, too, wondering what exactly had transpired all those years ago to lead his family to lie to her? Or was there something else she wanted to know?

He couldn't help wondering what their relationship

had been like, and if she'd been disappointed when he hadn't returned. If she'd mourned him.

Had he been in love with her, fully and passionately, the way he'd come to suspect he was no longer capable of being?

It was so long ago it felt silly to bring any of it up now, but he envied her the memories. And he was once more frustrated by the blank space in his head, where Elise van Hagan, and who knew what else, once resided.

"How did you end up back in Canada?"

He slanted her a glance and had to tear his gaze from her curious gray eyes to look back at the surgical site.

"I got married a couple of years after the accident, but it didn't work out. I felt as though I needed a change and applied as a skilled worker to migrate here."

So easy to distill some of the worst years of his life into two succinct sentences. Harder though to deal with the residual pain and guilt of his eight-year marriage. The knowledge that he was unable to give his ex-wife the love and affection she'd wanted. That she'd so desperately needed.

She'd begged him. For love. For the chance to stay together. But he'd known neither of them was happy and hadn't been able to see any way they ever could be. It was the hardest, and best, decision he'd ever made, but no one else thought so.

The divorce had caused so much anger and turmoil he'd had to get away.

Mostly from his father, who couldn't stop haranguing Rohan about how he'd brought shame down on the family. How he'd once more been a disappointment.

Thinking about that time in his life brought up so many emotions—none of which he wanted to deal with.

"Okay," he said, dragging his mind back to the task at

hand and giving the repair site one last inspection. "I'm ready to close, and then I'll stitch the laceration on his side. After that, we can put him in a kennel to recover."

Elise didn't reply but silently handed him the needle, already prepared for suturing, and watched as he closed the incision site.

To forestall any more questions about the past, he asked, "Are you ready for Christmas?"

He glanced at her as he spoke, and saw a little frown pinch the skin between her brows.

"Originally I was going to work, but HR told me I needed to take my accumulated vacation time over the holidays. Other than the annual Christmas party put on by the SAR team, I don't have much planned."

"No family to celebrate with?" He didn't know why it was so important to ask, especially since her plans sounded suspiciously like his own. It had been years since he'd enjoyed Christmas—so many that sometimes he wondered if he ever had. Yet he wanted to know as much about her as he could.

"None nearby," she said cryptically, and with the kind of finality that said she didn't want to talk about it anymore.

They finished working on the dog in almost complete silence, and Rohan noticed that the frown didn't leave Elise's brow. In fact, it seemed to deepen as they transferred the husky to a recovery kennel and cleaned up. That, along with the lull in conversation, created a suddenly stifling atmosphere.

When they'd put the last of the instruments into the autoclave, Elise preceded him into the outer area of the clinic. Baxter immediately got to his feet and walked over to his mistress. As she leaned down to ruffle behind his ear, Rohan saw that a muscle in her jaw was twitching, as though she was grinding her teeth.

She straightened, and instead of heading to the coat-rack for her outerwear, she took a deep breath and said, "There's something I need to tell you. Will you sit down for a moment?"

Her expression—serious and yet strangely bland—made him think it was the one she used at work when delivering bad news, and he took her advice, lowering himself into a chair. It didn't even occur to him to wonder what she was going to say, as she took a seat opposite him and Baxter placed his head on her lap.

"When you left...all those years ago... After you were gone..."

She stumbled to a halt and shook her head. Then she lifted her chin and met his gaze. Her eyes were darker, smoky gray, and for some reason it made his already galloping heart pick up its pace.

"There's no easy way to say this, so I'll get to the point. You—we—have a son."

He heard the words. She spoke clearly, decisively, yet his brain refused to give her declaration meaning, even as waves of cold and then hot rushed through his body, making him light-headed.

"What? I'm sorry—"

"When you left and didn't contact me, I thought you'd dumped me. Then I realized I was pregnant, and that's when I called Trinidad and was told you were dead."

"Pregnant?" He knew he sounded like an idiot, but the information floored him, leaving him reeling. The only question he could come up with was, "But why didn't you tell my father you were pregnant? There's no way he would have lied to you like that if he knew..."

Her face tightened for a moment, and then softened, became almost sympathetic.

"I did. He said he didn't care—just said I wasn't to call there ever again."

CHAPTER FIVE

ELISE SAW THE emotional struggle play out on Rohan's face as her revelation sank in, and her heart ached for him. Hers was an old, hardly remembered distress, soothed by the years of having and raising her child. This pain she'd visited on him by telling him about his father's betrayal was fresh, and the effects were clear to see in Rohan's expression.

"Why would he do that?" It was barely a whisper, and she could see the shock in his wide eyes and the pallor of his skin. "Lie like that, disavow his own grandchild?"

"I don't know," she said softly, unsurprised when Baxter abandoned her to go to Rohan and nudge his hand. Even though his gaze never left Elise, Rohan's fingers turned to scratch under Baxter's chin. "But you always said your father was manipulative."

"That's not manipulative." Rohan's voice rose slightly. "That's cruel."

They contemplated his words in silence, and Elise wondered what he was thinking, whether what she'd said had truly sunk in yet. Then his eyes widened further, and the hand below Baxter's chin stilled.

"A son?"

It was a question, and yet said with such wonder that she knew he wasn't questioning whether she was telling the truth or not. Somehow, that acceptance filled her with pleasure.

"Yes. Jeevan."

"Jeevan was my grandfather's name."

"I know," she replied quietly. "I named him that because you always said how much you loved your grandfather, and I wanted our son to have some connection to your family, no matter how small."

The corner of his mouth twitched. "My grandfather didn't like his name, because there was an Indian actor who used it, and he was always the villain in movies."

"I looked it up somewhere or other, and saw that it meant 'life.' I thought then it was even more appropriate."

Back then, she'd thought Rohan's life had ended, just as his son's was beginning. She'd been struck by the symmetry of it.

Before she could say anything more, Rohan sprang to his feet, making Baxter jump aside in surprise.

"Where is he?" Rohan looked around, as though expecting Jeevan to appear suddenly, beside him.

"He's been in Indonesia and is probably on his way to Australia right now. He's an ornithologist and was on a research mission that ended a couple of days ago, but a friend invited him to spend Christmas in Sydney."

"An ornithologist?" Rohan sank back down into the chair.

"Yes. I even have his noisy African gray, Titan, to prove it. Jeevan would have turned the house into an aviary if I'd allowed it, but I let him keep just one. He was a rescue."

Rohan seemed to be digesting all she'd said, his thousand-yard stare hiding his thoughts. Then his gaze sharpened on her again.

"Is his being away why you said you weren't planning on celebrating this Christmas?"

The perceptiveness of the comment should have surprised her but didn't. Rohan had always had the ability to see the bigger picture.

"It's the first time we'll be apart for the holiday, so yes, I didn't feel like fussing."

"I haven't enjoyed Christmas in years," he said. "Not since the accident, really."

She nodded, looking away, suddenly awash with all the pain she'd experienced over Christmases past.

"It's not my favorite time of year," she admitted. "So in a way, it's a relief not to have to go through the motions."

He was silent for a moment, making her glance back at him, only to have her gaze once more snared. "Because of what happened with me?"

"Partially." It wasn't something she wanted to discuss, and she sought a way to distract him.

But before she could think of anything, he asked, "Tell me what happened, after I left to go back to Trinidad."

She could remember the devastation she'd felt, but now it was distant, and it didn't hurt to tell him the truth.

"You called the first night after you'd arrived, and said you'd call me the next day. When I didn't hear from you for a couple of days after that, I called, but everyone kept telling me you weren't there, or not available. I just thought you'd dumped me. You'd said you'd be back before Christmas but didn't show up. And then…"

She paused, and he said the words for her.

"Then you realized you were pregnant."

Elise nodded and took a deep breath, wondering why that part of the story had been so difficult to articulate.

"I called one more time, and that's when I was told you were dead."

Anger sparked in his gaze.

"I need you to know I never abandoned you. The accident happened the first night I was there. My cousin and I were hit head-on by an oncoming vehicle. He died on the scene, and I was in hospital for almost two months."

He touched his face, running his fingers along the scars, and then abruptly dropped his hand back into his lap.

"I'm sorry," she said, a wealth of pain in the low words. "But I'm glad you didn't die."

All of that was in the past. Now was the time to look to the present, and the future.

So she asked, "Will you be willing to meet Jeevan, once he gets back to Canada?"

"How can you even ask that? I can't wait." His reaction was swift and clearly heartfelt. Then he frowned as he continued, his anger evident. "But I can't blame you for asking, after what my family did. That's the most despicable, horrible…"

His voice faded and, rising suddenly, he looked around, tugging at the neck of his Henley. Elise saw the perspiration that popped out on his brow and upper lip, the sudden, intensifying pallor fading his skin to a muddy gray, and she rose, too.

"Are you okay?" Crossing the room, she took his wrist between her fingers, immediately feeling the racing pulse. "Sit down. Take some deep breaths."

"No," he said, his voice hoarse. "I just need some air."

"Take Bax with you, if you don't mind. He probably needs to go out." She hoped the dog's presence would help him navigate whatever it was he was going through.

Rohan was tugging on his coat, his movements jerky and uncoordinated.

"Of course," he replied politely, as if by rote, already

reaching for the door handle. "We'll be back in a minute. Come, Baxter."

And, with a swirl of cold air, man and dog slipped out into the frigid morning.

He hadn't had an anxiety attack like this in years. Not since leaving Trinidad and coming back to Canada. His heart pounded, as though trying to push its way out of his chest, and his skin was on fire. As Rohan strode through the snow, taking deep gulps of cold, fresh air, his mind whirled with all the information Elise had given him.

He had a son, whom he'd never seen, never gotten to know. A child who'd grown up thinking his father was dead, because of a lie told twenty-seven years ago.

At least that was what Elise had said.

Rohan stopped walking, shaking his head. Something about the way she'd sounded, the expression in her eyes, told him she was telling the truth. Besides, if she hadn't thought him dead, why even bring up the fact she had a child with him, instead of keeping quiet?

The need to find out exactly what had happened all those years ago was overwhelming, stifling his ability to sort out any of his emotions about having discovered his son. The only way to deal with it was to contact the one person who could tell him how the whole situation had unfolded.

Chandi.

With his father's present mental state, there was no way to ask him anything, but Rohan was almost completely sure his cousin could fill in at least some of the gaps.

Pulling out his phone, he scrolled through his contacts and pressed the call button once her name came on the screen. Although she had retired to Florida with her much older husband, she should be up. And even if she wasn't, he didn't care.

She answered on the second ring.

"Rohan!" she almost shrieked in his ear. "Merry Christmas! What's happening, cuz?"

"I have to ask you something," he replied without preamble. He was in no mood for catching up. "Do you remember a woman named Elise van Hagan?"

She hesitated, and in that small moment of silence, he knew she did. Chandi never thought too much before she spoke, and if she had nothing to hide, she would have answered quickly.

"Why you asking?"

"Do you, or don't you remember her, Chandi? It's a simple yes-or-no question."

He'd gotten to the snowmobile, and eased down to sit on it, sidesaddle.

"I think I might," his cousin finally answered. "There was a chick on my dorm, and I think that was her name."

"On your dorm?" he questioned. "You knew her from school?"

"Well, I wouldn't say I really knew her *that* well." Rohan could hear the evasiveness in her tone, and the background sounds of TV and conversation suddenly cut out, as though she'd gone into another room. "She was a couple years ahead of me, and in the medical program or something. A real swot if I remember right. Man, that was years and years ago. Why you asking me about her after all this time?"

"I just met up with her today, Chandi. She thought I'd been dead for twenty-seven years. How the hell did she hear *that*?"

He heard her curse, even though she tried to cut it off before it fully emerged, and Rohan clenched his phone so tightly his hand began to throb. Yet, when he spoke, his voice was as cold as the winter morning.

"Tell me what you know, Chandi. Everything."

"Rohan—"

She paused, as though trying to figure out what to say, and Rohan cut in before she could come up with something ridiculous.

"You introduced us, and told her I was dead, right?"

"No, no! Your father told her you were dead. I just…"

"You just what?"

He heard her take a deep breath and blow it out. "I confirmed it when she asked me."

Rage swamped him, and in that moment, he was glad his cousin was thousands of miles away, because he didn't feel he could be responsible for his actions.

"Tell me exactly how it all went down. Don't leave out one damn thing."

Chandi sighed, and all the vivacious spark was drained out of her voice as she said, "A bunch of us were going out one night, and we asked Elise if she wanted to come. She had told us she'd just passed with honors, and we got her to come celebrate." She huffed. "I mean, who gets through medical school and doesn't go party afterward?"

"Just get to the story." Rohan wasn't inclined to put up with her commentary and didn't mind her knowing that was how he felt.

"Well, to cut to the good part, you and she went home together that night. And next thing I know, you've taken off with her to parts unknown, and your father is raving about how you're ruining your life, letting some Canadian hussy lead you astray."

"So, Dada did know about us…"

"Yes, you never hid it. And he was *mad*, sah. He wanted you to go home and get a government job, or set up practice to make a ton of money, and here you were, gallivanting around all 'bout with Elise."

Rohan could picture his father ranting, hands swinging through the air, as though looking for something to hit. It was a scene he'd been witness to too many times in his life not to be able to conjure in his imagination.

"Then what?"

"Then you went home at the beginning of December and got into the crash, and your father told Elise you were dead when she called, asking for you."

Just from the way she said it, he knew there was more.

"Don't mess with me, Chandi. I know that's not the whole story, and I'm mad enough to get on the next plane to Miami and get the rest out of you in person."

"Rohan, after all this time—"

He got up, the same rage that had made him sit propelling him to stand, to pace.

"After all this damn time, I deserve the truth." He didn't care whether he was being rude or pushy. "This is my *life* we're talking about, not some abstract scene from a movie or a book. My *life*."

"Okay, okay." She tried to sound as though she was just placating him, but there was a note of fear in her tone, too. "I wasn't there, but I heard you went home and told your father you were going to marry Elise and stay in Canada. He lost his temper, and there was a screaming match between the two of you. That's when Sanjay came by and took you out of there. He wanted to let you cool off."

"And that driver crashed into us."

He'd never known where they were going, he and Sanjay. No one had said, and he'd come to assume that since he had just gotten back to Trinidad, his cousin had come by to see him and take him out.

"Yeah."

No doubt she'd be happy to leave it there, but Rohan wasn't letting her off the hook.

"And?"

"When you were first in the hospital, your father told everyone in the house that if Elise called, they were to say you weren't there, or weren't available. I think he was hoping she'd think you dumped her and stop calling. Then, when you woke up, your father realized you'd lost those months of memories and you'd need extensive rehabilitation, and he knew you wouldn't be able to go back to Canada, so he told her you were dead."

What would his father have done, had the memories returned? The doctors had held out hope that eventually they would, although they never had.

Then Rohan remembered how his father kept pressuring him to marry Suvarna, mostly because of her family's wide connections and wealth. For a man of his father's generation, divorce wasn't a viable option. No doubt he'd thought once his son married someone else, even if he regained his memories it would be too late to do anything about them.

When he'd awoken from his coma, Suvarna had been at his bedside, and had stayed there almost as much as if not more than Rohan's own mother had. It hadn't been long before he was so used to her support that he thought they'd be a good match.

As it turned out, they weren't. She'd been waiting for the "old Rohan" to come back. Their life together had been rocky, with her increasingly frantic emotions met by his stony, unyielding calm.

No one deserved to live with a man like him, and he'd eventually insisted they divorce, knowing she'd be better off without him.

"So that's it," Chandi said, trying to sound like her old self. "That's the story."

"Not quite. You haven't explained why you told Elise the same lie."

"Because your father told me to." Her voice was strident, defensive. "And he promised to pay for the rest of my schooling if I did. Your family was rich, and mine was talking about me coming back to Trinidad to finish there, because it would be cheaper. I didn't want to go back, and get stuck marrying some boy from Sangre Grande, and give up my dreams. You didn't remember her, so what was the big deal?"

What was the big deal...?

Rohan couldn't even answer her, with all that was swirling in his head.

The big deal was not having someone who cared about him, at his side, while he tried to recover.

Not knowing he was a father, until his son was twenty-six years old.

Maybe even missing what it felt like to be loved and supported as he fought for his life.

Something about Elise told him she would have flown to Trinidad to be with him, when he needed her.

But he didn't bother to say any of that to Chandi, because he knew she wouldn't really care. All she would do would be to try, once more, to justify her behavior.

"Well, at least she wasn't pregnant, like I'd heard." Chandi sounded cheerful, as if imparting great news, and Rohan froze.

"What?"

"I said, 'At least she wasn't pregnant, like I'd heard.' There was a rumor going around at school that she was, after she'd left, but no one knew for sure."

"Did you tell my father?" Referring to the old man

as "Dada" was beyond Rohan's capability just then. He might never be able to again.

"Sure," Chandi said. "He told me to mind my own business and never mention it again."

He hung up without saying goodbye, the gesture feeling like putting a period on a part of his life that had haunted him in so many ways.

It was then he realized Baxter was by his side, leaning on his leg. When he looked down, the dog was staring at him with such concern that he had no choice but to stoop and hug the animal.

"I'm okay, Bax," he muttered into the warm, slightly pungent ruff. "I'm okay. Or hopefully, I will be."

Rising, calmer and resolute, he took another breath of the fresh mountain air, then turned back toward the clinic.

He had a son, absent at the moment, but soon to return. An adult, with whom Rohan would have to connect, create a bond, despite the lies and secrets that had kept them apart all these years.

Just knowing Jeevan existed gave Rohan the kind of joy he hadn't experienced in years, even as the questions of how to proceed awoke his deepest fears.

After his accident everyone said how much he'd changed, but they couldn't understand just how difficult it had been, battling with the effects of his head injury. During that time, he'd found it easier to distance himself from everyone, so as not to be overwhelmed, and the solitary man he was had grown from that seed of self-preservation.

Somehow, he'd have to break through the shell he'd built around his emotions, if there was to be any hope of a good, solid relationship with his son.

As he walked back toward the clinic, Bax close by

his side, he thought perhaps, if he were lucky, the capable and calm Elise van Hagan would be the key. There was something about her that spoke to a part of him he'd thought was gone, but which now seemed merely to have been locked away.

Not that he was at all looking to rekindle their long-ago romance.

Even if she had any such hopes, which he had no reason to believe she did, he'd long accepted relationships weren't for him. All his focus would be on building a bond with his son, and to do that, he'd need to know as much about Jeevan as he could before they met.

That was all he needed from Elise, he assured himself, as he pulled open the door.

But the beaming smile she turned on him, which lit up her face and turned it from attractive to breathtakingly gorgeous, stopped him in his tracks and made his heart race all over again.

Not with anxiety this time, but with desire.

"He's coming home," she said, the gleam in her eyes capturing his gaze and holding it effortlessly. "Jeevan's coming home for Christmas after all!"

CHAPTER SIX

TWO HOURS LATER, Elise waited in her kitchen for Rohan to arrive from Trail's End. The road had been ploughed, and he'd said he'd come by as soon as he felt comfortable leaving the husky he'd operated on in the care of Janice's employees.

Her head was full of plans and lists of what needed to be done now she knew Jeevan was coming home. She'd got another message from his friend, that Jeevan was running to catch a flight and had some tight connections, so there was no way to know exactly when he would arrive. She'd discussed it with Rohan, and they'd agreed not to say anything to their son until they could do it in person. It seemed logical, and less stress-inducing than having him flying back perhaps worried about what he'd find when he got home.

Elise was determined to have everything ready for Christmas before he got back to Canada, but instead of focusing on that, she found herself thinking about Rohan.

There had been no way to predict how he would respond to Jeevan's existence. Nor was she confident about how things would pan out, especially when she'd seen Rohan have what she thought was an anxiety attack while talking about the situation.

But when he came into the clinic from outside, and

she'd told him their son was coming home in a few days, he'd smiled fully, joyously, for the first time that day, and he'd seemed as excited as she was. "Will you still be here, when he arrives?" she'd asked. "You could stay and celebrate Christmas with us."

He hadn't hesitated.

"I'd like that. A lot."

"I don't know exactly when he's going to arrive. The message I got was from his friend—the one he was supposed to go to Australia with. Apparently, Moe's mother has taken ill, and he didn't think it made sense for Jeevan to go back there with him, when he didn't know what was going to happen. Jeevan was trying to get a last-minute ticket, which could mean they route him through half of Asia before he gets to Vancouver."

Rohan had sat in one of the chairs, still smiling. "Doesn't matter to me how long he takes to get here, I'm just happy I'm able to meet him sooner than expected. I'll have to book a hotel room, though. I'd told Janice I'd leave today, and she has a sled team arriving tomorrow. Between that and Ben being in hospital, I don't want to be an additional problem."

"You might have a problem finding a room at this time of year. Banff's really popular at Christmas. I have a spare room, though. Why don't you come and stay at my place?"

He'd hesitated, then said, "I wouldn't want to impose."

"No imposition," she'd replied, keeping her voice brisk and matter-of-fact.

He'd slanted her a glance, and then, when she thought he wasn't going to reply, he'd said, "I'd like that. Thank you."

"Of course," she'd joked, ridiculously lighthearted at his agreement. "You'll have to put up with Titan, the African gray, and his squawking."

"I'm used to it," he'd said casually, rubbing the side of his face. "I have a macaw, and she's a chatterer, too."

"I guess the apple didn't fall far from the tree, then."

The grin he'd sent her had her heart racing.

There. There was Rohan.

The devil-may-care smile that showed he had the world by the tail and wasn't afraid to tweak that appendage whenever he wanted.

"I guess not."

She'd grinned in return, and the unwanted trickle of awareness she felt when his smile widened had made her look away.

"I pulled up some pictures on my phone," she'd told him, unlocking the screen as she spoke. "But, of course, at home I have many more of him when he was young."

She'd handed him the phone and seen the way his eyes tracked across the screen, as though trying to see every small detail of each picture he looked at.

"He looks like me," he'd said softly.

"A lot," she'd confirmed, her heart melting at the yearning set of his face. "It'll be wonderfully strange to see the two of you together."

"What is he like?"

Warm fondness had flooded her as she sought the right way to describe their son. It was so hard to be objective, but she felt she owed Rohan all the honesty she could muster. At least on this topic.

"He was a scoundrel and hell-raiser as a child. I never knew what he was going to get up to next. But at the same time, he could be just this quiet, sweet little boy. For a while I wasn't sure how he'd turn out, and I worried about that all the time. One minute he was skateboarding with his friends, and I was hearing stories about the mischief they were getting up to, the next I'd find him crying over a dead bird he'd found in the garden."

She'd paused, and Rohan's gaze had lifted to hers, stealing her breath for an instant. Forcing a deep inhale, she'd cleared her throat before continuing.

"But as he grew, I realized it would be okay. He's good people, and I like him as much as love him, and I know not every parent gets to say that about their children, so I'm happy."

Rohan had nodded without comment, just looking back down at the phone, and she'd been acutely aware of all she hadn't said.

He not only looks a lot like you, but in so many little ways he reminds me of you. The way he walks, his wide grin. How he so easily connects to other people, even with just a smile or a few well-chosen words.

For all his life, Elise had watched Jeevan grow more and more like his father, or how his father had been when she first knew him, and she'd been fiercely glad. Rohan had been the kind of man she wanted her son to become: kind, considerate, easygoing, but still strong and always ready to stand up for what was right.

It was left to be seen how much of that man still existed under the stern, contained exterior Rohan now wore so easily.

Then he'd surprised her again, by asking, "Since you have such a short time to get ready for Christmas, and I'll be at your place anyway, can I help with anything?"

There'd been no hesitancy in his voice, but he'd lifted his hand briefly to his cheek again, making her think he wasn't as calm as he seemed. That one gesture made her not want to refuse.

Besides, against her best intentions, she was looking

forward to spending more time with him—getting to know the new Rohan better.

"I'd appreciate it, actually, since usually by now I'd have everything done, and this year I haven't even started. But I have a few things I have to take care of, as well as the Christmas prep, so we'll have to coordinate."

He'd raised his eyebrows. "I don't mind tagging along, if I won't be in the way." The corner of his mouth quirked, and he admitted, "I volunteered to bring the huskies up to Trail's End to get away from the Christmas fuss, so it's not as though I'm needed here, or anywhere else. Nathan can keep an eye on the husky we operated on this morning and call me if needs be."

"I have an appointment at half past twelve, so if you can come down, we can leave from my place."

Which was how she found herself walking out to his car dressed like one of Santa's elves, with Baxter behind her wearing a pair of reindeer antlers.

When she'd got Baxter's harness fastened in the back seat, she got into the truck to see Rohan's eyebrows up at his hairline and his lips twitching, as though he were trying his best not to laugh.

"I'm due at the nursing home with Baxter, and then I thought we could pick up a Christmas tree before we go back to the house and then you can help me decorate."

"Why are you going to the nursing home?" he asked as she fastened her seat belt.

As he put the SUV in gear, she told him, "After Bax and I retired from search and rescue, I decided to train him as an emotional support animal. I didn't want him to get bored and fat just sitting around the house all the time."

"Ah. That's why you told me to take him out with me

earlier, because you knew I was having…problems with what we were discussing."

She slid him a glance, found him staring resolutely through the windscreen, his jaw tight.

Why couldn't he even say the words *anxiety attack*? Did he think it made him weak to have them?

Not feeling it was appropriate to press him on it, she replied, "And why I called him into the barn when the husky was guarding Ben. I thought he might be able to calm her down."

"You were right." His voice sounded less stiff, but he lifted his hand to briefly touch his cheek. "And Bax and that female husky led me right to the other, injured dog. Do you think the husky might be trainable as a search and rescue dog?"

Elise frowned, considering it. "Huskies aren't usually trained for that. Her dominant skill sets may not be appropriate, but that's a question Tom, the volunteer SAR captain, would be better able to answer."

"How did you get into search and rescue anyway? Being an ER doctor wasn't exciting enough for you?"

"It was something I'd been interested in since I was a child. I never really wanted to study medicine, but my mother insisted. Once I got into it, I wanted to be where the action was, so emerge was the best fit."

He made a sound in the back of his throat, and she interpreted it as one of amusement when he asked, "A thrill seeker, huh?"

She snorted, then had to smile at the inelegant sound. "I guess you could put it that way. All I wanted to do was search and rescue, but Mom kept at me until I agreed to her plan. She was of the opinion it was too dangerous, and not a job for a woman. Besides, by then she was sick, and

I know she wanted to make sure I would be able to take care of myself after she was gone, so I went along with it."

"Did I ever meet your mother or your father, back when we were together?"

He was trying to sound casual, as though just making conversation, but she got the impression he was trying to fill in the blank spot in his brain with facts, since the memories were gone. It made her wonder how he'd coped after the accident, when no one could, or would, offer him any lifeline to his immediate past.

"No," she said quietly. "You never met any of my family. By then both my parents were gone, and my sister was in Calgary, where my mother's family originally came from."

"Is she still living there?"

"No. She and her husband moved to BC a few years ago. Make a turn here."

He put on his indicator and made the turn into Banff. The ploughs had been busy, and downtown was already filled with people shopping and enjoying the crisp, late-morning air. Not wanting to talk about her family any more, Elise searched for another, less painful topic.

"I used to bring Bax to the home in the afternoons, but the residents requested that he come earlier. At first, I thought it was because they weren't as tired as they were closer to the end of the day, then I realized it's because they like to sneak him little bits of their lunches. I have to keep a sharp eye on them."

Rohan chuckled, and for some reason the sound went straight to her heart.

Had she heard him laugh, even once, all day? She didn't think so.

"There you were, training him so he wouldn't get

bored and fat, not realizing the danger of becoming obese would come with the new job."

"Exactly," she replied, letting amusement color her voice as she directed him into the nursing home parking lot.

When he'd parked, and she was unbuckling her seat belt and gathering up the bag of gifts she'd brought, Rohan exited the vehicle ahead of her and let Bax out the back door. As they met at the front of the vehicle, he held out the leash for her to take. Neither of them was wearing gloves, and as her fingers brushed his, a sweet tingle of awareness rushed through her.

Before she could make sense of it, Rohan's hand closed over hers, and he said, "I have one more question, and I hope you don't mind me asking."

She raised her eyebrows, trying to pretend his touch wasn't giving her goose bumps.

"Why did you give up search and rescue, really?"

Tugging her hand free, she set off for the lobby door, saying over her shoulder, "That's a story for another day."

Knowing full well that if she had her way, that day would never come.

As they walked into the home and were greeted with cries of welcome, she saw Rohan retreat to a spot against the wall, his stoic mien firmly in place. As Elise allowed Baxter to work the room, greeting all the residents, Rohan stayed to one side, watching. But as she well knew, no one visiting was allowed to remain aloof for very long.

"Who is that young man?" Mrs. Ferguson waved at him. "Come here. You remind me so much of someone, but I can't think of who it is."

"I think he looks like Elise's son," Mrs. Durrant said. "Do you remember, Ada, when he came with her to visit?"

"Oh, yes," Mrs. Ferguson said, peering at Rohan over her glasses. "That's right."

"He looks like Jeevan, because Rohan is his father."

Elise didn't even hesitate. The words flowed from her lips so easily even she was a little taken aback by it.

And then she met Rohan's gaze, and his expression was one of mingled wonder and surprise. Then it morphed into something else—something hot and wild—which caused desire to flash through her so hard and fast she had to turn away so he wouldn't see it reflected in her eyes.

It reminded her of how, even as she'd kept an emotional distance from him all those years ago, he'd been able to turn her inside out with lust with just a look or a single touch. He was the only man who'd made her mindless with need. Who'd made her forget just why love wouldn't be something she counted on to be happy.

No. No. No.

They weren't going there. This chance meeting had nothing to do with what they'd once shared, beyond the fact that it had produced Jeevan.

The only thing that mattered was uniting father and son, and she refused to allow echoes of the past to muddy the waters.

Especially not the kind of echoes that made her want to tumble into Rohan's arms the way she used to, and allow him to set her ablaze.

CHAPTER SEVEN

BY THE TIME they left the nursing home, Rohan couldn't believe how much fun he'd had.

Watching Bax work had been a treat as he allowed himself to be petted, hugged and kissed by resident after resident. He'd delivered little presents to each person, carried in a basket he proudly held in his mouth, and his tail had hardly stopped fanning the air.

At the end, Rohan was happy to escape the old ladies' interrogations, and had tagged along with Elise and Bax while they went to visit a resident who'd been bedridden for a few weeks.

"He fell and broke his hip," Elise explained. "And, as it is for many patients with dementia, the hospital stay caused a marked deterioration in his mental acuity. Mr. Robson is almost completely nonverbal now, except when he sees Bax."

It had sounded so much like what he'd found the last time he visited his father that Rohan was tempted to wait for them outside the room. But the nurse had held the door open for him, and by then it was too late to avoid going through without it being obvious.

Despite his misgivings and the lingering sense of being thrust into a situation he felt unequal to handle, he couldn't help being touched as he watched Bax interact with Mr. Robson. On opening his eyes and seeing the dog next to his bed, the elderly man's face had lit up, his trembling hand reaching out. Bax had shifted, putting his head in the proper position to be petted, and then, on Elise's command, he'd placed his paws on the rail at the side of the bed so he was face-to-face with the patient.

"Oh, you beauty," the old man had breathed, his voice little better than a sigh. "You gorgeous boy. You've come to see old George again. I love you. I love you."

That moment, Rohan knew, would stay with him for a very long time. He'd always known and accepted that animals had healing qualities, but seeing it displayed so clearly moved him deeply.

But the experience that lingered even stronger in his mind was when Elise had, so calmly and matter-of-factly, named him as her child's father.

Hearing her do so had caused his heart to stutter, warmth to fill his chest. The emotions released had swamped him, threatening to drown him in joy so intense it was frightening.

And in that instant, she was even more beautiful to him than she'd been before.

He'd even imagined that something special and wonderful had passed between them as their eyes met, but now he dismissed the thought. She was intelligent, kind and beautiful. Everything any man could want or need, but he had nothing to offer in return.

Not when his emotions were so stunted, and almost impossible to process.

The focus needed to stay squarely on Jeevan. Although his son was no longer a child, as parents it was their obligation to ensure that Rohan's meeting with him went smoothly.

There was no room for error, nor for complications, like his growing attraction to his son's mother.

After his accident he'd been told over and over how different he was, how he was no longer the young man people knew and loved. The changes had been pointed out in detail. How solemn he'd become, how he lacked the laughter and joking ways of his youth. He'd been unable to give affection easily, locked in a cycle of simply trying to survive the effects of his head injury, and it had shown in how he treated those around him.

Elise would remember that younger man, and perhaps even now wondered at the transformation. He had no urge to hear those kinds of comments again, especially not from a woman he now knew he would be forever tied to.

"Okay," Elise said briskly once they were back in the SUV, breaking him out of his not-so-happy thoughts. "Let's go get a tree, and then head back to my place. I was thinking of going by the hospital to see Ben, if they're allowing him visitors, but I refuse to go there dressed like an elf."

Her stout declaration amused him. "But you'll go tree shopping like that?"

"Downtown Banff is Christmas central. No one will even bat an eye. But I'd hear about it for years if the staff at the hospital see me like this."

He wouldn't blame anyone for mentioning the outfit. He'd been trying to ignore just how snugly it fit her athletic form, and how the tail of her tunic swung enticingly when she walked. Her body was toned, but with womanly curves he longed to put his hands on. Soft, round breasts beneath her clingy costume showcased a still-narrow waist, which then flared into rounded hips.

The maturity of her figure was a turn-on he couldn't

ignore, especially when she walked ahead of him, bottom swinging with each long, confident stride.

Not even the funny shoes and hat made her look anything less than completely desirable.

The tree market was busy, but Rohan appreciated the swiftness with which Elise made a decision, and it wasn't long before they were back on the road, heading to her house.

"We'll get the tree set up, and then cut some branches before getting the decorations out of storage." Rohan got the impression she was mentally running down an already prepared list. "This evening, if you're up for it, I'll need to do some food and gift shopping. We could go by the hospital then, too."

"Sounds like a plan," he agreed, settling back, trying to ease the tension out of his shoulders.

When they stopped at an intersection, Elise pulled off the elf hat, and once more he saw a few wisps of hair escape her bun. Without thought, he gently swept them back, tucking them behind her ear. She didn't say anything but slanted him a quick glance, and he silently cursed the impulse that had made him touch her so intimately.

He'd have to watch himself going forward, to make sure he didn't do anything else like that.

Bax whined from the back seat, and Elise turned to say, "Yep, almost home, boy."

Her house was a neat bungalow, which, with all the snow they'd had the previous night, seemed to be floating on a sea of white. One side had been cleared, the driveway and walk shoveled, making paths through drifts three feet high in spots. She directed him to park near the garage door.

While Baxter found a spot that needed watering,

they wrestled the tree out of the SUV, and then they all went inside.

In the kitchen, they stopped to take off their shoes while Baxter made a beeline for his water bowl. Obviously, cheering up the elderly was thirsty work.

"Help yourself to a drink, if you like, and go on through to the living room." She pointed him to an archway on the other side of the kitchen as she walked toward a hallway. "I'm just going to change out of this costume."

He took a moment to look around. It was no surprise to him that everything was tidy, spic-and-span. Elise struck him as a person who probably wouldn't abide too much clutter.

"Bax! Bax! Mom wants you!"

The squawk of a parrot drew him into the living room, and he saw the African gray in its cage first. Then, as he started to cross the room to take a closer look, he realized the room was filled with photographs. They were on the walls, on the shelves surrounding the television, the mantelpiece—everywhere—and that became more interesting and important to Rohan just then.

On suddenly shaky legs, he moved closer to look at them. Most were of Jeevan in different settings, with a few of Elise thrown in. A chronicle of Jeevan's life, from him as a baby, round, damp and sandy, a lake or ocean in the background, to some of him at university graduation. One of Elise, proudly wearing her search and rescue uniform, Baxter at her side. And then, on the wall, Rohan came face-to-face with himself.

It looked like an autumn day, with a wash of orange, red and yellow leaves forming a backdrop to his face. He was laughing, head thrown back, sunlight glinting in his smiling eyes.

The only thing he recognized in the picture was the

scarf around his throat. It was covered in smiley faces, and he'd worn it all through college, been teased about it numerous times.

Intellectually, he knew it was his face, and was touched that Elise had kept his image in front of his son's eyes all those years, but the person in the picture was, deep inside, a stranger to him.

"Who were you?"

He said it aloud to the photo, struggling not to let the doubts and fears overtake him and cause him to botch this important moment in his life, as he knew they had done at other times.

Unable to bear looking at it anymore, he turned away and drew in a deep breath. Blowing it out, he straightened his spine.

Seeing the pictures brought the wonder of it back.

He was a father. Had a son.

A son named after his beloved Baba, the grandfather who'd taught him how to be a man and a decent human being.

Your father thinks prestige is the most important thing in life, Rohan, but he's wrong. And money isn't important, either. What is important is that you do the right thing, always, and bring joy to others. Only then can you be truly happy.

Remembering Baba's words brought calm, and a new resolve to make this work.

He'd doubted his ability to love, to care deeply for another, but already he knew he'd do anything for his son and fight to the death anyone else who tried to come between them again.

Elise stood in the doorway, watching Rohan examine the pictures on the wall, knowing he hadn't noticed her and glad for it.

Now she could clearly see the emotions, as though the only time he could let them free was when he was alone. She'd seen sorrow, joy, confusion, tenderness, and her heart ached for him, even as her body insisted on reminding her how sexy he was.

Being around Rohan—even this new, different Rohan—was doing crazy things to her equilibrium.

When he'd brushed the hair back from her cheek, his fingers warm against her skin, she was transported back in time. The intervening years fell away, as though they'd never existed, leaving her feeling like that young, carefree girl who'd desired him beyond reason.

"Why doesn't your hair ever stay where you put it?"

He'd slicked her hair off her cheek, tucking the strands securely behind her ear.

"It's because it's so fine and straight. Nothing keeps it in place for long."

"You know what? I like that it flops around like that."

"Flops around?" She'd feigned annoyance. "And why on earth would you like that?"

He'd moved closer, nuzzling her so his breath rushed, warm and exciting, over her cheek, as he replied, "Because it's one more reason to touch you."

He raised his hand, not to his face this time, but to the back of his head, and once more memories swamped her, brought on by the cowlick at his nape. How many times had she swirled her finger through it, or snuck up behind him and kissed him just there? Too many to count, but she remembered as if it were yesterday. And when Jeevan was born with a full head of hair, and she'd seen the same swirl of baby-fine hair at his nape, it had brought her to tears.

Elise drew a long breath into her lungs and held it for a beat before letting it out silently.

This wasn't then, and she wasn't that relatively naive

twenty-six-year-old, she reminded herself stoutly. And Rohan Khan wasn't the man she'd fallen for and mourned. They'd both been changed, fundamentally, by the events of that year and all the intervening ones. Now the best they could hope for was to find some way to co-parent so no one got hurt.

Especially Jeevan.

She stepped into the room, drawing his attention. As though watching a curtain fall, she saw the expression leave his face, and it hurt her more than it should.

"Do you have a tree stand?" he asked, as though that was the most important thing in the world.

"I'll get it," she replied, turning away so he couldn't see her silly pain.

"Do you need a hand with getting it out?"

"Not right now," she called back to him, although his superior height would have been useful in getting at it on the top shelf.

Carrying a chair over to the storage closet, she climbed up to get the stand, glad for a few minutes to herself.

"I could have gotten that for you."

She'd been so lost in thought she hadn't heard him come in, and the suddenness of his voice behind her startled her into spinning around and she toppled from the chair.

Rohan caught her, bending over her to shield her from the cascade of wrapping paper and boxes that came down around them.

"Are you all right?" he asked, slowly straightening, although his arms remained around her. She told herself to move, to step back, but her head filled with his scent, and her entire body awoke, tingling and heating.

How can he still smell the same?

"Elise?"

His voice was cool and controlled, and she was made aware of how stupid she was being, getting lost in memories of a time so long gone it could have been a different life.

"I'm fine," she said, stepping back and having to suppress a shiver of sudden cold. "The tree stand is right there. Thank God it didn't fall on one of our heads."

Although, she thought as he easily pulled the article in question down, it might have knocked some sense into her, if hers was the head in question.

CHAPTER EIGHT

THE AFTERNOON FLEW by and ended up being a lot more fun than Elise had anticipated. Once they had the tree set up, they put back on their outdoor clothes and went to the woodlot to cut branches to decorate the house.

"Jeevan and I usually decorate the tree together," she explained when Rohan asked about ornaments. "But there's still lots to do. I like to have fresh pine boughs above the cupboards in the kitchen and along the mantel, and we can decorate those if not today, then tomorrow. If you're available," she added quickly, suddenly aware of how easily she assumed he'd be around.

It wouldn't do to start thinking that way. At all.

But he replied, "Sure," without a hint of anything untoward in his tone. "Later, I'd like to go up to Trail's End and look in on the husky we operated on, just to make sure he's doing okay."

As they were cutting boughs and putting them on the sled, Rohan said, "So Jeevan is an ornithologist, huh? Couldn't get him to choose veterinary medicine?"

Elise chuckled. "He swung between the two for a while, but birds were always fascinating to him, although I never really understood it. I don't mind them, but he was obsessed. Made it easy to buy him gifts, though, which isn't always the case as a parent."

Rohan glanced over, and his eyes were smiling. "Never thought he'd go into human medicine?"

Elise gave a decisive shake of her head. "No. Never. He worked at the hospital, to get his volunteer hours in for school, and he hated having to be inside all the time and complained that there were too many 'crotchety old people' to interact with."

That made Rohan chuckle.

"I'd feel the same way," he said, amusement still evident in his voice. "Although I mostly do small animal work now, some of my favorite jobs are when I get called out to do house calls at farms or ranches. A few weeks ago, I had to attend on a birth at an alpaca farm. Mind you, I would have preferred if it were summer, but, hey, at least it got me out of the office."

"I love working in the emergency room—the bustle of it, and never knowing what will come in next."

"You have the mind and temperament for it, I suspect."

Surprised, she asked, "What do you mean?"

He shrugged. "Not everyone can keep cool under stress, or be open to all possibilities, which you have to when you're trying to diagnose patients. From what I've seen today, those are both qualities you possess in spades. They must have served you well in SAR too."

"I guess," she replied, ridiculously flattered by his factual tone.

"Do you miss it? Search and rescue?"

"Sometimes," she replied honestly. Somehow it was easy to talk to him out here in the open, the cold prickling her face, the smell of pine in the air. "The comradery, and the act of helping people under tricky situations. But there are parts I'd rather forget, and unfortunately, those are the ones that stick with me."

He tossed the branches he'd just cut onto the sled and turned to her, their gazes meeting, snagging.

"What parts?"

She wanted to turn away, refuse to tell him, but something inside was clamoring to tell the story, to try to leach some of the constant fear away.

Would he judge her as a coward, if he heard what had happened?

"Bax and I were on the slopes, looking for a skier who'd gone off the marked trails. There was an avalanche warning in effect, but the team can't think about that when they're trying to find someone."

She paused, took a deep breath, trying to slow her racing heart.

"We got caught in an avalanche, and buried. Bax was injured, but he still managed to dig me out."

"God, Elise." He took a step toward her and then stopped. "I'm sorry. You must have been terrified."

"I was, at the time, and even after a few months, I realized I still was. Even today I froze, coming through the tunnel, because I had a flashback when I heard the rumble of snow falling from the barn roof. There's no room for error or fear when you're on a rescue, and I knew I'd be a danger to the team, so I quit."

Those dark eyes of his surveyed her, seeming, as they so often did, to be looking into the heart of her.

"Do you want to go back to it?"

"I don't know," she said, shaken to honesty by his question. "Sometimes I do, and then I know I'm too scared to risk it. Yet it feels like I gave up on something I was so proud and happy to do, and that's almost worse than the fear."

He frowned, his brows coming together for an instant. "You're going to have to decide what's more important,

I think—the fear or the determination to get past it. But you're the only one who can make that choice."

"You're right, but it's not a choice I feel strong enough to make right now."

He nodded before turning back to his chore. "Give yourself some time."

At his words, something eased inside, as though she had just been waiting to hear that advice to be able to relax. And the pangs of guilt and loss she usually felt when talking about it were softer, somehow more bearable.

When she decided they had enough boughs, and they were heading back to the house, she worked up the courage to ask a question that had been nagging at her all day.

"Is your father still alive?"

"He is, but he has advanced dementia."

"I'm sorry."

He shrugged. "He's had it for a number of years, and it progressed slowly at first. Then he had a series of strokes, and all at once, his condition deteriorated rapidly. He's nonverbal and barely ambulatory now."

"I'm sorry," she said again, knowing how inadequate the words were, but unable to find any better.

Rohan slanted her a look. "That's kind of you to say, considering what he put you through."

"Whatever he did, whatever his reasons, that's no way to end your days."

"I know."

There was something in his tone—sadness and anger all mixed together into the type of pain she knew all too well—that brought her to a halt and made her wish she could alleviate it in some small way.

"Do you want to see something totally ridiculous?"

she asked, as he stopped walking, too, to turn a questioning gaze her way.

"Sure."

Elise bent to pick up some snow, saying, "For a dog as smart as Bax is, he completely loses his marbles around a snowball."

Even as she spoke, Bax noticed what she was doing, and came running, barking his head off. As he got closer, he screeched to a halt, then started jumping and prancing in a frenzy of delight.

"Bax, catch!"

Elise threw the snowball, and Baxter leaped to intercept it, biting at it in midair. The loosely packed ball disintegrated, of course, but after it did, the dog looked shocked and began a concentrated hunt for it. As he turned in circles, snuffling on the ground, Elise prepared another ball.

"Bax, look."

His comical expression of surprise on seeing what he obviously thought was the same ball, magically back in her hand, never failed to amuse her. And she was happy to hear Rohan snort with laughter, too.

"He looks that way every time," she said, throwing the next snowball. "As though I've tricked him, and he can't figure out how."

When Baxter reacted the same way the second time, Rohan's amusement turned to actual laughter. Encouraged by the sound, and the joy on his face, Elise threw the next ball at him instead of for Bax. The situation quickly devolved into an out-and-out snowball fight between them, with Baxter jumping about, barking and capering.

It was a much-needed moment of levity, and they were still laughing as they finally pulled the sled into the garage.

Yet, despite her laughter, Elise almost wished she hadn't seen this side of Rohan again. One that was so redolent of his younger self it made her yearn, wanting something that no longer existed.

Even with the laughter, Rohan couldn't shake the disquiet he'd felt as he spoke about his father. There were so many unanswered questions regarding their relationship, and about why the older man had done the things he had in life. Rohan had always intended, at some point, to sit down with his father, perhaps over a glass of rum, and talk about their shared past. Ask all the questions he'd known his father wouldn't have answered in Rohan's youth, in the hopes they could talk as men rather than as parent and child.

Of course, now it would never happen, and with the kind of role model his father had been, Rohan couldn't help wondering what kind of father *he*'d be.

The fear that he wouldn't know how to relate to his son, that he'd mess up somehow, was nagging at him, eating away at his insides.

They hung garlands of boughs in the living room and festooned them with lights, to the accompaniment of Titan's running commentary. Then, while he arranged more boughs above the kitchen cupboards, Elise noted, "You're very quiet."

He stepped down from the ladder and stood back to view his handwork. "Just wondering how Jeevan and I will get along."

He tried to keep his voice light, but he didn't think she was fooled, since she put her hand on his arm and looked at him with compassion shining in her eyes.

"I think you'll get along fine. Yes, you're his parent, but it won't be like meeting him as a child. You're both adults, and both fine men. It might take a little time to find common ground, because of the situation, but I think you'll find it."

"Do you have an adult relationship with him?"

Her smile was soft, a little rueful.

"It's hard for me right now, because it was always him and me, and I was always the one in control. Once he went off to university, I had to start stepping back from my role as parent and give him the room to become whatever he wanted to be."

She sighed and glanced away. "Everyone seems to think there's some particular point in life when parents stop treating their kids as children and accept them as adults, but it's not as clear-cut as that. He'll always be my baby, but now I have to walk a fine line on a slippery slope, so he doesn't think I'm interfering in his life too much."

"I don't have the best experience on how fathers and sons relate to each other," he told her, knowing he had to be as honest as he could be, if he hoped for her help. "And I've become less and less social over the years, so my interpersonal skills are rusty, at best. I just want to do the right thing by him, and I'm not sure I know how."

There were so many other things he worried about, including the aftereffects of that long-ago accident, which seemed set to stay with him forever.

Although he'd retained most of his memory, was able to recall all he'd learned in school, knew his family and friends, something else had happened to his brain as a result of the crash. Something above and beyond the loss of those crucial seven months.

He couldn't remember having emotions about anything prior to awaking in the hospital. Couldn't recall how he'd felt during important times of his life.

In a way, he couldn't remember what it meant to be loved, and on the whole, accessing emotion had remained difficult.

Oh, he'd felt things—anger, sorrow when his mother died—but always at a distance, as though the hole in his memory banks had created a barrier between him and the world.

She squeezed his arm, her expression one of understanding.

"It's an unthinkable situation you've found yourself in, and it'll take time to figure it all out. Be kind to yourself. I'm sure everything will be fine."

Her assurance was generous, but was she comparing him to the young man he once was? The one who no longer existed?

The sensation that washed through him was familiar.

It was the urge to escape—an instinct to flee that came over him any time talk of his younger days surfaced. That urge to turn away, both from the conversations and the people wanting to have them, had led him into a solitary life.

Yet he couldn't do it now. Not when it meant forgoing a chance to meet his child.

And to spend a bit more time with the woman who'd given him this unexpected, glorious gift.

Again, honesty propelled him to say, "I'm not the man you knew, twenty-seven years ago. I've changed and—according to some—not for the better."

Her eyebrows rose, and her gaze searched his. Then the corners of her lips tilted up.

"If you were, after all this time, I'd say you suffered from a severe case of arrested development. Everyone changes, as life goes on, but I can say that the best qualities you had when I knew you are still very much in evidence. If they weren't, I'd probably not have said anything to you about Jeevan."

Her forthright words and acceptance made something warm bloom in his chest and spread its heat out through every vein in his body. He didn't know what the sensation was—could put no name to it—but perhaps a shadow of it crossed his face, for her eyes widened.

Once more he couldn't help noticing the sweet curve of her mouth, the way it softened, and the tip of her tongue briefly peeked out to touch her lower lip.

He wanted to kiss her, pull her into his arms, but fought the impulse.

"Nothing good can come of this." He hadn't planned to say the words aloud, but they echoed between them, and Elise nodded slowly.

"You're right, of course," she whispered, but Rohan realized their lips were closer together than they'd been before. So close he felt the rush of her breath, warm against his mouth.

Had he moved? Or had she?

Did it really matter, when his hands had already found her waist, and hers gripped his forearms?

"Elise." He'd planned to say more: *We can't. Tell me to stop.* Anything, in a last-ditch attempt to stem the tide of desire trying to drag him under. But his voice caught in his throat, and her name came out more like a plea.

The muted chime of a phone sounded from the table behind them, and they both froze. Almost simultaneously they stepped back, and he saw a warm rush of color stain her cheeks before she could turn away.

Walking to the table, she picked up her phone.

"Jeevan is in Hong Kong. He's been bumped from his original flight but hopes to get on another soon."

Rohan let out a long, silent breath, battling to get his wayward libido under control.

The best thing he could do would be to get away, try to make sense of what was happening between them.

He cleared his throat.

"I'm going to run up to Trail's End and check on the husky."

That would give him a little time to himself to work out what to do.

Elise nodded, her gaze unclouded, seemingly clear of the doubts and worries—and the lust—swirling through him.

"I'm going to put on dinner so it'll be ready when you get back."

He nodded. "Sounds good. And after we've eaten, if you want, we can go do the shopping."

"Okay," she said, giving him a little smile before turning to open the fridge.

As he put on his coat and headed out the door, what struck him was how homey the conversation sounded. Almost domestic.

And how damned right.

CHAPTER NINE

ELISE COULDN'T BELIEVE she'd almost kissed Rohan, and
each time she thought of it, tingles spread up her spine,
and desire ran, warm and sultry, through her entire body.
She couldn't even find solace in the mundane, like she
usually did, and as she fixed dinner, her mind kept going
back to those thrilling moments.

Her response to his closeness didn't surprise her. Not
really. Rohan was as attractive to her as he'd been all
those years before, and the day had been an emotional
one, filled with revelations and drama.

She was also discovering much to like about the older
Rohan. His calm and compassion, the way he listened to
her, his full attention focused on her words and expression. More than once he'd caught her off guard with his
insightful comments and questions.

But even more important, she liked how much thought
he was obviously putting into meeting Jeevan and what
he could do to make their relationship a good one. His
eagerness made her heart sing and boded well for the
future.

What wouldn't bode well was the undercurrent of lust
flowing between them.

It wasn't hard to tell he wanted to keep some distance between them, and she was quite sure doing any-

thing about their attraction would be a bad thing in the long run.

Once the novelty of their reunion wore off, having slept together would make things uncomfortable.

She'd made a big pot of chicken stew the week before and frozen it in batches. Now she heated some up, planning to add dumplings once it was simmering. As she mixed the dough, her thoughts turned once more to Rohan, and her breath caught in her throat.

He'd looked so uncomfortable, almost shocked, at their near-kiss, but she'd also seen the desire shimmering in his eyes. It was a look she recognized, even after all these years, and it still had the same effect on her as it had before.

Turning the burner down to low, she decided to have a shower while Rohan was gone.

While Ben's rescue had happened just that morning, it felt as though days had passed since then, and somehow the thought of a warm shower to wash away the day was infinitely appealing.

Having enjoyed her shower, she checked the pot and then went to make up the bed in the spare room and put out towels for Rohan. Wondering if he still liked an extra blanket when he slept, she went and got one, laying it out, just in case.

It was weird to know so much about a man but still consider him something of a stranger. Yet that was exactly how this crazy situation felt.

They'd somehow found their way back together after almost thirty years, their story almost perfectly bookended by accidents—one that tore them apart, the other reuniting them.

But she reminded herself that it wasn't a reunion, really.

More a reintroduction—happenstance that fortunately also gave back to her son the father he'd never known.

That was what was important.

Nothing else.

By the time she finished, it was time to add the dumplings to the stew. After putting some rolls in the oven, she set about making a salad. As she went to open the fridge, she caught sight of the picture of Jeevan she always kept on the door.

Love for her son overwhelmed her, brought her to tears. She'd missed him so much. It had been a constant ache in her heart. At least when he was at university, she'd known he was in the same country, although miles away. While he was abroad, she'd fretted and worried every day. Now she wondered how he'd feel when he discovered his supposedly long-deceased father was actually still alive.

When he was growing up, she'd tried to gauge how he was dealing with not having his father around, but he'd always assured her he was fine. During his rebellious teenage years, she'd wondered if having a solid father figure, or even a male influence on a day-to-day basis, would have curbed some of his wilder impulses.

Jeevan had had his Uncle Ray, Elise's brother-in-law, while they lived in Calgary, but once they'd moved to Banff when Jeevan was fourteen, it had just been the two of them.

How would Rohan coming back into their lives, and hearing why he'd been absent, affect their son?

There was no way to know until Jeevan got home and found out, but Elise couldn't help worrying anyway.

As she was cutting up cucumbers, her phone rang. It was Rohan.

"Everything okay?" she asked, wondering if he'd changed his mind about staying there after their near-kiss.

"Yes, but I wanted you to know I'll be a little longer."

"The husky isn't doing well?"

"The one we operated on is fine, but the female has been acting up since the barn collapse. Nathan thought she was missing the male, and took her in to see him briefly earlier, but it didn't help. She only settled down when I went and took her out of the kennel, and I thought I'd just stay with her a while and see if I can calm her down enough to not have her howling all night."

"Bring her back here," Elise said. "Maybe having Bax for company will help."

There was a short silence, and she wished she could see his face, to perhaps get a hint of what he was thinking.

"She isn't house-trained, Elise."

"Bring some pee pads with you, and we'll keep her and Bax sequestered in the kitchen overnight. I'm not some shrinking violet who'll get upset over a bit of a mess in the morning."

The sound he made was something between a snort and a chuckle.

"Are you sure?"

"Definitely."

"Well, then, I'll see you in a few minutes."

"And for goodness' sake, give her a name. We can't expect her to listen to us if she doesn't know we're talking to her."

He laughed then, before hanging up, and the sound turned her insides to molten desire, and her legs to jelly.

What was it about that laugh that affected her this way? And had her thinking the kinds of thoughts she'd firmly told herself she shouldn't have?

Like if making love with him would be as magical and fulfilling as it had been when they were young. He'd instinctively known where to touch her, how to seek out her pleasure zones and, after taking her to the edge of orgasm, bring her to completion. Just thinking about it made nerve endings she'd almost forgotten she had roar back to life, and pushed tingling heat to all her erogenous zones.

During those heady months, they'd spent hours exploring their sexuality together. Neither of them had been virgins, but he'd often said he'd never had the type of satisfaction he'd found with her, and she'd readily admitted it was the same for her. Just kissing him had been an exercise in pleasure back then. One of her favorite memories was of them sitting on a bluff in Algonquin Park, surrounded by glorious autumn colors, kissing and kissing, and stopping only when they heard others coming up the trail.

That was where the picture of Rohan in her living room was taken, when she'd caught him in a moment of joy and impulsively snapped the shot. It showed, she thought, the essence of the man she'd fallen for so hard.

But he remembered none of that—and in a way she was glad. While he worried that she may be judging him against the person he was then, she didn't have to consider how he would view the changes in her—both physical and emotional—in return.

The young woman who'd luxuriated in delicious, rebellious passion no longer existed. In her place had grown a woman who'd learned to be steady, calm, controlled.

That was the woman she now needed to depend on, to put aside her erotic, potentially destructive impulses and keep him at arm's length.

With that pep talk, she went back to fixing the salad,

but the heat that had flooded her stubbornly refused to abate, and her heart gave a little stutter when she heard his vehicle arrive.

The husky took some coaxing to get inside, and it was Baxter who seemed to have convinced her eventually, but once she came in, she swiftly settled down, sharing a bed with the golden.

"See, I told you Bax would help." Elise couldn't keep a hint of smugness from invading her tone as she put their dinner on the table. "Have you decided on a name for her yet?"

"Yes, you told me, and no, I haven't given her a name. We usually wait for either the fosterer or adopters to do that."

He pulled out her chair for her, waiting until she was seated to sit down.

"Well, I think that's silly. She needs rehabilitation, which also means learning her manners and basic commands, as well as socialization. I don't see how that's possible if she doesn't have a name to respond to. I'm going to call her Phoebe."

He just smiled and, picking up his spoon, said, "This smells delicious."

She knew a change of subject when she heard one, so she started on her salad. Swallowing the first bite, she said, "Chicken and dumplings is one of Jeevan's favorites. I was telling myself off for cooking as much of it as I did a couple days ago and was resigned to eating it for weeks. But since he's coming home, I won't have to worry."

He glanced up, his eyes gleaming. "Maybe you had a premonition that he would be here for Christmas after all?"

"Nope." She shook her head as she reached for a roll. "I was absolutely sure he wouldn't be. He was so excited to see Australia—all those birds." She chuckled. "I asked him whether he'd go to the Great Barrier Reef, or travel to Sydney to see the Opera House or Bondi Beach, but he said probably not. His friend had some bush treks arranged so they could go bird-watching."

"I think I'll have to have words with him. I've heard the bird-watching on Bondi Beach is pretty amazing."

"Ooh…" Elise gave his deadpan expression a narrow-eyed glare, even though she saw the devilish humor in his gaze. "Don't you become a bad influence."

"What?" He tried for an innocent look and failed. "He likes birds."

She swatted his hand before going back to her meal. "Watch yourself, buddy."

As he was eating, Rohan couldn't help watching Elise even while they joked around—the way she moved, the shape of her lips, the delicate yet strong hands.

No matter how he tried to force himself to stop, his gaze tracked back to her again and again, taking in all the nuances of her expression.

Just as they finished their meal, a huge yawn took him by surprise, and she gave him a knowing look.

"It's been a long day. I think we can leave the shopping for tomorrow, don't you? Why don't you take a shower and go to bed?"

"It's too early for bed. If I turn in now, I'll be up at three in the morning, but I could use a shower. Besides, I want to see Jeevan's pictures."

"Sure. If you like."

The memory of her smile, as she agreed, followed him down the corridor to the room she directed him to.

She seemed so happy that he wanted to see the pictures. Didn't she realize how amazingly special that would be to him?

But how could she, really?

Jeevan had been a part of her life since he was born. An unbroken chain of love connected them in ways Rohan could hardly fathom. There was no way she could begin to understand how it felt for him, after all those lonely, somehow barren years, to be presented with the gift of the chance to know—to love—his child.

It was like being given a second chance, a new lease on life, and he was going to grab ahold of it with both hands.

Going to give it everything he had.

He felt a bit better after his shower and wandered back out to find her in the living room, a stack of photo albums beside her.

She'd turned on the lights in the garlands they'd put up that afternoon, and Rohan wondered what her Christmas tree would be like when decorated. Would it be filled with colorful, silly toys, remnants of Jeevan's childhood, or would it be elegant and color-coordinated? Somehow, he thought the former. She struck him as a woman of sentiment, behind that no-nonsense, strong exterior.

As he sat next to her on the couch, she said, "I got in the habit of putting albums together and kept doing it even when the digital revolution took over, although I have hundreds of other pictures on the computer."

She placed them on his lap and said, "The years they span are on the spines, and I think they're in order, but you can check." Straightening, she stretched. "I'm going to take the dogs out. If there's anything you want to know about, just ask."

"Thank you," he said, battling disappointment that she wasn't sticking around to look at the pictures with him.

Yet that same sense of excitement he'd felt earlier superseded discontent soon, as he opened the first album and found a record of Jeevan's birth, complete with foot and handprints.

That was when he knew he was in trouble—that what he'd thought of as an interesting way to learn a bit more about his son was going to be an emotionally devastating event. The knowledge almost made him close the album and walk away, but he fought the impulse.

All this time he'd thought he'd lost the ability to feel emotion, but maybe he'd just been too frightened to feel. Too hurt to want to. Looking at the pictures would hurt, but perhaps also, in some way, heal.

So he forced himself to focus, to accept the pain of loss.

Those tiny hands and feet that he'd never got to see. Toes he'd never got to kiss. Palms he'd never got to wash.

He wanted to go back, to experience it all. To be there for the middle-of-the-night feedings. For rocking baby Jeevan to sleep. Even for diaper duty.

Elise had had to do it all herself, taking on the full responsibility of motherhood without him, and the knowledge tore into him like a lance through the heart.

For a long time he couldn't move, except to run his finger over the inked lines until, eventually, he forced himself to turn the page.

Elise, younger, disheveled and pale, and a wrinkly, obviously just-born Jeevan lying on her breast, his face turned away from the camera. He had a full head of dark hair, and Rohan lifted his hand to touch his nape, just where his hair swirled. The spot every barber complained about, because it was impossible to cut it so the strands lay flat.

"Who has a cowlick at the back of their head?" one had complained.

Rohan did. And so did his son.

What else did they share? The shape of their toes or fingers? Perhaps an affinity for sweets, or seafood?

He wanted to know, even as each revelation, every discovery, would tear at his heart.

With a deep breath, he turned another page, trying to hold it together, taking his time to view the photos, noting the subtle changes as Jeevan grew. One thing never wavered, though, and that was the love clearly visible in Elise's eyes whenever she was looking at their child. There were other people in some of the pictures, but Rohan hardly spared them a glance. The only people he was interested in were his son and the woman who'd given him life.

"How're things going?"

Lost in the moment, in the pain, he hadn't heard her coming back, and looked up. She was a blur, and he blinked to clear his vision. And it was then he realized he'd teared up, looking at this record of all he'd missed.

All he'd lost.

"Oh, Rohan. Don't."

And then she was there, holding him, and he could let go, somehow sure she wouldn't let him fall.

CHAPTER TEN

"IT'S OKAY. IT'S OKAY."

Elise didn't know what else to say to the man trembling in her arms, or how to comfort him. She thought he was crying, but he did so without sound, just the silent, quaking body expressing sorrow and regret.

Because she knew there was no real comfort she could offer.

What he was seeing, what it appeared he mourned, was the past, and the lost chance to be a part of all that was laid out two-dimensionally before him in the albums. To experience what was pictured in real time, as she had.

She remembered the feel of holding Jeevan as a newborn, a baby, a toddler. Remembered the weight of him, the scent, as he went from baby powder sweetness to grubby little boy, to the teenager who wouldn't leave the house without the stinky cologne he favored at the time.

There'd been fights over clothes, about how he wore his pants, and the ugly hat he'd found on sale somewhere and wore until it started to unravel. Strong words exchanged over report cards and inappropriate friends, rumors of him sneaking cigarettes—which he thankfully didn't become addicted to—and the snake she once found in his room.

Elise knew she wouldn't change any of it, although there were parts she would prefer not to relive.

Rohan, she now realized, would give anything to have been there for all of it, and was grieving the inability to do so.

So there really were no words to ease his anguish, or to make it right. All she could do was hang on and try to see him through.

In a way, she'd been where he was, just in a different way.

She was eternally thankful for her sister, Emma, who'd taken her in and held her while she wept for Rohan. Emma had traveled the road of loss with her, encouraging her to think of the future, not just of the past. Perhaps Elise could do the same for Rohan now.

"You can't go back in time, Rohan, but you have a lot to look forward to. I know it hurts to know what you missed, but there's time to start over, to build a relationship with Jeevan, and be happy."

He lifted his head from her shoulder. His eyes were red, and the long, dark lashes damp, and her heart ached for him even more.

This close she could clearly see the fine lines of his scars, noticed for the first time how close to his eye one of them went. Without thought she touched it, thankful the laceration had stopped short, and he hadn't been blinded.

"Were we in love, Elise—back then?"

The truth was hard to admit, but it was the only way to help him move forward.

"Yes, we were. Very much, although I held back as much as I could, too frightened to give in to it completely. You wanted us to make a life together, and we were to discuss how we would move forward after you came back. You said you'd wait and see where I would be doing my residency before looking for a job, because you wanted me to go wherever I wanted, rather than follow you."

His gaze searched hers, and she held it effortlessly, needing him to see she was willing to tell him whatever he wanted to know.

"Was Jeevan planned?" He hesitated a beat, then continued, "I mean, we're both doctors. It's not as though we didn't know where babies come from."

That made her smile, just a little, as she shook her head. "Not planned, but not avoided, either. We were in Algonquin Park, and one of our bags fell out of the canoe and got swept away. My birth control pills were in it, and we both knew the possible consequences but didn't take any other precautions."

It had been, she'd realized long after, the beginning of capitulation on her part, the start of admitting how much she loved him. But she hadn't gotten the chance to tell him, and that, as much as anything else, had intensified her grief.

His gaze turned inward for a moment, then it sharpened back on her, his expression one of regret—sadness.

"I wish I could remember it all. I wish I had been there for you, and for Jeevan. Knowing I can't go back doesn't lessen the regret and the guilt."

"I know." Unable to tame the impulse to touch him, she pressed her palm to his cheek, as she had so many times all those years ago, the nostalgia of it almost too much to bear. "But neither of those will help you now. Look to the future, rather than pining for a past that's long gone."

As if by instinct, he twined his fingers around hers and turned his head to kiss the inside of her wrist. Elise's breath caught in her throat at the tender sensation, so achingly familiar.

When he looked back at her, his eyes were even darker, slumberous, as if he, too, recognized the connection to the past, although she knew he didn't.

Never could.

But before that thought could take root and cause her to pull away, he leaned closer and laid his lips on hers. There was no attempt at mastery or coercion, both of which would have caused her to resist.

Instead, it was a gentle salute, a question and a subtle seduction, all in one. His mouth was firm and warm and intensely exciting, drawing out within her all her desire, the longing she'd been wrestling with all day. And as his lips moved softly over hers, it was like slipping into one of the dreams she still had about him, where they laughed and loved, expressing the passion that had burned so bright between them.

The need to be with him, even just one more time, was too strong to resist. So, instead of drawing away, she looped her arms around his neck and drew him in closer, deepening the kiss.

She wasn't sure how Rohan would react. He had no way of knowing, as she did, how much pleasure they had found in each other before, the perfect way they melded, the satisfaction they could achieve. It wouldn't have surprised her if he had set her aside, think it a step too far.

But he didn't.

And anticipation turned to bliss as he returned her embrace and took over.

Just a kiss. One kiss more, and then I'll stop.

But those were lies he told himself, because he didn't want to stop.

Ever.

And Rohan kept kissing Elise, sinking deeper and deeper in the rushing passion swirling around them.

Sweet. She tasted sweet, the flavor unlike any he'd encountered before, but more intoxicating than twelve-year-old rum.

The sensation of her body against his was almost too sublime to be real.

They fit together perfectly, aligning as though made just for this purpose.

For each other.

For loving.

He shifted, distantly aware of the albums sliding off his lap onto the floor, and urged her to straddle his thighs. Without hesitation she nimbly complied, and he groaned into her mouth as she settled over him. Her nipples pressed into his chest, even through the layers of their clothing, and the crux of her thighs against his erection generated mind-blowing friction.

And still they kissed, mouths slipping against each other, tongues tangling together.

He didn't know how far she wanted to go, or when she'd tell him to stop. All he knew was he would make love to her as much, and for as long, as she'd let him.

When he slid his lips along the line of her jaw, she tipped her head back, offering the long line of her throat, and he didn't hesitate to comply with her silent request. At the first touch of his mouth on her neck she moaned, low and sweet, and shivered, the sensation of her pleasure traveling through her and into his hands.

His fingers moved restlessly against her back, wanting to dip under her clothes, but he was unwilling to take the chance to do anything to make her retreat. With his pulse racing, breath sawing in and out of his chest, he kept nibbling, licking and sucking at her throat, reveling in the passionate sounds she made and the way her hands clutched at his arms.

Elise leaned back so suddenly he was taken by surprise, and his heart missed a beat as he feared she'd had enough. Then she reached down and grasped the hem of her sweater and pulled it off over her head.

Transfixed, Rohan stared at the bounty of her breasts, clad only in a lacy bra, peachy nipples clearly visible under the sheer fabric. His hand trembled as he used his index finger to trace along the curved edge of the cup, and she gasped softly, goose bumps breaking out across her chest and arms. When he dipped beneath the lace and touched one puckered areola, she shivered again, and a rush of color stained her skin, rising up into her throat.

Entranced, Rohan slid his hand across to the other side, repeating the teasing caress. The contrast of his darker skin against her lighter one was sublime, as was the softness of her flesh beneath his finger. Heat rose along his spine and filled his belly as the desire between them flared even hotter.

He was taken by surprise when she reached back and undid her bra, sliding it down her arms so she sat before him bare to her waist.

He wanted to tell her how beautiful she was, how he ached for her, but his voice had deserted him, unable to function in the storm his need created within.

Her hips moved against him, making him groan her name, and when she cupped her breasts, offering them to him, and he bent to take one nipple between his lips, he knew himself lost.

And somewhere at the back of his mind, he hoped never to be found again, if it meant returning to the bleak existence he'd been living just the day before.

There was no way to measure how long he spent lavishing attention on her sensitive flesh. It could have been hours, or minutes. He didn't care. Time had no meaning. All that was important was the way she trembled and moaned, her hands on the back of his head, holding him there.

But then she lifted his head so as to kiss him again, and again, pulling up the back of his shirt, obviously wanting no more barriers between them.

As she broke the kiss to remove it, a cold finger of fear trickled down his spine.

His body wasn't as it had been all those years ago, when she'd first known him. Now it was scarred, pitted with the evidence of the accident and the operations needed to put him back together.

It had never mattered to him before, but now embarrassment made him want to cover himself, so she, who had known him whole, wouldn't see what he'd become.

"Elise…"

But it was too late. Her darkened gaze wandered over his body, and her fingers trailed across his belly, chest and shoulders, seeking and caressing each raised ridge, mark and scar. Just as she had touched his face, tracing the passage of his physical injuries, as though reading them like braille.

When her eyes met his, she must have seen his shame and fear, because her lips, so full and lush from his kisses, lifted into a gentle smile.

"You're still beautiful," she said softly. "And I want you."

Then she slid off his lap to stand in front of him, holding out her hands.

There was a dreamlike quality to the moment, which had him putting all caution aside and standing to take her outstretched hands. Turning, she led him down the corridor and into a dimly lit bedroom, which smelled like her.

Far in the back of his mind were all the worries, the questions arising from what they were doing.

Was she just lost in nostalgia, forgetting the present? Would she compare him to what he used to be, and find him wanting? Or regret this impulsive, passionate encounter? Tomorrow, would she want him gone, because they'd given in to lust instead of being sensible and thinking only of their son and his reactions?

Rohan tried to find the right words to ask all those questions, to find out if she was sure about what they were doing, but Elise turned to pull him close, and everything fled his mind.

Except her.

CHAPTER ELEVEN

DEEP INSIDE, ELISE knew she shouldn't allow herself to fall into fantasy, but it was impossible not to accept and welcome the surreal quality of once more loving Rohan.

She had never tried to forget him over the years, feeling that to do so would be a betrayal of all they'd shared, an insult to him and their son. There had been times when she'd believed it would be best to let his memory fade, like the old photographs in their album, but she could never quite achieve it.

And at night sometimes he came to her in her dreams. Then she would awaken with a familiar ache around her heart, and physical frustration as her companion for the rest of the day.

Even now her head stumbled over the thought of him being alive and in her arms, and she found it simpler to believe it a lucid, arousing figment of her imagination. Not even the sight of his scars brought her back to her senses. Instead, they filled her with tenderness, and gratitude for his survival.

It made it easier to be bold, demanding. To tell and show him what she wanted, and to revel in the perfection of his response and attentions.

Easier, too, to put aside questions and doubts.

This moment might never arise again, and Elise refused to let it pass without making the absolute best of it.

She turned on the lamp beside the bed, wanting to see him, as well as touch. He stood just inside the door, his expression dazed, but the dark fire in his eyes was thrillingly familiar and grew even hotter as she took off the rest of her clothes.

Then she lay on the bed and said, "Aren't you going to undress?"

He didn't reply and didn't take his eyes off her as he swiftly removed what he had on. When the last garment fell away, Elise held out her arms. Without hesitation he came to her, embracing her as though never to let go.

There. There. At last.

She pulled him in as tightly as she could, wrapping arms and legs around him, almost in tears at the feel of being skin to skin with him, as his scent inundated her head. Her heartbeat, already racing, quickened, and her body trembled as jagged shards of arousal fired through her system.

They kissed, and for Elise it was as though the intervening years hadn't existed, the sensations so familiar she was thrown back to the time when she was his love, and he was hers. And she allowed herself to forget the pain and heartbreak, concentrating only on the now and the echoes of then.

It may have been a long time, but she still knew how and where to touch him, the muscle memory intact. Running her fingers down the valley of his spine made him shiver, low sounds of pleasure flowing from his lips into her mouth. And as they shifted, twisting against each other, she found the spot, just beside his hip bone, and made him jerk in reaction.

Yet it was, in a sense, poking the bear, as his previously leisurely lovemaking morphed into a dedicated campaign to drive her wild.

He'd always been a deliberate lover, slow of hands, tender of touch, but now he seemed determined to stretch his caresses out until she lost control. She arched and stretched, mewls of delight and excitement breaking unfettered from her lips as he tasted and explored her, as though intent on learning her body's every secret.

He lingered for a long time over her stomach, his tongue tracing back and forth across her skin, the heat from his mouth making her bow up with the promise of what came next. Opening her eyes, she looked down and watched in rapt fascination, wanting to have a visual memory of the moment.

Then she realized what he was doing, and tears threatened. Beneath the tender, erotic trail were the stretch marks she'd been left with after giving birth to Jeevan.

As though sensing her regard, he lifted his gaze to hers, and in it she saw the same pleasure, desire and sense of loss she felt deep inside. It made the moment sweeter, hotter as his lips drifted lower...

Everything slowed for a moment, and at the first soft touch of his lips between her thighs, she cried out, her need suddenly building, her body tightening. His hold on her grew firmer, his sole focus seeming to take her to the brink of insanity and then ease her back, letting her catch her breath before beginning again.

She heard herself first pleading, then demanding, and then begging for completion. But when it came it was like a lightning strike, taking her by surprise, sending sharp currents of almost unbearable ecstasy over and through her, so she wept at the power.

Shifting up on the bed, he held her until the final

tremors of her orgasm ceased, then he lifted her chin to look deep into her eyes.

"Thank you," he said.

But before she could ask him for what, he was kissing her again, and the swift rise to desire began once more.

This time she wasn't letting him take the lead, and she set about arousing him as thoroughly as he had her. When they were young, he used to like her to take charge whenever she wanted, and it seemed that hadn't changed. He didn't stop her as she rolled him onto his back and began her own form of loving torture.

Finally, he twined his fingers into her hair and gave a gentle tug.

"If you don't stop, I'm going to lose control."

She heard it in his tone, his accent thickening, his already deep voice little more than a growl, and it made her smile. Working her way up his body, she planted kisses at random intervals, watching the goose bumps feather up over his skin, pleased with the effect.

She straddled his thighs, her gaze taking in the ruddy tone staining his cheeks, the tension evident in his posture. Both face and body were different—older, scarred, battered—yet he was still Rohan, her lover.

Her love.

In that moment she made the choice to think of him that way, even though she knew there would be adjustments to be made in the morning, realities to be faced.

It was simpler, since he didn't remember her and didn't have the same battles to fight. She was fine with that—glad of it—and tonight was just for her.

Not for Jeevan, or even for Rohan.

Just for her.

Her last chance to feel young again, and in love. To feel as though the rest of her life stretched before her, too long to contemplate the ending. The way she'd felt the last time they'd been together and hadn't ever since.

She shifted over him, took him deep, gasping at the sublime sensation, lost in the passion and the love flowing in her veins. Lost, perhaps, just a little in the past, too, although she kept her eyes open so she could watch his face tighten, his eyelids droop, as he surrendered to her lovemaking.

Rohan held her hips, helping her rise and fall, letting her set the pace. This time she felt it coming, the orgasm teasing her as it built, making her frantic.

"Elise…"

She knew the sound of her name, said just that way, was a warning. Rohan was close, trying to hold off, for her sake.

He reached between her thighs, his thumb seeking, finding her clitoris, and with a touch, he sent her skyrocketing, and immediately soared with her.

She pitched forward, boneless, onto his chest, and he caught her in his arms. Rolling to one side, he struggled with the sheet and comforter, finally getting it out from under their bums so he could pull it up to cover them.

Neither spoke, and he turned off the light, leaving them in the shifting shadows of moonlight on snow coming in through the drapes. It was a companionable silence, and in it Elise came to peace with what had happened. No regrets. Although it had been mind-blowing, it had also been a one-off.

Being the only one mired in the memories of the love they'd shared, she had no urge to make Rohan feel sorry for her, or as though his relationship with Jeevan was dependent on them being together.

No. Tonight really had been just for her—for sentiment, and for pleasure. For one more sweet memory to savor.

But as she dozed off, sadness crept close, and she turned away from the warmth of Rohan's arms, as though not to get used to the comfort she found in them.

Rohan listened to Elise's breathing deepen as he lay beside her, wide awake and wondering if her turning away was an omen of things to come.

It wouldn't surprise him if it was. He'd seen the struggle she'd gone through today, coming to terms with him being alive, accepting he was—no matter the capacity—back in her life once more.

Who could blame her if sleeping with him was just an impulse born of an emotionally shocking day?

Yet their lovemaking had been more beautiful and heartrending than any he'd experienced before. Holding her had felt right. Touching her had awakened in him instincts—of tenderness and caring—he'd long thought dead. And while it hadn't brought any memories to life, at the same time it was familiar, comfortable. His mind might not recognize her, but his body seemed to, and the intimacy of that had almost undone him.

Once more his thoughts turned to the loss he'd sustained, not of his memories, but of the time he could have shared with this beautiful and remarkable woman. And with his son. The anger at being cheated of a life he was sure would have been more fulfilling and satisfying than the one he'd been living bubbled once more to the surface.

Yet what good could come from yearning for the impossible? He had to accept the night, her lovemaking, as another gift, one he probably wouldn't be given again.

That was a good thing, on the balance. Establishing a relationship with her outside of the parental one left him vulnerable to the kind of pain he never wanted to feel again.

The agony of being a disappointment, of not being the man she thought or hoped he was.

Restless, his anxiety rising, he quietly slipped from the bed and the room, grabbing his pants as he went.

Putting back on the rest of his clothes, he went into the kitchen, stepping over the temporary barrier they'd set up to keep the husky from having free rein of the house. Both dogs looked up at the sound of his entrance, and when he went toward the door, got up to follow him.

Pausing to put on his coat and slip his feet into his boots by the back door, he contemplated whether the husky needed a leash, but decided it would be okay to let her run free. None of the rescue dogs had much experience with wide-open spaces and tended to stick close to what they considered safe territory. Of course, she'd only been here for a few hours, but with the way she closely shadowed Bax, Rohan thought she wouldn't stray far.

The cold air stung his cheeks, and he wrapped his scarf tighter around his neck, aware of the fact he wasn't as warmly dressed as he should be, but the need to be outside was almost primal. Something about the winter night spoke to his soul and eased his anxiety.

While his body continued to hum with pleasure, his mind swung in dizzying circles, thinking about Elise, Jeevan, the past, the future.

He knew without a doubt that there was no future between him and Elise. There would be no encore to the lovemaking. He couldn't afford to open himself up that way. Not when his relationship with Jeevan might be affected.

At one point in the past he'd thought about being a father, yet had never been sure he'd be any good at it.

The aftermath of his accident, the way everyone criticized who he'd become, had made him believe himself unworthy of being a parent.

How do you love, when you can't seem to feel anything too deeply?

Yet, with the revelations of the day, that theory had been blown out of the water.

He was nothing but a mass of emotion right now, and the thought of meeting his son brought equal parts fear and pleasure crashing over him.

The knowledge of all he'd already lost in life was a constant refrain in his head, and he couldn't risk putting himself in a position to lose even more.

His sole focus had to be Jeevan, and making sure the lessons Rohan had learned from his own father showed him what *not* to do, so he could be, at the very least, a decent one.

And being that kind of man didn't include causing pain or disappointment to the child's mother.

Recalling how his father had become increasingly overbearing as time passed, while his mother faded to a kind of quiet shadow in the glare of her husband's bullying, made his stomach clench in disgust. He knew he wasn't like that, but there were myriad ways to hurt and to harm those closest to you.

Then he shook his head, trying to think of the future instead of the past.

Elise deserved better than him—as a lover, or more—but for Jeevan he'd have to find a way to be the best he could be, as a man, so as not to destroy his only chance of a good relationship with his son.

Calling for the dogs, he let them back inside and,

after taking off his outerwear, went back into the living room. He picked up the albums again, losing himself in the pictures.

CHAPTER TWELVE

ELISE AWOKE EARLY on the day before Christmas Eve, her mind too sluggish and slow to bring up the list of her daily chores the way it usually did.

She knew she should get up—there was so much to do—but lay still for a moment more, wondering why everything felt so strange. Slightly askew.

Then it came to her.

She'd had another dream about Rohan making love with her, but this time, instead of feeling bereft and frustrated, she felt happy. Satiated.

Absolutely wonderful.

Then her heart started racing, as she remembered it hadn't been a dream. Rohan was not only alive but here in Banff, and her bed.

Or he had been in her bed.

A quick glance told her he was no longer there, and a rush of disappointment made her sigh.

When had he left? Stretching out her hand, she found the sheets were cold, so she knew he'd been gone for at least a while.

Had he slept beside her? She wished she knew.

Then she forced herself to come back down to earth and leave the fantasyland she was tempted to remain in.

It didn't matter whether he'd slept there or not. In fact,

them making love didn't matter, either, regardless of how magical and special it had been.

She'd recognized how selfish she was being, even while reveling in his touch, and now it was time to let her common sense and parental duty take precedence.

In the cold light of morning, the only matter of importance was breaking the news to Jeevan and giving him and Rohan a chance to develop a good relationship. Well, realistically, any kind of relationship would be a start, but it was up to her to step back—from them both—to give them the leeway to bond.

Elise wasn't naive enough to think it would be easy or happen in a flash. There'd already been one Christmas miracle; no need to be greedy and hope for another.

And there was the rest of her Christmas preparations to consider, she thought, swinging her legs out of bed with a decisive move. As she rose to her feet, she was determined that nothing would change, or be missed, of their traditional festivities, except that Rohan would be there, too.

But that realization had her suddenly plunking back down onto the bed, almost light-headed.

All those years ago, he'd promised to be back for Christmas, and hadn't come. That first year, heartbroken, she'd locked herself away from everyone but her sister and family, unable to bear the thought of Rohan no longer being with her, or able to return.

Then Jeevan had been born, and he'd filled some of the holes left in her heart. Given her a reason to go on.

But Christmas had never been the same.

She'd forced herself to celebrate every year, to give Jeevan the kind of Christmases children dream of, but her heart was never truly in it. Not for herself anyway. Oh, she'd enjoyed them through her son's eyes. His childish wonder had buoyed her spirits, and his laughter salved her wounded soul.

As he'd gotten older, he'd come to expect their holidays together to be mostly the same, and she'd complied, because by then it was tradition. Once they'd gone on a Caribbean cruise, her gift to him when he graduated with his first degree, but they'd agreed that while it was fun, it wasn't really Christmas. Home was where they preferred to be.

After all, she was his family—all there was locally, since Emma, her husband and kids had moved to British Columbia—and he was hers.

Now, after all this time, Rohan had showed up, and Elise had to accept nothing would ever be the same.

Part of her almost wished he'd been to blame for his desertion, so she could flippantly think, *Twenty-seven years late and a dollar short*. But he hadn't been, and for him, finding out he'd had a son whose existence had been kept from him was painful. She'd seen it in his eyes, in his expression, when he was looking at the photographs, and she'd known she wouldn't do anything to hurt him more.

Like give Jeevan a reason not to like him. And Jeevan, being very protective of his mother, would definitely have something to say if he thought they'd slept together and Rohan wasn't serious about the relationship.

And why would Rohan be inclined to be serious?

Sure, their sexual chemistry clearly was still off the charts, but he didn't *care* about her the way she cared about him. Not when he couldn't even remember her—when he couldn't remember the love they had so passionately shared.

Because it had never been just sex between them, all those years ago. Instead, there'd been an instant, mutual connection of their hearts and souls, although it had taken losing him for her to admit it. Having lost so much already in her life, she'd been loath to trust in the longevity of their relationship, and it had taken having Jeevan to prove she could never really love too much.

No matter the potential cost.

Elise remembered what Rohan and she had shared. Too bloody well, really. But there was no way she was going into a new relationship with him, knowing she was the only one capable of having that depth and strength of love rekindled.

Best to keep it friendly and light, and to forget about her romp down memory lane, even if the night together was best described as incendiary, and the chemistry between them combustible.

Decision made, she got up again and set to making the bed, trying to ignore how her stomach flipped and heart raced as Rohan's scent rose from her sheets.

While in the bathroom, she looked out of the window, and in the early morning light saw Rohan walking along the driveway, Baxter and Phoebe following him. For a moment she allowed herself the luxury of watching and remembering the erotic, ecstatic night just gone.

The way he touched her had lit a fire within, and even now, despite knowing it shouldn't be repeated, she felt it smoldering beneath her skin.

Phoebe, who'd been slinking along behind Bax, suddenly paused, head cocked. Baxter stopped, too. The two dogs trotted over to the edge of the driveway, and then jumped over the snowbank to inspect something on the other side.

As Elise reached for her toothbrush, she noticed Rohan look back and realize the dogs weren't following. Of course he strode over to see what had them so interested and, once on the other side of the mound of snow, he stooped down.

What were they all looking at?

Hurrying through her morning routine, Elise pulled on a cozy sweater and pair of jeans and was on her way to the kitchen when she heard the back door open.

"Elise, can you come here a moment, please?"

"I'm here," she replied as she stepped through the door to find him cradling something in his hands. "What is that?"

"A raven. The dogs found it. It's still alive, but just barely."

Drawing closer, she saw the pitiful mound of black feathers cupped in his palm, and all her recent worries faded into the background.

"What do you need?" she asked, even as she was crossing to the utility cupboard to pull out a clean towel. "I have a hot-water bottle we can put it on."

He glanced at her with eyebrows raised. "I see this isn't your first avian rescue."

She snorted, folding the towel. "Nowhere near the first. Jeevan had a knack for finding injured birds and bringing them home. And he has a soft spot for the Corvidae family."

"It looks to be a youngster, probably a yearling," Rohan said, putting the raven gently on the outstretched towel. "And the wing is injured. Where can I put it, so I can examine it better?"

"Use the kitchen table," she replied, already halfway to the hall closet, where the hot water bottle was stored. "I can disinfect it later. And I think we still have a small cage in the garage. I'll go look."

"Could you get my medical bag out of my car, too,

while you're out there?" Rohan had pulled off his jacket and scarf and was rolling up his sleeves.

"Sure."

First, though, she filled the hot-water bottle, and as Rohan lifted the bird, put it between the folds of the towel. To her surprise, the bird was already exhibiting some signs of life, but it wasn't struggling or showing fear, which made her wonder just how badly it was injured. Ravens usually fought to be free and away from humans, even when hurt, but this one was terribly lethargic.

By the time she got back with the cage and bag, Rohan had the raven covered by a drape of the towel, and the bird's dark eyes flickered.

"The poor fellow has a coracoid injury, and he's very thin," Rohan told her as she set his bag next to him.

"Broken?"

"No. From the swelling, it seems to be muscle damage, and it's probably been hurt for a while. I'm going to apply a figure-eight bandage to keep the wing immobilized, but we'll need to get it to a wildlife rehabilitation center. Is there one here?"

"No, I'm afraid not. I think the closest one is in Cochrane, about an hour away."

"I'll take it there, then, once I get it bandaged," he replied. "Rehabbing a bird like this is a full-time job— one I'm not prepared to take on right now."

"Thankfully Jeevan learned that quickly, too," she said. "He'd go and volunteer at the rehab center but knew he didn't have the time to take on too many cases himself. He also realized that we weren't set up to rehab and release, and he's a huge proponent of that, although he's aware not every bird can fend for itself in the wild once injured."

Rohan cut a long length of vet tape, and Elise moved closer to hold the raven while he wrapped the wing against its body. Their fingers brushed, and a shiver fired along her spine, making her breath catch in her chest.

He glanced up and his eyes gleamed for an instant, as though he was remembering the night before, and then the shutters came down, leaving his expression bland and unconcerned.

"Hold it just here," he said, showing her what he needed, his voice cool.

It shouldn't hurt. After all, wasn't she just not long before telling herself it would be better that there was nothing physical between them? She'd even been going over in her head what she'd say to him so he knew there'd be no repeat of their lovemaking.

But his coldness did sting, although she refused to reveal that to him. She would be her usual self, no matter what, and just be glad if he took the onus off her by making the decision not to push for a closer relationship.

As he wrapped the bird's wing against its body, her stomach grumbled, probably annoyed at not even having had a cup of coffee yet, and the corner of Rohan's lips twitched.

"I'm going to make breakfast when we're finished here," she said. "Want some, before you head to Cochrane?"

"That would be great," he replied, his skilled hands making short work of immobilizing the raven's wing. "I'm not sure this little guy is going to survive, so it makes sense to watch him for a little while before making the drive."

They prepared the cage with a liner, and once the bird was ensconced, she washed her hands and poured herself a cup of coffee. Rohan was at the sink, and now that she had a chance to really look at him, she realized he looked tired. Drawn.

"Are you feeling okay?" She used her doctor voice, although it was very much the woman worried about him. But before he could answer, she held up her hand and said, "And don't give me a stock 'I'm okay... I'm fine,' answer either. You look like hell."

He shook his head, brows coming together for an instant. "I'm just tired. I was too keyed up to sleep last night, and spent a few hours going through the pictures."

Was he worried about what had happened between them? He'd been put through the wringer the day before, and she didn't like the idea that their sleeping together was adding to his stress. Although before she'd thought to not say anything unless he brought it up, now she decided it was better out in the open, so it could be resolved, once and for all.

"About last night," she began, making sure to keep her voice clinical. "I let old emotions and nostalgia get the better of me, and I knew, even when it was happening, that it wasn't a good idea. But we're not kids, so let's talk about it and make sure we're on the same page."

"Okay," he said, in a distant, noncommittal tone that set her teeth on edge.

Then he just looked at her, eyebrows raised, as though waiting for her to continue. Tamping down her annoyance and hurt, Elise took a breath and said, "I can't allow my baggage to jeopardize your chance to build a relationship with Jeevan. I know he's an adult, but I think he needs to see us as separate units at this point. We shouldn't muddy the waters by fooling around, making him think, even for a second, that we might get together."

He gave her a long look, while nodding slowly.

"Thank you for the candor, and I think you're right," he said, finally. "It wasn't a good idea."

She'd said it first, so why did his agreement wound her so much? But they'd started down this road and needed to get to the end.

"I think the main things we need to concentrate on are how to tell Jeevan and how to be supportive of his reaction, whatever that may be."

"I agree. Our son has to be our first concern."

He looked away, and she noticed a muscle jumping in his jaw. Realizing he wasn't as calm as he appeared, she reached out without thought and touched his hand.

"It'll be fine. I'm sure of it."

"I'll keep hoping you're right," he replied, his voice cool, as he eased his hand free. "So what's on the agenda for you today?"

She followed his lead, turning to open the fridge, pretending casualness and a deep interest in picking out sausages and eggs. "As soon as I'm finished here, I have to run out to the supermarket, since I need baking supplies, as well as groceries. I'm planning to make all of Jeevan's favorite treats later this morning. Do you think the raven might want to eat? We could try it with an egg."

"Not right now," Rohan replied. "I don't think it's recovered enough for food just yet. And they'll have mealworms at the rescue, which might be better for it at this point."

He walked to the window and stood looking out, rubbing his cheek.

Then he turned back toward her and said, "While you're out shopping, I'll run the raven over to Cochrane, and then go up to Trail's End for a bit. I thought I'd give them a hand, since Janice has more than enough on her plate."

"Okay," she replied, thinking he sounded glad to be getting away. Almost relieved. "By the way, would you like to come to the SAR fundraiser tomorrow night? It's usually a lot of fun. There are silent auctions, and the dinner is catered by a really great company. You could ask Tom about Phoebe then, too."

"What's the dress code? I didn't bring anything but jeans when I came up here."

There it was again, that flatness in his tone, as though he were simply being polite, and not totally engaged in the conversation.

"It's dressier than that. You'd definitely feel out of place in jeans. Most of the men wear suits, or sports coats at least."

He shrugged. "I'll buy something. It's been a while since I bought a new suit, and I know it won't go to waste."

"We can go into town later," she said as she turned on the stove. With everything else going on, she had yet to make out her shopping list. "I need to buy a few gifts."

He walked back to the cage and bent to look at the raven.

Without glancing at her, he said, "I was thinking... I want to get a gift for Jeevan, but I don't want him to think I'm trying to buy his affection, or anything like that. Will you give me some advice on what he might like?"

"Sure," she said lightly. Despite the hurt caused by his renewed coldness, her heart melted at the thought he was putting into how to treat his son. "We'll go out this evening and take a look around the shops. You can get your suit, too, then."

"Excellent," he said.

But although the conversation sounded normal, even

friendly, she saw the way all expression had fallen from his face, and felt the distance between them widening.

And telling herself not to be stupid about it didn't ease the pain.

CHAPTER THIRTEEN

AFTER DROPPING THE raven off in Cochrane, Rohan spent the rest of the morning at Trail's End, checking on the huskies and talking to some of the dogsledders who'd arrived earlier. It wasn't a sport he'd ever been interested in, but speaking to the racers, he found himself intrigued.

When he asked about the chances of Phoebe training as a search and rescue dog, they looked a little skeptical.

"If she were trained from when she was a pup, then maybe, but huskies tend to have high prey drives, and that could be a distraction," one member named Ron said.

"And some are stubborn," his son, Tyler, added. "They don't always obey commands the first time around, and that's imperative in any type of emergency situation."

"She was part of a hoarding situation, and I estimate her to already be over a year old," Rohan replied, somewhat disappointed.

"Well, there was that one guy, in Denmark I think, who was training his dog for SAR, remember, Dad? He was on one of the husky forums, sharing videos and talking about it."

Ron glanced back at Tyler and nodded.

"Yeah, I remember that, but he'd started training him from the time he got him at eight weeks old. It'll probably be very different with an older animal."

"Especially one who only just got a name," Rohan added. "She still doesn't even know it yet. She's smart, though. Where she is now, she's hanging out with a golden retriever, and she follows his cues."

"You should put together a sled team," the father said, but he chuckled as he said it, and Rohan joined in. "And if you're around in the next few days, I'll take you for a ride and teach you a little about the sport."

"Dad, it's Christmas. Dr. Khan's probably spending it with his family. Not everyone's as obsessed as we are."

Rohan was about to say, no, he had no one to spend the holidays with, then it struck him that he actually did.

The reality of it, the sweetness, sank in, making him smile.

"Yes, I'll be pretty busy with family, but maybe when my son comes home, I can bring him with me, if you're still here."

Just saying the words started a warm, silly glow in his chest, and he was grinning like an idiot as he excused himself to answer his phone.

It was Elise.

"Hi, I'm just about to make myself some lunch and wondered if you wanted anything."

There it was again, that feeling of hominess. Of domesticity.

Of rightness.

"I'd love some lunch," he replied, hearing the smile in his own voice.

"Oh," she said, as though surprised. "Well, it'll be ready in fifteen minutes."

"I'll leave here in a short time."

After they hung up, he said goodbye to the sled team and headed for his vehicle.

He knew why Elise had sounded so surprised at his

upbeat tone. When he'd left that morning, he'd been curt and distant.

Elise had talked about the night before with such calm it was infuriating. She'd made it sound as if he was a dress she'd found at the back of her closet and, remembering how much she'd once liked it, wore it one last time, for old times' sake.

Fooling around.

Hearing her classify what they'd shared that way was like having ice water thrown in his face.

While she was perfectly sanguine about it, making love to Elise had opened a floodgate inside him, swamping him emotionally and mentally. Ratchetting the tension inside him tighter and tighter.

Yet she'd been right about the need to think only of Jeevan at this point, and putting much-needed distance between himself and Elise was the wisest thing to do. He had to think of her only as Jeevan's mother and nothing else, no matter how hard that was turning out to do.

The walls around his emotions had taken years to build, and seemingly had fallen in just one day, battered down by a woman he didn't remember, and a son he never knew he had.

During the night, while he looked at the photos, he'd found himself desperately searching for any memory, any hint of Elise, of the connection they'd shared. It was as though his brain insisted that before he could move forward, he had to remember the past.

Not hear about it. Not dissect it, as if it were something outside of himself, but actually *remember*.

The compulsion to search, to keep trying, was driving him crazy, and being around Elise amplified the feeling.

How could he have loved her, made a baby with her,

set out to alienate his family for her, and have no recollection of any of it?

How could she elicit so many feelings in him, and be, in every sense of the word, a stranger?

But when he'd realized he actually had family—one of his own—to spend the holidays with, there was no separation in his mind between her and Jeevan. They were to him a package deal, and he could see no way around it.

And although the thought was terrifying, it also filled him with satisfaction.

That was a dichotomy he wasn't willing to examine. While the sensible part of his mind tried to remind him of the need to be on guard against getting too involved with Elise, other parts of him were saying it was already too late.

When he got back to Elise's place, she was at the stove, making grilled cheese sandwiches. He inhaled the delicious scent of baked goods and eyed with interest the results lined up on the counter to cool.

"I got so caught up in the baking I almost forgot about lunch," she said. "I hope this is okay."

"You could just feed me some of those butter tarts instead," he replied, wanting to keep the conversation light. Spending the morning obsessively going over everything that had happened had been mentally exhausting, and he didn't think he could deal with any more serious conversations.

She sent him a look over her shoulder.

"So you still have a sweet tooth, eh?"

"Definitely," he replied, going to the sink to wash his hands as Baxter and Phoebe wound around his ankles, looking for his attention. He gave them both pets and rubs before squirting soap into his hand. "I think those look terrible, and I should try one of each to make sure they taste okay, before Jeevan has any."

That made her laugh and, when they sat down to eat, it was in a far less weighty atmosphere than the one in which they'd had breakfast.

As they ate, he told her about the conversation he'd had with the dogsled team members, and she told him about her phone call to the hospital.

"Ben's out of the ICU, and in a room, but they're still restricting visitors for the time being."

"Is that normal?" he asked, concerned for the young man's well-being.

She shrugged. "It depends. That could be on doctor's orders, or it could be a family request. If it's the former, they could be just particularly worried about infection, or keeping him undisturbed. He's listed as stable, and being out of ICU makes me a little less worried about his prognosis."

"Before we leave to go shopping, we should check and see if he can have visitors yet."

She nodded. "Sure. I thought we could leave around three, which will give me a chance to finish up what I need to do here."

"So what can I do to help?"

"Untangle the lights for the tree," she said without hesitation. "They're a mess, and I lose patience with them. Every year I promise myself I'll put them away properly, and every year I end up just tossing them in the storage bin."

"Sure," he replied, glad to have something to do. "Should I put them on the tree, as well?"

"That would be amazing. I usually get Jeevan to do it, and then we put the ornaments on together. I thought we could take the boxes out this evening, and if he doesn't make it home tomorrow, you and I can decorate it so it's done when he gets in."

There she went again, making him feel as though this was all normal and he was an integral part of her life—and Jeevan's. Feeling ridiculously pleased, even as he reminded himself not to, he excused himself from the table and, after she said she'd wash their plates, took himself off to do battle with the lights.

Elise set about prepping for the Christmas Day meal, one ear open in case Rohan needed any help, but besides the occasional soft curse, he seemed to be handling the chore without too much fuss.

She shook her head, still trying to adapt to having him around, her wild swings in mood and attitude not helping.

Yesterday morning she'd been filled with rage when she realized he was still alive. That had morphed to sympathy and sadness when she realized the pain his accident had put him through. Traumatic brain injuries often left people floundering to figure out the world again, since the changes they wrought could manifest in a myriad of ways. Alterations in personality and loss of cognitive or physical function, along with long-term issues with fatigue and sensory overload could make patients and their families struggle to cope.

From what she remembered him telling her about his family, and what she'd found out over the past two days, Elise suspected Rohan hadn't had the support and understanding he needed. Yet he'd recovered and moved on with his life so well, and that filled her with admiration.

She didn't find herself grieving anymore for the man he'd been. Instead—far more dangerously—she was beginning to truly like and respect the man he was now.

As well as desire him.

So although she'd achieved her goal of putting a stop to any further amorous encounters with Rohan, it was a hollow victory. Sleeping with him hadn't extinguished her desire, only heightened it.

"Hey," he called from the other room. "Do you think Jeevan would be interested in going dogsledding? The team up at Trail's End invited me to come up and try it out, and when I said I'd be with family, they said I could come up after Christmas, and bring other people with me."

"He might," she said, tamping down a rush of unreasonable annoyance at being excluded. "He's pretty adventurous."

"Like his mother. Would you like to come, too?"

"Perhaps," she said, now exasperated with her own contrariness. Not two seconds ago she was fussing about being left out, and then, in the next moment, she was hiding behind a noncommittal response.

Of course, she wanted to go. Not because she was terribly interested in dogsledding, although it would be fun, but because she really wanted to spend more time with Rohan.

This new, enigmatic Rohan, who seemed set to steal her heart all over again, once more against her will. However, whereas before she'd been afraid of love and abandonment, now she feared the effect on her son, and on Rohan. She never wanted him to think he had to be with her just so as to be able to see his son on a regular basis.

How was she going to manage being around him for the rest of the holidays? Even with Jeevan in attendance, it was going to take everything she had to stay sane and detached.

"Is Jeevan into sports?"

Rohan's question pulled her out of her own thoughts

and made her realize she'd been operating on autopilot, instead of concentrating on what she was doing.

"Watching them or playing?" she called back.

"Either."

She heard the hunger behind the words, the need to start understanding his child, years and years later than he should have done. The pathos of it made her have to stop and catch her breath before she could reply.

"He's pretty athletic, so yes to both, really. He played hockey up until high school, and was pretty good. Used to skateboard and snowboard and, of course, ski. Oh, and he's a mean tennis player. I had to stop playing with him by the time he was in his midteens. It was getting embarrassing."

His soft laughter warmed her aching heart, and she wished she could see Rohan's face so she could know what he was thinking.

She waited for more questions as she worked, but he went silent, leaving her far too much time to think.

On a whim, she'd taken out the album she had of the two of them together, while he was out earlier. She didn't know what she was looking for, or hoped to find, but when she opened the cover tears prickled the backs of her eyes.

The love was there in every picture, every glance, each touch of one body against the next, whether just in the clasping of hands or an arm wrapped tightly around a waist.

On the final page in the album, she found the last picture she had of them together, taken in Toronto on the day before he left to go back to Trinidad. He'd taken her camera and asked a passer-by to take the shot as they stood outside the airport.

"You'll wait for me?"

He'd asked her that question at least twice before he left. While she'd said yes, she'd seen the skepticism in his eyes. She'd made no bones about not believing in love everlasting, but he'd sworn to make her change her mind, even if it took a lifetime.

And he had changed her mind, although not in the way he'd thought. From the first moment she held their son in her arms, she'd understood what it meant to know love that would never falter. Never die.

Of course, she hadn't waited for him for twenty-seven years. But looking at the pictures, she thought perhaps she'd been looking for someone who could make her feel the way he had and had never found that.

He wasn't the same, but she'd so easily stopped looking for signs of the old Rohan and just accepted the new, seeing the essence of the man she'd loved just beneath the cool veneer.

The twenty-seven-year-old Rohan had been supremely self-confident, or at least had given that impression. But she'd seen wariness in his eyes last night when she'd taken off his shirt, revealing the heartrending signs of what he'd been through. Had the accident knocked some of that bravado away, leaving him vulnerable in ways she'd never seen him be in the past?

How else had it changed him, deep inside?

And with all he'd been through the last day and a half, how was he truly coping?

She knew what the long-term effects of traumatic brain injuries could be. What emotional toll had yesterday's events taken on Rohan? Had what she'd seen as cold stoicism been a defense mechanism against feelings he didn't know how to handle or his brain wouldn't let him process properly?

If that were the case, was there anything she could do about it?

Or would he resent her for even trying?

"Hey, Elise," he called from the other room. "Do you have a knife, or a hand grenade?"

Laughter burst from her throat before she could stop it, and glad to have the tension ratcheting inside relieved, she grabbed a towel to wipe her hands, and headed into the living room.

"Don't go blowing up the house, Rohan."

"Well, it seems like a good option," he said, looking up as she entered the room. "Or I could buy new lights so I don't lose what's left of my mind trying to untangle this mess."

Her heart did a flip as her gaze met his laughing one, and it took all her power to not bend and kiss his smiling lips.

So instead, she frowned ferociously and plopped down beside him, holding out her hand.

"Give it here. I'll do it."

"Oh no," he said, moving it out of her reach. "*We* can do it, together."

CHAPTER FOURTEEN

HIS WORDS STAYED with her the rest of the afternoon, and although she tried not to dwell on them, she thought of them each time she looked at Rohan.

She was seeing him differently, she realized, as they walked to her truck to go into Banff. Before she'd been caught up in seeing the shadows and reflections of the young man she'd known. Now she saw the man he'd become and had no interest in comparing the two.

Not anymore.

Here was someone who'd weathered adversity, been blindsided by life when he'd least expected it, and somehow refused to break.

And she knew it was a struggle for him—had seen it for herself. Yet he kept it all together, and even though she had dropped the bombshell on him, raking up matters he no doubt would have preferred to stay in the past, he could smile and laugh, be silly with her.

She'd seen his outer scars and glimpsed his inner ones, but none of them held him back from accepting the idea of having a son. Indeed, he'd done so without protest, which was another mark in his favor.

Since Ben still wasn't allowed visitors, they went straight to the Banff Avenue shopping area.

It was ablaze with lights, which glinted off the snow

even in the waning afternoon light, and festive decorations hung from every streetlamp and in all the store windows. Carolers, dressed like something out of a Dickens novel, walked among the shoppers, stopping periodically to serenade them.

"I know you said Christmas isn't your thing, and this is as festive as it gets," she told him as they strolled along. "But this is where the shopping is best. There's a suit store right over there."

"I'm actually enjoying this Christmas," he said, his voice casual. "For the first time in a very long time."

She didn't reply, as a wave of pleasure engulfed her, causing a lump in her throat.

At the clothing store, the sales woman was happy to help Rohan find a suit he liked, and that fit without needing alterations.

A little too happy, in Elise's estimation.

"This one is perfect," she all but purred, rubbing her hands across his shoulders from behind. "And the color really goes well with your skin tone."

Rohan turned to Elise, who was sitting on the sidelines, trying to appear unconcerned and hide her annoyance at the saleslady's over-the-top, touchy-feely pitch.

"What do you think?" he asked, raising his eyebrows. "Like it?"

"You look great," she said.

In reality, he looked fantastic.

Scrumptious.

Everything the saleslady said was true, but Elise knew firsthand exactly how the body beneath the fabric looked, and could see just how the navy-blue suit emphasized its best attributes. The jacket hung beautifully from his broad shoulders, and the dress pants did nothing to obscure his lean hips and wonderfully muscled thighs.

Just looking at him made her mouth water.

He'd picked out a light blue dress shirt and a blue tie with discreet red stripes, while a pair of black dress shoes completed the outfit.

The effect was both distinguished and sexy, and Elise realized how proud she was going to be, walking into the dinner with him the following night. Thank goodness she'd bought herself a new dress last week, instead of planning to trot out one of her "old faithfuls."

"I'll take it all," he told the beaming saleswoman.

Once they were back out on the main road, they took their time looking in the shop windows they passed.

Suddenly, Rohan paused in front of a gallery and said, "I want to go in here."

When she followed him in and saw what had caught his eye, she couldn't help smiling.

It was a small, stylized painting of a blue jay, done by a local artist whose name Elise recognized.

Rohan turned a questioning gaze her way. "Do you think Jeevan would like this?"

"I'm sure he'd love it," she replied, getting a little misty-eyed. "That's one of his favorite local artists, but he only has some prints, not an original."

Rohan immediately picked it up. "Plus, you said he likes corvids, right?"

"Right," she agreed as he went toward the cash register.

"Would you like this wrapped?" the gentleman manning the store asked.

"Yes, please," Rohan replied, adding, "It's for my son, and I would hate for it to get damaged."

Elise turned away so he wouldn't see how touched she was, how much his words meant to her.

And how much she wanted him, right then.

Not just in a sexual way, but in every way she could think of. She could try to tell herself it was just echoes of love long gone that made her feel this way, but she already knew that wasn't true.

When she first fell for him, it was because of his sunny, winning disposition, his humor, along with his handsome face and young, fit body. While they'd had serious conversations, it was his open personality and the unfettered joy of him she remembered best.

He was still handsome despite his scars, and kept himself in good shape, but in many other ways he'd changed completely. There were flashes of humor now, not the constant smiling banter she'd so enjoyed. And he kept most of his thoughts and emotions to himself, when before they'd been freely shared, or visible in his expression.

Yet that didn't stop her from wanting him, just the way he was.

By the time the gift was wrapped, she had herself back under control, after a stern reminder that this wasn't about them, and Jeevan was their main—only—concern.

Outside, he looked up at the dark, cloudless sky and remarked, "It's gotten colder. How about a coffee or hot chocolate, before we continue on?"

"Sure."

They waited for a horse-drawn carriage to pass, before crossing the busy street toward a café. As they stepped up on the sidewalk on the other side, a commotion broke out a few meters away.

"Hey, watch where you're going!"

"Mama? Mama?"

"Are you all right?"

"I think she's probably drunk."

At the cacophony of voices, Elise instinctively turned

to see a young woman stagger to one side, putting out her hand to stop her momentum and steady herself against the building. It didn't help, as she lost her footing, going down in a heap.

A little girl standing nearby screamed, "Mama!" and rushed toward the fallen woman.

Elise was moving before she'd even thought about it, aware of Rohan coming up just behind. Getting to the woman, Elise parted the gathering crowd and said, "I'm a doctor. Let me through."

By the time she went down on her knees beside the woman, Rohan was coaxing away the little girl, who was crying for her mother.

Cursing the lack of her medical bag, Elise began her examination, although the woman weakly flailed with her right arm, as if trying to push her away, and mumbled unintelligibly.

"I'm calling an ambulance," Rohan said, his voice calm, controlled.

The woman's mumbling got louder, but Elise couldn't make out the words. She took her pulse, finding it rapid; the patient's breathing was shallow. Fear radiated from her eyes, which blinked and flickered as though she was having a hard time focusing.

And Elise saw a marked difference in her eyelids: the left one was drooping.

Perhaps an aneurysm or a stroke?

"It's okay," she said. Keeping the patient calm was imperative. There wasn't anything she could do out here on the sidewalk. They had to get her to a hospital ASAP. "Your daughter is safe, and I'm a doctor. Let me take care of you."

"Take my coat." Rohan handed it down, adding, "Ambulance is on the way."

Elise put Rohan's coat over the other woman, then held her hand, straining to hear the sound of sirens and heaving a sigh of relief when she heard them approaching.

"We're going to get you fixed up, okay?"

The chilled fingers squeezed slightly around Elise's, just as the emergency vehicle pulled up.

Looking up while digging her car keys out of her pocket, she said to Rohan, "I'm going to the hospital with her. Meet me there."

"Will do," he replied, still calm, the little girl now safely ensconced in his arms, her head on his shoulder, thumb in mouth. Bending, he took the keys from her hand. "You go and get her through this."

And somehow, the way he said it, with assurance of her abilities, made her feel like a million dollars.

Rohan had to hand the little girl, who'd told him her name was Brenna, over to the two police officers that attended on the scene, but Brenna wasn't happy about it.

The cops weren't happy, either, when the little girl started to wail.

"I'll come to the hospital," Rohan told her as she reached out her arms to him, after one of the officers had taken her from him.

"There's no need for that, sir," the other officer told him, sounding stern. "We'll take care of her until a relative can be found."

"I have to go there anyway," he responded. "I was shopping with Dr. van Hagan and I have to pick her up from the hospital."

Hearing Elise's name made them relax, and neither objected again when he told Brenna he'd see her in a few minutes.

He hurried back to the truck and stowed the packages on the back seat. Suddenly realizing he didn't know where the hospital was, he had to take a moment to look it up with his GPS. Then, with the tinny voice giving him directions, he made his way there.

Going in through the front entrance, he paused, looking at the signs, trying to figure out where the emergency room waiting area was located. Following the arrows, he was about to make his way down a corridor when he spotted the gift shop.

Brenna was so scared. Maybe a stuffed toy or a book would make her feel a little bit better?

He went in and chose a virulently pink bunny and a picture book, after asking the lady at the register what would be appropriate for a three-year-old, which was his estimate of the little one's age.

Setting off, he took the corridor indicated, but soon realized he must have missed a turn. He'd just turned back when, from behind him, a voice said, "Jeevan! You're home early!"

But it was only when he felt a hand on his arm that he registered the woman dressed in scrubs was actually talking to him.

"I'm sorry," he said. "You've got the wrong person."

"Oh," she replied, looking both startled and chagrined, her gaze searching his face intently for an instant. "I'm so sorry. I thought you were someone else. Can I help you?"

As he walked away a moment later with the directions to where he needed to be, the knowledge of being a father struck him in a way it hadn't before.

Oh, he'd believed it, but until that nurse or doctor had mistaken him for his son, he'd thought of it in an almost academic way.

At one time, he and Elise van Hagan had been intimate, and that coupling had produced a child—Jeevan.

One plus one equaled two.

Nothing truly surprising about that, and because Rohan remembered nothing of his son's conceiving, Jeevan hadn't actually seemed real. Not even when he looked at the photographs, or heard Elise speak so lovingly of him.

But somehow, having the woman mistake him for his son brought the entire situation to life in a new way. Took it from the theoretical and made it completely, heartachingly factual.

It felt as though he were walking on air the entire way down to urgent care.

I'm a father. And my son looks like me.

As he was approaching the door to the waiting area, Elise came through another one farther down the hallway, and he went over to her.

"How is the patient doing?"

"She's holding her own, but I've called for a specialist."

"Elise. Rohan."

Hearing their names, they turned in unison to see Janice approaching from the opposite direction. She hugged them both, one after the other, as she got to them.

"How's Ben?" Elise asked.

"He's doing all right. Awake now after brain surgery and an operation to pin his leg. They've transferred him out of ICU into a room, and I just popped over to the cafeteria for a bite to eat." She smiled, but it didn't reach her tired, worried eyes. "He's not talking yet, but that's probably the effects of the anesthetic. Although the doctors keep talking about cognitive impairment, I'm sure he'll be fine. He'll be out of the hospital in no time."

The determination in her voice as she averred her son would recover worried him. He didn't want to frighten her, but at the same time, it was a situation too close to his own to let it pass.

"I'm sure he will, too," Rohan said gently. "But it might take some time."

"No, no." Her hand waved, as though telling him to go away. "Ben's strong. He'll be fighting fit before we know it."

"I hope you're right. But head trauma can be tricky and take a while to heal." He found he'd raised his hand to his face and was tempted to drop it, but instead he lifted it higher, to the rear of his skull. "I know that from personal experience. And I know how frustrating it can be to be unable to rise to other people's expectations, when you're trying your best."

Janice's gaze searched his, and she nodded as tears filled her eyes.

There was nothing to do but put his arm around her shoulder and let her lean her forehead on his chest as she cried, probably for the first time since they'd got Ben out of the destroyed barn.

Looking over her head, he met Elise's gaze and found there an expression of such warmth that he had to look away. The conversation left him feeling exposed, vulnerable. He didn't want Elise's sympathy. In fact, he would go so far as to say that it was the last thing on earth he wanted.

But what she seemed to offer was understanding, and it almost undid him.

"Here," Elise said, thrusting some facial tissue into Janice's hand.

"Thank you." Janice stepped away, looking a little ashamed. "I'm sorry for crying all over you like that, Rohan."

"You've had a long, stressful day," he said, then cleared his throat. "It's fine."

"I need to get back to Ben, but I'll remember what you said." She straightened her back, as though getting ready to do battle, but her lower lip quivered. "As a parent, sometimes you want the best for your child so badly that you push too hard, but I'll remember not to make Ben feel inadequate if he doesn't recover as quickly as I hope."

"That's the best thing to do for him, I think. Let him recover in his own time and support him as he does."

"I will," she said, giving them both quick hugs before heading for the elevators.

"That was good advice," Elise told him, her gaze warm, but probing.

"I hope she takes it," he admitted, knowing he was laying a painful part of his soul bare to her, and not caring anymore. "Or she could do more harm to Ben than good."

Someone popped their head out of a door and called for Elise.

"I have to go," she said before giving him the most heart-twisting smile and then hurrying off.

CHAPTER FIFTEEN

ELISE CAME OUT of the cubicle where her patient was, about ten minutes after she'd seen Rohan in the corridor. A glance into the emergency waiting area, to see where he was, had her heart aching with a combination of wonder and sorrow.

The patient's daughter, who was maybe two or three years old, was sitting sandwiched between Rohan and a police officer. She was clutching the rabbit she'd seen in Rohan's hand earlier, and the two men on either side of her were taking turns reading from the book perched on her lap.

That was the kind of father Rohan would have been to Jeevan: kind, gentle, willing to be involved. Knowing they'd both missed that opportunity was heartbreaking.

"That's your patient's daughter," a nurse said, following Elise's gaze. "Those two calmed her down and the man on her left even bought her that stuffie from the shop. They've been keeping her entertained while we try to figure out where the family is staying. She doesn't know the name of the hotel, but she did say her father is here with them."

Of course, Elise already knew most of that, but she made the nurse none the wiser.

"No sign of a room keycard in Mom's purse?"

"No, and her phone has one of those manual locks on the screen, where you have to know which pattern to draw before it'll let you in. I have one of the NAs calling the hotels, but it might take a while."

"Mom's had a minor stroke," Elise said. "And I've called for a neurosurgeon to consult, so we need to find Dad ASAP."

"We're doing our best," the nurse advised.

"I'll see if I can find out anything useful from the daughter," Elise said as the nurse hurried away.

Taking a deep breath, Elise made her way over to the little group, and she almost faltered when Rohan looked up and saw her—and smiled.

It was the kind of smile that was almost a grin, and did all kinds of crazy things to her body and her heart. Once more, in an inappropriate place, she wanted to grab him and kiss him.

Ignoring her reactions was almost impossible, but she had to put them aside.

Until later, at least.

Stooping down in front of the little girl, she said, "Hi, I'm Elise. What's your name?"

"Brenna," the little one replied. "Wanna read my book wif me?"

"I'd like that, but maybe later, okay?" Elise smiled, glad the men had already put Brenna at ease, which would make asking her questions that much simpler. "But first, can you tell me what you, your mom and dad have done since you got here?"

Brenna scrunched her forehead and then said, "We played in the snow and petted the aminals. There was a donkey and some goats and a bunny like mine." She held up the object in question. "But the bunny was white, not pink."

"The George's Inn, out by Chester Road, has an indoor petting zoo," the policeman said quietly. "I've taken my kids out there a time or two."

Elise nodded. She'd come to the same conclusion, too, when Brenna spoke. She got up and touched the little girl's hair. "I'll get them to try there. Thank you, Brenna."

But even while she was giving instructions for someone to call the inn, it was the image of Rohan reading to Brenna and the beauty of his smile that stuck in Elise's mind.

The smile, in particular, had thrown her system into overdrive. There was something different about it, but she couldn't put her finger on what the difference had been.

All she knew was that it had set her senses on fire and made the wanting she'd been fighting all day almost impossible to subdue.

But they'd agreed that Jeevan had to come first, and their relationship, whatever it became, was far lower on the list of priorities. Some might say Jeevan was a grown man and should be able to handle anything that came along, but Elise refused to put him in a position to have to choose between his parents.

He was, and had to continue to be, her first consideration.

Nothing else could be allowed to matter.

Not Rohan, who increasingly took up more of her headspace than was wise and had the ability to turn her inside out with a look, a word, a shared confidence.

And not her own selfish desires.

"I found him, Dr. van Hagan." The NA put down the phone. "Mrs. Pilar's husband is on his way here."

"Excellent," she said, gathering up her chart and heading back to the cubicle to check on the patient. "Please call upstairs and ask for an ETA for the neurosurgeon."

But she couldn't resist one more glance into the waiting room, and could only smile, heart melting, at the sight of Rohan holding the shocking pink bunny and pretending it was reading.

And once more she experienced a wave of anger as she realized all she and Jeevan had lost, the day Rohan went back to Trinidad.

But that was dangerous, too, she knew, because there was no way to go back and change the past, and to hanker for something that never was, and never could be, was unhealthy.

Best to be thankful for the present and not wish for anything more than what she already had.

With that bracing yet somehow depressing thought, she hurried back to her patient.

By the time Elise handed off Mrs. Pilar to the incoming doctor and neurosurgeon, Brenna's father had arrived, and Rohan was released from his babysitting job.

Brenna hugged him tight as her father thanked him, over and over, and Rohan just said it was fine.

The truth was, though, interacting with Brenna had been a joy, not a chore, and had made him happy and sad in turns. It had made him think that perhaps he might have been a decent father to a child that age, although he completely understood spending a couple of hours with her wasn't really a good indication.

He was still on a high from being confused for Jeevan at the hospital, too. Although to anyone else it might seem silly, for him it was a true turning point. Yet part of him hesitated to share the moment with Elise, wanting to hug it to himself a little longer.

As he and Elise walked to the pickup, she said, "Thanks for sitting with Brenna." Her smile just increased his sense of well-being. "She must have been so scared."

"She was, and the police officer was doing his best to console her, but it wasn't working."

They got into her truck and were fastening their seat belts. Elise's smile softened into something so sweet, so glorious he couldn't help staring. Staring and wanting.

He wanted to kiss it off her lips, feel her mouth go from smiling to passion-filled.

Dragging his eyes away from her face, he fumbled with the buckle, getting it latched just as she put the vehicle into gear.

"The bunny and book were masterstrokes. Which female can resist something soft and fuzzy, and having two men cater to her?"

He tried to laugh, but it was a rusty sound, roughened by his lust for the woman beside him.

Stop it. Behave. That's not what any of this is about.

But the self-chastisement did nothing to tamp down his desire. Only the habits and control of years kept his hands unmoving on his lap, and his mind firmly on the conversation.

"Will her mother be okay?"

"I can't discuss the specifics with you, but I think in time she will."

She sounded grim, and he wondered what had happened.

"Can you at least tell me if it were a substance abuse issue or physical disease?"

She sent him a sidelong look, then sighed. "Disease."

Probably neurological then, or perhaps a diabetic episode. Whatever it was, Rohan was glad that sweet little girl's mother hadn't been drunk or on drugs.

"Home now, I think, to get something to eat," she said. "I'm getting hungry again."

"Why don't we get some dinner here in Banff?" She'd been busy all day, and he didn't like the thought of her going home and having to cook.

"It might be hard to find somewhere that isn't full, although… There's one place that might find us a table."

He wondered at her hesitation but realized the source when they got to the small restaurant, which was full, and the hostess came out from behind her podium.

"Dr. van Hagan, welcome! It's been ages. Dad will be so happy to see you."

She immediately led them to a secluded table, chattering away about her family. Not long after she left to get their drinks, a gentleman in a chef's uniform came out of the kitchen and made a beeline for them.

"Dr. Elise." When she got up to greet him, she was enveloped in a huge hug. "This lady saved my son's life," he said, loud enough for some nearby patrons to hear.

Elise blushed and tried to downplay it.

"It was a team effort, Mr. Kitterly."

But he was having none of it.

"If you weren't there, on the slopes where you found him, he wouldn't have made it. The surgeons told me so."

By the time he left to go back to the kitchen, Elise was beet red.

"His son was an excellent skier," she said, grabbing her menu and not meeting Rohan's gaze. "Was a world-class athlete before his accident. It's such a shame."

"You did a lot of good in SAR. Why are you embarrassed when people acknowledge that?"

"I didn't do it for the accolades," she said, adding a little huff for good measure.

"Why did you do it?" he asked, keeping his voice gentle.

She sighed and put down the menu. "It was actually all I ever wanted to do, from the time I was a little girl and saw a documentary about a SAR team. But like I said, my mom talked me out of it because she didn't think I could make a living if that was all I did."

Rohan considered that for a moment, waiting until a waiter had brought their drinks and left again. Then he said, "It's a shame you decided to give it up. I know your capabilities, firsthand, even after you've been away from it for a year."

He saw the anguish in her eyes as she leaned forward to say, "But even yesterday, I froze. That can't happen during a rescue."

"But it did," he said, mildly. "Then you unfroze and continued on, rescuing a young man who might have died if you hadn't acted as decisively as you did, and saving a dog's life, too. Even though you must have been terrified, you got the job done."

She stared at him, eyes wide and luminous, and his breath caught in his throat at her beauty.

When he could speak again, he said, "I think it was Nelson Mandela who said, 'Courage is not the absence of fear, but the triumph over it.' You've triumphed, and I think you would again, if you wanted to."

"Like you did," she said, taking him off guard at the swift change of subject.

"What do you mean?"

"I heard what you told Janice this evening, and I remember the things you said about your family when we were young. I can only assume you didn't get the support and understanding you needed after your accident. Not everyone would be able to thrive the way you have, after going through all that."

"Thrive?" He would laugh, but the bitterness surrounding the subject made it stick in his throat. "I don't know that what I've been doing over the last few years could be categorized that way."

Just then the waiter came back, and they ordered, Rohan choosing quickly, since he'd hardly looked at the menu. He was hoping once the young man was gone, Elise would change the subject, but she went right back to their prior discussion.

"You don't consider being a partner in a business, doing what you've always loved, as thriving?"

"Maybe on a materialistic level," he said, even as he wondered why he was compelled to speak so frankly about it. "But socially, I've distanced myself. My coping mechanisms aren't very…friendly. When I'm having a hard time, I retreat. Hide in my head. It destroyed my marriage, because Suvarna couldn't deal with it."

She nodded, the sympathy in her eyes almost more than he could stand. He never talked about it, but somehow he wanted—*needed*—her to understand.

"I would have liked to give her what she wished for, but my remoteness, the wall between me and the world, which included her, was just too large. I couldn't connect emotionally, and the harder she pushed the further I stepped back. If I feel as though things are out of my control, or if I'm stressed, I back all the way up until I can regroup."

"I've noticed that. But at the same time, you pull yourself out of it and start communicating when you're ready." She smiled slightly, her gaze warm on his. "That's the important part, isn't it?"

"Is it?" he rebutted, his chest aching. "I want to connect with my son, not shut him out if he asks the hard questions."

"Just…be you," she answered quickly. "He isn't a child

without any experience of the world. Don't pretend to be anything you're not comfortable with, and he'll accept you as you are."

"How do you know that?" he asked, with fierce swiftness. "How can you know how he'll react?"

She took a deep breath.

"Because he already loves you, even though he thinks you're deceased. I raised him to. I wanted him to know who his father was, and what a good man he was. Jeevan will accept that you're older, maybe a little sterner than I described you. But from his perspective, the emotion is already implanted. All you have to do is accept it."

Rohan froze, his fingers clenched so fiercely together they began to ache. Elise put her hand over his, and the warmth that flowed between them made his chest tighten with a mixture of pleasure and pain.

"How could I have forgotten you, Elise? Loved you and then wiped the memory from existence?"

He hadn't meant to ask, but the words were out before he could stop them. She shrugged, and although there was a hint of sorrow in her eyes, she looked serene, at peace.

"That wasn't your fault, Rohan. The brain is a complex organ, and no matter how hard you try, once the damage is done, it's rare it can ever be reversed. Just… put that aside as something we have to accept and move forward from."

"We?" He shot the question at her, not angrily but in surprise.

"Yes, *we*. Don't you think I've been struggling to deal with that, too? It hurts, deep down, that you didn't know me, have no recollection of the time we spent together. But I know it wasn't willful on your part, that it was a side effect of an event that still haunts you, and I'm coming to terms with it. You've had longer to accept it, but I get the feeling you never have."

He looked away, letting his gaze roam the room, seeking some modicum of calm before facing her again.

"I avoided thinking about it, for a long time. When the internet became more accessible, I was still trying to figure out where I was, and what I was doing during those lost months. I contacted old schoolmates, friends I hadn't seen in years, and asked them if they knew. When no one seemed able to give me an answer, I think I decided I'd never know."

He paused, shook his head. "But the hole—the gap—in my memory banks was a constant ache, one I've never been able to soothe. And now it hurts even more, because I know if I could find the piece of my memory that's missing, it would have you in it. You, and your love, and the joy we shared together."

Now it was she who looked down, as though hiding. It popped into his head to say that perhaps they could find that love and joy again, but he bit the words back, frightened by the impulse.

Hearing her admit she was struggling with his amnesia, too, somehow made his own fight a little more bearable, and the whole situation sadder.

While he was oblivious to the emotional nuances, she would remember everything. All the little gestures, the inside jokes, the patterns they'd formed together. After all these years he knew she didn't still love him the way she had. To think she might would be ludicrous. Yet no doubt some of the old emotions would linger, causing her additional hurt.

And causing her to make love with him, as she had the night before.

But he couldn't afford to think about that, since she'd made it clear a repeat wasn't in the cards.

So he was relieved when the waiter approached with their food and put an end to the conversation.

CHAPTER SIXTEEN

WHEN THEY LEFT the restaurant, they were both quiet, lost in their own thoughts, and Elise decided not to pursue any deep conversation again.

She felt raw, ragged around the edges, and unable to cope.

It had become clear to her as they spoke that she was falling for Rohan again, and she didn't know what to do. What she really wanted was time to think, but with Jeevan hopefully on his way home and Rohan staying at her house, there really wasn't any. Not the kind of solid alone time she needed.

When they got to the house, it was too early to go to sleep, so she said, "Want to play some cribbage?"

He smiled, but it was just a tiny upturn of his lips. "I haven't played in years, but sure."

Playing cards was definitely preferable to getting back to their discussion.

She lit the fire, and they set up the cribbage board on the hearth rug. Rohan seemed lost in thought, and because he wasn't concentrating, she beat him around the board the first time, and when he called for a rematch, she beat him again.

The nice thing was that as they played, they talked. Not about heavy subjects like amnesia or surprise parenthood, but about their lives and jobs, where they'd worked, and how they'd ended up where they were.

"I would have pegged you more for a Toronto type of guy," she said, being honest. "You used to love the city."

He shrugged. "I started out there when I first moved back, but just found myself drifting farther and farther west. When I got to Calgary, it felt good, so that's where I've been for about eight years."

"I moved here from there about twelve years ago, when my sister and her husband went to Vancouver. I wanted to try my hand at search and rescue, and this was a great place to volunteer."

Simple, easy conversation, but the entire time she was so aware of his every move, gesture and breath. There was something compelling about him that she found almost irresistible.

Before they started a third match, she went into the kitchen and came back with a plate of Christmas treats.

"Oh," he all but groaned with delight. "Those look delicious."

She grinned. "Just a few lemon squares, Nanaimo bars and butter tarts to tempt you."

He took a bite of a butter tart and closed his eyes as though in ecstasy.

After he swallowed, he said, "I just remembered, someone at the hospital mistook me for Jeevan from behind."

Elise watched his expression and asked, "What did you do?"

He shrugged as his hand hovered over the plate, while he decided between a lemon square and a Nanaimo bar.

"Told her she was mistaken. But I have to admit, it brought everything home to me in a way just talking about him hadn't."

She didn't want to go back to serious conversation, she was having way too much fun just chatting and laughing with Rohan. It was, in many ways, just like the old days, although she didn't want to tell him that, in case the reminder of his amnesia caused a resurgence of his stress.

But there was something bothering her, and she vacillated between saying something and letting it lie. He'd spoken with such sadness about his experiences with his family after the accident, and she remembered how upset he'd been when he discovered how his father and Chandi had acted.

That kind of anger ate away at you, and she hated the thought of him carrying it in his heart.

As they finished the third cribbage match, she said, "Are you still angry about what happened all those years ago?"

"How can you ask me that?" He gave her a fierce glare. "Of course I am."

She held his gaze, feeling his pain and sympathizing.

"I think," she said slowly, "you should forgive your family."

The look he gave her could have felled an oak, but she didn't look away, refusing to back down.

"What they did was unforgivable."

He said it with such finality she almost gave up. But at the same time, she knew she couldn't.

"True," she agreed. "Do it anyway. For your sake and Jeevan's. Don't you think he's going to want to meet your side of his family at some point?"

"Yes, but—"

"What are you going to do if you take him to meet them? Cherry-pick who he gets to talk to, and who gets greeted with a glare?" She shook her head and continued softly, "When this all sinks in, he'll have anger enough of his own to deal with, don't you think? Why add yours on top of it?"

"He has a right to be angry. We do, too. Aren't you angry, Elise?"

"Sure." She fiddled with the cribbage pegs, trying to find the right words, giving her hands something to do to stop them from reaching for him. She wanted so badly to touch him, hold him so as to ease his agony, but she didn't dare. Her emotions were too close to the surface, her desire for him too strong.

"Part of me is livid about the entire situation. But realistically, none of that anger will give me back any of what I'm upset about losing. It won't let Jeevan have his father growing up, or give me back a minute with you, or stop you from being in the accident. So what's the use of holding on to it and letting it rule my life? Worse, why pass it on to Jeevan?"

"You can forgive my father and Chandi, and just move on?" He shook his head. "That's crazy. I can't do it."

It came back to her, in one of those full-circle moments life occasionally tosses up. She looked over at him to say, "I'll tell you what you once told me: 'I don't know what forces in his life caused your father to act the way he did, but sometimes you have to accept people are the way they are, and there's nothing you can do about it.'"

He'd been lounging on his side, one hand propping up his head, but now he sat up, curiosity sharpening his gaze.

"When did I say that?"

"After I told you about my father abandoning us when I was small, and never looking back once he left."

She took a deep breath, trying to hold on to her composure. "When we met, my mother had only been dead for a few years, and I was still grieving. You asked me about my father, and I told you he'd taken off when I was eight. What you said to me that night helped me realize I really didn't know the full story, so a few years later, Emma and I did some research. We couldn't find our father, but we located a sister of his, and she explained that our father had mental health issues since he was a child. Medication would help for a while, and then either stop having any efficacy or he'd come off it, thinking he was cured.

"She hadn't seen him in decades. He'd just taken off one day, and none of his family heard from him again, just like what had happened with us. We all figure that his need to disappear is part of the pathology of his disease, but that doesn't make it any easier to deal with, especially when I don't know what ultimately happened to him."

"I'm sorry for all you and your sister went through." He brushed the back of her hand with his, and the jolt of electricity she felt up her arm was way beyond what she should, with such a gentle touch.

"I didn't tell you that to get sympathy. I told you so you'd understand how hard it was for me when I thought you'd died. It was like being abandoned all over again, and I grieved like any one would, including getting angry with you. But the truth was, you were the father of my child, and I had to forgive you so I could raise him to be proud of who he is, and where he came from. I could have poisoned him against you with my grief and anger, but I refused to do that. Don't poison him against your family with yours."

He looked into the fire as though unable to meet her gaze a moment more, and he shook his head but said, "I'll think about it, but I can't promise I'll be as magnanimous as you are."

And with that she had to be content.

* * *

Rohan watched Elise get up, her fluid movements reminding him of her strength and flexibility. Remembering other ways those attributes had been displayed caused a rush of heat up his spine, and he turned his gaze back to the fire, to hide the desire he was sure was reflected in his eyes.

As she walked around the room and turned on the Christmas lights, which they hadn't bothered with before, she said, "I'm going to make some tea. Do you want some? Or coffee?"

Getting himself under control, he turned to her with a smile. "Coffee would be great, thank you."

He was starting to understand her, he realized, watching with frank appreciation the swing of her hips as she went out the door. After one of these deep, uncomfortable conversations, she wanted to get up and move. Find something to do. Be active, even in a small way. As if by doing so she was able to release some of the stress or digest all that had been said.

God, he was lucky to have her as the mother of his child.

Somehow she'd been able to shelve her own pain and anger and raise Jeevan to love a man he'd never met, and—as far as they knew at the time—had no chance of meeting.

Rohan still got those washes of hot and cold in his belly each time he thought about meeting his son, but now they heralded more excitement than trepidation.

Not that all his fears had been put to rest. But at least now he had good reason to hope they would be able to forge a bond.

No pressure, though. Not from Rohan's side. It had to be at least somewhat organic.

Titan whistled and the bell in his cage, put there for stimulation, rang wildly for a few seconds, then went silent. Rohan looked his way, and the parrot bobbed up and down on his perch, doing a little dance.

"Good birdie," Titan said, tilting his head to one side and then the other. "Pretty Titan."

"You're a ham," Rohan told him, chuckling, and realizing how easily the laughter came in the moment.

It wasn't always like that, for him, and especially after the emotional wringer he'd been through, it felt strange, but good. The simple pleasure of amusement filled him with calm contentment. Being with Elise eased the pain he always carried in his heart, lightened his soul.

Had it been that way before? Somehow he thought it might have been. He could imagine speaking to her about his father and having his anger and discontent at their relationship leached away. He'd never know for sure, but he knew loving her had given him the courage to face his father head-on, when in the past he'd have been more subtle, or just given in for a peaceful life.

Elise's phone rang, and he heard the murmur of her voice from the other room. Figuring she'd be a while, Rohan looked around for something to divert his thoughts away from her, and his ever-present desire to kiss her, make love to her again.

The photo albums were on the coffee table, and he reached over and took the one off the top. He felt better equipped to look at them now than he had been last night. Then he'd been a mess of tangled, shocking emotions, while today he was steadier, mentally stronger.

Then he opened the cover and froze.

These weren't pictures of Jeevan, but of him and Elise.

Younger. Oh, so heartbreakingly young, but smiling at each other with the kind of love that was unmistakable.

Without conscious thought his hand went to the scarred side of his face as he looked at a photo of himself with unmarked, unblemished skin. When he realized what he was doing, he let his fingers fall away again and rode out the painful moment.

Elise had said everyone changed as they got older, and Rohan realized she'd accepted him as he was, now, just as she had in the past. Somewhere along the line, he'd forgotten that self-acceptance was important, and had continued to resent all the changes the accident had brought.

Seeing himself as he used to be helped Rohan reconcile himself to the loss of the young man staring into the camera and be okay with the older, hopefully wiser one he had become.

Flipping the pages one by one, he realized something else. Something that had him going back to the beginning, and taking another, closer look.

His heart started to race, disbelief making him flip back and forth through the album. What he was seeing made no sense, and yet there it was, right in front of him. As far as he was concerned, there could be only one explanation that made any sense and, in doing so, account for everything he'd been feeling about Elise.

"That was Jeevan on the phone." Elise walked in carrying a tray, which she put down on the table. "He's finally got a flight out of Hong Kong, but he won't be here until Christmas morning."

Rohan looked up at her, and he didn't know what she saw in his expression, but it made her abandon the drinks and kneel beside him on the rug.

Putting her hand on his shoulder, she asked, "What's wrong?"

"It might sound weird," he said, his voice suddenly

hoarse from the lump that had gathered in his throat. "But I think I've been looking for you."

Her hand fell away and she leaned back, as though distancing herself from his words.

"What?"

"I've been looking for you since I returned to Canada. Not consciously, but everywhere we went twenty-seven years ago, I've been to since I came back."

She shook her head. "That does sound weird. You're just imagining it."

He didn't know why, but her down-to-earth common sense just made him even surer.

Pointing to a picture, he said, "This is Corner Brook, Nova Scotia, isn't it?"

She looked at the photo and slowly nodded. "I think so."

"And that's Tignish, PEI. That one is Truro, and this one—" he flipped a few pages "—this one is Moncton. I know, because about fifteen years ago, I decided I wanted to travel through the Maritimes. I didn't know why, but I felt compelled to go. I went to all those spots, plus Halifax and Quebec City." He found the pictures of those cities, pointing them out to her. "Then, the following year, I spent a month in Algonquin Park, canoeing and camping."

"Rohan, it could be just a coincidence." Elise sat cross-legged beside him, a wary look in her eyes. "A bizarre one, but a coincidence all the same."

"I don't think so. After I'd worked in Toronto for a while and made those trips, I got restless and decided to move. The first place I lived after that was Guelph."

"Not surprising, since you went to school there, and it would be familiar."

He shook his head. "I still wasn't satisfied. I kept moving, farther west each time, staying a year, sometimes less, until I got to Calgary. Then I stopped. Why, after years of wandering, did I stop there, if not because I knew, deep inside, that was where you came from, and probably would be?"

CHAPTER SEVENTEEN

ELISE STARED AT ROHAN, taking in the smile on his face, the gleam in his eyes. It was like seeing a mask fall away to reveal someone you'd known long ago and never thought to see again.

Despite the scars, he looked like the man he'd been twenty-seven years ago.

And it frightened her on a visceral level, as did what he was saying.

Surely he didn't believe he'd been subconsciously trying to find her for almost twenty years?

"You're talking crazy, Rohan. That makes no sense."

His smile actually widened. "It makes perfect sense to me, Elise. Why else would I find myself drawn to you in a way I can't remember ever being attracted to anyone else before? And last night, when we made love, why did it feel so natural, so incredibly intimate? I think…we were made to be together. And no matter what we do, we'll always find our way back to each other."

She shook her head vehemently, the fear in her belly churning, making her nauseous. "I don't believe that. That's not how memory, how the brain works."

Tipping his head to the side, he surveyed her with a look so loving it almost was her undoing. "Didn't you say the brain was a complex organ? Why wouldn't something as important to me as the love we shared be stored somewhere, even if the memories of us being together were lost?"

"I don't know, but I won't believe you've been searching for me, or that there's still a connection between us other than the past, or nostalgia, and the fact we have a son together. That's all nonsense."

Yet a part of her wanted to believe it, desperately. She couldn't let it overwhelm her, in case he decided, sometime later, he'd made a mistake and leave her again.

A few strands of her hair had come loose, and he slid them behind her ear with his fingers. She gasped, heat fanning out from where he touched, the familiar gesture making the conversation that bit more surreal.

"I don't remember any of that past, so I can't be nostalgic about it, and I know your reactions to my touch are from more than just good memories. Why are you afraid?"

She couldn't articulate it, terror holding her vocal cords hostage.

The specter of loving, of giving her all only to once more be abandoned arose in her mind, and she whispered, "Stop, Rohan. Please don't..."

He reached for her, and she wanted to resist but couldn't. Instead, she found herself collapsing, almost boneless, into his embrace, craving the security of his arms as much as she feared him going away, never to return.

"When we're like this, how can you doubt we should be together?" he whispered into her ear, sending shivers along her spine. "We still fit perfectly—the way those pictures show we always have."

How could she explain? All day they'd spoken of his

fears, especially about being a father to Jeevan, but they'd only briefly touched on her own.

Then he said, "Are you afraid I'll leave you again, like I did before?"

She lifted her head to search his expression, tears threatening again at the tenderness in his eyes.

And it was that gentle regard that gave her the courage to reply, "Yes."

His arms tightened around her, and he bent to place a gentle, loving kiss on her lips before resting his forehead against hers.

"I don't blame you. I promised to be back for Christmas, and it took me twenty-seven years to keep my word. I wouldn't trust me, either, under those circumstances. How about we take it slow, date for a while, so you have time to learn to trust me again? Even if you never do, I'll always be here for you. I don't plan to desert you again."

"And what do we tell Jeevan? I don't want him to be hurt by whatever we do."

"He's an adult now. I think he'll probably understand that there's still something special between us, but we're not going to rush into anything. And we can make sure he knows he'll never have to choose between us. We'll both always be around for him, whenever he needs."

Elise tried to call on her steady head and common sense so as to make the right decision, but the conflict in her mind was too strong. One part wanted to immediately agree to take one more chance on loving Rohan Khan, but another part insisted on caution. Loving him had almost broken her, had left scars that, although they weren't visible, still ached deep in her heart.

Could she really risk it all again?

Then she remembered all the advice she'd given Rohan during the day, about leaving the past behind and moving forward in life. While he'd been stuck because of his accident, she'd been too afraid to risk being hurt again.

It was time to break free from the past, for both her and Rohan, and maybe they could, over time, heal each other with love and forgiveness.

She took a deep gulp of air, for courage, and said, "I'd like to try your idea of dating, although it's a bit of a haul from Calgary to here and back."

Rohan gave her a squeeze and she heard him blow out a breath, as though he'd been holding it in while she deliberated.

"An hour and a half isn't too long a drive. But I have all that accumulated vacation time, too. I could book a hotel room here for a couple of weeks. Give us a chance to figure out how we want to arrange things."

Leaning back slightly, she looked up at him. "Why not just stay here?"

His eyebrows rose. "In the spare room?"

She shook her head. "No."

"What about Jeevan? I thought you didn't want to give him any ideas about us getting together?"

"Honestly, it's time I stop using him as an excuse not to have a life. And I think it would be good for him to see us try, even if eventually we decided it isn't working. After all, he's heard me say all his life what a wonderful man you are. If I let you get away again, he's going to think either I'm a liar or a fool."

Rohan laughed, and her heart sang to once more see a glimpse of his old self, which before had been so overshadowed by the cold mask he wore.

That deep, joyous laughter, more than almost anything else, gave her additional hope for the future. If they could talk and laugh and love, share their fears and their dreams like they had so long ago, everything would come right in the end.

Reaching up, she cupped his still-smiling face in her hands and, with her heart full of thankfulness for the second chance they'd so miraculously been given, laid her lips gently on his. When he pulled her closer, deepening the kiss, she allowed herself to let go of the past and all its attendant pain so as to be completely and totally present with Rohan.

The Rohan of now, and hopefully her future.

They made love in front of the fire, slowly, his tenderness almost moving her to tears.

He touched her as though she were the most precious thing in the world, kissed her as though he never wanted to stop.

"You're so beautiful," he told her, his hands cupping her face, his eyes gleaming in the firelight.

"So are you," she told him, tracing his lower lip with her finger.

They caressed with long, leisurely strokes, taking their time as they relearned each other's bodies. Somehow, now that they'd come to this point, the rushed intensity of the night before wasn't necessary. They could spend as long as they wanted and needed, letting their passions build.

But the power of that desire was immense, and Elise whimpered, caught on the almost painful line between arousal and culmination.

And when he tipped her over into ecstasy, she cried out and hung on to him as if she would never let him go.

This time, when they were satiated, she didn't roll away but curled up beside him, her head on his arm. He was facing her, his hand on her hip, their legs intimately intertwined.

"I wish I'd seen you pregnant with Jeevan," he said, a touch of melancholy in his tone. "Or found you sooner, so we could have had more children."

Rubbing her hand over his chest, she said, "No regrets. We're looking ahead now, not back."

"I know, but— What the—"

He sat up so suddenly Elise was left lying in a confused heap, having banged her head on the floor. When she sat up, it was to see Rohan glaring at Baxter, who was standing next to them, a querulous expression on his shaggy face. Phoebe stood in the doorway, keeping her distance, yet very much interested in what was going on.

"He...he *goosed* me," Rohan accused. "And his nose is damned cold."

Elise tried to tell him that was Bax's way of reminding them it was way past his walkies time, but she started giggling instead, and couldn't stop. Rohan's outrage, when he turned his accusatory look from the dog to her, just made it worse.

Finally, as though unable to help himself, Rohan joined in, his laughter ringing through the house, sweet to her ears.

Baxter stalked off, obviously unimpressed.

Getting to her feet, still giggling, she started putting back on her clothes.

"Where are you going?" Rohan grumbled.

"The dogs need to go out," she replied.

Rohan yawned and stretched, then grabbed his jeans before rising also.

"I'll go with you," he said.

Once they had on their outerwear, Elise turned on the light above the back door and let the dogs out. As she followed with Rohan, he reached out to take her gloved hand in his, and something about that simple gesture melted away the last of her fears.

Except for what would happen when Jeevan got home.

As though sensing the change in her mood, Rohan squeezed her finger.

"Any regrets?"

"None," she answered honestly. "Just a little worried about how what's happening between us will affect Jeevan."

"I am, too," he admitted, as they watched Phoebe and Bax play a game of Keep Away in the snow. "We'll take it slowly, as we agreed, although I have to tell you, it won't be easy."

"Why not?"

He turned to look at her, and even in the low light from the single bulb, she could see the gleam of rekindled desire in his eyes.

"Because just looking at you makes me want you," he said, low and sweet. "And I don't know how to stop the entire world knowing that, whenever we're together."

What had happened to the stern, stoic man? The one who'd admitted to locking his feelings away and retreating from entanglements?

When she asked him as much, he snorted, the sound one of laughter and bemusement combined.

"I have no idea. Over the past two days, he's slowly faded away. Not that I think I'll revert to the person I used to be before the accident. Just that somehow the burden of the past, the weight of it, seems to have lifted."

"I'm glad," Elise said, "if it makes you feel better. But there's nothing wrong with taking a step back—mentally, or emotionally—if you're uncomfortable in a situation or conversation. That ability has helped you through the years, and it's a good one to have."

He turned his face up to the night sky, inhaling deeply. Then he dropped her hand and put his arm around her waist, pulling her in tight against his side.

When he spoke, his voice was little more than a whisper.

"For years I've believed the man I am now is far inferior to the one I was. People told me so, over and over, and I absorbed that, like a slow-acting poison."

He turned, guiding her around, so they were face-to-face. His expression of wonder, of joy, made tears gather in her eyes.

"You've given me the antidote I needed, and I'll always be infinitely grateful for that."

He pulled her in closer and kissed her, their lips going from chilled to hot between one breath and the next.

There was no need for more words between them, so she called the dogs in, and led Rohan straight to her bed. Although nothing had been completely settled, she knew, if she had her way, there would be very few nights that they slept apart going forward.

Yet as she tried to drift off in Rohan's arms, the worry that Jeevan might find all this unfathomable held sleep in abeyance.

Jeevan was a scientist through and through. The type of man who needed evidence to support any theory. Elise, who was the same way, couldn't help thinking that he'd find the events of the last days crazy.

If anyone had come to her with a story like the one she would have to tell their son, she'd caution them to be careful, to make sure they weren't letting old emotions cloud their judgment.

It was what she'd told herself, over and over, since recognizing Rohan, but now it couldn't sway her from the course she was on.

"You okay?" He asked it gently, stroking her arm. The soft caress unraveled the tension that had built inside, and as she kissed the soft skin on the inside of his elbow, the last of it melted away.

She loved him, and everything would come right in the end.

"Perfect," she replied.

He tugged her closer, so her back was snug against his chest, and, cocooned in his warmth, she fell asleep.

CHAPTER EIGHTEEN

THE NEXT MORNING, awaking with Elise still wrapped securely in his arms had Rohan smiling before he'd even gotten out of bed.

When she rolled over and wrapped her leg over his, while pulling his head down for a kiss, his happiness turned to passion and eventually to ecstasy.

They took the dogs out together, holding thermal coffee mugs in their mittened hands. Clouds were massed on the horizon, although the weather service said there would be no more snow until late that night.

He knew Elise was worried when he caught her staring westward, where the weather system would come from.

"He'll make it," he said, not needing to elaborate.

That drew a smile. "I'm sure he will."

But a little shadow of concern lingered in her eyes.

To cheer her up, he put down his cup and started throwing snowballs for Bax, while Phoebe, who'd probably never played catch in her life, tried to get in on the action. The problem was, she had no idea what exactly the action was, and her comical antics, on top of Bax's continued confusion over the disappearing balls, had them howling with laughter.

When they went back inside, Elise started breakfast

while Rohan dried off the dogs and then gave them their food and fresh water.

After his chore, he washed his hands at the sink, but his attention was completely focused on Elise. He couldn't help it. If they were in the same room, she was all he could see.

Even now he couldn't believe what had happened. In the space of two days, he had gone from closed-off loner to a father, head-over-heels in love with his child's mother. Or maybe besotted lover was a better description.

He felt lighter, freer and happier than he could ever remember being. It was like he'd been living in a twilight world for years, and then, suddenly there was light all around him.

Christmas lights, at this point. And carols playing on the stereo.

And he loved it all.

But he was still stressed about the meeting between him and Jeevan, just as he knew Elise was, too.

Things might be wonderful between him and Elise, but Jeevan was still, to Rohan, an unknown quantity. Any number of things could go wrong. Jeevan could hate him, which would potentially put stress on the relationships between mother and son, and definitely between his parents.

Jeevan might be an adult, almost the same age Elise was when she gave birth, but he also was still Elise's main concern. And Rohan wouldn't want it any other way.

How would he react, should his son despise him? Would he be willing and able to give up the happiness he'd only just found with Elise, so as to not interfere with the bond between mother and son? Would she expect that of him?

"Hey," she said, pulling him out of his rambling, whirling thoughts. "It'll be okay."

"Yes," he replied and even nodded, although he wasn't at all sure.

"I have a hair appointment at two," she said, flipping pancakes on the griddle. "You can stay here if you want, or come into town with me."

"I'll go," he said, trying not to sound too eager. He'd planned to go to Banff later, to find her a Christmas gift, and this way she wouldn't be suspicious. "While you're getting your hair done, I can walk around and see the rest of the place."

After breakfast he helped her in the kitchen and then took down the boxes of ornaments from the attic. It was nothing exciting, but the peace he felt as the two of them worked together—the rightness of it—made him happier than he could have ever imagined.

Who would have thought something as normal as peeling and cutting up potatoes could feel like a benediction, when done in the right company?

The rest of the day passed in a blur, although when he thought about it, besides the trip into Banff they'd done nothing extraordinary. Yet before he knew it, it was time to shower and dress for the SAR fundraiser.

When he was ready, he sat in the living room waiting for Elise, and picked up the photo album once more. While looking at the images still brought pangs of regret for the time they'd lost, now they also reassured him that what was happening between them wasn't completely crazy.

The way they'd looked at each other clearly showed the love they'd felt, and he knew, although the memories were gone from his head, they'd somehow remained in his heart.

When he heard the tap of her heels coming down the corridor, he closed the album and stood up, just as she came into the room.

Stunned, he stared, until she lifted a hand, self-consciously, to her throat.

"What?"

"You look gorgeous," he said, wondering if she'd agree to forgo the dinner so he could take his time exploring how to get her out of that red dress. "Everyone is going to hate me, for having the most beautiful woman in the room on my arm."

A tinge of rosy color stained her cheeks, and she smiled.

"Thank you. You're looking mighty fine yourself."

"Right now I want to kiss that lipstick right off those luscious lips, but I figure you'll beat me up if I did."

Her eyes got slumberous, and aforementioned lips came together in a sexy pout.

"I can always put more on," she said.

And that made them late leaving the house, because that was an invitation Rohan had no intention of passing up.

The hotel where the dinner was being held was decorated like a Christmas wonderland, and the ballroom was already full of people by the time they got there.

A tall, barrel-chested man came to meet them as they walked in, a relieved smile on his face.

"Elise. I thought you weren't coming."

"I told you I would be here, Tom," she said, tilting her cheek up for a kiss. "Let me introduce you. This is Dr. Rohan Khan. Rohan, Tom Harding, the head of the SAR team."

As they shook hands, Tom Harding gave Rohan a long, searching look.

"I heard that you went into that barn with Elise, to help bring Ben Sullivan out."

"Yes."

"Janice was so grateful to you both she called me from the hospital to tell me."

"I'm sorry I haven't filed a report yet, Tom," Elise interjected. "I haven't gotten around to it yet."

He waved his hand, as though brushing the words aside. "It's Christmas, so it can wait a few days, but I was wondering if Dr. Khan might be interested in volunteering for the team. We can always use another pair of hands."

Rohan shook his head. "I don't think it's in the cards for me, although I'm flattered you asked. Besides, I live in Calgary, so I wouldn't be of much help to you here."

"Shame," Tom said, sweeping his hand toward the front of the ballroom. "I was hoping you'd join and bring Elise back with you. She's one of the best we ever had."

"Actually, Tom, I wanted to talk to you about that."

Tom Harding's face lit up.

"You're ready to return? Put an end to this ridiculous retirement?"

"I'm thinking about it," she admitted. "But if you want me to handle a dog, I'll need a new one. I won't endanger Bax's health by putting him back in the field."

Tom rubbed his hands together, as though someone had just offered him a million dollars, and he was contemplating how to spend it.

"We'll talk about it, after we get all this holiday malarkey out of the way, but this is the best news I've had in weeks."

Elise laughed. "You've been just fine without me."

"But we're better with you." He glanced around as

someone called his name, and then continued, "Go mix and mingle, and put in some bids. There's something special coming up in a few minutes, so listen out."

He hurried away, and Rohan realized he was beaming at Elise and couldn't seem to stop, even when she lifted her eyebrows, and asked, "Why are you grinning like that?"

Moving close to her side, he put his hand on her waist and bent to whisper in her ear.

"I'm just so damn proud of you right now."

Lifting her hand, she touched his scarred cheek, the gentle brush of her fingers making his heart sing.

"I wouldn't have found the courage without you."

Elise reveled in the moment with Rohan, so glad he was pleased with her decision to go back to the SAR team. It might have sounded spur-of-the-moment to him, but she'd found herself thinking about what he'd said about courage, and realized it was the right time to find hers.

She'd given up her dream out of fear but knew in her heart that she'd regret walking away from it forever.

After all, she might be on the other side of fifty, but there was a lot of good she could still do. And if the day came when she physically couldn't do the job anymore, that would be the time to retire. Not when she was still fit—and still wanted to be involved.

When he kissed her cheek, his lips lingering warm and tender against her skin, she also knew being with him was, as he'd intimated, her destiny.

That her love had never truly died but stayed dormant in her heart, until he'd returned to awaken it again.

"I have to tell you something," she whispered, putting her palm on his cheek to keep him close.

"Go ahead," he said, equally softly, pulling back just far enough to see her eyes.

"I love you. I always have, and always will."

His face went blank for a moment, and her heart dipped, and then, before she could backtrack, he smiled, his entire face lighting up with love equal to her own.

"I love you, too," he said. "But couldn't you have waited just a little longer to tell me, so I wouldn't be tempted to embarrass you in front of all your colleagues?"

"No," she replied, stroking his cheek. "I've waited long enough."

He took a deep breath, his fingers tightening on her waist.

"Later, we'll discuss this in depth," he said, dark eyes gleaming, promising sweet retribution. "And I think I might need a demonstration, just to be sure you mean it."

Elise huffed a laugh, which was curtailed by the rush of desire melting her insides.

"Agreed, on both our parts," she said before stepping back. This really wasn't the place to grab him and kiss him, no matter how badly she wanted to. "Let's get something to drink, shall we? It's suddenly really warm in here."

He laughed and agreed, settling his hand at the base of her spine to guide her toward the bar.

As they strolled around the edge of the ballroom drinks in hand, looking at the auction items and bidding on a few, she was aware of the curious stares they were getting, but she didn't care. Soon enough it would be common knowledge that Jeevan's father was back in the picture, and back in her life.

Intimately.

Forever.

No one they spoke to was bold enough to ask any

questions outright, which amused her no end, since she knew there were a few people there who probably were speculating.

Anyone who knew Jeevan, and most of the folks there did, would see the resemblance.

As they were talking to one of her former SAR colleagues, Kaylyn, and her husband, the PA system squawked, and they all looked up to see Tom at the podium.

He tapped the mike, then said, "Good evening, ladies and gentlemen. Thank you all for coming out tonight to support our annual Christmas fundraiser. In a little while we'll get dinner going, but tonight we're starting with a little surprise."

The crowd murmured, and Elise whispered to Kaylyn, "What's going on?"

When the other woman shrugged, Elise looked back at Tom.

"Last year, as you all know, we lost a valuable member of our team to retirement. Dr. Elise van Hagan was, and is, one of the finest and most valuable rescuers I've worked with in my career."

Shocked, Elise could hardly hear what Tom was saying, and when Rohan put his arm around her, she gladly leaned into his side, needing his support.

"When the committee met to plan this function, talk turned to how much we respected and admired Dr. van Hagan for her service. After surprisingly little debate, it was decided that tonight, we would honor her with a small token of our appreciation. Elise, would you come up here, please?"

"Go on," Rohan whispered as people started clapping. He took her glass from her hand and gave her a little nudge, when she didn't immediately move.

Reluctantly, but keeping her head high, Elise made her way to the small raised stage and then up the stairs. Tom was beaming at her and held out his hand to pull her close to the microphone.

"Elise, this was planned before you told me, just this evening, that you're thinking of returning to our SAR team—"

He had to pause as applause broke out again, and wait until it faded before he could continue.

"That decision on your part is more welcome than you can ever imagine, but it doesn't detract from the amazing work you've done over the last ten years." He turned to the audience and said, "A couple of days ago, I called on Elise, asking her to go to the site of a barn collapse, because the team couldn't get there as quickly as she could. Without hesitation, she went, and saved a young man's life."

The applause was louder this time, with a few whistles thrown in, and Elise felt heat flow into her cheeks.

"Come on, Tom," she said pertly, giving him a smile, wanting off the stage. "Cut to the chase. I'm sure all these people are starving."

That drew laughter, even from Tom, who was shaking his head.

"Okay, then. The doctor has spoken. Elise, on behalf of the SAR team, and all the people you've saved over the last ten years, we'd like to present to you this plaque celebrating both your long service to the team, and to our community."

There were footsteps behind her, and she turned, expecting the committee chairwoman or some other dignitary. Instead...

"Jeevan!"

His smile was wide, but she knew him well enough

to see the question in his eyes. But none of that mattered as she threw her arms around him and he hugged her in return. The thunderous applause drowned out her words, but it didn't matter.

"You're home!"

CHAPTER NINETEEN

ROHAN STOOD ROOTED to the spot, staring at the man who'd walked out from the wings to surprise his mother. He couldn't stop the smile spreading across his face, and his heart was pounding. Thankful for the column beside him, he held on to it, needing something solid to lend support to his suddenly shaky legs.

My son!

As mother and son hugged, warmth flooded Rohan's chest, and they were all he could see.

There was so much love there he could hardly bear to watch. Elise had tears in her eyes, and Jeevan touched a finger to her cheek, laughing at her shock.

But then they both turned, in unison, and looked at him, and suddenly his joy was curtailed.

Jeevan might still be smiling for the crowd, but his eyes were flinty, interrogative.

He must have been watching from behind the curtains and wondering who it was with his mother. And just like Elise when she first saw him, he hadn't recognized who it was.

The group walked off the stage, Tom still beaming, and disappeared behind the drapery flanking the opening.

What should he do now?

Go to them? Stay where he was?

The suddenness of Jeevan's appearance, the public nature of it, had his anxiety rising, and the urge to slip away almost overwhelmed him, but he stood his ground, waiting. The man who retreated from life, from emotions, took a distant second place to the father—and the lover—who would wait a lifetime to be with his family, if necessary.

Elise's head popped out from behind the curtain, and her gaze found his unerringly. There was no need for her to wave. Rohan was already moving, walking toward one of the most important and pivotal moments in his life.

His stomach was in knots and his mouth was dry, but nothing could stop him going to her, and his son.

"There never was an Australia trip. I planned to surprise you all along, with Tom's help," Rohan heard Jeevan say, as he walked up the steps to the stage. "Who's the guy? You look really into each other. Did he get you to go back to the SAR team?"

Rohan paused behind the curtain, suddenly unsure again and wishing he had the right to the kind of hug Jeevan had given his mother, full of love and joy.

"He's..." Elise caught sight of Rohan as he stepped fully out into her view, and her voice faltered to a stop.

Jeevan turned.

This close, Rohan could see how much they truly looked alike, and realized they were almost the same height, with his son an inch or so taller.

Rohan's heart was pounding so hard he felt almost light-headed, but he held his son's gaze, seeing his brow furrow and his mouth tighten.

"Mom?"

Elise seemed unable to move, to speak, and it was then that Rohan realized she'd been equally nervous about this moment.

"How this all came about is a long story, but I'm your father."

Jeevan turned to his mother and said again, "Mom?"

She was shaking, but she nodded and tried to smile. "It's true. He's alive, and he found us."

Jeevan faced Rohan again, the bewilderment in his eyes tearing at Rohan's heart.

"How... I thought... I thought you were dead."

"I'll explain it to you," Elise said, and her words pushed a rush of cold through Rohan's body.

Not we. But just her.

Yet wasn't that her prerogative? She'd raised Jeevan by herself, taken care of him and nurtured him into the man standing between them, looking from one to the other.

They had a relationship, while he—he was still the outsider looking in, hoping to be accepted.

"I'll let you two talk," he said, fighting to keep the coldness out of his voice, unable to stop his expression from going blank.

Some habits were harder to break than others.

He turned to go back to the ballroom.

"Wait."

Two voices, calling out at the same time, stopped him in his tracks, and he turned back to see Jeevan coming after him.

Then he was enveloped in a hug so tight he heard his ribs creak, but he didn't care, as Jeevan's voice, muffled but audible, said, "Dad. Daddy."

And when he hugged his son in return, everything felt right in the world.

Elise wasn't sure how she made it through the dinner, and the three of them left immediately afterward, needing time for Jeevan to sort through it all.

He peppered them with questions the entire way back to the house, stopping only for the time it took for him to go in and pick up his bags from his friend's house, where he'd been staying.

They had to go back to the beginning, explaining about the accident, and the way his grandfather had manipulated the story to get Elise out of Rohan's life.

"Wow," he remarked. "That was pretty low. Do you know why he did it?"

"I think, because he wanted me to marry a friend's daughter so the two families would be tied together. My father always was all about business and money, which equal prestige for some people."

"Yeah," he said. "I know some of them."

He was quiet for a moment, then asked, "Did you? Marry the woman your father wanted you to?"

"Yes, but it didn't work out."

Another brief silence, and when Elise looked in the rearview mirror, she saw Jeevan shaking his head.

"I'm sorry you went through that, Dad."

And her heart ached when Rohan lifted his hand to his face, not to touch his scars as he habitually did, but to swipe at his eyes.

"Thank you, son."

"Holy crap!" Jeevan's sudden shout almost made Elise drive off the road. "I have my dad back. Well, I have my dad." He laughed, and the joyful sound had her blinking back tears, too. Thank goodness she was pulling into the driveway. "Hey, Dad, wanna teach me how to throw a baseball?"

"Sorry, son." The amusement in Rohan's voice was apparent. "I grew up in Trinidad, so I could maybe teach you how to play cricket. But baseball? No. And don't even think about hockey."

The three of them were laughing as they got out of the car, and Elise had to stop for a moment, too thankful to move.

It would work out. She knew it would. And the relief was almost paralyzing.

"Come on, Mom," Jeevan said, putting his arm around her shoulder. "I'm sure there must be a butter tart with my name in the house somewhere. Otherwise, it just isn't Christmas."

"If your father hasn't eaten all of them," she replied, and on hearing her words, they all paused, as though letting them soak in.

Then Rohan said, "Hey, don't have him hating me already. At least let him get to know me first so his dislike is an honest one, not over baked goods."

"I've never hated you." Jeevan's voice had lost all mirth and was serious. Almost grave. "And I never will. So that part of the father-son bonding experience won't happen."

"Glad to hear it," Rohan said. Then, as though unable to help themselves, they hugged again.

Baxter went wild when Jeevan walked in, scaring Phoebe in the process. By the time Rohan and Jeevan had them both settled down, Elise had made hot chocolate, and they went into the living room to drink it.

When Jeevan saw that the tree wasn't decorated, he insisted they get on it. It couldn't be bare on Christmas morning.

"You should write a book." Jeevan considered where on the tree to put the glittery ornament he was holding, then reached up and hung it on the topmost bough, before looking at his father. "It's like a soap opera, or a Bollywood movie. The hero is dead, and then, when you least expect it, he isn't."

When Rohan laughed, Elise felt now familiar warmth fill her chest. She would never tire of hearing that sound.

"When you put it that way, sure. But no one would believe it actually happened. They'd think I made it up."

Elise nodded her agreement as she hunted for some more ornament wires. Every year she misplaced them and ended up buying more. They should be drowning in them by now. If she didn't know he was too well trained to do something like that, she'd think Baxter was hiding them somewhere.

"People nowadays wouldn't understand what it was like when it was all landlines, and local newspapers and TV. You hardly knew what was happening one town over, much less a thousand miles away," she said. "Now everyone has a cell phone with video capabilities, and are posting selfies all over the internet, and even the smallest countries have their newspapers online. Anyone who didn't live before the worldwide web would think it was the most ridiculous story they'd ever heard."

Jeevan obviously was still trying to make sense of it all, and Elise knew it would take some more time. But when she'd seen him spontaneously hug Rohan, she'd known it would be all right in the end.

They still hadn't broached the subject of his parents being together again, after having reconnected only a couple of days ago. She and Rohan had already agreed that, for at least these first few nights, they'd sleep apart. One shock at a time was enough for their son.

Yet she didn't really want to wait. Not now, when Rohan and her had admitted to their feelings. She was chomping at the bit to start the rest of their life together, as a couple, as well as a family.

"Gosh, I love Christmas." The contentment in Jeevan's voice mirrored the feeling that blossomed in her chest as she watched the two most important people in her life interact so easily. "And this year is the best ever."

"I can't wait to hear all about your trip to Indonesia and Borneo." Rohan handed Elise a plastic bag filled with the wires she'd been hunting for. "Did you get enough data for your doctorate?"

"Yes, I'm sure I did. It was amazing there, but rough living most of the time. I can understand why some scientists only want to do field work, but jungle living isn't for me. At least not all the time."

As the two men talked more about the trip, Elise allowed herself a little moment of relief. She'd been worried Jeevan might decide that adventures in faraway places suited him perfectly and then end up living in inaccessible locales all the time. Hearing him say it wasn't for him made her happy, even though she knew he wouldn't stay in Banff.

For now, she was perfectly content with what she had, and knew she shouldn't be greedy. No matter where Jeevan settled, they'd still be in touch, and visit regularly. At least, she'd visit him regularly, whether he wanted it or not. When she was ninety and he was sixty-three, he'd still be her baby. And Rohan would still be the love of her life.

Christmas had definitely taken on a new sparkle. Where before she'd associated it with loss, now it had become what it was always meant to be: a season of hope and joy and love.

"Were you the one who encouraged Mom to go back to SAR?" Jeevan asked Rohan. "I've been telling her for the past year that she shouldn't give it up. Do you know she passed the physical at forty-two, and some of the people half her age flunked it?"

Rohan gave her a look that heated her to her toes, and

she was glad Jeevan was once more deciding where to hang an ornament, and not focused on them.

"I didn't know that, but I'm not surprised. And no, I didn't encourage her, per se, just told her I thought she was amazing at it."

And that led to them telling their son about the joint rescue they'd effected, and their being on site to help Mrs. Pilar, when she collapsed in Banff, as well as the raven they'd rescued.

"You guys have been busy, eh?"

"You could say that," she replied.

The tree was almost completely decorated when Jeevan turned to his father and said, "It just struck me—you told Mom you'd be back for Christmas, but it took you twenty-seven years to keep your promise." Jeevan quirked an eyebrow at his father. "I guess better late than never."

"I'm a man of my word," Rohan said with mock gravity. "Just a little tardy sometimes."

They exchanged almost identical grins, which they turned on Elise, making her heart ache with happiness. Her eyes got damp and she smiled back, shaking her head at their silliness. Mind you, she might as well get used to it. They were more alike than not, and she could almost bet they'd be ganging up on her sometimes. She resolved to stay on her toes, and ready for anything.

"I still think you could have a bestseller on your hands," Jeevan said, sending his parents another teasing glance. "And if you cap the story off by getting married, then you could tap into the romance market. I hear it's huge."

"Jeevan!"

Elise put as much outrage as she could into her voice,

but Rohan completely spoiled the effect by muttering, "Hush, son. Don't spook her. I'm working on it."

"Definitely the best Christmas ever," Jeevan said happily.

"The first of many."

The surety and love in Rohan's voice was patent, and Elise got up from her chair to lean down and kiss him lightly, no longer concerned with how Jeevan might interpret her actions. He obviously already knew his parents were back in love and had no problem with it.

There would no doubt be more discussions about everything, later. But right now, she had to express all the love in her heart.

Rohan pulled her down into his lap and, under Jeevan's teasing gaze, wrapped both arms around her waist.

"Yes," she agreed, snuggling in, at home again in Rohan's embrace, contentment making her smile. "The first of many merry Christmases. Together."

* * * * *

MILLS & BOON

Coming next month

FALLING FOR THE SECRET PRINCE
Alison Roberts

'Roberto Baresi is our father.'

Emilia actually shook her head. 'But your surname's Di Rossi, not Baresi.'

'I go by my mother's maiden name. I didn't want my background known when I came to study and work in America. I didn't want special treatment or media attention. I wanted to be like everyone else. Like you, Emmy... Being able to work hard and achieve my dream of becoming a doctor.'

Emilia's head was spinning. 'Wait...you're telling me that you're the son of a king? That would make you a...a prince?'

He was holding her gaze again and she could see the absolute honesty in his eyes. 'Yes.'

A single word but one that suddenly opened a gulf between them that was wider than an ocean. He was nothing like her. They were suddenly so far apart that they could have come from different planets. He was a prince. Part of a royal family that could be traced back for centuries and she was a girl who hadn't even known who her father was and had to be taken away from her mother's damaging lifestyle. He was a man who'd always had a privileged lifestyle and a future to look forward to, whereas she was a girl who'd been labelled wild enough to get shunted from foster home to foster home, becoming more and more lost until someone—that amazing teacher she'd had in the eleventh grade—finally believed in her enough to let her dream of a different future.

So she'd been bang on the mark in thinking she didn't know very much about Dom, hadn't she? It was, in fact, so much of an understatement that it should have laughable. But it wasn't. This wasn't remotely funny. Emilia couldn't quite identify the swirl of emotion that she could feel building inside her head—and her heart—but it wasn't pleasant. And it was powerful enough to be preventing any speech right now. Having opened her mouth and then closed it again, she had to give in and wait for the initial shock, or whatever it was that was paralysing her, to wear off.

Continue reading
FALLING FOR THE SECRET PRINCE
Alison Roberts

Available next month
www.millsandboon.co.uk

COMING SOON!

We really hope you enjoyed reading this book.
If you're looking for more romance, be sure to
head to the shops when new books are
available on

Thursday 29th October

WE'RE LOOKING FOR NEW AUTHORS FOR THE MILLS & BOON MEDICAL SERIES!

Whether you're a published author or an aspiring one, our editors would love to read your story.

You can submit the synopsis and first three chapters of your novel online, and find out more about the series, at **harlequin.submittable.com/submit**

We read all submissions and you do not need to have an agent to submit.

IF YOU'RE INTERESTED, WHY NOT HAVE A GO?

Submit your story at:
harlequin.submittable.com/submit

MILLS & BOON